Out for Blood

The Second in the
Cycle of the Aphotic World

THE APHOTIC SERIES

Bad Blood
Out For Blood
Blood Loss
Blood Pact
Blood Relations
Flesh and Blood

Out for Blood

Tobin Elliott

Luminous Aphotica Publishing

ISBN 978-1-77826-297-5 (hardcover)
ISBN 978-1-77826-292-0 (paperback)
ISBN 978-1-77826-293-7 (ebook)

Cover Design by Camille Codling (Instagram: @codling.creations)
Interior Layout by Jennifer Dinsmore (jenniferdinsmoreeditorial.com)

This one goes out to all those I hung out with during the last three years of high school. We've mostly gone our separate ways, and the fire of friendship is now nothing but cooled, scattered ashes, but you'll all never know how much you saved me back then. And it all started with a bit of gambling…

Also, this one's also for all my teachers during those same three years. It's been over four decades since I saw you last, but your faith in me and your small, daily kindnesses helped an insecure kid begin to believe in himself.

ACKNOWLEDGEMENTS

As with my note in the previous book, thank you to everyone in my life who keeps me sane. You are my family. My blood…

To the Hickey family…you find the broken things and show them their worth in the world. That's a powerful gift.

To Dale Long…writing partner, confidant, and dad-joke black belt, you've had a hell of a few years, and yet you helped keep my broken parts together. Near! Far!

To Jennifer Dinsmore, whose brilliant editing and suggestions make me look better than I am. You are a treasure and a magician.

To my daughter Madison and her husband Devyn, and to my son Hunter and his fiancée Camille. You're all incredible human beings and I'm proud to be a parent to all of you. You all make me proud, and I love you all more than you'll ever know.

Finally, and most importantly, to Karen Elliott. You don't get what I do in front of my computer, but you're encouraging and supportive just the same. You put up with all my shit, and there's not many who would.

Doubt thou the stars are fire
Doubt that the sun doth move;
Doubt truth to be a liar;
But never doubt I love.

— William Shakespeare

Part One
Dark Ride

"I know always that I am an outsider; a stranger in this century and among those who are still men."

The Outsider
H. P. Lovecraft

TRAGEDY AT DISTRICT HIGH SCHOOL

New Hope—June 13, 1981—The small town of New Hope was rocked this morning by the grim discovery of at least thirty dead at the local district high school.

The local police department received several calls about missing teens—all students at Clarington District High School—last evening. Almost all the students were reportedly staying late to work on decorations for the upcoming musical to be presented later this month.

"Who would do this?" a shaken Nathaniel Bostash, parent of one of the students, and brother to one of the high school staff, asked. "I just don't..."

(Story continues on Page 3. See "Death Toll")

Prologue

THE MAN BEHIND the bar was aware of the massive, scarred fist arcing straight at his face, and thought, *Again?* The scene played out in slow motion as he continued to wipe down the countertop, his movements never hesitating or deviating. He did not flinch as the flesh-and-bone missile continued its collision course.

Yet another regular night at the drinking establishment—it couldn't really be termed a bar—until Stanley had become overzealous in his quest for intoxication. The trouble started when the man behind the bar refused his barely decipherable request for just one more.

The incoming fist stopped about four inches from the barkeep's face and simply hung there, trembling. Stanley stared at his mutinous hand as though it was something separate from his body. His disbelief and confusion would have been comical had he not been trying to put that fist through the smaller man's skull.

The barkeep finished wiping down the last bit of the bar, then cleared his throat and the entire room stilled. Stanley continued to hang, fist locked up in thin air, unable to do anything but stare at it. With a noncommittal glance at the suspended fist, the barkeep addressed the owner of the fist.

"Time to go, Stanley," he said, his tone more bored than anything. "When you start swinging at the guy who pours your beer, you've definitely had too much to drink."

"Aw jee-zuz," Stanley said, his voice shaking as much as his still-hanging fist was, "I was…I was jesh feckin' joshin' ya." His words slipped from his throat like a car on an icy road, all sloppy and skittering. The man behind the bar looked at Stanley's watering eyes, the way a few strands of his greasy hair danced a jig as they hugged his jawline. He saw the white hairs like potted plants sprouting from Stanley's ears and nose. And he saw so much more about Stanley as well. More than he ever wanted to see about anyone.

Turning away, willing himself not to see anymore, the barkeep balled the cloth and wiped at a stray wet spot on the bar. "Time to go, Stanley."

"Nah," Stanley pleaded. "Nah, doan. Doan kick me out. I'll be quiet, promish."

The wiping stopped. Their eyes met.

"It is *time*," he said, "to *go*." Though it wasn't stated, everyone in the place heard the threat. Things never went well if he had to repeat himself.

Stanley's fist slowly dropped back to his side, fully in his command again. Without another word, he spun—almost too lightly for his parka-encased bulk—and headed for the door. The barkeep followed behind. Though no one was near it at the time, the door opened as Stanley approached and he walked through without another word.

"You say hi to that pretty wife of yours," the barkeep said. Stanley's wife was not what anyone would consider pretty, and Stanley often referred to her as "the feckin' poster child for Save the feckin' Whales," but he chose not to correct the barkeep. One hand came up in a backhanded wave as Stanley continued to concentrate on trucking right. It wasn't so much that the road was long, as it was the width that was causing the problem.

The barkeep watched his ping-ponging for a few seconds more, said, "See you tomorrow, Stanley," then slammed the door and stalked back behind the bar. Picking up the cloth that was more holes than material, he went back to wiping down the bar. "And you *will* keep those fists to yourself tonight," he muttered as his motions became more violent and his knuckles whitened. Though it was spoken low, and to nobody in particular, it still sounded like another warning. A couple of the regulars moved from the bar to the tables, knowing his mood would not improve tonight and distance was the better part of valour.

♦♦♦

THE BARKEEP, THOUGH slim and unmuscled, seemed to carry an air of command about him, as though wise beyond his years. This did not go unnoticed by a relatively new, but regular, patron of the bar.

"Lookit that guy! Can't believe how all y'all kowtow to 'im. He doesn't look old enough to shave, let alone pour, fer chrissakes!" Greasy Eddie said. He turned to his new best friend, an older man with a face like an ashtray. "What's his story, Willie?"

Blind Willie—so named due to the unfortunate insertion of a fork that had robbed him of sight in his left eye, the spot since covered with a dirty patch—took a long swig of his beer before wiping the foam from his whiskers with his sleeve. Willie took his time doing it, as though savouring the smell of a fine cigar and not snot- and beer-encrusted flannel.

"Guy's been here damn near twenty years."

Greasy Eddie turned in his seat, the legs of his chair scraping across the rough lumber floor, as he tried to get a better look at the man behind the bar. Man? No way, that was a boy! A teenager at best, all lanky hair and peach fuzz. Twenty years?

"Bullshit, you say!" Eddie retorted, turning back to Willie.

"Hey, you don't gotta believe me. No skin off my ass," Willie said, throwing his hands up in placation as his whiskers picked up the dim light from the lanterns placed around the drinking area, gleaming whitely in the semidarkness. "Believe it or don't. That's your call, but I ain't shittin' you. Showed up in the early eighties, ain't that right, Red? Eighty-one, eighty-two?"

Red, one of the drinkers who had just moved from bar to table, simply nodded morosely into his beer. "Yup."

Greasy Eddie was having none of it. "You mean he showed up as a young pup, right? Still sucklin' on his mama's teat?" His face screwed up in a grimace of such tight concentration that the single tear tattooed near his eye nearly disappeared into the folds of skin.

"If he was still suckin' tit at that age, he was a lucky man indeed!" said Willie, laughing. His voice was a sandpapery rasp. "Ain't that right, Red?"

Red addressed his beer again. "Yup."

Eddie looked between the Red and Willie. They were jerking him around. He spun again to face the bartender, mentally calculating the man's—the boy's!—age, figuring he would have to be on the ass end of thirty, minimum, probably more like early forties. He watched the bartender brush the hair—not a spot of grey in the patch—away from his unlined forehead with his wrist as he wiped at a sign posted behind the bar. *This is a dark ride*, it stated.

They were jerking him around.

Greasy Eddie's eyes travelled around the room, noting details. Hell, he'd been in more luxurious fishing huts. But what did anyone really need to drink away the memories of their day, their job, their spouse, or their life? It was all here: a very simple square enclosure made from rough planks and wood panelling on the walls, some mismatched tables and chairs, a big woodstove in one corner and the bar itself in the other. The walls were unadorned with the exception of the propane lanterns hung on nails spaced every six feet or so, giving the room what little ambience it may have possessed. No dart boards, no pool tables, no neon signs, no beer posters, no fancy-ass appetizer menu. Not even a big fridge that he could see. Hell, the place didn't even have a sign outside to declare name or nature of the establishment. Just that weird plaque above the door.

The fact that Greasy Eddie had stumbled in and ended up sharing beers with Red and Blind Willie was down more to luck and curiosity than anything. But that's what this place was. A serious drinking room. Come in, drink up, and get the hell out before the fight starts. Or, get a good seat for it, if you're so inclined.

After spying the dozen or so faces currently in the bar, none familiar to Eddie as yet, he had no other sources of information to draw from. But he was sure he was the brunt of the joke.

As his gaze came back around to Blind Willie, the old man spread his calloused hands in front of him and over the scarred tabletop. "Like I said, I ain't shittin' you. I don't know you well enough to give you any shit, or to be takin' any shit from you. We all got our own shit, and I personally got enough shit to last me." Willie rubbed a grubby hand against the side of his capilleried nose, his dirty fingernail making a quick deke inside his left nostril, checking for anything worth mining. Finding nothing of note, it popped back out. He never wiped it. "I think our buddy at the bar probably has more than enough shit to go round, by the looks of him."

Eddie took another look at the bartender. There were traces of lines around his mouth and too-old eyes, most Eddie would have guessed were from smoking, though not all. They weren't laugh lines, and they looked out of place on such a youthful face. It looked like he hadn't found the humour in anything in years.

Maybe Blind Willie wasn't jerking him around. At first glance, he did look young. But those eyes...they'd looked into darkness. And they'd seen more than most. Eddie was well acquainted with the darkness, having seen a fair share himself. The fact that he'd always been able to slide out from under it had earned him the "Greasy" tag. But this guy...

"What do they call him?" Eddie asked. "What'ziz name?"

"Dunno."

"'Dunno'? Whaddaya mean, 'dunno'?"

"I don't know. 'Guy at the bar' or 'bar guy' or whatever."

"That just don't make sense."

"Dunno," Willie repeated. "We ask, he pours. Never asked fer no name an' he ain't never offered, ain't that right, Red?"

"Yup."

"In fact, you din't even ask 'im when he borrowed your truck that time t' git t' California, didja? I'm right, ain't I?"

"Yup."

Eddie turned to Red, still plumbing the depths of his mug of beer. His salt-and-pepper hair hung limply around his face, reminding Eddie of that donkey from *Winnie the Pooh*. "You tellin' me you guys have been drinkin' here for twenty-odd years and you never caught his name?"

"Yup." Red's head barely moved.

Greasy Eddie was beginning to wonder what kind of weird-ass town he had stumbled upon. "Don't that strike either a' you as a bit unnatural? Not knowin' a man's name?"

"Ain't nuthin' natch'rill 'bout No Hope," Willie replied.

"'No Hope'?"

"The bar." Willie spread an arm to encompass the establishment. "This place is No Hope. The No Hope Bar, y'might say. Din'ja notice the thing with the sayin' above the entrance?"

"Yeah," Eddie said, curious. "So what?"

"Says, 'Abandon all hope, ye who enter here'?"

Eddie snorted. "Like that 'dark ride' sign over the bar?"

"Yup," said Red.

"Yeah, so?"

"So. Abandon hope. No hope." He spread his hands to take in the room. "The No Hope Bar."

Greasy Eddie nodded, getting it now. "So what's so unnatural about this place?"

"The clientele."

"Oh yeah?" Eddie snorted again. "Like ol' Stanley, there? Guy he just turfed?"

"Nope. Lots worse'n him." His voice lowered to a whisper as his eyes darted to the man behind the bar. "Monsters, Eddie."

"Willie, c'mon," Eddie said, thumping a thick calloused hand down on the table and wobbling the beer mugs precariously. He lowered his voice to a stage whisper. "Got news for ya, man. There ain't no such a thing."

"After sittin' in this seat for so damn long, I'm gonna have to beg to differ with you." Blind Willie's single good eye narrowed down to a slit. He brought his face close to Eddie's, close enough that Eddie could smell his beer breath and his unwashed body. "I only got one good eye, but I seen 'em. They're real, all right."

"So you're sayin' this is like…a monster bar or something?" Eddie asked.

"Well, I guess you could say that. I'll tell ya though, the goddamn vampires are the biggest pain in the ass, always havin' to be invited in alla time." Willie shook his head. "The worst. Ain't I right, Red?"

"Yup," said Red morosely.

Eddie slumped back in his chair, unbelieving. But Willie had not smiled, not even a little. And Eddie could usually sense a liar, but his spider-sense wasn't setting off any alarms right now. So he sat back and said nothing.

Blind Willie told him about the various visitors to the No Hope bar. The regulars—some here tonight, some making their appearances only on the weekend, others only on payday.

Then there were the stragglers, the one-timers, the "where the hell am I's?" These last were the easiest to spot, entering the bar tentatively, eyes wide with apprehension, looking around as though they were expecting someone to harass them or to pick a fight, starting with the "you ain't from 'round here" line.

"That hardly ever happens," Willie said.

Then there was the special breed that always seemed to somehow find the little bar in the northern expanses of nowhere. Some found it out of desperation, or determination. Whatever the reason, this place attracted them. Those who needed confirmation of what they had seen, or experienced. To relate the story, to spin it and weave it into something that made some sort of sense. To unload it on someone else who gave more than a cursory nod or a suspicious glance. Someone who could affirm that, yes, that was real. That really happened. To give credence to what they had seen or done.

Over the years, Blind Willie explained to Eddie, he had met people who claimed to have seen vampires, werewolves, spirits, succubae and incubi, demons and angels, and things that had never been imagined in any book or movie. Hell, some of the things they mentioned demanded belief because they couldn't be imagined. Some shit just couldn't be made up.

There were also the ones who were looking to understand what they themselves had become. They were the fringe element that claimed not that they had seen these things, but that they *were* these things.

Then there were the legends. Willie had heard so many of those. He figured it was just a matter of time before they too would cross the threshold of this most unusual sanctuary: the two-century-old demon hunter whose only wish was to die, an avenging Angel of Death, the wicked thing that intruded on the dreams of those who slept, the Roswell man, the plant woman who fed you her tongue, the special ones who travelled backward through time.

Willie had heard all of these stories, and more just as improbable. And he believed them. All, without question. Because so many came looking for the nameless bartender, the guardian of the spirits.

"Yeah, well," said Eddie, unnerved by it all, and still not believing the whole nine yards, "I didn't come lookin' for no bartender or monsters or freaky people. All's I wanna know is why I bin here a week an' I still can't find a decent one."

"A decent one what, Eddie?"

"The best game in the world, Willie. Poker! I'm tryin' to find where's the best poker game in town?"

The bartender dropped the bottle of Jack Daniels he was holding. It shattered on the floor, silencing the bar yet again.

PART TWO
OUT OF THE LIGHT

"Unhappy is he to whom the memories of childhood bring only fear and sadness."

THE OUTSIDER
H. P. LOVECRAFT

CHAPTER ONE

AS HE HUNG suspended above the ground where the twisted metal and broken concrete lay, he wondered. As the water dripped like a metronome, his mind ticked over the infinite possibilities of what might have been. As the puddles of water reflected the dim light—only slightly brighter than the surrounding darkness—off shattered mirrors and cracked porcelain, he strained to see brighter outcomes.

If only…

As his broken body floated in mid-air and his twisted mind slid between the various realities, Stinky Pete pondered what might have been. What could have been.

If, just a few hours earlier, he had said yes instead of no.

If only he'd chosen a different path.

If only he had chosen, instead, to play a little poker…

♦♦♦

PETE AWOKE TO a loud bang.

Then there was cursing from the hall, just outside his bedroom.

"Fuggin shoes!" His father's bitching came through muffled beyond Peter's bedroom door. His voice was sleep-mushy in a dopey, semi-drunk way. "Who lef fuggin shoes out'na fuggin hall?"

A few hours earlier, Pete had heard his father come back from his Friday night out, and, with a quick glance at Cheryl Tiegs's bikinied bosom hanging on his wall, he had extinguished the light on his night table. Next, the clock radio was silenced. Pete Townshend's plaintive voice cut short during his request to allow his love to open the door.

Francis Wilson, the man Pete's mother once referred to as "Peter's donor, not his dad," had stumbled past Pete's closed door and into his own room. Peter, under the covers and faking sleep, heard nothing after that and fell into his normal, cautious, hair-trigger sleep.

Until the bang.

♦♦♦

"ARE YOU FUCKING serious? Four fucking natural aces? I call bullshit!"

"Toad," said Crouch, "dude, keep it down! My old man's upstairs."

"Sorry man." The Toad turned a suspicious eye from Crouch back to Stash. "Stash's just too goddamn lucky." The Toad had both arms wrapped around his torso and he was rocking as though in physical pain. He was losing money, so he probably was.

"Yeah, it must be hard to sit there with all those horseshoes up your ass," Theo agreed.

Stash ignored them both. "Read 'em and weep, suckers," he said, sliding his cards across the table to the still-rocking Toad with a theatrical flourish, then raking the poker chips toward him. They merged into an already remarkably large pile. He wore a shit-eating grin, carefully crafted to piss off the Toad even more. It worked.

Another Friday night, another poker game. The four friends exchanged money with each other on a weekly basis. Usually it was painless, but tonight Stash was gleefully flaying the Toad, one hand at a time. They all were, in fact, but none of the others had fallen to the depths of destitution the Toad was approaching. Stash, sixteen years old, a full year younger than the rest of them, was on a roll. "Kickin' ass and whaddayacallit takin' down names," he kept saying, grinning teeth clenching an unlit Colt cigarillo.

It had to be unlit. Crouch's father was cool, but not cool enough to permit underage smoking or drinking. He would tolerate no more than a modicum of swearing—it was poker after all, some swearing *was* necessary—and the music had to be turned down after ten p.m.

Though there were limits, they usually got away with more at Crouch's place than at any of the other teens' houses. Stash's parents were also reasonable, but no swearing and no cigarettes, unlit or otherwise. No poker was ever played at the Toad's house. His mother, an avid bingo player, disapproved of gambling. Theo's house usually had the least restrictions, only because they played when Theo's parents were absent altogether. The downside was they never knew when his parents would show up. Could be early, could be late. Either Theo's dad struck out on all his attempts and belligerence, then came home raging drunk and looking for the fight he didn't get at the event he had left, or he found the fight early—likely due to an unwanted come-on to another man's woman—and came home more pissed that someone else had taken a strip or two off him. He was a fighter, but the only fights he won were the ones he picked at home.

Either way, bad news. But the four had gotten quite adept at keeping watch for the headlights coming down Theo's drive. At the first sign of his parent's return, they would scoop their individual winnings into their untucked shirts, the pot of poker chips went into a box top they kept handy, and the cards were quickly gathered and tucked in a back pocket. Theo would place the vase and the placemats in their proper positions as the others slipped out the back door.

If Theo was fast enough, he'd join them. If not, he suffered the wrath of his old man, taking the beatings and abuse to deflect the violence from his mother.

Some nights, he just had to let her fend for herself, knowing he could not take his father's rage, knowing the guilt would affect him the next morning just as bad as the beating would have as he watched his mother fix breakfast with a swollen lip or eye, bruises purpling around her wrists.

Most of the time, she would have an excuse for it. "Your dad didn't mean to hit me. He was just so mad, Theo, and he just lashed out. I shouldn't have pushed him. I shouldn't have opened my mouth. He didn't mean it, not really. He said he was sorry and promised not to do it again." Then she would look at him with that pleading look he'd come to despise so much and say, "You know he loves us, don't you? You understand, don't you?"

Theo really didn't know any such thing. But he still felt the guilt just as bad.

Tonight was a good night, though. Tonight was guilt-free. Theo's dad had a furious head cold and was confined to bed, where the probability of violence was minimal. He would not lash out when he needed Theo's mother to tend to his needs. Tonight, Theo could enjoy himself.

If only he could win some damn money.

"Come on, Toad!" Theo said. "Quit your damn cryin' and deal, for chrissakes."

Toad gathered the cards and began to shuffle. He had lost the pained expression and now looked simply thoughtful. The others prepared themselves. It only took the Toad a few seconds, then he unleashed it.

"You guys ever notice how incredibly loud a fart sounds in the shower?"

"Dude," said Crouch, "where'n the hell do you come up with this shit?"

"The shower, obviously," replied Theo.

"No, seriously! Like, Cheech and Chong should be recording that stuff, man! I'm gonna write them. Give 'em a heads-up, like."

Stash, ever the thoughtful one, said, "Yeah, but they probably don't because have you ever noticed how whaddayacallit *wicked* it smells when you fart in the shower?"

"Yeah," said Crouch, a one-sided grin crossing his face. "But my farts smell like little purple flowers."

"Right." Toad look pained again.

"But really, no one minds the smell of their own trouser coughs. Am I right?" Crouch looked around the table. The other three nodded seriously. The man had a point.

The Toad, shuffling finished, began to deal. No game had been called as yet, so they knew not to look at the cards. Sometimes it took a few minutes to call the game. The Toad was still in scatology mode.

"Speaking of smells, I gotta tell ya this! It was so fuh—"

"Dude! My dad!" Crouch angled his head to the upper floor and dragged his lower lip to one side.

"Sorry man," the Toad continued, not missing a beat, still dealing. A lot of cards out now. Baseball maybe? "Anyway, it was so freakin' cool. I had Cheerios for breakfast this morning and—check this out, it's so cool—when I had a piss a couple of hours later?" His face could barely contain his excitement.

"Yeah?"

"Yeah, a couple of hours later, what?"

"A couple of hours later, when I had a piss…*it smelled just like freakin' Cheerios*!" His expression was triumphant.

There were mixed expressions of disbelief and awe from the other three. Okay, they collectively agreed, that *was* cool. It was also something to be tested.

"Sum'n tells me all our moms'll be purchasing *that* particular brand of cereal real soon," Crouch said, a sly smile sliding across his face. "Gonna smell so much better than asparagus piss."

The four sat quietly, savouring the thought of the upcoming tests. But only briefly.

"Okay, Toad," said Theo. "I need some cash! Call the game!"

♦♦♦

BY TWO IN the morning, Stash had stripped them all of their money and they had turned to pool, then darts, and now they were surfing the channels looking for something good. Preferably with a lot of sex or violence. Preferably both.

It didn't take long to check the four available channels. Squat. Diddly. Nada. Bupkis.

"Man, this town sucks for TV," said the Toad. This coming from the guy who thought *B.J. and the Bear* was world-class entertainment.

"Isn't *Charlie's Angels* on soon?"

"Not 'til three."

"The first season? Farrah?"

"Farrah."

"Oh yeah! I'm there," said Theo. Farrah was the best. The hottest woman in the world. And she never wore a bra.

Theo had her poster in his room. He stared at those nipples almost every night. She was unbelievable.

"So, what do we do until three?" Crouch asked.

"We could figure out a fifth poker player."

"Yeah," said the Toad. "Someone who can lose! Stash's fuckin' killin' me." Crouch let that one slide. His dad would have been in bed hours ago.

They all considered again. This was an old topic. Since they had lost Moose. It had been a tragic loss. Moose had a decent after-school job, loved poker, and played like shit.

But he refused to play anymore, ever since they had taught him a lesson.

♦♦♦

THE FUGGIN SHOES.

Pete knew the shoes weren't his. His were safely tucked in the front hall closet as normal. They must have belonged to—

His father threw open Pete's bedroom door, making Pete flinch. A millisecond later, the doorknob punched through the ever-growing hole in the drywall. He never subscribed to the Pete Townshend manner of opening the door with his love.

"WHO LEF' FUGGIN SHOES INNA HALL?" His father was pissed. Pissed off. Piss drunk.

Pissed.

"HAH? DIDJOO LEAVE EM THERE SO'S I COULD FALLUN MY ASS?" Had his father not been so furious, he would have been laughable, barely standing, one hand on the punished doorknob for support, his naked body swaying in the moonlight.

"HAH? GET A LAUGH AT YER OL' MAN'S EXPENSE?"

Peter was immobile, up on one elbow, the sheets in disarray. He could only stare at his dad, knowing anything he might say would only make the situation worse. Choosing the occasionally safe path of keeping his mouth shut, he simply stared at his father's bloated nakedness. His dad looked corpse-like in the bluish lunar light.

I wish, he thought. *I wish he* was *a corpse.*

♦♦♦

MOOSE WAS A heavy drinker. But he was usually a fun drunk.

On poker nights, he usually had a few beers before heading

over to the Friday night game, and he usually smuggled a few more in, stuffed into the waistband of his jeans and covered by his overlarge plaid lumber jacket. He would usually be tanked by ten. And that's when he would start.

Moose was well over six feet tall. He was probably north of two hundred pounds, all of it muscle earned from his work on the family farm. He had a steady girlfriend and by all accounts—both his and hers—was sexually voracious.

In no way did he ever exhibit any signs of homosexuality whatsoever. Until he got all liquored up on poker nights.

On those nights, when intoxicated, the Moose would start up his overly-familiar request. It was a request that used to gross out the other four teens, each and every time.

When intoxicated, on poker nights, the Moose would bug the other four incessantly to play strip poker with him. Needless to say, each time the request came up, they rejected it immediately. Not one of the others ever felt a burning desire to get up close and personal optically with the Moose dick. There were no girls, for chrissakes!

The lack of female players never seemed to slow him down though. Week after week, Moose continued to harass the others. It really began to grate on their nerves. The Toad was almost moved to violence on a couple of occasions.

Three weeks back, Moose couldn't make it. Date night with the girlfriend to see some shithead romantic comedy. The other four took advantage of his absence.

After the poker playing finished, the Toad had broached the topic in his usual subtle way.

"What are we gonna do about Moose and his fuckin' strip poker? He's really starting to irritate my crotch." He didn't mean that literally. It was a go-to expression the Toad busted out on occasion.

The others agreed, though none so vociferously.

The four of them had heard about homosexuality, sure. It

was 1981, who hadn't? And it wasn't that they hated anyone of that persuasion, it was just that New Hope was a small town. If there was a homosexual here, no one knew about it. And god knows they'd seen enough nakedness, having to change in cramped changerooms at school. No, it wasn't hate so much as fear of an unknown. Then again, they'd all been born and raised here, and in their seventeen years—sixteen in Stash's case—they hadn't even seen anyone of a colour other than white, unless they travelled two hours to the closest large city.

Yes, New Hope was a sheltered, backward town, existing in the eighties, but stuck in a value system twenty years out of date. Which made them uncomfortable at the idea of a guy—and a friend, at that—wanting to play a game where five guys ended up in various states of nakedness.

Over the next hour or so, the four hatched a plan. It was initially Theo's idea. Theo always seemed to be the man with the plan. Maybe it came from all the scheming he did to keep himself out of his old man's shit. Maybe it was just the way his mind was wired. Regardless, it was a good plan, a righteous plan.

It would be executed the following week, when Crouch's dad—who was the coroner for Clarington District—would be out of town on business.

♦♦♦

THE NEXT WEEK, Moose was back, drinking his face off, regaling them with stories of his sexual exploits from the week before. "Those romance movies make Cyn hot!" he explained. "Works for me."

The others acted as though nothing was out of the ordinary. They let him drink himself into his normal semistupor.

Then they waited. It would come.

They weren't disappointed.

"Hey guys," slurred Moose, "I got 'n idea. Le's play strip poker."

The others didn't want to make it too obvious, so they put up a token resistance. Just enough to lull Moose into a sense of security.

They gave him fifteen minutes before they relented.

"Come on, dudes," Crouch said, barely hiding the smirk. "Every week Moose asks us, and every week we say no. Come on, let's do it." He put a hand on Moose's shoulder. "Let's do it for Moose."

The others made a show of reluctantly agreeing.

"All right, I guess so…"

"Yeah, but just this once, man."

Moose was incredulous. He could barely contain himself.

"Really? You guys'll really play? Aw, that's so cool! Thanks, guys! You're the best!"

They dealt the cards, and encouraged Moose to have another beer. They kept him talking and he never noticed the surreptitious transferring of cards between the other four.

They cheated their asses off, allowing only the occasional loss. A sock here, a watch there. Moose was drunk enough that he didn't realize exactly how bad he was going down. Each time he lost, it was greeted with a chorus of "Whoooaaaa!" and "Take off something else!" He would giggle like a girl and remove another article of clothing.

When he got down to the removal of his underwear, Crouch stipulated that he had to put his T-shirt on the chair first, before his naked ass hit it. "There is no way I'm gonna explain skid marks on the furniture to my dad," he said.

By now, Moose was sloppy drunk and pliable as Silly Putty. That's when Phase Two of Theo's plan kicked in. He gave a slight nod to Stash.

"Okay, guys, here's a 'what if?' for ya's," Stash said.

"How long do you think it would take to run from Crouch's front porch to the whaddayacallit stop sign at the end of the road?"

"Oh, a good couple of minutes, I would think," answered Theo.

Moose fidgeted.

"You think?" said the Toad. "I don't know…maybe a minute and a half, tops. What do you think, Crouch?"

Moose's head wobbled from one person to the next, his eyes trying to track the conversation, his booze-soaked brain trying desperately to calculate the distance, wind speed, velocities, and time factors.

"I've lived here a while, dudes," Crouch answered. "I know I could make it in about a minute, easy."

Moose was practically dancing in his seat, the student who knew the answer, but the teacher wouldn't call on him. That wriggling and wiggling would have been funny had he not been as naked as the day he was born. "Butt nekked," Theo's grandpa would have said.

"Guys! Guys! I could do it in less 'n a minute!" he said, his voice twittering with excitement.

Hook.

Stash looked at him in disbelief. "You really think so? I don't know…"

"Oh yeah. Guaranteed, guys!" His enthusiasm was contagious.

"But could you do it…naked?" Theo asked.

Line.

Moose straightened up, puffing out his chest. He almost looked insulted.

"Yer damn right I could!" he said.

"Right now?"

"Damn straight!"

And sinker.

♦♦♦

THE FIVE OF them stood at the front door of Crouch's modest house. The big door hung open, but the aluminum storm door still separated them from the outside. Moose was valiantly attempting to put on his running shoes. He wasn't having much luck.

The Toad looked over at him. "Theo, help the man," he said.

Theo looked at Moose, then at the Toad. They both looked back at Moose. It was impossible not to look at his cock flopping around like a dying fish as he hopped on one foot, pulling a shoe on the other.

"Ain't no way I'm goin' near that," Theo said. "Looks like an ugly ass snake falling out of a nest."

"What? My trouser hoagie?" Moose asked, still hopping, still having no luck.

"Yeah, whatever," Theo said. "Your wiener and beans."

"The purple-headed yogurt blaster," the Toad said.

"Throbbin' Hood," added Stash.

Moose, now on the floor pulling at his second shoe, took time out to say, "Guys. It's the Hipcracker." Then he grabbed at his dick and tugged it in the direction of the others. "Woo woo!" he said. His hairy balls jiggled obscenely with the motion.

"Hey! No bacon strips on my carpet," Crouch said. "Get your ass off there!"

"Okay okay! I'm ready. Le's do it!" Moose was pumped. Woo woo.

"Okay," said Stash. "Let's make sure we're straight here. As soon as you open the door, we start timing. You gotta run down to the whaddayacallit stop sign, touch it, and run back again. When the door's closed, we stop timing. Got it?"

"Got it."

"Moose, you have your mission," the Toad said solemnly. "Godspeed, young man!"

"Don't catch your pecker in my door," said Crouch.

Theo just turned away, unable to hide his grin.

And so began Phase Three.

♦♦♦

"GO!" THE DOOR clattered open and Moose stumbled outside and hit the ground running. The other four moved out to the porch and yelled encouragement at the top of their lungs.

The four of them made an awful racket. Enough to raise the dead.

It was almost two a.m.

Moose's legs pumped, twin pistons propelling him forward in the cool night air, his

(butt nekked)

ass quivering as he ran.

"Go! Run!" they shrieked. Down the street, lights began to appear in windows as neighbours, awoken by the yelling, looked out to see what the fuss was all about.

Moose continued to run, finding his stride, his long legs scissoring, his nakedness apparently not an issue. Stash said, wonderingly, "Goddamn. Even drunk, that boy runs like a fucking gazelle."

"Run, baby, run. Go go go!" The four increased their volume, their efforts rewarded with more lights coming on. Crouch would catch hell for this, but it was an acceptable loss. They would all share in the blame if necessary. Besides, Crouch's dad would appreciate the simple elegance of the plan. He wouldn't stay mad for long.

Moose approached the stop sign at top speed. He jumped up and slapped it with a loud *bong* and spun triumphantly, his bat and balls slapping off both thighs as he prepared to return.

Apparently, that's when he noticed the lights. The faces at the windows. Billy Joel has a line in the song "Piano Man" that says something about a smile running away from a face. The line came to Theo as he saw that exact thing happen to Moose. Suddenly, he bent over, trying to cover his genitals.

Then he bolted—*really* booking it now—back to the house, one arm pumping and the other attempting to cage his wildly flailing Hipcracker.

Woo woo, Theo thought.

From the porch, they didn't cut Moose any slack, continuing to yell at him all the way back.

He batted his free hand at them. "Shut up, guys!" he begged.

Across the street, old Mrs. Fletcher opened her door and, brandishing an umbrella with extreme prejudice, yelled at Moose. "You get back inside and cover up your foo-foo, you pree-vert! I know your parents, Kenneth, and they're going to hear about this!"

Moose gave up any pretense of hiding his trouser hoagie and broke into an Olympic-calibre run. Mrs. Fletcher had a dog.

"Come on, you whaddayacallit pree-vert!" Stash yelled.

"Cover up that nasty foo-foo, dude!" Crouch yelled.

Theo and the Toad couldn't contribute. Their lungs were too busy sucking oxygen to fuel their laughter.

"Okay guys, he's getting closer," Stash warned.

"Got the door," said the Toad. He had his thumb on the handle. Moose, looking like he was going to cry, hit the edge of Crouch's yard.

"Okay guys. Back inside." The Toad opened the door and the four of them scrambled inside. Moose scrambled up the porch steps.

As he put his hand on the storm door, Crouch smiled, then slammed the big door in his face. It was locked.

Moose was locked outside, butt nekked.

Theo, Stash, Crouch, and the Toad fell about the living room, laughing uncontrollably as Moose's muffled pleadings filtered through. Muted thumps on the door made tears squirt from their eyes. Moose panicking out there with old Mrs. Fletcher yelling about his foo-foo. Oh, it was too much! Stash ran for the bathroom, unconsciously mirroring Moose as he clutched his own crotch, giggling hysterically all the way.

Then the thumps and the pleadings stopped.

"Shit! The back door!"

Crouch ran through the dining room, into the kitchen and down the stairs to the back door entrance off the patio. He locked the sliding glass door seconds before a frantic Moose grabbed at it. He looked in, framed in the moonlight, his face red with fury, visible even in the faint light. "Let me in, you sonsabitches! I'll kill you all!"

"Not a real convincing argument, Moose."

"Let me in!"

That was when they all heard the barking.

Fletcher's dog!

Moose spun, his hairy butt pressed obscenely against the glass.

"Oh look, there's a full moon tonight," the Toad said sweetly.

"LET. ME. IN!" There was no trace of drunkenness left in him. His sweaty ass cheeks squeegeed back and forth over the glass. *Glad I don't have to clean that in the morning,* Theo thought.

"You gonna ever bug us to play strip poker again?" Crouch asked.

"Never! Never! Swear to god! Come on! Fletcher's dog is coming!"

"Ooo, he's gonna eat yer foo-foo, Moose!"

"I'LL NEVER ASK AGAIN! *LET ME IN!*"

Crouch popped the lock and Moose blew the door open, slamming it just as Fletcher's ugly mutt came bounding around the corner. It came up to the glass, snuffling and grumbling, its claws making clicking noises on the surface.

Moose kicked at the mutt from his side. "Fuck off!" he said.

"Yeah, go pick on some foo-foo your own size!" the Toad said.

It was then that Stash had the unfortunate timing to come down the stairs, the sound of the toilet still simmering in the background.

"Hey guys," he said, still laughing. He imitated holding his dick and yanking on it. "Woo woo," he said, reaching the bottom of the stairs. That's when Moose spun, death in his eyes. Even naked, he looked mean. The others ran, screaming for their lives.

Stash had never anticipated being attacked by a naked man. It wasn't pretty.

♦♦♦

"NOTHING TO SAY? HAH?" Peter noted with distaste that his father's sagging testicles shook and swayed like rotted fruit in the moonlight.

"IT WAS YOU, YOU LIL' PRICK!" Spit flew on the last word. *That's the weather, now back to Bob for the sports scores,* Peter thought stupidly.

"GONNA TEACH YOU A LESSON, YOU LIL' PRICK!"

Then his father released his grip on the doorknob and bounded across the small bedroom.

Peter had never anticipated being attacked by a naked man. It wasn't pretty.

♦♦♦

AND THAT WAS how they had succeeded in curing Moose of his strip poker fetish—at least with guys. Unfortunately, he flat out refused to ever play poker again, so they were down to four. They needed a fifth.

And that's where they were now.

"Who else is there?" Crouch asked.

"What about Dan Holt?" the Toad offered. "Seems like an all right guy."

"He does," Theo said, "but dude's always either working at *The Last Word* bookshop—"

"Or he's workin' on Lila Pirsig," Crouch said.

"Can you blame him? Lila's *smokin'*."

"She's no Steph Nolan, but yeah, can't blame the lucky bastard."

"So, Dan the Man's out," Crouch said. "Who else?"

"No one that I know of," the Toad said.

"Well, Theo has a whaddayacallit idea," offered Stash. "I don't know what you'll think, though."

"Who, Theo?"

"Well," Theo started. He swallowed, knowing he would have to convince them. "I was thinking about Pete."

"Pete?" asked the Toad. "Pete who?" Suspicion darkened his voice. His blue eyes looked out from behind the thick plastic-framed glasses at Theo.

Theo sighed. "Pete Wilson." All hell broke loose.

"Peter? Peter fucking Wilson?"

"Stinky Pete?"

"Yes! Yes!" Theo said, his hands up, palms out, placating. "Yes, Stinky Pete. Hear me out, willya?"

The other three settled back in their chairs. Stash put the Colt back in his mouth, even though the brown cigarillo was beginning to droop in its plastic holder. *Convince me,* their looks said.

"Look, the poor bastard has an asshole for a dad, he's got no friends, and in the past couple of months he's really seemed to go downhill, y'know?"

"Theo," Crouch said, "it's a stinkin' poker game, not a charity event."

"And he stinks, man!" added the Toad.

"So do you, Toad. Ever smell the trouser coughs that come out of your ass? And Crouch, you remember what you said when you asked me to join into these games a few years back?"

"...yeah."

"You said, 'You look like you could use a night out.' You remember?"

"...yeah," he said again. "I remember."

"Well, you know what? I *did* need a night out. My dad's an asshole, too, so I think I know what the guy's going through. And I think he could use a night out too, okay? What do you say, guys?"

They were silent.

"Stash?" Stash was Theo's best friend. He would back him.

Stash ran his hands through his curly brown hair, wrinkled his nose to push up his glasses. "Yeah, what the hell."

"Crouch?"

"Sure. Maybe we can get him drunk and running naked in the streets."

"Toad?"

The Toad just sat there. It had to be unanimous. That's how they worked.

"Toad?"

Nothing.

"He might lose. He might lose better 'n Moose."

The Toad was still quiet. He sat there for a full minute.

"I don't like the guy, Theo. There's something about him I don't like. But, sure, yeah, I'll take his money."

"You're all heart," Theo said dryly. "Okay. I'll ask him for next week."

CHAPTER TWO

STINKY PETE STALKED cautiously through one of the many halls of hell.

This particular hell was known as Clarington District High School to the great unwashed, but Peter knew many hells. His entire life was hell—start to finish. School, home, it made no difference. No matter where he was, he was always the different one, the outsider who didn't belong, didn't fit in. No matter where he was, it was hell. No matter what he looked at, he saw hell.

Currently, hell happened to be in between third and fourth periods, so Peter was making his way from the English class he had just drifted through to his locker to dump his books, and from there he would go to calculus. Jesus! Like anyone needed to know this shit to survive. Like a running comparison on the differences between the dystopias in *Brave New World* and *1984* was going to give him an edge at the local lumber mill when he went looking for a job. Like anyone in No Hope had any need for a knowledge of integers. Yeah, that knowledge would get him out of this fucking town and the money rolling in his pockets.

Like knowing what a prime number is helps me see my dad as anything less than a prime asshole.

Stinky Pete shook his head as he worked his way down the north stairs from the second-floor English class to his locker, located in the science wing. This goddamn school had more wings than a flock of budgies: the science wing, the mathematics wing, the languages wing, the tech wing, the athletics wing. What the hell was that? The athletics wing was the goddamn gym, for chrissakes! Peter guessed the architects must have thought the place would seem more *learned* with all these damn wings. Nice try, but useless with a school located in Buttfuck, in the nether regions of the sunny state of Indifference. Even his town's name was cheese—New Hope. The only thing worth hoping for was a quick exit, but that was an old hope. No Hope was the more appropriate name, and the one most frequently used by anyone under the age of twenty-one.

New Hope was anything but. The town had been around forever, and every year the population dropped by another few souls lucky to have found a way out, be it death or the persistence to escape the town's clutches. Most people either worked at one of the three regional lumber mills, or in town at one of the bullshit little stores. Stores that sold steel-toed boots and thick winter coats with reflective material on them. Stores that sold dynamite caps for those occasions when your yard work needed that extra *oomph*. Stores that sold Day-Glo ball caps so your drunken hunting buddy wouldn't blow your head off. Stores that did a brisk trade in pain medication and alcohol. Gotta numb those pains.

Hell, even the *Mayflower*—the Lake Kwanashishing ferry that used to run the north-south route from New Hope to Carry's Cove—decided to commit suicide rather than come back to this shit town for the winter. And that was over seventy years ago.

Yee-haw, he thought. *God bless New Hope.* He could see *that* one on some sort of a cross-stitched doily. Or maybe a T-shirt with the sinking *Mayflower* on it. *New Hope. Where hope comes to die.*

Pete squeezed his body through the throng of students congregating in the hallway, making the most of their ten-minute break before last class. He might as well be invisible for all the notice he received from his schoolmates. That suited him just fine. The last thing Pete wanted was to be noticed. He got enough of that shit at home. He didn't wear clothes that would make him stand out. Jeans, T-shirt, lumber jacket over top, and finished off with a pair of nondescript running shoes in the summer months and tan workboots in winter. It wasn't name brand, but it was ample camouflage.

The smell of hairspray, acne medication, and teenage sweat was thick in the brightly lit hall. A million inane conversations went on around him, unnoticed. *Are they really dating? Did you see the top she was wearing? Think I can score some before Saturday? Did you see* Dallas *last night?* Didn't they realize they were in hell, too? Couldn't they see it all around them?

Pete forced the sounds away, hunkering his chin tighter into his chest as he pushed through. He felt like a cancer cell in the student body.

It was a strange sensation, but he could feel himself getting closer to his locker. A humming buzz

(could use a night out)

started up in his head as he approached it. A light layer of sweat broke out under his arms, at the small of his back, and in the dead zone between his balls and asshole. A sensuous tingling roiled all along his scalp, like a lover massaging his skull. As weird as it was to admit, it was erotic. He wiped at his greasy forehead, pushing his wavy hair out of his eyes.

Pete reached locker number 1086 and tucked his binder under his arm as he spun the dial on his combination lock. He had performed this action so many times now it was done without thinking. He could, in fact, dial the three numbers—48-22-6—without looking—a talent no one knew or cared about. So what? He knew he could do it. He popped the lock with a metallic bang and opened the door. *Stinky Pete sux big cock* had been crudely scratched into the sickly orange paint months ago. Pete ignored the commentary as it swung by his eyes, having become numb to it by now. He ditched his English books and grabbed his calculus text and binder. His eyes caught a glimpse of the other book sitting up on the top shelf, partially hidden by a brown paper lunch bag with an uneaten Spam sandwich inside. The book that called to him, that tickled his brain. The book that made him pant slightly and gave him a hard-on. The book that offered its secrets up like a virgin on her wedding night. The Book.

Soon, he thought. *Soon it will be time, my friend. Time to use You.*

And then we'll teach someone about hell.

♦♦♦

THE TOAD APPROACHED Theo and Stash, a big smile threatening to wrap around his ears. It could only mean trouble.

"What'd you do?" Stash asked, a note of dread in his voice.

"Oh man, you shoulda been there! It was the best!" The Toad was so excited he was almost vibrating.

"I was just at my locker, and there was Brian Brandt and all these cheerleader types around him—"

"As usual," Theo and Stash said in unison.

"Yeah," the Toad continued, not even registering the interruption. "So anyway, Mr. Studley Wellhung's chattin' up the chicks..."

Suddenly the Toad's posture changed. He straightened, flipped up the collar of his jean jacket, smoothed back his limp, blond bowl cut and leaned against the locker in a display of completely out-of-character machismo.

"...So he's like this and he's like, 'oh yeah, my dick's big and my hair's perfect and blah blah fucking blah.'"

"So he's acting whaddayacallit normal," Stash interjected.

"Yeah! Exactly, so I mean, he's gotta be dropped a coupla notches, right? Right." He gave them no time to answer themselves. "Cuz he's a goddamn jock and all jocks are assholes. So I dropped an SBD right there at my locker, like, two feet away from his ass!"

Having been around the Toad this long, Theo and Stash knew SBD meant Silent, But Deadly. As in flatulence. Crouch called them "shits without the mess." Stash just called them "sharts."

Stash was already laughing. Theo had a wide grin on his face as well.

"So what happened?" he asked.

"So, some of the girls are grabbing their noses and they're like, 'ewww.'"

"Well…yeah," Theo said. "Been there, buddy, and it ain't no fuckin' rose garden."

"Yeah well, I made out like I'd just caught it too—and it wasn't bad, either, one of my better brands—so I'm looking at Studley and I'm like, 'ewwww, dude, somethin' musta crawled up inside you and *died*, man!'"

"Yeah, and?"

"And what?" The Toad looked incredulous. "I walked away!"

Theo and Stash really began to laugh then.

"What?" the Toad asked. "What's so damn funny?"

"You really think anyone whaddayacallit thought Brandt farted?" Stash said.

"Yeah, Toad, you really showed him!" Theo fell back against the locker, his arms around his shaking stomach. "No one would ever have suspected it was you. Jesus! What a criminal mastermind!"

Still laughing, Theo slid into Bugs Bunny mode. "Wot a maroon."

"Wot a whaddayacallit ultra-maroon." Stash pulled off his wire-rimmed Lennon glasses and wiped tears from his eyes.

"Whatever," the Toad said, pissed. "You guys have no sense of humour. God! I gotta get a higher class of friends…"

Still laughing, they started down the hall.

"Hey!" Stash nudged Theo in the ribs. "There's Steph."

"Where?" Theo almost sounded panicked that he couldn't see her.

"See that creepy Talia chick? To the right."

Theo nodded. "Oh man! Check out the sweater. Look at that rack! I could climb right in there and get lost!"

The three picked up the pace. As they approached her, the Toad noticed Peter at his locker.

"Hey, Theo," he said, "there's Stinky Pete. You talked to him about Friday yet?"

"No, not yet. I thought you weren't crazy about letting him in—why you asking?"

"Cuz my wallet's still sore from the reaming Stash gave it last week. I need cash."

"Your wallet's likely just pissed off from the whaddayacallit stealth bomb you just dropped on Studley Wellhung," Stash observed.

"Shut up and stay here, both of you," Theo said. "I'll go talk to him now."

♦♦♦

PETER SHUT THE locker door and threaded the lock. Turning to leave, he watched Stephanie Nolan walk by. Everybody watched Steph go by. All the guys wanted her—Stinky Pete included—and the girls all wanted her to be ugly. Or flat chested. Or fat. Or stupid. Hell, anything to bring her down a notch. But she was none of those. Small, well built, with a dazzling smile, she could have almost any guy in No Hope.

She was one of the only bright spots, the one angel in Peter's hell. But Pete didn't have a chance. He was the invisible man. The greasy, smelly, invisible man. The guy they smelled but never really saw.

He looked down the hall, past the prom banners—*Why is this man smiling? Because he's already got a date to the PROM!*—and the crowd of girls just outside the washroom. Sure as shit, there was Theo,

(no catch pete)

Stash, and the Toad cruising in their cords and concert shirts. They were Stephanie's little lambs, and everywhere that Stephanie went, the lambs

(me and the guys)

were sure to follow. It was a school-wide joke, especially when it came to Theo, since he'd broken up with Marcia, but none of them seemed to care. Neither did Stephanie, for that matter. She talked to them, even hung out with them from time to time. Just enough to keep them on the hook. Just enough to keep them salivating.

What a bunch of idiots, he thought. Peter allowed himself a rare smile as he dropped his gaze and headed off to another class he wouldn't be able to concentrate on.

Before he could walk more than a few steps, he felt a tap on his shoulder. Turning, he was surprised to see Theo standing there, a tentative smile on his face.

"What…" he started. No one ever talked to him. He didn't know what to say. "What?" he said again.

"Hey, Peter, how you doin'?"

Peter was too surprised to answer, and only stared dumbly at Theo.

"Yeah, okay, listen," Theo said, "I know it's kinda last minute, but me and the guys"—he hooked a thumb over his shoulder at Stash and the Toad—"we were wondering if you were interested in playing some poker tonight. We're all getting together at Stash's."

Pete was so shocked, he was at a loss for words. Someone was offering an invitation to him?

Finding his voice, he said, "What's the catch?" He had a lopsided grin on his face that held only suspicion.

"No catch, Pete," Theo said. "You, uh, you just look like you could use a night out."

Peter sucked in a breath. Yes, he did need a night out.

Theo stood there, forgotten.

A night out. A night away from his miserable life. A night of laughter, of jokes at someone else's expense. A night of fun. A night where he wasn't dreading the next minute.

A night out.

Yes. Yes, he could use that. He needed that!

"Pete? You okay?"

"Huh? Oh, yeah. Yeah, I'm good. Uh, tonight, right?"

"Yeah, we get together around seven every Friday night. TGIF and all that good shit."

The school traffic continued to swirl and flow around them. The two of them were an eddy in the stream. Peter stood there, scratching his still-clean hair. He really wanted to go. He really wanted to be amongst others again. It had been so long.

Peter opened his mouth to say yes. He had held off this long for his father—this plan of his, couldn't it wait until Monday? Maybe what he was doing was wrong. Maybe this was some sort of sign to abandon this whole mission. He was only seventeen. He would be away from here soon. He could go anywhere he wanted. There was no real need to stay in No Hope. He would escape soon. Maybe having something to look forward to every Friday would help him over the rough spots, make the other six days tolerable. He had heard about Theo's dad. Maybe he and Theo could be friends…

All of this passed through his mind as he opened his mouth to say yes. But what came out of his mouth surprised him as much as that erotic tingling of his scalp.

"No."

Theo looked surprised. If he had been reading Peter's expression correctly, Peter could understand why. Why had he said that?

"Ah, okay. Shit. Yeah. Maybe some other night, then," Theo said, looking genuinely disappointed. Crestfallen. Not a normal word in Peter's vocabulary, but crestfallen fit the bill.

Peter felt rising panic. *No! No, that's not what I meant to say! I want to come! Ask me again, I'll say yes! Just ask me again! Don't turn away! No!*

Peter's eyes pleaded with Theo to not go, to not accept the answer. But Theo just nodded and, with a mumbled "see ya 'round" turned back to Stash and the Toad. Peter was frozen to the spot. Theo turned back once and looked to Pete again. "You take it easy, okay?" Again, that look. Crestfallen.

Why did I say no?

Eventually, Peter was able to move again, and he slunk off to the last class of the day. Nobody noticed him, as was usual, but if they had, they would have thought Peter was in physical pain.

But, as usual, no one noticed.

♦♦♦

THEO WALKED BACK over to where Stash and the Toad were waiting for him.

"What's up?" Stash asked. He could see that Theo was obviously troubled.

"I don't know. He *looked* like he wanted to come. I would have bet cash money that he was going to say yes."

"But?"

Theo shrugged. "But nothing. He got this weird look on his face and said no."

"Hey, no skin off my bag," said the Toad. "I tol' ya, man, there's somethin' about him I just don't trust. I just wanted his cash."

But something about the whole exchange left Theo with a bad feeling. There was something screwy. It was like having a puzzle with a couple of missing pieces. But this felt like an important puzzle.

Theo felt like he could identify with Pete. They both—from what Theo had heard—seemed to come from similar home lives. If that was true, then Theo definitely knew where Stinky Pete was coming from. He knew what it was like to be the linchpin between his mom and dad—two trains trying to go in opposite directions. Or maybe a more apt analogy would be one of those Chinese crackers. Pull too hard in opposite directions and it was going to explode.

God knows there were many times Theo felt like he was going to explode.

Looking at Pete's receding back, Theo wondered which of the two of them was better off.

He figured Pete was in a tug-of-war where one side had given up. He was a flag, flapping in a desperate attempt to get away, but always tied to that pole. So, really, which one of them was better off?

Which one was going to explode first?

Everything in him said to go back and ask Peter one more time, just to be sure. He said this to his two friends.

"Nah, maybe you should leave him alone," said Stash. "Hey, you never know, he may come around. Don't whaddayacallit stress on it. He may just want to be alone right now."

Stash was usually good at reading people. Theo trusted his opinion, and—again against his own better judgment—decided to go with Stash's advice.

Theo headed off to class. He passed a poster—*Why is this man screaming? Because he didn't get his prom ticket in time!*—and, as he looked at the caricature of a screaming student, he got a chill that ran straight down his spine.

Which one was going to explode first?

CHAPTER THREE

MR. POPPER WAS talking, but Stinky Pete, safely camouflaged at the back of the room, only caught the odd word. He was mostly tucked up deep inside his head, wallowing in his own personal shit heap.

It didn't seem to faze Popper. He was in his glory, preaching to the masses about the new era they were entering – the computer age.

Pete caught that. *Big shit,* he thought.

"I'm sure you will all recall the assembly we had a couple of months ago, where we announced that Clarington High School was one of only five schools in the country that had won the competition to link up to a nationwide network of computers through USENET."

Some of the students nodded. Yeah, they remembered being able to goof off for half an hour or so. Damn straight! The nodding was enough to keep Popper going.

"Well, we now have the infrastructure and equipment in place!" He rubbed his hands together, as though he was about to tuck into a big meal. *Goddamn, what an ass,* thought Pete.

"This is a heads-up," Popper continued. "We will be looking for some students to participate in a special study group next year. This is the primary component of the competition.

"We will be looking for applicants and the guidelines will be posted shortly, but it's something I want you all to keep in mind over the next week. This is a very important and exciting opportunity for some lucky students. This," he said, rubbing his hands together again, "is the future!"

Peter caught some of what Popper was saying—enough to know what he was talking about, but also enough to know he didn't have a hope in hell of being chosen. No one would ever pick Stinky Pete for an "important and exciting opportunity."

Funnily enough, Peter would have made an excellent choice.

Peter probably knew more about the computer system installed in the school than most of the teachers did. Before his mind had turned to…other interests…

(all the things we can do)

he had done a lot of reading and research on computer technology and the advancements that were being made. He had found he had a knack for the computer languages. Some people were adept at learning Latin or French—Peter had grasped COBOL and FORTRAN with a speed and proficiency that had astounded him. He'd read up on ARPANET and CSNET and, yes, even USENET.

It also pleased him greatly. Something he could do! Something he was *good* at!

Something else ol' Francis will never know about me, Pete thought as he rubbed at a bruised rib.

Pete's eyes drifted off Popper to settle on…what? His mind was floating again and he realized he had been staring at Daniel "the Donkey" Dunkey's Adidas shirt.

Adidas. What was the phrase all the students used? *All Day I Dream About Sex?*

Pete knew that, like calculus and physics and algebra, none of his knowledge of computer technology would ever help him either. He needed to deal with a violent father, and that required different knowledge.

So that horny Adidas phrase didn't apply to Pete. His would be more like *All Day I Dream About Survival…*

♦♦♦

IN HIS MIND, his father's face loomed, all red with bloodshot eyes and nose, hair as wild as the wind, his voice low and guttural, full of all the hate and malice he could summon. He was letting his only son know his exact standing in the world.

"You little piece of shit! I've pissed on better than the likes of you!"

The commentary was nothing new. It used to be that his dad's attacks were infrequent bursts of anger, supernova-like explosions that flared up fast and died just as suddenly. Peter could put them down to a bad day, money problems, whatever. But over the past few months, they had steadily increased in frequency and intensity, with the added bonus of violence at no extra charge. Without warning, his old man would just snap, take aim, and unleash on whatever was closest at hand. Sometimes it was a piece of furniture, sometimes it was a wall, and sometimes it was Peter. To Pete, he had lately felt like he lived with a human bomb that never gave a warning when it was going to blow. And, like a bomb, his attacks were loud, violent, and the effects felt for days.

Lately, though, the bomb went off almost daily. Pete's home life was a minefield. One outburst would cause another. His dad had punched a hole in the wall with the toaster one day. The next morning, he was not able to make his Eggos so he had snapped again.

That time, Peter had been the closest thing at hand.

♦♦♦

"I THINK HE carried that book in his pocket because he thought he *was* the Catcher in the Rye. He thought he was saving the world's children from the evil inherent in John Lennon's music, because he was the guy who said the Beatles were more popular than Jesus," she said.

"Of course, what he didn't count on—what he obviously never considered—was that he killed the *man*, but not the *music*." Helmsley stopped and the class was quiet for a moment, considering her unusually interesting words.

Quite simply, Miss Helmsley wasn't that cool. In fact, Marcia generally considered her to be one of the least cool teachers—with the possible exception of Mr. Trask—currently employed at Clarington High.

Not cool, but definitely a contender for the title of weirdest. Theo referred to the class where Helmsley taught English as "Transylvania."

Theo. She sighed. Better to not go there.

Marcia looked around the classroom, trying to find something else to think about. Anything other than Theo. Her eyes settled on an empty desk in the second row, third from the front.

Crouch's desk. Definitely shouldn't go there, either.

Where the heck is he?

She looked away from the desk once more in a futile attempt to find something that didn't remind her of ex-boyfriends.

The classroom was so obviously an English teacher's room. There was the usual overhead projector and related school paraphernalia. Books were stacked anywhere a flat surface presented itself. No one doubted Miss Helmsley loved the subject, but what caught the attention of anyone entering for the first time were the photographs and illustrations of Miss Helmsley's favourite writers posted all over the room: J. D. Salinger, Harper Lee, Jack Kerouac, Mark Twain, Oscar Wilde,

Shakespeare. In between the portraits, she had laboriously written out some of her most-loved quotes. When she had run out of wall space, she began putting large sheets of bristol board on the windows and posted more words and pictures there.

Like she didn't want the sun in. Weird. *Transylvania.*

To Marcia, Helmsley seemed like a bear wandering in her cave. She immediately felt bad about the thought. Sure, Helmsley was a big woman, but she could hardly be called a bear. She was always so pleasant, with a large round face that seemed to naturally go to a smile.

Weird. Uncool. Overweight. But definitely pleasant.

"…isn't that right, Miss Mayer?"

"Hmm?" Marcia said. Darn! Helmsley had caught her daydreaming! "I'm sorry, what was the question?"

Miss Helmsley smiled. "Marcia, summer's almost here, but we still have to pay attention." The last word came out with a musical quality that only jovial people could successfully manage to make sound both joyful and sarcastic.

Marcia lowered her head and nervously doodled in her notebook. "Yes, Miss Helmsley," she said. "I'm sorry."

Helmsley seemed appeased, and continued on with her dissemination of *The Catcher in the Rye*.

Oh well, at least it had got her thoughts off Theo and Crouch.

Marcia's eyes drifted back to the empty desk. *Where is he?*

She figured Crouch was out drinking again, or maybe vandalizing in the name of Damage Inc. Those two pursuits worried the heck out of her. His drinking used to be confined simply to his extended lunches on Wednesdays, but in the past couple of months since Marcia and Crouch had split up, the drinking had accelerated. She didn't think he was an alcoholic. An "alky" as her mom termed it, usually when referring to Theo's dad.

No, Crouch wasn't an alky. At least, not yet. He wasn't even eighteen!

And this Damage Inc. thing. Sooner or later, he was going to make a mistake—get caught stealing a street sign or whatever the heck he did—and then he'd be in real trouble.

She never did understand why Theo even hung out with Crouch. They didn't seem to have anything in common—not really. But there they were. Like two peas in a pod, as her mom said.

Seems her mom had a lot to say when it came to Theo, now that she thought about it. Her mom really didn't like Theo. She would likely have a lot to say about Crouch had she known her daughter had been with him as well, a fact that Marcia kept hidden despite lies of omission being a sin.

She probably should have taken the same tactic with Theo.

Theo. Marcia didn't really understand her mother's dislike of him. Though, there was one thing Marcia didn't like about Theo. Well, maybe *not like* was too strong a term. Maybe it was more something she didn't understand about him—his fascination with Stephanie Nolan.

Well, okay, if she was honest with herself, she *could* see some of it. She'd heard the boys calling Steph "Jocelyn," and she wasn't stupid. But Steph didn't really seem to be Theo's type.

Then again, she was no expert on Theo—what was "his type"?

Marcia?

Apparently not. At least, not lately.

Though it was something Crouch and Theo had in common. Marcia sighed. Seventeen and already two ex-boyfriends to her credit. It didn't bode well for a good Catholic girl's reputation.

At least, that's what her mom said.

Marcia looked around the class, glancing at Miss Helmsley and nodding every once in a while to let her know she was still dialled in to the conversation. She settled on Cynthia Fuller—Moose's girlfriend.

How that girl put up with him, Marcia didn't know. They'd been an item since Grade 6. But what she was going through now...

Marcia suppressed a grin. Stupid Moose running naked down a street, a dopey little dog with a bow on its head snapping at his quivering butt...

As bad as Crouch was, at least he hadn't been caught doing something that stupid yet. So he wasn't *that* bad, was he? But that was probably Theo, Stash, and the Toad's influence on him. They were more of a calming influence.

Then again, she realized, they *were* the ones who put that bug in Moose's ear to run naked in the streets in the first place.

A calming influence, Marcia thought. *Yeah, right.*

Why were guys so hard to understand?

Miss Helmsley was mentioning something about picking up reference material for an impending assignment. Marcia sighed inwardly and dutifully turned her attention back to Helmsley's words.

♦♦♦

PETE ENDURED POPPER'S class as best he could, considering the maelstrom that spun in his mind. All the black thoughts, all the plans, and off by itself in a slightly less dark corner, Theo's offer. Just a little while longer and it would be over. All the shit. All the beatings.

Mr. Popper, like most of the faculty and students at Clarington High, seemed oblivious to Peter. The teacher knew just as well as Peter did that it really didn't matter how well he did in school because that summer job in the Madawaska Mill would very likely turn into a rewarding career in the lumber industry. Which, in turn, would probably spur the profits of the breweries and local weed dealers to even greater heights. So, really, who cared if he just sat at the back of the class marking time like any prisoner on death row?

Except for having to endure the occasional ridicule or prank, Stinky Pete was just one more of the non-entities that inhabited the school, drifting through classes like smoke, never leaving an impression or even a sign that he had ever been there. His only mark would be a bad picture in the yearbook.

Yeah, well. Pete checked his watch. *That's all gonna change in an hour or so.*

All he had to do was survive the class and get back to his locker. He needed to get back to the Book. He could hear It singing to him right now. It was a sweet, plaintive Siren's song, begging him to come back.

♦♦♦

IN THE PAST couple of years, Peter had picked up the unfortunate tag "Stinky Pete." He was a normal seventeen-year-old male—he perspired. The problem was his dad's fucked-up obsessions: a few years ago, around 1977, the summer *Star Wars* was released, and a year after his mother had abandoned ship, and all those people from town had disappeared, his father got it into his head that the shower could only be used once a week—Thursdays. Peter was expected to get all his chores done on the weekend. Chopping wood, cutting grass, shovelling snow, raking leaves. He spent most weekends willing his body not to sweat, but sweat it did. For a while, he snuck in some showers at school, but then the

(leggo my fuckin' eggos, you fuck)

beatings had started.

Soon, it was easier to be known as Stinky Pete than to show the world his purpled bruises and ragged scars, to let his peers know he was being tortured on a regular basis. As cruel as teenagers could be, they were little league compared to Peter's father.

So, Stinky Pete Wilson found himself applying his mother's five-year-old makeup to the still-developing bruise on his left cheek on a beautiful Wednesday

(twenty-four hours to cleanliness!)

morning in March just over two months ago. All because his father couldn't toast his goddamn waffles.

The teen ego is a fragile thing at the best of times. When Peter found himself staring in the mirror at his obvious patch-up job to his cheek, he realized something had to be done. Any love that Peter had held for his father had been shouted, beaten, and tortured out of him with all the care and sympathy of dog shit being removed from the bottom of a boot. Peter could not handle his life anymore. Something had to give.

Something had to change.

The tears had flowed then, allowing the bruise to come to light again. As the bruise flowered, something inside Peter just died. The light flickered out in his eyes and his heart turned black. He watched the face of his reflection darken. And in that moment, he came to a place that had been just out of reach until then. It was a barren, hardened place where dreams could not live and hope could not grow.

Revenge.

Peter realized, once that place of no hope had been reached, that he only had one clear choice.

He was going to kill his father.

♦♦♦

LAURA DAVIS WAS having a hell of a time teaching today's art class.

Kenneth Birch—Moose—was late and had come running into her class.

As he had bustled through the overgrown garden of easels, stools, and students to an empty spot, Diane Beam spoke up.

"Oh!" she said in mock surprise, "I didn't realize we were gonna do *nudes* today!"

That had started the class going. An avalanche of laughter rolled over the entire room. Moose's face and neck reddened as he suddenly found something interesting behind his easel. Laura watched him drop his head in a defeated, when-is-this-gonna-end pose.

"Diane!" Laura had barked. "EEE-nough!"

Laura's tone said she wouldn't stand for anymore shit. She sincerely hoped none of the students noticed her fighting a smile as she turned away to gather the drawing materials for the day.

Poor Moose. Laura was sure he had signed up for her art class only because his girlfriend Cynthia had done so. Then Cynthia had run into a scheduling conflict and had to drop out of the class.

Moose had tried as well, but all the other classes he had applied for were either conflicted or full. He was stuck.

All he seemed to be interested in drawing were muscle cars or World War II fighter planes. Thankfully, he wasn't bad. There was some talent there. Just enough to keep him coming back.

She looked over at him now, careful to show only concern in her expression. She gave him her best "you okay?" face. His look of desperation kicked her into gear and she got the class started.

But every so often during the class, she had to pause, turn away, and smile. It was a curse that her imagination put together a great visual of Moose running down a darkened street, his shadow sliding under him as he crossed from one streetlight to the next in a panicked bid to get back inside, his hands hiding his naked...what had they called it?...His foo-foo?

She did her best to cover her smirk with a cough and blamed it on an oncoming cold.

"Summer colds," Diane Beam said sweetly. "They're the worst." She turned to Moose. "I hear you get them from not dressing warm enough when you go out at night."

Laura sighed. It was going to be a long class.

♦♦♦

"AND THAT, MY friends—"

The 3:15 P.M. bell rang.

"—is the sound of roughly four hundred teenage brains shutting down. Enjoy your weekend." Mr. Popper sat down at his desk as his students finished packing up their notes with the gusto that only comes from Friday-afternoon liberation. Peter took his time, wanting to savour the next few minutes. By now, Theo's offer of friendship was pushed low and back into a bottom shelf of his mind. He only had thoughts for the coming event.

After all, the life he saved would be his own. For the second time today, he allowed himself a

(why is this man)

small smile.

CHAPTER FOUR

THE 3:15 P.M. BELL rang.

"Oh thank god!" the Toad shouted from the back of the class. "I gotta pinch a loaf most serious! I'm tasting chocolate, man!" Though he ducked his head, Theo saw Smilin' Johnny chuckling, which actually was fascinating. Normally, the physics teacher's interests ran less to shit jokes and more to looking down the girls' tops. The guy was a fucking perv of the first order.

"All right…well…ah, class? You all…ah…have a nice, ah, weekend? Okay? But, ah, not…too nice?" The way Smilin' Johnny Trask spoke, with those weird pauses and everything sounding like a question, drove the students bugfuck crazy. But damn, Stash could imitate him *perfectly*.

Always harassing his female students, it was a wonder he'd never been busted for some sexual misdemeanour. Everyone knew the ones who got the best marks from him were the chicks who wore low-cut tops that showed a decent amount of cleavage. That lack of cleavage pretty much left Theo and his friends in the dust.

Theo reached under his desk to get his books. The Toad, his workstation partner, did the same, cutting a fart in the process. Ignoring it, Theo instead tried to come up with even one advantage to having a fecal-obsessed partner in physics. Nothing came to mind, even as the stink came to his nose. "Jesus, dude, you need help," he said, waving a hand in front of his face.

"Seriously, though," the Toad continued as he nonchalantly pulled out a banana and began to knead and squeeze it. "Haven't you ever had a serious hurt-on to take a major league squamp, and your body's crying out to just let off a little gas—just a *little*—and you know if you push out one trouser cough, you're gonna shit yourself? Haven't ya?"

Theo laughed. The Toad knew damn well that he had. "You telling me you just—"

"No, man," the Toad said. "Do I look like I'm two?"

"I mean, you're the one who brought it up."

"Whatever." He continued to manipulate the banana. "Just trying to make conversation."

This banana thing now. The Toad's eating habits grossed Theo out. He had found out from somewhere—maybe *National Geographic* or something—that there was some tribe in Africa or someplace that smooshed their bananas and then ate them by squeezing out the innards like toothpaste. Theo was convinced the Toad hated his bananas this way, but was too enamoured by the gross-out factor to ever give it up.

"Man, you're sick," Theo said.

"Eat me," the Toad replied good-naturedly. "Better yet, eat my banana!"

Mr. Trask ignored their comments. "Ah, don't, ah…forget? To put your, ah…stools on top of, ah…the stations? The, ah…cleaners are doing the, ah…floors tonight?"

"Heh," said the Toad, "how about I just leave my stool in the handy porcelain receptacle down the hall. If it's all the same to you, sir."

"Oh, yes, yet another whaddayacallit lame innuendo from the Toadster," said Stash. "Please, do carry on."

Theo chose to ignore both of them, because Stephanie Nolan—the Orgasm Machine, as far as Theo was concerned—was not leaving the class. Oh, no. Instead, she was walking toward Theo, looking right at him. Right at Theo! Tight jeans, soft sweater just sheer enough to catch a glimpse of bra gently cradling her breasts.

"So there was this time? I had to sh—"

"Shut up, Toad," Theo said, his voice low and hoarse, his eyes never leaving the vision walking toward him.

Theo tried, really tried, to look in her eyes, but good god, those tits had just the right amount of jiggle and sway to divert his attention. She was in possession one of the finest racks Theo had ever seen, aside from Farrah.

Theo was sure that it was a set of mammaries like Stephanie's that first inspired James Brown to come up with that "G' GAWD!" thing he did. It was definitely that particular set of bodacious ta-ta's that inspired a few of the No Hope guys to nickname any well-endowed woman

(jostlin')

Jocelyn.

Ohmigod, Theo thought, *what I wouldn't give for five minutes alone with those—*

"Theo?"

He came back to reality with a thud. *Look at her face, just her face and you'll be all right,* he thought, but things were already stirring in Penisville.

"Hey, Steph," he said. Oh, yeah, he was cool. *Breathe, buddy. Now, breathe again.*

"Listen, I was wondering..." She lowered her eyes. Her delicate face angled downward

(toward those mouth-watering funbags)

and she looked at him through long eyelashes and a few of strands of hair. Her eyes were green.

"Uh, yeah?" he asked, showing off his incredible cache of words for any occasion. "You were wondering what?" *If you could play hide-the-sausage with me? Hell, yeah!*

"I was wondering if you were busy right now. You know, was there anything pressing?"

The only thing pressing right now was Theo's trouser hoagie against his fly. All thoughts of the poker game vanished. He felt the blood rushing to his head in a blush of excitement. Stephanie was asking *him* if he was busy. Reality geared down and everything came into focus. Theo saw the Toad's eyes widen. Stash grinned like an idiot. Smilin' Johnny had even stopped and lowered his glasses to the tip of his nose so he could watch the proceedings. Even Brian Brandt—Mr. Studley Wellhung himself—looked like he might choke. The room had gone quiet enough to hear the faint buzz of the fluorescents. This was a dream come true! Was he busy? Not a chance!

Toad said, "Actually, we're all playing po—"

"*ShutupToad,*" he said. Then, summoning all the cool he could, Theo managed to croak, "No, my schedule's pretty open, Steph. What'd you have in mind?"

The tension was a living presence in the room. Not a breath was drawn. Time slowed and took the off-ramp. Theo imagined he could feel his pupils dilating as he anticipated her next words. The green-eyed goddess had come down from Olympus in a golden chariot and was about to proffer a porcelain-skinned hand to him before ascending back to the heavens. This was it. From Geek to Love God with the passing of a few silken words from Stephanie's perfect mouth. He was in.

Oh, yes.

"Actually, the set crew is running a little behind on the stage set-up for the musical. You know, *The Sound of Music*? We've just got a week left, and we need some more help with the papier-mâché and the painting. D'you think you and the guys could help us out for a couple of hours tonight?"

"Wha…?" Theo said stupidly.

In Theo's head, Stephanie still gave off the "I need to get you into my bed" look, and the actual words entering his ears sounded nothing like what he heard north of his eyebrows. His fantasy was so strong that Theo didn't kick back to reality until about halfway through her question. By then, nothing she said made any sense.

It only got worse. Stephanie gave him a look that clearly questioned his mental stability. Studley Wellhung exited the class chuckling, his reputation intact. Stash and the Toad were considerate enough to look both embarrassed and amused for Theo, even as they hung around to enjoy the show.

"Look," Steph said, sounding miffed. "I'm sorry if I've said something funny. I just thought you guys might be interested in showing a little school spirit for a change."

"Woo-hoo! Way to go, stud muffin! Steph's gonna open a can a' whoop-ass on yo' head!" The Toad could always be counted on for the colour commentary.

Stephanie turned on the Toad, finger in his face. "And you! What's your problem? You could volunteer too, y'know...you...you..." Her face reddened with the flash of anger. It was obvious she wanted to swear, but wouldn't.

"...Poo-boy!" she finally finished. The Toad didn't seem interested in any more colour commentary after that.

Then, Stash got lined up in the path of the fickle finger of fate. "Robert, your uncle's a teacher here. You'd think you would get your butt in there from time to time. God! The spirit in this school sucks!"

This is getting ugly, Theo thought. *Time to diffuse it, dial it back a bit. Cool the jets, so to speak.*

"Whoa, whoa, Steph!" he said. "Take a pill! Relax. We'll be there. *All* of us." He looked at Stash and the Toad, doing the exaggerated say-yes nod. "Won't we, guys?"

"Oh yeah, we're there, man."

"Definitely. Definitely there."

"Absolutely. Yep, we're there as we speak."

"Oh yeah! I can damn near taste that whaddayacallit papier-mâché goop now."

"Mm-mmm! Goop! That's goooood eatin'!"

"Yessir, ma'am." Stash looked to the Toad. "Poo-boy?" Stash extended an arm in a grand gesture toward the door, eyes expectant. "Shall we?"

"Mm-hmm, yes. Quite!" the Toad exclaimed in possibly the worst British accent Theo had ever heard. "Twice around the park and a quick stop at the loo, Jeeves. And don't spare the horses. And that's *Mis*ter Poo-boy to you, Jeeves"—and here, he whacked Stash upside the back of his head, making him giggle stupidly—"you forget your place, you impertinent fool." He linked arms with Stash and the two of them skipped—actually skipped—out of the classroom. In an exquisite display of Vulcan mind-melding, they launched into a horribly off-key, completely spontaneous version of "We're Off to See the Wizard." All the way down the hall, the echoes of "becausebecausebecausebecauseBE*CUUUUUZZZ*!" were heard, along with catcalls, whistles, and a "fuckin' dickheads" comment.

Theo looked back to Stephanie and smiled. He had his arms spread out in a see?-I-told-ya pose. She had a big beautiful smile coming right back at him. "I guess they still have some spirit after all," he said. "C'mon, let's go paint some greenery. Can I be in charge of bushes?" He scooped up his books and they headed out of class. "Would that make me a plant manager, or a branch manager?"

Stephanie rolled those emerald

(we're off to see the wizard)

eyes, and Theo was sure that maybe, just maybe if he could play it cool, he might have a chance at something more than friendship here. That would be nice, now that the whole thing with Marcia had fallen to shit. Yes, it would be good to have at least a *hope* of another girlfriend.

If he could just keep his eyes off her

(the wonderful wizard of)

breasts.

♦♦♦

STINKY PETE SLID the Book into his gym bag and closed the locker door. As he threaded the padlock back through the holes, he rested his forehead on the

(sux cocks)

cool metal.

This was it. This was the day the pain, the humiliation, and the torture were going to end.

This was the day he got his life back.

This was the day his father would die.

♦♦♦

PETE MADE HIS way upstream through the throng of exiting students. Maybe it was the Book, or maybe it was just his frame of mind, but everything seemed sharper. More in focus.

Normally drab and muted, the halls now seemed a riot of colour. He found himself able to focus on and pick out a conversation, no matter if it was near him or down the hall. He could smell the lunches

(peanut butter and banana, cream of mushroom soup, peas)

in the lockers, the industrial cleaner on the floors, the sweat, the testosterone, and the cheap perfume.

What was going on with Nicole Davidson? Oh. Pregnant. Huh. That sucked. Just past her, he could tell Susan Tomlinson was on her period. How the hell he knew that was a mystery. But he *knew*. Bet Nicole was wishing she was on hers, too.

Pete caught a deeper, muskier smell from Lila Pirsig. Pete knew there was a couple of cells tucked just behind Lila's frontal lobes that would turn into a nasty little tumour. Pete knew it was a patient, ticking bomb that would kill her in a little over a decade. She walked with her boyfriend, Dan Holt, who had a strange, unreadable aura of darkness over him. It wasn't the first time Pete had caught this, but it was the first time it had truly bothered him. Like that darkness was something he should *know* but didn't.

He thought, *Fuck it,* and kept walking. He had things to do.

Then, further along in the throng of students, he saw an area of quiet, of darkness that he couldn't penetrate. As though a shadow walked amongst all the lights. Very different from the one around Dan. Pete felt, heard, smelled, tasted, and saw everything going on around that one dark spot, but nothing within it.

Then, as he pushed through the hall, he felt the shadow coming toward him as well. *What the hell?* he thought.

Then she passed him. Talia Davis.

Spooky Talia.

She gave him a look of such hate, such fury, such…menace, that he stopped dead in his tracks. He was used to being ignored. He was used to being noticed only to be ridiculed. But he was not used to unbridled loathing.

As she passed, he couldn't help it, he extended a hand, it brushed her

(hate you hate you hate you fucker you took it away stole it stole it like i'll steal your fucking TEETH)

shoulder as she passed him.

And in that second, he thought he might have worked out the difference between Dan's and Talia's darkness. Though it made no sense to him, the only way it fit in his mind was to think of Talia's darkness as a *past* darkness, and Dan's as an *upcoming* darkness.

Which was fucked up.

Then she was past him, and his mind cleared. He noticed that a path seemed to spontaneously clear for her as people shrank away from her. Pete knew they didn't do it consciously.

He heard their thoughts. She didn't register.

They just shrank away from her.

Would they do that with him soon too?

♦♦♦

STILL WONDERING ABOUT Talia and Dan, Pete plodded down the hall past the science classes on the left and the school offices on the right and worked his way to the north stairs leading to the third floor. As he pushed open the door to the stairwell, he noticed Stash and the Toad

(pop goes the weasel)

skipping down the hall—*arm in arm for chrissakes*—singing some dumbass song from *The Wizard of Oz* at the top of their lungs. And everyone thought *he* was a loser. "Fuckin' dickheads," he muttered.

And yet, somewhere deep down, he didn't agree with that. Something inside him wanted to be a friend to them, to experience that kind of camaraderie. Then, as though a black fist—a shadow—clenched around it, that feeling died.

♦♦♦

MARCIA MAYER WATCHED as Theo, Stash, and the Toad followed Stephanie as she came through the cafeteria doors. *Jeez! Did they have to make it so obvious? Are all guys this bad?*

Was Theo really that pathetic? Marcia really didn't think so, but sometimes it was hard to know for sure. Since they had broken up last summer, theirs had been a strange and stormy relationship.

Marcia shook her head and turned away. There was no need to think about any of that stuff now. She was here to help with the sets. Mr. Hasselton said they weren't too far behind, but they would be soon if they kept at the same pace. Hassy had to know what he was talking about. He was the maestro behind all the musicals at the school for the past ten years.

Why couldn't boys at the school be more like Hassy? Marcia wondered. Though he wasn't a really good-looking man—more on the cute side of average than anything—Marcia had a bit of a crush on him. Nothing serious, and nothing she lay awake nights pining over. He was just a nice man.

Average height, average build, with steel-grey hair that didn't seem to make him look older, just a little more…what? Experienced? Mature? Marcia didn't know exactly, but it sure didn't hurt his appearance. He had a slightly rough complexion that spoke of his battle with acne when he was younger, but again, it worked to his favour, giving him a slightly tougher look. He looked manly. Marcia liked it.

Maybe the male species just had to mature before they became attractive.

Whatever the case, when Hassy had come to the actors and actresses in the musical and asked if they could lend a hand, Marcia couldn't say no.

That's how she had ended up sitting on a stepladder painting the wall of what would be the von Trapp childrens' bedroom. Hassy had shown her how to get a decent-looking effect for wallpaper. It looked awful up close, but when you got some perspective on it—twenty or thirty feet back, like an audience would see it—it looked great. She had done a section, asked Hassy's opinion, and he had proclaimed it good.

"But it looks so bad from up close," she had said.

"Ah yes, the illusion of the theatre," Hasselton had proclaimed grandly. "Far from good, but good from far." They had both shared a warm laugh and he had moved on to the next student, navigating through the pockets of activity, always encouraging and sharing a smile.

She had watched him glide amongst the students, moving comfortably and easily through the groups, effortlessly dealing with each issue. God! She wished she had that same kind of confidence.

She wished there were some boys her own age who showed that kind of confidence.

At one time, Marcia thought she had sensed some hint, some promise, of that confidence in Theo, back around the time they had started dating. It wasn't readily apparent, not like Hassy, but it was there nonetheless. She had been sure of it.

But it had frustrated her that it never manifested itself. Just once, she wanted him to show her the confidence she knew he had. Marcia had just wanted Theo to make a decision. His friends always seemed to call him the man with the plan, yet when it came to her, he seemed hopeless. Why couldn't he just grab her and kiss her, instead of being so damn polite all the time. Polite was good, but sometimes she just wanted to be a little bad.

Not a lot. Just a little.

But she had never known how to tell Theo that. How does a supposedly good Catholic girl ask someone to be less polite, to be a little more forceful, without coming off sounding slutty or just plain weird? Though sometimes she thought she caught that same feeling off him, too.

Not a lot. Just a little.

Unfortunately, too little. He had never mooned over her like he was doing with Steph.

Five weeks after they had started dating, Theo and Marcia had stopped dating. Theo had pulled the plug on them. His first real decision. Marcia didn't even know if he knew why he had done it.

Even then, he hadn't seemed confident about the decision.

She gave him one last look, just a quick one as she dipped the tip of her paintbrush into the can beside her and then turned to apply more to a pattern that couldn't be seen until she got some distance on it.

Sort of like relationships, she thought as she placed the brush against the surface.

♦♦♦

ROGER WATERS'S PLAINTIVE voice faded off after asking if that damn wall needed to be so damn high, and the sound of the needle sliding into the playout groove rumbled over the speakers of the caf.

"Throw on the whaddayacallit second record, Sparky. Side three, dude," Marcia heard Stash say.

"Oh, please," Ann Marie said, "can't we hear something a little less depressing?"

"*The Wall* is the finest album ever made, young lady," Stash said, adopting the tone of a learned music critic. "How dare you disparage the tale of one man's tortured whaddayacallit descent into madness."

"Madness, schmadness. It's boring and it's depressing. Sparky, put on my Little River Band album. It's got "Reminiscing" on it. Or REO Speedwagon."

Stash rolled his eyes as though he were in serious pain.

"Little River *Bland*? Oreo *Gag*wagon? No wonder it's women who drove Pink to madness. Hassy. Back me up here. Are all women blind to art? Seriously, dude!"

Mr. Hasselton smiled. "Robert, women aren't blind to art." He paused, obviously for effect. He wanted their attention and he got it. The man knew theatre. "Robert, women *are* the only works of art. All else is a pale imitation."

Marcia turned back to her painting; her mouth in an exaggerated "o" and her eyes squinted. "Busted," she said under her breath, reminded again why men were so much sexier than boys.

Bested, Stash quietly turned back to his task.

The next record started up, and Marcia smirked at Stash's overloud groan.

The mid-tempo sounds of the Little River Band suddenly seemed louder for some reason. Marcia turned as she realized the entire caf had gone quiet.

Moose had entered the room.

In the last couple of weeks, the story of Moose's hundred-yard flash had circulated the school like a case of the measles. Some believed, some didn't.

Theo, Stash, and the Toad also turned to face Moose as he came in.

Obviously rehearsed, in three-part harmony, the three said, "Woo woo!" as they made jerking gestures at crotch level.

Snorts and chortles and sniggers sounded out as the students turned back to their duties. From their half-hearted actions, though, it was obvious everyone was waiting to see what transpired.

Marcia let out a guilty hiccup of laughter, but it was buried under the full-out assault of guffaws from the woo-woo boys themselves.

Moose, blushing furiously, didn't rise to the bait. Instead, he looked at Cyn with a do-we-really-have-to-be-here? look. Cynthia, ever the dutiful better half, rose to the challenge.

"I gotta get some books off Miss Helmsley. Maybe we should check her room to see if she's left yet." It was totally fake and said way too loud—so everyone would know that they weren't leaving for any reason other than the one just stated—but it was a reasonably respectable exit, under the circumstances. Moose and Cyn shambled back over to the caf doors and bid a slow retreat. It appeared to Marcia that Cyn was trying hard to ignore everyone's snickers.

"All right, boys and girls!" said Hassy. "Playtime's over. Back to work!"

As Marcia turned back to her labours, she saw Moose give the guys the finger. Even as he did so, she saw him fighting off a grin. Embarrassed or not, he was still a celebrity enjoying his fifteen minutes of fame.

And Stash thought *women* drove *men* to madness? Marcia was beginning to realize she would never understand the male species.

♦ ♦ ♦

STINKY PETE HIT the third floor, walking into the washroom and straight to the wheelchair stall at the far end of the room. There were a couple of seniors taking a piss at the urinals, but their quick, throwaway glances told him he would never be remembered. He was too low on the food chain.

He entered the stall, gently placed his gym bag on the floor, being careful to avoid any wet spots, and sat down on the seat of the toilet. He waited for the seniors to leave.

Little folded pieces of toilet wipes littered the piss-stained tiles. Rolls of toilet paper were no longer allowed since the girls' can had been streamered last year. So now the student body got their bum-wipes in handy individual sheets.

The stall was painted the same puke-orange as the lockers. Must've had a sale on that particular shade or something. *Terri Parr titfucks for a buck,* was scratched into the metal divider to his left. Below it, someone of similar wit had added, *fifty cents if you cum in her mouth.* On the inside of the door, just at eye level, was another. *Stinky Peet sucks dick for bus fare than walks home.*

It didn't even faze him anymore. Not even the bad grammar. It wasn't even worth scratching out.

He heard the urinals flush. Finally, the damn seniors had finished pissing or jerking off or whatever they were doing. Neither of them washed their hands before they left.

One of them had gonorrhea. Good for him.

This was it. Pete's last chance to bail. Once he started, he couldn't turn back. *Okay, buddy, do we really wanna do this?* he thought. He remembered Theo's expression as he had refused the poker invitation. Then he remembered his father's words. "I've pissed on better than the likes of you."

There was no question. One more deep breath, eyes closed, he reached for the gym bag.

As he lifted it, the bag's weight shifted in his hand. The Book. It was the Book. It was getting impatient. Again, he didn't know how he knew, but he *knew*.

Then he heard It in his head. A low, raspy tone like some dirty, unshaven drunk trying to snuggle up and whisper in his ear. All slow and sultry in a sick sort of way.

~...doooo iiiit...~

Pete's hand reached for the zipper when he heard the washroom door swing open and Mr. Austin, the good-looking French teacher came in.

Isn't that weird, that I know who it is? Pete couldn't see to the door. And then it hit him again. Instant knowledge of things he should not know. Had no right to know. But there it was.

Austin's freaking because he's been fucking one of his students

~...iiiitttt's nnnnicoooollllle...~

who told him she needed to talk to him

~...nnnnicoooollllle daaaavvvvidssssonnnn...~

and he's worried she might be knocked up and he's damn close to just bolting town. Well that cleared up one mystery, didn't it?

~...maaaayyyybeeee sheeee juuuusssst neeeeds a gooood ssssooooollllid kiiiick toooo theeee sssstoooommmmach...theeee liiiitllle cuuuunnnnt...~

Peter shook his head to clear it. *The sooner I've got this done, the better,* he thought. *Then I'm done with this damn Book.* The fucking thing gave him the willies.

Mr. Austin splashed cold water on his face, and stood looking at himself in the mirror. It looked like he might be here awhile. Pete felt his nerve slipping away.

Just then, the Book shifted again, enough to make a noise. It was enough to make Austin uncomfortable and he left, his dress shoes clacking and echoing off the tiles. The door made a soft thump as it closed.

Pete prepared himself. He sure as hell hoped nobody else would walk in on him. With what he was going to do, he didn't need any more interruptions.

Besides, he wasn't exactly sure how long it took to raise a demon.

CHAPTER FIVE

MARCIA NOTICED THAT Theo, Stash, and the Toad had moved closer to the stage where she worked. They were preparing the papier-mâché paste to make some hills. Hills that would soon be alive with the sound of music.

Marcia caught Theo looking at her a few times. Each time, she turned back to her work, her long brown hair slipping off her shoulders to hide her smile. He really wasn't good-looking. In fact, he wasn't even on the cute side of average, like Hassy. A crop of pimples on his forehead and one or two on his nose—not that she could complain, she had a pretty good monster zit of her own that had cropped up right between her eyes this morning—and his hair was at that in-between stage, like he couldn't decide to wear it long or to cut it off. Most of the guys in the school wore it like that. The hairstyle spoke of an ongoing war between a parent that demanded it cut and the owner doing his best to push the envelope. The ones who lost the war walked the halls with crew cuts or, more tragically, bowl cuts.

The Toad was one of those tragic cases, his mother having cut his hair herself and thus controlled his hairstyle. But the Toad was also the only one Marcia had ever seen who actually suited it. That was almost tragic in its own right.

Marcia brushed her hair behind her ear and caught another glance in her direction.

She liked that Theo still looked at her. That meant he was still interested. So was she. But this back and forth thing with the eyes was never going to go anywhere.

Let's see if we can escalate this a little. He wants to look at me? I'll give him something to think about while he's doing it.

She got down from the stepladder she had been sitting on and, grabbing the paint can and a paint-smeared rag, she walked over to the side of the stage where the thick velvet curtains hung. Theo was working with the others about fifteen feet from the front of the stage. Nothing but a piece of velvet between her and them.

She looked around, and seeing no one in her field of view, she unbuttoned her oversized paint shirt.

♦♦♦

PETE STOOD NAKED in the stall. Not the most comfortable feeling. There was just no way to feel at ease while not wearing clothes at school. Something about all those students out there who lived to bring him down, to skewer any self-worth he may have built up. All he needed was one of them to show up right now, while his cheese was in the wind.

As he got himself ready, Pete looked down at the Book. It was big—a foot by a foot and a half, at least. Thick leather covers darkened by the oil of thousands of nervous, sweaty hands through centuries of use. Scuffed and tarnished gold metal adorned and reinforced the corners. The pages were thick, and made of some parchment

~...iiiitttt'ssss sssskinnnn...~

that Pete had never seen before. It ran thick, at least three hundred pages, all handwritten with ornate script and many illustrations. Whenever Pete opened the Book, he actively avoided the pictures. They gave him a sick feeling in his gut, and his bowels turned to water.

Pete opened the Book on the toilet seat, carefully positioning It so It would not slip, and knelt before It on the piss-stained tiles like he was about to pray. He was almost ready to start.

More accurately, he was almost ready to finish the task he had decided on two months earlier.

♦♦♦

AFTER THAT DAY in March, when Pete decided his father should die, he spent long hours with various murderous scenarios roiling around his mind, none of which ever seemed feasible.

He wanted the bastard dead, but he sure as hell wasn't going to go down for it.

That left him stuck until about a month ago, when, in desperation, he hit the school library, searching once again for a course of action. He had lost all contact with the few friends he had since he had begun swimming the dark waters of revenge. He found it easier to prowl alone in the quiet corridors between the library's shelves of books. The school library became his sanctuary.

And that's when he found the Book. Or rather, when the Book found him.

♦♦♦

"HEY GUYS," MARCIA said, "how's the hill coming?"

Theo looked up at her with a wariness in his eyes. *What are you up to?* they seemed to ask.

He really does have beautiful eyes, she thought, somehow noticing them for the first time.

The Toad turned to her, his hands covered in paste. "Hey Mar, it's going goo— Holy shit!"

That brought Stash around. "Fuck me whaddayacallit *hard*!"

Marcia could see that Theo still hadn't clued in. That's because he was watching her face, trying to read her. So she purposely looked from him to the Toad. Theo followed her gaze over to the Toad.

The Toad was still standing, his hands dripping goo, his mouth hanging open. Theo looked at the Toad's face, then followed his eyes to their target.

Right to Marcia's chest. Marcia watched his eyes widen. *Now he's got it,* she thought.

♦♦♦

PETE HAD BEEN looking for more information on ethyl and methyl alcohol. He had been in chemistry class when Mr. Matter had finally said something to catch his attention. Somehow, Matter had gotten on the topic of his school days, and he mentioned that two of his classmates had broken into the chem lab and stolen the alcohol there, but had grabbed the wrong one. Instead of getting drunk, they got dead.

Unfortunately, Pete had missed which one was the fatal one. And it wasn't like he could ask. But he now had the beginnings of a plan to off his dad.

Pete had been aimlessly walking the rows of books, knowing he would eventually find the information he needed. What he found instead was a completely different solution.

There was a big-ass book on the floor in the middle of the aisle. Biggest fucking book he had ever seen, in fact. *Gold friggin' corner reinforcements? What's the deal with that? Probably a Bible or something,* he thought.

Big deal. He had stepped over it and continued on his way. Let the fuckin' librarian pick it up. Not in his job description.

He rounded the main aisle that divided the rows in half. He crossed over and continued up another row.

And there was the same goddamn book. Right in the middle of the aisle again.

It was two weeks too late for April Fools' jokes. Pete quickly walked back to the other aisle, where he had first seen the book. Nothing.

There were three other people in the library. The librarian and two minor niners mooning over some teen magazine devoted to that guy from *Welcome Back, Kotter*. He was in that new movie...*Greased,* or something like that. John Revolta, whatever.

No one else was in the library. No one.

What the fuck?

Mind racing, Pete walked back, fully expecting the book to be gone. It wasn't. It was still there, like it had known he would be back.

This is some kind of bullshit joke, he thought. What he did not want to admit was that he was seriously creeped.

Fuck it, I'm gone, Pete thought as he turned his back on the book and headed for the exit. Whoever was doing this could get their jollies off on some other loser.

Pete strode past the two girls and the librarian to the doors. He pushed them open and started up the short flight of stairs to the main foyer.

Then he stopped dead in his tracks.

On the third stair from the top, the book waited for him.

The doors had been in sight all the time he had crossed the library. No one had come in, or had left. The hairs on his arms stood straight out and a weird fluttering rattled in his chest.

What else could he do? Obviously, the book wanted him.

That was the strange thing: it wasn't even a case of taking the book. It was the firm knowledge that the book *wanted* him to take it. That they could help each other.

Pete slowly, cautiously, and reluctantly reached out and picked It up. Though its weight surprised him, he found he could heft it easily with one hand. Like the Book made him suddenly stronger.

And it wasn't a "book." No, It was the Book.

Aside from the weight, Pete got another immediate surprise. The Book was *warm*. Warm like a living body was warm. Then the Book pushed that revelation aside and replaced it with something more staggering.

~...yoooou'vvvve goooot hhhheeeellllp...~ the Book whispered.

~...iiii caaaannnn hhhheeeellllp yoooou wwwwiiiith yoooour proooblemmmm...~

A warm soft buzz enveloped him.

~...iiii caaaan beeee yoooour friennnnd...~

♦♦♦

THE NEXT FOUR weeks were hazy. Pete retained few solid memories. Just flashes, images, and impressions like slightly out-of-focus snapshots.

Pete remembered opening the Book for the first time. He had been in his bedroom, his dad safely passed out for the evening in front of Johnny Carson. He had made sure a school textbook was nearby so he could do a fast switch in the unlikely event that the bastard woke up.

There, with the *Close Encounters of the Third Kind* movie poster on one side of his bed, and Cheryl Tiegs and Farrah in all her nippled glory on the other, he used trembling fingers to open the thick cover and browse through the pages. He watched as the words shifted and ran like blood in water. It made his eyes tear up. When he got them clear, he was surprised to find he could read the Book easily. Every time he flipped pages, though, the text would swim around briefly, then clear.

It's translating itself, he thought.

The Book showed him things. Loathsome, incredible things that made his head hurt. But, as he flipped pages, It kept whispering.

~...weeee cooooould doooo thiiiissss toooo yoooour daaaaddddyyyy...~

~...orrrr thiiiissss...~

~...orrrr thiiiissss...~

He found the illustrations disgusting, nauseating, yet exciting in some weird way. Sort of like how he got excited by the women's lingerie section of a department store catalogue. Only this was like looking at some department store catalogue from hell. He took in repulsive acts and sickening scenes...and it fucking turned him on.

Pete initially felt real dirty having a full-scale four-alarm erection all the time he was contemplating what death he should go with for dear old dad. But he got over it and learned to enjoy it.

Then he found the Demon.

He read the pages quickly, knowing this was what he had been looking for all along. Finally, head spinning, he carefully hid the Book behind a pile of Fantastic Four comics and fell asleep.

Above him, as Cheryl and Farrah smiled on, the poster with a roadway leading to a plateau called the Devil's Tower quietly reminded him he was not alone.

♦♦♦

IF HE UNDERSTOOD the Book correctly, Pete could summon the Demon, offer it a living sacrifice, and it would do whatever it was asked. But only by the summoner.

Him. Stinky Pete Wilson.

Well shit, that was easy enough. He already had the sacrifice. He just wasn't sure what he would ask it to do afterward. Maybe he would just let the Demon kill his old man, and then he would banish it back to Hell, or wherever the hell it came from.

Aside from picking up the Book, this was Stinky Pete's second error in judgment.

♦♦♦

MARCIA STOOD INNOCENTLY as the three boys stared at the two large handprints on her paint shirt. One handprint on each side, as though the hands cupped her breasts. The blue paint stood out very clear on the paint-splattered white fabric.

Theo's face reddened.

"Can I talk to you? Alone?"

"Sure, Theo," she said.

She headed back up to the stage where it was quieter, Theo smouldering a few feet behind her.

"Damn! Hand-picked funbags! Dem's gooood eatin'!" the Toad said. Stash punched him on the shoulder and the two of them turned back to the bucket of goo. Marcia saw them both shaking their heads.

Well, I wanted a reaction. Guess I got one, she thought.

They reached the stage. Theo caught up with her and, grabbing her arm, spun her around.

"What the hell was that all about?"

"What was what all about?"

Theo strutted around her, pushing his chest out. "'Hey guys, how's my *hills*?'" he asked. His act was exaggerated, but pretty accurate all the same. He stabbed a shaking finger in the direction of her chest. "I'm talking about *that*," he said. "Flaunting your tits."

"That's *not* what I said, and oh yeah, I was really flaunting it, wasn't I? Is that why you were the last to notice?" she asked, her voice rising slightly.

Theo kept his voice to an angry hiss. "Yeah, I was the last to notice. So what? I see you as more than a pair of tits. That's just fuckin' awful, isn't it?"

Darn it. This wasn't going the way she had planned. Not at all.

But Theo wasn't finished yet.

"So, really, what the hell was that about? What, you wanted to freak me out by having someone put their hands on your tits? Who did it? You enjoy it?"

"No! No, Theo, that wasn't it at all! I did it myself!"

Theo was still mad, but he now looked confused as well.

"I went over there," she explained, pointing a blue hand to the curtain, "and took my shirt off and dipped my hands in the paint and—"

"You took your shirt off here? In the open?"

"Yes, I…" She hadn't wanted thinking she didn't want to get any paint on the T-shirt.

They both looked over to the area again. The can of paint was there, and so was the T-shirt she had originally been wearing underneath the paint shirt.

"So, you took off the paint shirt, the T-shirt, made the handprints, then stuck the paint shirt back on." Theo looked back at her. "Shit, Marce. Did you at least keep your bra on?"

Her eyes welled up with tears. This hadn't gone anything like she had planned. She had just wanted him to be a little jealous. Not a lot. Just a little. Maybe she had wanted him to see somebody else notice her. Notice *her* for a change instead of Steph all the time, dammit! Maybe she had just wanted him to grab her and kiss her.

"Did you?" Theo asked again.

One of the tears slipped free of her eyes and slid down her cheek. "Yes," she said, hating the tremble in her voice. "Yes, I kept my damn bra on."

"Well, congratulations on showing *some* self-restraint," Theo said, sarcasm bubbling over. "I just wish I knew what the hell you were trying to prove." He turned and walked off the stage, never looking back at her.

Her tears flowed freely as she walked back behind the curtain and grabbed up her T-shirt.

She went to the back of the stage, where small cubicles had been set up as dressing rooms for the quick changes necessary between scenes. She took off her paint shirt and picked up the T-shirt, unfolding it to reveal the bra hidden inside.

Damn him! she thought as she used the shirt to dry her eyes.

She got dressed quickly and headed back to the stage. Though she would still be doing more painting, she threw the paint shirt in the big green garbage can that sat off to the side of the room.

Damn him!

♦♦♦

ON HIS KNEES in the washroom on the cold tile, Pete flipped the pages to the section he was looking for—It almost fell open to the right page. He had no idea what language it was that he had to speak during the summoning incantation, but he thought it was very cool that the words had been broken down and written phonetically for easy reading and pronunciation. Seriously. *all'Gueroth?*

Pete ducked down and took one more look around the washroom from under the stall. *Nope, no one here but us sorcerers,* he thought. *Well, here goes. Time to get me a hit demon.*

He crouched, studied the sounds for a few seconds, rolled the syllables around on his tongue, just to get a taste, then rose. He made a complicated gesture, as shown on the illustration, and uttered a few unintelligible sounds. As he did, the temperature in the washroom seemed to drop a few degrees. His naked body broke out in gooseflesh and his balls shrivelled up tight between his legs. His breath fogged out with each exhalation.

"Surr-sirilioch mak chandos mak y siriliache..."

He flipped the page and continued. Another gesture, more phonetics, more gestures, more mumblings. The room got colder still.

"Surr-sirilioch mak bitineesh kak rontys siriliache..."

The quality of the light in the room changed. Like the air before a big rain, the atmosphere appeared darker, yet at the same time, it took on a glow.

"Qomt ayleeth het all'Gueroth elisveph Nyar La Hotep..."

Then, the wall behind the toilet split and opened. There was no cracking tiles or breaking concrete. One second, the room was normal, the next, Pete faced a hole with swirled, out-of-focus edges.

Holy shit! thought Pete. It was working! A big part of him truly thought it would not. A smaller part—the sane part, the part with a conscience—had hoped this whole thing would not work. That he'd just mumble a few phrases, naked, make himself feel a little stupid, and that would be the end of it.

He took a brief moment to sober himself.

"Kolot shyliq Petrain hek-Wil mak all'Gueroth y Kar kosa."

Okay, that was the end of the language lesson. Now came the weird part.

He now needed to "give of himself" as the Book said. A small opening sacrifice to show he was serious. Something that held life, however briefly: a finger, a toe, some blood...

Sperm.

Nothing says "I love you" like a small living sacrifice.

He had decided a while ago that it would be best to whack off. It was definitely the least painful option, and the thing he was most experienced at.

But now he thought, *How the hell do I get myself going with all this shit going on? What if someone walks in while I'm spanking the monkey?*

~...juuuusssst do iiiit...yoooou wiiiillll beeee heeeellllped...~

Yeah, right.

Pete took his cock in his hand. Even with the cold, his fingers felt warm and they definitely knew their way around down there. Despite his current location and circumstances, he felt himself getting hard.

As he worked his shaft, he glanced down at himself.

~...noooo doooo nnnnot llllooook...cllllooooossse yoooour eyyyyessss...~

Pete did as instructed. Without warning, something changed. Suddenly, it no longer felt like his calloused fist on his dick anymore. Instead, the strokes were warm, soft, wet.

Vaginal.

"Oh geez." His breath puffed out in surprise and pleasure. He couldn't help himself. Pete was a virgin, so it wasn't like he had a lot of experience in the area, but damn! This felt better than any pussy he'd ever imagined.

~...jussssst cloooose yoooour eyyyyessss...~

Pete began to thrust himself enthusiastically. His breath came in short gasps timed to the motion of his hand and hips. It only took a few more strokes for him to feel his balls tighten, for his cock to swell. His head began to pound, his legs to quiver. It was almost painful, but in a good way. He rose to his toes, pushing hard. He savoured a final delicious instant where he tried to hold it back, then it was gone. His jizz exploded out of him and pulsed into the hole in the wall before it could hit the toilet or the floor, crossing the three-foot gap as though vacuumed up.

Pete's knees buckled, and he dropped back down to the piss-stained floor, gasping like he'd just run a marathon. His hand was still on his cock, but it was just his hand again, and he quickly lost his erection, his dick bobbing in time with his pulse. All thoughts of demons, school, his dad, and revenge were gone, replaced by the buzz only a truly spectacular orgasm could create.

The buzz didn't last long. Pete opened his eyes at the sound of ripping. What he saw made him forget all thoughts of anything else. His mind turned white. He crab-walked backward fast enough to break the stall door off its hinges. His backward plunge ended with an ungraceful drop on his ass at the far side of the washroom.

The quiet blasted away in a frenzy of sound and motion as dozens and dozens of small black creatures pattered out onto the tile floor and scampered around, apparently getting the lay of the land. They were about the size of a big rat or a small dog, like a Chihuahua, but more muscular and with *way* more teeth. Most of their bodies shone with a chitinous shell, like an insect, and thick, short hair sprouted from around their eyes. And the eyes! Massive black orbs bulging frog-like from a noseless, vicious face. In fact, the things were pretty much eyes, teeth, and claws. And, aside from the scrabbling of their claws on the tiles, eerily quiet.

They were fucking Chihuahuas from hell. But they were nothing—just a warm-up for the main event. And Holy Christ, what an entrance.

Pete stared, frozen and wide-eyed, as the stalls exploded apart and shredded like pages from a binder. When he brought his forearm down from protecting his face, Pete's overloaded brain could only think *big* and *dark*.

In the middle of the boys' washroom on the third floor of Clarington High stood the Demon. It was forced to stoop forward to keep its head from hitting the ceiling. It wasn't just black, it radiated darkness, various qualities of black on black. On parts of the body, like one side of the head and down the neck to its chest, the skin caught the light, pimpled and shiny, like plastic. On the opposite side of the head and down one arm, on side of its torso, and its leg, the covering was rough, scabrous and peeling. Its back and face looked like granite. Its mid-section ran insubstantial, like smoke from burning rubber. The Demon's arms were multi-jointed and ended in claws that looked like they could rip through a bank vault.

Teeth jutted from its mouth. Some thick clumps of bone, others jagged shards, and all black as ebony, clotted with remnants of what looked like flesh. From what, Pete didn't want to guess.

The Demon had a wide, lumpy nose pushed tight to its hideous face and a low, sloping forehead that drooped down to craggy cheekbones. No eyes. The monster was blind.

No it's not. It's the little rat-dogs, thought Pete. *They are its eyes. Seeing-fuckin'-eye rat-dogs.*

That's all he got before the thing swung a massive arm out and tore the overhead fluorescent light fixture out of the ceiling with a shower of sparks and twisted aluminum and glass shards. They were thrown into a darkness that took Pete a few seconds to adjust to.

The Demon was taking in its new surroundings, sniffing at the air, its thick fleshy tongue lumbering over its teeth, twisting this way and that, all without seeming to notice Pete. There was no sign of urgency in its manner. It seemed to have all the time in the world, like appearing in a third-floor high school washroom was a normal thing for it to do. After it finished scanning the entire tiled wasteland, only then did the Demon all'Gueroth acknowledge the figure slumped in the corner.

Its nostrils flared and it advanced toward Pete with an unexpected grace. The Demon bent lower on its haunches and extended one clawed digit to Pete's still-dripping penis. Delicately, it lifted the shrivelled member and sniffed the air. It nodded once, almost as a confirmation that, yes, this was the human who had called it to this world.

The Demon ran a claw as long as a forearm up Pete's quivering belly to his hairless chest. Almost a caress, it left no trace. Then, with a clawed finger over Pete's pounding heart, it pushed, almost imperceptibly.

"Ow! Hey!" Pete exclaimed as he looked at the pinprick of blood on his chest. The Demon cocked its head to the side briefly and snorted. A fetid blast of air in Pete's face. Then it showed its teeth. Was it smiling? It was a repulsive thing to see.

I hope this isn't some sort of mating ritual, Pete thought, eyeing the creature's shockingly huge, barbed penis. *At least we know he's really a he.*

Though still terror-stricken, the Demon's grace and gentleness—aside from that poke—helped to put him a lot more at ease. Pete had brought him here, after all. Shit, he *owned* this thing.

The Demon slid its huge, three-fingered hand behind Pete's head and neck and gently eased him forward until their foreheads touched. The Demon's granite-like skin surprised Pete with its slight stickiness, like it was coated with a thin layer of snot. Underneath, its skull was hard and rough, like a concrete sidewalk. Its breath was heavy, moist, and pungently unpleasant, like the smell of a skunk—okay for just a whiff, but overpowering when he sucked a lot of it in.

With no normal focal point on the beast's face because of the absence of eyes, Pete could get no read from it. This close, Pete stared at the thing's enormous cheekbones, one sprouting an afterthought of a horn, like a large, hardened pimple. But black, all black.

As their heads met, Pete got that same warm buzz the Book had given him. He felt himself relaxing, all the tension leaving him. *Yes,* he thought, *this is it. This big son of a bitch is going to kick my father's ass. I'm gonna be the boss. I'm gonna do what I want to do. Maybe I'll even ask Steph out on a date.*

Everything is going to be al –

The screaming snarling tearing wall of pain ripped through Pete's head like a rabid animal, shredding his thoughts, chewing his memories, cracking his skull and sucking the marrow of his mind dry. He didn't have time to make a sound. It swallowed his mind.

The Demon pulled Pete's head back with a wet pop, the mucus layer between them stretching like caramel. Pete's mind ran on base, primitive instinct now. All knowledge now in the Demon's mind, but still Pete's body lived. To look at his shivering, naked body, there was no visible damage—only a wet spot on his forehead and pool of piss expanding outward from where he sat. He slumped against the wall, a wrung-out sponge. His mind was white and blank, but his body could still function. It could still experience pain.

And yet, in that emptiness, something still worked. Pete's mind was now connected with the monster's. And Pete knew, as much as the Demon was tempted to visit death upon him, this soft meat—for that was all Pete was to all'Gueroth—had summoned it. This meat had released it. Yes, the Demon's father had wanted through the portal, but all'Gueroth had heard the call and got there first. The meat had pulled him through instead of Nyarlathotep.

For that, the meat would be rewarded.

Then Pete knew what came next.

Slamming its claws through Pete's chest, the Demon lifted him off the tiles. With its free hand, it ripped into Pete. Its reward would be to live. But not without knowing what mad well he had been foolish enough to dip into. Not without knowing what power he had tapped into. Not without understanding what that power could do.

Pete's eyes snapped open. Though he had lost virtually all reason and intelligence for the moment, some primal instinct kicked in. He looked down to see gobs of himself splashed about the washroom. Neurons connected and allowed his mouth to open.

And he screamed.

As the Demon contorted and twisted him, Pete watched the last of the remaining light creeping under the door fall away as the power failed throughout the entire school.

Then he saw nothing for a long time.

He was too caught up in the betrayal the Book had led him to so willingly.

CHAPTER SIX

MARCIA WENT BACK to her painting. The boys left her alone.

Ten minutes later, Theo, Stash, and the Toad were laughing like hyenas at some stupid joke, probably involving genitals, excrement, or Moose. Marcia silently fumed. Her paint strokes became violent, slapping against the cheap plywood like a beaver tail signalling imminent danger.

They didn't seem to notice. That pissed her off even more.

Why is it that when there's a fight between the sexes, it's always the guy who snaps out of it first? she wondered. And the problem with that was the sooner the guy snapped out of it and began to enjoy himself again, the more the woman became enraged that the guy was having fun. This only seemed to increase his fun, which pissed her off even more…

Then, to make matters worse, Crouch came in. And he was drunk as a skunk. Stash and the Toad had coaxed him into the caf from the looks of it.

"Hey, Crouch! You gonna help us or what?" she heard the Toad say.

"Yeah." Crouch giggled, stroking the peach fuzz on his chin. Marcia remembered laying close to him, playing with those hairs. He used to preen like a cat when she did it. He pointed up at the metal support beams that ran the length of the ceiling. "Gimme a paintbrush. Gonna paint a Michael-fuggin-Angelo onna roof!"

"More like you'll be swingin' from the damn rafters."

"Inna gadda da vida, baby!" Crouch responded. No one knew what he was talking about, but they all laughed anyway. Marcia's mood sank lower and lower.

So both her ex-boyfriends were here now. Together. And happy. Best of buddies, darn it!

And she knew that Crouch would hear about the shirt thing. Her only hope was that he would be too drunk to remember it. It usually went that way with Crouch—through the late summer to the early winter that she had dated him, he was probably drunk more often than not. That was why she had finally abandoned him. Well, one of the reasons.

The boys were laughing and joking over the bucket of paste when she saw them jump back suddenly, like they had discovered a man-eating crocodile in there.

No, she was wrong. Not all of them had backed up. Crouch was bent over the bucket, a weird smile on his lips. And something else as well.

And now, she had graphic proof of why she had made the correct decision to break off with Crouch.

♦♦♦

CROUCH THREW UP violently into the big plastic garbage bucket. That wouldn't have been so bad, but the bucket already contained the papier-mâché paste—better known as goop—intended for the *Sound of Music* set.

He was drunk again. Actually, "drunk" did not cover it. He was bombed, wrecked, smashed, totalled, blotto, ruined, shit-faced. Superlatively inebriated.

Crouch—also known as Ben by those who didn't know him well—had gone out with some of his less studious peers who shared the same third-period spare on Wednesdays. This spare provided Crouch and friends with a full two-hour span in which they could consume vast quantities of illegally-obtained alcoholic beverages. Once they had discovered the hard-worn, Black Russian-drinking, mess of a bartender at the Pine Lodge, a seedy little dump of a motel just down the road from the school, cared less about proof of age and more about drinking partners, the group became regulars.

It had started out as a weekly event known to the participants as "wenzdayin'," or Wednesdaying, used as a verb instead of a noun, much as the term "party" or "partying." Crouch was proud to have been the one to coin the term. But over the course of the school year, wenzdayin' began occurring more frequently. Such as today, for example. A Friday.

Crouch was the badass of Theo's little group, and Theo's mother constantly worried about Theo hanging around with him. "That boy's trouble," she always said. "He's going to end up in a whole peck of trouble one day, you mark my words." All this for a guy who was polite to her to a fault. It was always "Yes, Mrs. Clarke," "No, Mrs. Clarke," and "You're looking very pretty today, Mrs. Clarke." Theo figured his mom's bullshit radar worked real well in Crouch's vicinity. *Too bad it doesn't work as well for my whore of a father,* Theo thought.

Crouch did push the envelope more than the rest of the group, with the possible exception of the recently departed Moose. Though it could never have been recognized by Crouch's home demeanour—the one that avoided swearing and most sex talk while his dad was around—Crouch was the resident wild one. He had another stable of friends that he kept company with. The Wednesday group. It was like he was always trying to reconcile two separate personalities residing in one body. The Wednesday group, as far as Theo was concerned, would be considered Crouch's enablers.

The only one with his own vehicle—a beat-up ex-telephone company Dodge pickup that his old man got at an auction eight years ago—Crouch had more freedom than Theo and Stash, who relied on the mercy of their parents for use of the family sedans. The Toad always had to beg a ride because his mom didn't drive at all.

Any vandalism in the town of No Hope, or Clarington District for that matter, could usually be attributed to Crouch, and he was proud of it. Proud enough to autograph his work, Crouch was the Damage, Inc. vandal who the local paper constantly railed against, but who Sergeant Flewwelling—the local Barney Fife—could never catch.

Crouch was the one who would always come through with booze and joints if Moose failed. The Friday-night poker games were always more interesting for it. Just as long as his dad wasn't around.

But for all his loud noises and actions, he also had this other side that amazed and captivated Theo. He was an incredible artist. He had twelve fish tanks and could name every species of fish he owned, even the Latin. He had typed out lyrics to songs that dealt with loneliness and alienation and taped them to his binders, like a silent plea. Songs like Styx's "Man in the Wilderness" and Billy Joel's "The Ballad of Billy the Kid." Theo was so enamoured by this he did his own, though the lyrics Theo used leaned more toward escapism—the Beatles' "Tomorrow Never Knows" and Billy Joel's "Captain Jack." It was that lonely, alienated person who Theo liked to hang with. It was the one he identified with.

The wenzdayin' group generally tended to make it back for the final class of the day, though usually there was not much use in their attendance. Crouch's last-period class on Wednesday was English with Miss Helmsley, though he usually referred to her as Miss Piggy due to her striking resemblance to Kermit the Frog's porcine girlfriend. Usually, each Wednesday, the class passed with fits of drunken giggling, or members of the group passed out with their heads on their desks at the back of the class. Crouch likely didn't know what day it was. Or maybe what month.

From just inside the caf, Stash and the Toad had noticed Crouch—so named due to the brutal posture he inherited from his father, along with the shitty eyesight and bad teeth—as he attempted to sneak back into the school. He had lost all track of reality, and had truly believed he was getting back in time for Miss Piggy's Wednesday class. Stash and the Toad convinced him he was forty-nine hours behind schedule and coaxed him to the caf to help with set duty. They figured he would have some time to sober up before going home, maybe get some coffee into him.

Crouch came into the caf, pondered the information briefly while stroking his peach-fuzz beard, and proclaimed it a grand idea. He would stay.

Ten minutes later, he was throwing up into a big bucket of goop.

"Ah, fer chrissakes, Crouch!" Theo said. "Didja have to puke in the—"

"Puke in the what?" Stephanie came up. Crouch stood there stupidly, with the remnants of semi-digested beer dripping from his furry chin. Stephanie's eyes tracked from his chin to the bucket to the four of them. Theo, Stash, and the Toad looked down sheepishly. Only Crouch lacked understanding of the consequences of his regurgitation. Steph glared back at him with a look that almost caused Theo physical pain. All his plans were going to fall to shit if they didn't get Crouch out of here.

Stephanie's voice was low with implied threat. "Did you really throw up in the bucket of paste?"

Crouch, oblivious to the danger, seemed rather impressed with his feat. "Yep," he replied proudly. "I'm superlatively inebriated!" This came out as "spert-a-livly neev-a-braded." Theo could tell she had no idea what Crouch was talking about. Theo and the guys understood the fractured phrase only because Crouch said it every time he was drunk. He claimed that if he couldn't say it, he *was* it.

He definitely was it now.

"First, your friend Moose," Stephanie said, "and now...this." She rolled her eyes, then looked directly at Theo with an I'm-not-amused look. "Get him out, please." Again with the low, dangerous voice.

God she's hot!

"And can you please mix up some more paste while you're at it?"

Stash and the Toad took the bucket. Theo took Crouch. He had a feeling Marcia would be enjoying this, but he did his best to ignore her as he got Crouch out of the caf.

♦♦♦

THE BUZZ IN the caf died down reasonably quickly after Theo and the guys had removed Crouch. Steph went back to the set she had been working on. Marcia figured Theo realized that any chance he might have had with Steph, slim as it was, went down the drain along with the vomit-and-paste mixture. She didn't take any pleasure from seeing him embarrassed, but it was funny. How could she not laugh at someone who tries so hard and never seems to get a break.

Hassy made it quite clear that they had had all the entertainment they could possibly handle in one day, and that there was a show to prepare for. Everyone went back to their duties, but not without some final whispered comments, jokes, and smirks. They had been at it less than an hour, and it had already been one heck of a day.

"C'mon, Sparky," Hasselton yelled from the floor of the caf to the sound booth up above. "Let's get some working music! Something with a beat! And don't you dare put on Rush again! That singer sounds like a girl."

That brought some comments from some of the student body. Marcia noticed it was only guys who protested. Rush was a guy band. She didn't understand the fuss over them. They never sang about boy-girl stuff, so what good were they?

The good, solid rhythm section of the Destroyers kicked in, and soon the cigarette and booze-roughened voice of George Thorogood explained how he came to be in a bar ordering one bourbon, one scotch, and one beer. The pounding beat and growling guitar gave them the drive to get their asses into gear.

Right up until the power cut out.

♦ ♦ ♦

STASH AND THE Toad wrestled the bucket to the janitor's closet, located in an alcove just off the cafeteria. The girls' washroom was just around the corner, and the boys' was another twenty feet down the hall. The school day was officially over, so neither of the shitters would be needed all that bad. Not at this time of day. Theo looked at Crouch, who currently hung off his shoulder, thought, *fuck it*, and made a decision. He angled Crouch toward the girls' can.

Balancing Crouch with one arm, Theo pushed through the first door, then the second door—the "panty shield" according to the Toad, because it blocked his view of the girls in their panties—and worked him into a stall and let him drop to his knees in front of the toilet. Praying to the porcelain god.

"You gonna be okay here, Crouch?"

"S'pose so. Gotta tellya though, man—I really got a nasty case a' the zacklies."

Theo was lost. Zacklies? He squinted in confusion. "What the hell are 'zacklies,' buddy?"

Crouch's voice took on an impatient tone. "The zacklies, man! The zacklies!" He punctuated each word with that rubbernecked head bob that can only be achieved through the Zen state of total, superlative inebriation.

"I." Nod.

"Got." Nod.

"The *zacklies*!"

He said it like Theo could glean the information from the furious head bobbing. He said it as though he made perfect sense. Theo was still lost.

Crouch finally lifted his head and gave Theo a sidelong glance. "The zacklies. Y'know? When yer mouth tastes zackly like yer asshole?" Then he turned and vomited again.

Theo left him alone with his zacklies.

♦♦♦

BACK BY THE janitor's closet, Stash and the Toad had managed to dump the offending goop and wash it down the floor-sink drain. Stash had just righted the bucket and turned on the water to refill it. The water pounded the bucket with a forceful spray. They had to yell over the drumming noise.

"CROUCH OKAY?" the Toad asked as Theo approached.

"YEAH, GOOD. HE'S GOT THE ZACKLIES."

"WHAT?"

"Yeah," Theo muttered to himself. "Exactly." Then he smiled.

"SO, DUDE," the Toad said, "SERIOUSLY. HAVE YOU EVER HAD A SHIT THAT FELT SO DAMN GOOD THAT YOUR ASS JUST KEPT FEELIN' IT FOR, LIKE, *HOURS* LATER?"

Theo gave the Toad that look that silently asked what the hell he was talking about.

"NO JOKE!" he continued. "THAT CRAP I HAD A WHILE AGO? THAT SUCKER JUST SLID OUT LIKE IT WAS

GREASED, MAN. *SHOOOOMP!* SO I LOOK DOWN AND, I WAS LIKE, 'WHOA! I JUST GAVE FUCKIN' *BIRTH*, MAN!'"

He flashed a big smile and wiggled his butt. The proud papa. "MY ASS HAS BEEN SINGIN' A HAPPY TUNE EVER SINCE."

Stash and Theo traded pained expressions, then Stash punched the Toad's shoulder. "YOUR WHADDAYACALLIT ASS SINGS EVERY GODDAMN DAY, FROM WHAT I HEAR." The Toad being the fart king and all.

"YEAH, BUT Y'KNOW, FARTS ARE JUST—"

"—YOUR ASSHOLE CLAPPING." Theo and Stash finished in unison, nodding and clapping their hands for full effect. The Toad didn't look too disappointed. As the Jedi Fart Master he schooled Theo and Stash in the ways of the Force.

The Toad could mine this topic for hours. Theo needed a change and, as though reading his mind, Stash flashed him a grin full of perversion. "SO, THEO, DUDE. WHAT'S THE DEAL? YOU GONNA GET SOME WHADDAYACALLIT *SCHMEKKEN* WITH THE STEPH-MACHINE?" He wrinkled his nose to walk his glasses back up the bridge. It never worked.

"YEAH, MAYTE," the Toad jumped in, again with yet another bad accent. *A Clockwork Orange* British. "GONNA ENGAGE IN A LITTLE A' THE IN-OWT IN-OWT?"

Theo desperately tried to shush them. Christ Almighty, did they have to yell? He looked around to see if anyone was in earshot. When he turned back, the Toad had the janitor's mop out and was making kissy-face at the business end. "Toadman! TOAD! FUCKIN' QUIT IT!"

This just encouraged him. The handle went between his legs and he humped it furiously. "OH! OH YEAH!"

Stash bent forward to grab the faucet handle, ignoring him, the best course of action when the Toad was on a roll. "TAKE IT AAAAALL, BITCH!"

Stash cut the water. No more yelling was necessary, but still, the Toad continued. "I KNOW I ONLY GOT FOUR INCHES, BABY, BUT MOST OF MY BITCHES LIKE IT THAT WIDE!"

"Toad," Theo pleading, "Shut the hell up, f' chrissakes!"

Stash, as usual, laughed like a fool, wiping the tears from under his glasses. The Toad, too. Looking from one to the other, Theo tried to be pissed but couldn't work up enough steam. "*Most* of your bitches?" Stash said through huffs of laughter.

And that was it. First, the grin curled the sides of Theo's mouth, then he cracked up. Soon, the three of them giggled and snorted so hard the tears ran down their cheeks and their guts hurt.

"Oh. Oh god," said Stash, still laughing. He did the middle finger-poke-between-the-eyes move to pop his glasses back into place. "Stop! Stop it, guys! I'm gonna whaddayacallit...piss myself here!" Another wave of laughter broke over them. Stash cupped his nuts. He went into a crouch. Just looking at him got the Toad and Theo going again, and that got Stash going again.

Pulling it together long enough to lob it out there, the Toad asked, oh so sweetly, "Whassamatter, you gonna make lemonade?" That did it. Stash popped up like a jack-in-the-box and, both hands on his balls, he ran for the girls' can. There was no way he would make it to the guys'.

"Ooo!" the Toad exclaimed. "'Rushing to the Washroom' by Willie Makeit..."

"Illustrated by Betty Don't!" Theo finished.

Which was enough to finish them. They sat down on the floor, laughing and snorting until they dissolved into tears.

Right up until the power cut out.

♦♦♦

LAURA DAVIS'S LAST art student finished up and left the classroom. Time for her to close up shop in her oddball room—the artsy-fartsy class in the middle of the tech wing.

Normally Ann Marie, one of her mouthier, but keener, students helped with the cleanup, but she had begged off to go help with the sets for the upcoming school musical, leaving Laura alone with her chores. This involved putting away the art supplies, straightening the tables and chairs, and throwing out the prank drawings that these supposedly maturing individuals believed were funny. She had to admit the unsigned caricature she had found of her with the Wonder Woman breasts wasn't bad, though she hadn't shaved her genital region in quite the creative manner depicted. Apparently someone had taken Diane seriously about the nudes. *Thank god I got through the class without cracking up.*

And then, on the heels of that thought, *Poor Moose.*

She rinsed the paintbrushes absent-mindedly, her mind aimlessly drifting, a slight smile creasing her face.

Laura thought about Tom Popper. She rolled the idea around about finishing up here and heading up to the third floor, where she knew he would still be marking his Grade 12 calculus tests. He had let her know he would be up there for a while, letting the hint drop in his quiet, overly precise, soft-spoken way that had left no room for mistake—he was interested in pursuing something with her.

So was Laura. It had been a long time since she had been interested in…well anything. Companionship. Dates.

…Sex?

Yes, if she was honest with herself, yeah, that too.

And it had been far too long since anyone had been interested in her. She smiled. *Maybe I'd be better off with those Wonder Woman boobs.*

Jude Davis had brought his bride to New Hope when he had purchased some land just outside of town. Then he promptly died of a heart attack—he was much too young to have had an attack that severe, everybody said—while removing stones from the first of ten acres. They were for building a rock fence around the house. Bringing him something to drink, she had found him dead in the middle of their heavily mortgaged field, a lit cigarette still burning in his mouth.

Great. Recently married and relocated, newly widowed, all she had was a house she couldn't afford with two hundred and ninety-nine more monthly payments and ten acres of rock. That and a lighter that she had given him not long after they had started dating. Oh, Jude had been so handsome. But despite the obvious "Hey Jude" Beatles reference, he had always been much more passionate toward Jimi Hendrix. So Laura had gone out and bought him a lighter.

She took some liberties with the quote, just to make it a bit more personal to her and Jude. On one side, it read, *You're my one burning desire…*

On the other: *…forever standing next to your fire.*

And he'd loved it. Carried it everywhere. Corny as hell when she thought about it on the other side of a dead relationship. But oh, how she had wanted him then. She still did. But all that was left was the lighter. She didn't smoke, but now she was the one to carry it everywhere. Just like her wedding band. Just to remind her. The fire no longer burned, but she could, at times, bring up the memory of its warmth.

Gone, but not forgotten.

Sometimes the dragon flicks his tail. That's what her dad used to say when someone had a string of bad luck. *Thanks, Dad. Flick this.*

Initially, the plan had been for her niece, Talia, to live with them. But she was family on Jude's side, not hers, Laura had never actually met her, and with all the other stuff going on, Jude dying so short a time after his brother Charlie and Glen, three brothers gone in less than six months...well, it just sort of fell by the wayside. So maybe Talia had her own dragon flicking its own tail. She didn't know and, cold as it felt initially, forced herself to not worry about it.

So here she was in her classroom. Single, in debt, devoid of Wonder Woman-sized mammaries, and getting a curious quiver when she thought about the idea of Tom Popper's neatly trimmed beard brushing against her cheek...

Or the inside of her thighs. *Oh, you're wicked,* she thought, and followed it with a quick, not-quite-guilty smile. It quickly washed away when the power died.

♦♦♦

"ALL RIGHT, ALL right! It's just a power outage, happens all the time. Just keep doing what you were doing." Hassy was becoming more and more frazzled, Marcia could tell. His voice held that what-else-can-go-wrong? tone.

At least Bob and Anna, the other engaged high school sweethearts—there was also Dan and Lila—hadn't gotten into a fight yet. That was going in their favour.

With the power out, the few emergency lights strained to brighten the cavernous room. Hassy watched in frustration as the students tried to work in the murky semidarkness. One large section of the set that still needed leaves painted on the trees faced the wrong way completely and was in shadow.

"Mr. Hasselton, I can't see to do anything," said Ralphie. He was a Grade 12 student and was playing the head of the von Trapp family.

Others nodded in agreement. It was too dark. Should they just go home and come back when the power had been restored?

But Hassy wasn't beat. Marcia watched his face as he scanned the room, his eyes squinted against the harsh light. Then his expression changed. *He's got a solution,* she thought.

She was right.

"Ralph, Bob, Gerry, get a chair and get those emerge lights down. Sparky! Get down here and help them. We can use them as flashlights until the power comes back." The four teens went to it.

Hassy continued to mobilize the forces. "Okay, guys, we've got to make this light count. We've got three emerge lights, with two lights each. We can angle each of those lights, so we can basically have six spots. Let's angle some of the sets around so we can see what we're doing." The three emergency lights were brought down and positioned for maximum effectiveness.

"And someone please get the three stooges back in here." Marcia smiled. *Theo, Stash, and the Toad. The three stooges. No kidding.*

Seconds later, all those thoughts were blown out as hell dropped into the room.

♦♦♦

THEO AND THE Toad tried to get a grip on their laughter as they hauled the bucket back to the now-dark cafeteria. Then the screaming started from the washroom—great whooping shrieks. They looked at each other and smiled, their stomachs too sore to go for the full laugh again. Stash always had to get the last joke in. They left the bucket and walked toward the bathroom. What would it be? A roll of toilet paper hanging out of his ass? A sanitary pad stuck to his forehead? If Theo started laughing again, he was going to end up with a hernia.

Stash exploded out of the bathroom, spun, and began to fight the hydraulic closer on the door. He struggled to close the door behind him. It didn't even have a handle.

"HELP ME! FUCKIN' CROUCH IS DEAD!"

Theo and the Toad stood with puzzled expressions. This was all right, but not up to Stash's usual calibre. Then he turned and ran to the other two with wild eyes. He clutched at their shirts, hands spasming, and Theo saw spit on his cheek and chin from yelling. They couldn't get a handle on the joke.

"Stash, what the fuck, man?"

"CROUCH IS DEAD. WE'RE FUCKIN' NEXT! KILL IT, MAN! WE GOTTA FUCKIN' KILL IT!"

The wild, roiling terror in his eyes convinced them. Theo and the Toad saw he was serious. Serious enough to scare the living shit out of Theo.

Chapter Seven

A NASTY LITTLE thing looking like a hound from hell—*A very fucking* small *hound from hell,* Theo thought—scrambled out, snapping and gurgling like it was in danger of choking on its own tongue. It looked so stupid—like about eight inches of eyes and teeth—that Theo and the Toad actually laughed at it.

Theo's brain had jumped back to considering this a joke, albeit an elaborate one, and he felt himself relax slightly.

Until it launched itself at Stash and, with brutal ripping and growling noises, tore a vicious chunk out of his heel.

A terrible moment passed as they all heard the tearing sound, then a wet pop. The thing didn't seem to mind that it had a mouthful of plastic and rubber from Stash's Adidas running shoe along with his flesh and bone. It chewed it all with abandon. It happened so lightning-flash quick that Stash hadn't even sucked in enough breath to shriek in pain.

Though that followed. Oh hell, did it follow.

As the beast chewed and Stash wailed, Theo ran to the bucket, though the Toad was closer. "The water! Hit it with the water!" It seemed vaguely dumb to be throwing water at what appeared to be a land-piranha, but there was nothing else even close, except for a mop. The Toad didn't argue. He just bounded to the bucket as the thing swallowed what it could of Stash's foot. It was so small, Theo couldn't even imagine where the mouthful went once it left the thing's mouth.

What seemed so heavy only a minute before now seemed weightless with the twin assistance of panic and adrenalin. The two of them hefted the bucket and jettisoned the contents at the hell-rat. Their aim was perfect.

The thing stiffened, then the water hit it, forcing it to hunker down on Stash's leg. When the tide passed, it blinked once and continued clawing its way up Stash's leg, drawing fresh blood with each step. Stash writhed on the ground, screaming

(KILL IT KILL IT KILLLLLLIIIIIIIT)

screaming screaming in agony.

"Fuck man, we gotta do somethin'!"

But Theo was already bolting for the janitor's closet.

♦♦♦

MARCIA STOOD TO one side of the stage—stage left, if she had that whole thing right—when a swarm of beasts invaded the caf, snarling and barking.

With the darkness of the room, all she saw was a shiny black cloud spilling out of one of the big vents that supplied the caf with fresh air, then break into individual parts as it hit the floor. But *what* it was, or rather, what they *were*, was not immediately clear to her. The dark, her distance from the seething cloud, and the unreality of the situation hampered any sense she could make of it.

She did understand they were not good. As they clattered to the floor, bodies thudding and nails clicking, Mr. Hasselton ran over to them—Marcia would never know what he had been thinking, maybe to save one of the falling set pieces, maybe just to investigate—and became the first victim. As Hassy approached, Marcia got a scale on the creatures.

They were small, the size of a large rat, or maybe a small dog. They looked like neither. The only other thing her overloaded mind processed was teeth. Lots of teeth.

Hassy stopped just short of the horde. One of the beasts stood just in front of him, a little ahead of the rest. They sized each other up for a second, less even. Then, the beast sprang, mouth gaping.

Hassy's face disappeared in a spray of red, like someone had hit him with a blood-soaked sponge. The little dog-beast seemed to burrow into his face, shaking its body, its claws gripping and shredding Mr. Hasselton's jawline. Then, it appeared to get what it wanted, because it pulled out and jumped to the ground. It held a large, bloody piece of Mr. Hasselton clamped in its jaws. It could have been his tongue. It could have been his brain.

Marcia didn't want to know.

As Hassy's faceless body fell backward, the room erupted in sound and panic. Everyone ran everywhere, nobody knowing what to do, where to go. Everywhere they ran, the dog-beasts got there first, waiting for them, their dangerous black teeth flashing horrible grins.

Marcia ran to the side of the set, her only thought to get up above them, to hide where they couldn't see her. She needed to find a place where they wouldn't turn her face into pudding. She reached up to grab at the crude ladder that served as the backstage entrance to the second-storey von Trapp bedroom. She got two or three rungs up but, in her panic, her foot missed the next rung. She slipped, banging her chin painfully. She tasted blood from her bitten tongue—a flash of the beast pulling off Hassy's face, the torn flesh dangling—as her hand slipped over the rough wood and she lost control, falling backward, arms pinwheeling, grabbing uselessly at the dark air.

Marcia's head cracked against the worn stage flooring with a thud, lost amid the larger, more horrific sounds of feeding and adolescent panic in the main part of the cafeteria.

Her vision swam and it seemed as though someone was closing big barn doors on either side of her head as her vision narrowed. The last thing she consciously noticed was the dog-beasts forcefully knocking over the emergency lights, breaking them.

Why would they wanna be in the dark? she thought as a different darkness closed over her.

♦♦♦

WHEN THEO WAS ten years old, he took a baseball bat to the mouth. It was an accident. Hell, he hadn't even been playing baseball at the time.

The game had finished about a half-hour earlier, so Theo and Jimmy Baldwin—his best friend at the time—hung out waiting for Jimmy's dad to pick them up. They had been just screwing around, talking macho, or as macho as they could manage at the tender age of ten, when out of the blue, Theo had bent down to pick up the softball sitting on the ground at his feet.

In one of those tragic synchronicities that occur so rarely, and also completely out of the blue, Jimmy had decided he could wind up and piledrive that ball right into home plate. He told Theo later that he could almost hear the ring of the chain-link barrier as the ball smacked into it.

Theo's mind tried to sort out the confusion that followed. He bent and saw the ball. Suddenly, the ball was gone from under his hand. *Poof!* Then he was sailing backward and landing on his ass. Then nothing but blue. The sky. He was on his back staring up at the sky, something warm sliding down the back of his throat.

He hadn't completely clued in that something was wrong until Jimmy's face blocked out the blue. He was saying something to Theo, but Theo couldn't hear him over the ringing in his ears. He tried to tell Jimmy that he couldn't hear him, but something was wrong with his mouth. It didn't feel right anymore. All jagged inside.

Then the pain punched into him. It drilled into his face like shrapnel, tearing pounding ripping shredding like a fleet of jackhammers.

The damage from the bat announced itself.

Both the doctors and the dentists who treated him told him how lucky he was. Most of the force landed just under his nose, robbing him of only one tooth and shattering a couple more. He had several hairline fractures running up his skull almost to his

(orbits doc called them his orbits)

eye sockets, but, with the exception of a scar under his lower lip where the missing tooth exited, and two years of corrective surgery, he had been left with no permanent physical damage.

But he had never touched a baseball or a bat again. He couldn't even fake a decent swing without wincing. When that bat finished with him, dental nerves had been exposed and fresh air slid across them like the bristles of a wire brush, every breath a new and undiscovered agony. Seven years later, the memory was still fresh. The actual pain had been forgotten, as pain always is, but the memory of suffering and agony was just as clear as it had been when he was ten years old and staring up at his best friend's face wondering what the hell he was trying to say.

Many times in the intervening years, Theo swore that he would never have anything to do, ever again, with the game of baseball.

Up until this day, seven years later, he had kept to that promise.

Theo grabbed the mop that had so recently felt the Toad's carnal embrace and ran back to Stash. Without so much as a thought to his once-damaged face, or the pain that had been inflicted upon it, Theo wound up and

(sah-wiiiinnnngggg battah)

cranked that little fucker off Stash's leg better than any home run ever hit in the majors.

The hell-rat—as Theo was already beginning to identify it—flew, twisting through the air, then finally grounding about twenty feet downwind, skittering and scrabbling across the wet floor, for all the world like an insectoid Chihuahua. It finally came to a stop when its skull impacted loudly off the brick of the wall. All buggy eyes and tapping nails, it fought to find purchase on the slick, faux-marble floor, little chunks of Stash's flesh falling from its grinding teeth.

While it was still disoriented, the Toad didn't hesitate. With a weird nervous giggle slipping out from clenched teeth, he clomped after it and launched himself forward, coming down on it with all the force he could pack into a pair of size twelve steel-toed Grebs.

Long ropy sprays of black blood and hell-rat guts squirted out from beneath the Toad's boots. *Jesus,* thought Theo, *we thought Crouch*

(IS DEAD KILL IT KILL IT)

puking into a bucket was gross.

The Toad turned and looked at Theo. He was so caught up in the moment that he was about to equate the size of his feet with the length of his

(wait'll the chicks get a taste of the Hipcracker)

penis, completely forgetting Stash twenty feet from him. Instead, Theo watched as his triumphant expression washed away.

"Aw, Jesus, Theo! The caf! Look at the goddamn cafeteria!"

That's when Theo finally tuned into the wailing shrieks roiling out of the cafeteria.

♦♦♦

"SHIT," LAURA MUTTERED. *Goddamn small towns! Why can't we go more than two weeks without a power failure?* This is what her tax money got her? She stuck her head out of the class, looking up and down the hall. Strange shadows slid along the floor from the battery-powered emergency lights.

"Shit," she muttered again.

She continued with the cleanup. Hell, she was almost done, and was aware of the fluttering thrill in her belly at the thought of meeting Tom in a few minutes. He was going to ask her out. If she didn't exactly know it, she strongly anticipated it. Hell, maybe they'd go out later tonight. *Okay,* she admitted, *maybe working here does have a few benefits after all.* A power failure wasn't going to dampen her spirits. This was the first ray of hope she had had in a long time.

After Jude had died, she had been desperate. Her parents were both gone, and she had no other family to lean on. Oh, there had been a bit of insurance money, and what was left of the Davis clan sent some more so she wouldn't starve, but they soon drifted away, mired in their own issues with two dead sons and Talia's missing parents and sister. She couldn't be angry with them, knowing that every time they talked to her, it reminded them that their son was no longer around. It was just too painful.

Maybe it would have been different if she had given them a grandchild. But she hadn't. There was no glue to hold them together.

So she went back to what she knew: she had been in the graphic design industry before her husband had moved her away to live like Grizzly Adams. And she had been damn good. Well on her way to art director. But not in New Hope.

She had heard that the local high school's art teacher was due to retire at the end of the 1977 school year. That was all she needed to hear. She had rushed home, gathered up the best pieces in her portfolio, and left a trail of blue smoke belching from her ancient pickup truck as she hightailed it into town again. She felt herself slide into sell mode. She used to use that mindset to present the idea, then sell the shit out of it to the client. Well, now she would present and sell the shit out of herself. Thank god she'd picked up a teaching degree back before Jude. She'd thought she'd been wasting her time, going after it only to prolong the time she had before settling into a permanent job. Now? It was one more thing to sell the shit out of. Half an hour later, she'd walked out with the gig.

It wasn't what she had ever imagined herself doing, but it paid the bills and got her out among people again. Even if they were mostly under the age of eighteen.

It had been the only thing that had kept her sane the past few years. And now, with her shit slowly coming together, and not a dragon tail in sight, she had gained back a little hope.

New hope in New Hope. *Who'd'a thunk it?*

A large, full-length mirror leaned against the north wall of the class, normally used by students wanting to check the way a pose would look, or the way a particular appendage bent. It's main use ultimately ended up being for hair and zit checks. She walked over to it for a check of her own, watching her own approach in the reflection. Hell, if her kids could do it, why not her? Not the best illumination under the weird glare of the emergency lights, but she saw her long blonde hair hanging straight to mid-thigh—

There's that word again. *Thigh.*

—and the faint traces of laugh lines beginning to form around her mouth and brown eyes. She wasn't a beauty, but she was all right, as Springsteen said. Jude used to say she knew how to fill a pair of jeans.

She smiled at her reflection, a little touch of sadness creeping in at the edges. She *really* wanted this thing with Tom to work.

God, get a grip, girl! she thought. He had made a small overture, that was all. He hadn't even officially asked her out yet. *But I think he will today –*

She froze at the unexpected and not-right sound behind her. *What the hell was that?*

Movement in the mirror. Something had skittered across the floor. Something small, black, shiny—but she wasn't sure if it was dog-fur shiny or insect shiny. *Oh, let it be dog-fur shiny. Like a*

(chihuahua?)

little black puppy. Not bug shiny. She didn't like bugs, and this would be a *big* bug. No, a puppy would be good. A small dog. She purposely ignored the fact that there wouldn't be a dog in the school because— Fuck it, she could live with a small dog in her classroom.

But it had moved different from a dog. Not mindless and all over the place like a pup, all tongue and legs and tail. No, this had been more purposeful.

In the quick peripheral glance she had got in the mirror, Laura also got a sense that whatever shared the classroom with her wasn't good. It felt *wrong*. The light-blonde hairs on her arms stood up as her flesh creeped. She turned from the mirror as quietly as she could, breathing quickly but silently through her mouth.

Where was it? *What* was i—

Movement.

Off to her right. Behind the cabinets. They were set like an island toward the front of the class.

Whatever it was, it was between Laura and the door.

Fuck me, she thought. *Fuck me* hard!

♦♦♦

STASH'S SCREAMS RANG in Theo's head like a frenzied hunchback ringing a bell. His mind chugged away, still trying to process the fact that Stash's left foot flopped around like an unstrung marionette's. It just wouldn't compute. Like that *Star Trek* episode where the confused android kept repeating the line: "Norman, please explain." Theo couldn't wrap his mind around it. It was too unreal.

Then, just to spice up the stew, Crouch—poor drunken, pickup driving, cowboy hat and peach-fuzz-wearing, zackly-mouthed Benmont Devenish—was apparently dead, killed by some hopped-up hell-rat.

And then there was the Toad. Completely incoherent. Crouch would have said he was FUBAR, which was supposedly some military term that was short for "fucked-up beyond all recognition." Crouch would have been right on.

The Toad stood frozen in the same position amid the flattened remains of the hell-rat, grue staining his Grebs, not moving since his "look at the goddamn cafeteria" comment. His right arm pointed, still outstretched toward the caf entrance, his left hand nervously batting his thigh in some crazed disco beat, and demon-dog goo dripped from his aviator-style Coke-bottle glasses. His mouth worked slowly, and his lips moved, but no sound passed his lips. It almost looked like he was enjoying a particularly tasty morsel of something.

Screams—ear-ripping, teeth-gritting ones—clawed and tore their way out from the cafeteria.

Theo shook himself out of inaction and pulled off his stretchy polyester track jacket, one of the only cool things his mother had ever got for him. White with a wide navy-blue stripe running from the collar and down both shoulders to the cuffs; a very cool article of clothing as far as Theo was concerned. Up to now, it had only one minor blemish, received the previous summer when a bunch of the guys from school had got into a full-out firecracker war. Each one of them had a lit Colt cigarillo (cigarettes were simply far too blasé, and matches too damn slow) to light the 'crackers efficiently and quickly. Theo had come up against Moose and the two of them got into a duel, both of them furiously lighting 'crackers and pitching them at each other.

Theo had done well, having one explode right in Moose's face and another right over his crotch. Moose, who by now giggled wildly, threw one at Theo. Theo felt it hit him in the chest, but he didn't see where the tiny explosive fell. Moose apparently did because he giggled more furiously and his hands flapped ineffectually in Theo's direction, as though windblown. He even dropped his Colt in the confusion.

Theo still couldn't see it. Then it exploded in the pocket of his then-new track jacket. Goddamn! A small flame licked up from inside his pocket, which was beaten out as fast as it had come to light. When he looked up, Theo realized Moose had come over and beat his pocket until the flame died. Theo looked at his pocket. There was a large ugly hole inside, with a ragged brown-black edge. Fucking thing melted. Good ol' space-age fabrics.

Theo looked at Moose and, in his most serious tone, said, "Thanks, man. You saved my life." Then they both lost it. Luckily, his mom had never noticed the burn inside the pocket. Even with the flaw, or maybe because of it, that jacket had been Theo's favourite. Until today.

He lifted the torn pant leg of Stash's blood-soaked Levi's. His white sweat socks were red and shiny like Christmas wrapping paper, his hairs matted to his leg. The smell of blood, piss, and demon goo, and the adrenalin made Theo gag as he knotted the sleeve of his jacket around Stash's

(ohfuckohfuckohfuckohfuckohfuckohfuckoh)

ankle.

Blood pissed alarmingly out of the mashed heel of Stash's Adidas running shoe as bloody flowers blossomed on Theo's jacket sleeve.

"Toad! Quit fuckin' the dog and help me here! Stash is losin' a lot of fuckin' blood! Get me that mop."

The Toad reacted in a real low gear, moving as though caught in quicksand. He picked up the mop and looked at Theo as if to say "you want me to mop the blood?"

Theo made a disgusted noise, reached out, and grabbed the mop from the Toad's limp hold. He put the business end on the floor, with the handle on an angle, then motioned at the Toad, who broke it with one thrust from his construction-booted foot. It made a crack that sent a visible jolt through the Toad.

Taking the shorter of the two pieces, Theo jammed it under the knotted sleeve of his jacket and rotated the stick clockwise to add pressure to the tourniquet. When he thought he had enough, he aligned the stick with Stash's leg and pulled his pantleg back down to hold it in place. Through all of this, Stash slid in and out of consciousness. Mostly out. He kept making soft little "oh" noises.

To Theo, this whole operation seemed to take hours, but it was done in less than a minute. It was one of those extreme-panic times that taffy-pulled seconds into minutes, minutes into hours. Now that it was past, Theo and the Toad dropped where they stood and sat on the floor in a hazed-out post-adrenalin rush phase. The energy bled off, leaving only a copper aftertaste and a pounding heart.

Reality had just considered making a return when it took another kick to the head.

Everything went pitch-black so fast, Theo wondered if he had somehow died without knowing it. He looked up and around, eyes automatically searching out the windows facing the lobby into the parking lot. Something pushed a solid wall of nausea over on him and his body bucked forward in a violent fit of projectile vomiting.

(pizza and coke and snickers)

He heard the Toad doing the same thing. But below that rode more menacing sounds. Groaning, shifting sounds kneaded his skull as he continued to heave.

(cheerios and oj and toast oh my!)

Theo's world somersaulted, and the building trembled like a piss-shiver.

And then there was light again.

Sort of.

Still heaving, Theo looked out the windows at…nothing. Not a nothing as in pitch-black and can't-see-at-all. Nothing as in *nothing*. No black, no white, no colours, no grey. It was the absence of anything at all. The *everythingness* of reality had been sucked away and only *nothingness* was left behind. Theo wretched again, spilling strings of chunky saliva, his guts doing their damnedest to crawl up his esophagus.

He looked away. To look out on that void was to feel his brain being hoovered out of his forehead. It was total disorientation. It was a mindfuck.

Facing the wall, Theo cautiously cracked one eye. All he could see was the reddish-brown of the brick. And his stomach held. The Toad's obviously hadn't, from the sounds behind him.

"Toad! Don't look at the windows—"

More retching. Why did people always do exactly what you told them not to?

"—just look at the wall. Look at the wall and you won't puke, dude."

Rustling noises. Wet sounds of boots sliding on slick flooring.

"Toad! You okay?"

"…gah…"

Okay, he wasn't throwing up anymore. That was a good thing. But Theo heard some sort of low drone coming from his way. *Fuck it. He's not puking. We're okay for now.*

The two of them stayed where they were, snuggled up to the walls like grade schoolers being punished. Theo calmed slightly, felt himself get a small measure of grip when a high, sharp crack sounded and made him do a squirt in his BVDs.

Jesus! What now?

♦♦♦

MARCIA WOKE TO the sound of someone screeching. No…more than one voice…

As her senses slowly came back to her—she had never passed out before and waking up from it was highly disconcerting—she tried to make sense of the situation. Where was she? What was all that noise? Why was it so dark? Why did her head hurt so bad? And her tongue, was it swollen?

And why was it so damn cold?

Then Marcia, still lying where she had dropped, saw Stephanie run, wild and panicky, for the doors at the entrance of the cafeteria, her arms flailing. She hit the door like she didn't even know it was there, like she was determined to run through it like the Tasmanian Devil did in those cartoons, but it held tight, closed and apparently locked. From where she was all the way across the cafeteria, Marcia saw that the doors looked weird. Bunched up.

Marcia closed her eyes and shivered against the cold. Those dog-beasts herded and slashed and ripped at the students in the room.

Why not me?

She didn't know, but she was scared to move right now in case her movement attracted attention. But she would have to move soon. The cold was getting to her. *Why is it so cold? It's June!*

Marcia's eyes snapped back open at the sound of Stephanie. She thumped on the door and pleaded with someone outside to please just please God let her out.

She had her face pressed up to the little wire-reinforced window, still begging, when they came for her. The dog-beasts. They swarmed over her and tore her from the door like a wave pulling her away from a lifeboat. Marcia couldn't see it clearly, but it looked like she left a mark on the window. It was fogged, or smeared.

They dragged Steph a few feet from the entrance. They pulled her down and...Marcia closed her eyes again. She couldn't watch as they shredded Stephanie apart. The dog-beasts tore pieces off her like cotton candy. They *dismantled* her. To Marcia, it looked like they were all trying to get at some tasty morsel buried deep inside her, almost like they had with Hassy's face.

Whatever it was, they got it.

All the time this was happening, the other students were run down like sheep. There was no escape. When they bunched together, huddling for protection from the cold, from the horror, they were picked over like a turkey at a Christmas dinner.

The wailing scaled higher and higher as more mouths opened in terror.

Dear God, I've got to get out of here.

CHAPTER EIGHT

SCRABBLING NOISES.

They came from around the far side of the cupboards. There. Laura saw it.

Jesus! she thought, jerking back in surprise.

It launched at her like a shot, covering the distance between them before Laura could react. All claws and teeth and shiny black hide, it ripped at her slacks, not quite getting a grip on her leg. She went down in a forest of stools and easels. Her head whacked painfully against the floor as she landed on her back, legs kicking. The thing made a high, keening whine, like fingernails on a chalkboard, making Laura wince. The blow to her head made strange flashing spots

(stars I see stars)

in her eyes.

The thing finally got a grip and sunk its teeth into her calf. The spots flew away. Something on her chest. Another one? No. Her fingers wrapped around something long, hard, thin. Paintbrush. It was a paintbrush. She raised it, dagger-style. Her arm came down and she heard the wood snap, slivers driving into her palm as the wood cracked off the floor. *Shit! Missed it! Shitshitshit!*

One more go. Arm swinging in an arc. Whizzing past her

(don't hit your)

leg and the jagged point found purchase in something. The whine scaled up, higher and louder. *Got ya, fucker.* Scrabbling noises again and—

It was gone. No, still here, still in the room, but away from her. Good. Good enough for now.

Laura pulled herself up from the tangle of furniture while trying to dial back her panting to something resembling normal breathing. Her calf burned with pain. She stood and eyed the room, searching for any sign of the thing.

She knew it was still here. She could hear it, but she couldn't get any sort of direction from the sound.

Fuck it. I've got to get out of here. Right now.

She moved toward the door, half limping, half hopping on her good leg. Three hops closer to the door, she stopped.

There. On top of the island cabinet, perched among the paints and thinners, sat the…

The…what, dog-beast? What the hell else could she call it? It was the size of a small dog, a shiny black but not furry. All black eyes and black teeth and black claws, it was one of the ugliest things she had ever laid eyes on.

She also noticed, with some pride, that the dog-beast was in rough shape. The paintbrush was buried high in its hide, just forward of its pelvis, assuming it even had one. It leaked a blackish-purple liquid that looked like blueberry syrup and stank like cat piss.

Breathing heavy, its sides pumping, it stared at Laura and she imagined rage in its marble-black eyes.

Its mouth stretched too big for its face, like its teeth had been swapped for those of a much larger carnivore's. It kept swinging its head around, grabbing at the paintbrush, but each time the beast tried to pull the offending stick out, it only succeeded in kicking up the volume and letting go with a squeal.

"Got ya, didn't I? Yeah, well, you got me too, you little fuck."

It didn't move. It continued to watch her, diverting its attention only to bite and snap at the brush handle sticking out like a sundial.

She thought about yelling out, but her mind flashed on the empty hallway. *School's out. No one here.*

Could she outrun it? Probably not. The little shit had been able to jump up to that cabinet, even with the handle shish kebabbing its guts. Laura took another step. Pain

(oh yeah, that hurts)

shot up her leg. She crouched forward, hands going to her thighs.

Under her left palm, in the pocket of her slacks, she felt a slip of paper

(pick up milk and honeycomb cereal)

she had stuffed in there this morning in her rush to make it to work on time. God. This morning. How many years ago was that?

But under the paper she felt…

(one burning desire)

…oh thank god, she felt…

(your fire)

…her lighter.

♦♦♦

THEY STOOD, NUMBED.

Back in better times—God, how long ago was that?—Theo recalled a family vacation to Paradise Island. His family's last vacation. One day, while swimming, he had found the bottom of a broken pop bottle that had been pushed ashore by the constant pounding of the waves. He had marvelled at the broken glass because it had been worn completely smooth by the action of the sand and waves. There had been no sharp edges left.

That's how Theo felt right now. The constant pounding of the violence and the wailing waves of tortured human voices and the cold and the dark and the big nothing outside had worn him down. He was broken. Glassy and smooth, he had no sharp edges left.

Theo and the Toad still stared stupidly at the wall, breathing heavily, when the crack assaulted their ears like a sonic boom. The Toad did a spontaneous back-jump of about five feet, his arms curled to his chest. Stash was still out

(ladies and gentlemen the stash has left the building)

but he'd just winced. Theo continued to measure off panicked shots of piss into his underwear. What the hell good was it wearing clean underwear when he kept pissing in it during the emergency situation he'd needed clean underwear for in the first fuckin' place?

Theo and the Toad turned their attention to the big double sets of doors that provided entrance to the cafeteria. If they angled their heads right, they could see it without seeing outside.

Ice.

Fucking ice grew around the edges of the door. But it grew way too fast, like one of those time-lapse movies of a sunset or a flower blooming. It flexed and bulged like muscles and the sheer force of it twisted the metal doors, flexing and warping them under the sinews of ice.

Theo pulled his attention away for a moment, drawn by the sound coming from the Toad. It took a second to nail it down, because he

(...goestheweaselpopgoestheweaselpopgoesthe...)

whispered it so fast.

Pop goes the weasel. Repeated over and over like a mantra. What the hell was that?

Theo's face still showed his confusion as another noise stole his attention away. A thump. A new and different noise that made his heart quake with fear. Not a sharp crack this time—more dull and hollow. It came from the caf door. They both turned to look. The Toad still prayed to the

(…weaselpopgoestheweaselpopgoestheweaselpopgoes…)

weasel god. Behind the thump was a hand, a human hand, slapping the wire-reinforced glass of the cafeteria door. That was bad enough, but it wasn't the worst. Oh no, not the worst. That came next.

A face appeared at the edge of the frost,

(steph jesus god its)

eyes wild and beseeching. Green eyes. Steph's eyes. Get-me-the-fuck-out-of-here eyes. "Something in here wants to kill me," those eyes said. Her mouth moved, but he couldn't make out what she said. Theo caught all this in the half-second flash before she disappeared, as though wrenched away in an undertow, the glass so cold it kept a few layers of skin because it came off her face and hand easier than the frozen glass.

From beyond the frozen entrance came screaming screeching shrieking. Full-throated, totally panicked wailing.

"Toad, we gotta—"

"…theweaselpopgoesthe…"

"We gotta *do* something!"

"We can get a torch from automotive to melt it, but those doors may be so cold we might be able to crack them with a battering ram if we can find one."

Theo and the Toad spun at the mostly calm voice. It was Ms. Davis. Laura. Theo's art teacher. She looked like shit. Where the hell had she come from?

♦♦♦

MARCIA SLOWLY PICKED herself up off the ground with shaky arms. Her teeth chattered as she moved as quietly as she could to the backstage doors. From there she would get out to the tech wing hallway and find some help. Slipping behind another curtain, she found the doors.

They looked like a crushed pop can. The doors had the

same muscular bunching around them as the front doors.

Ice.

The doors were frozen shut. That's why Steph hadn't been able to get out. Why none of them got out.

Okay Marce, this can't be the only way out. There's gotta be other ways. Don't panic.

But Marcia knew it was only a matter of time before those things started looking for fast-food items up on the stage.

Peeking around the curtains, she tried to ignore the orgy of carnage, blood, and pain out on the main floor to seek a way out of here. All the doors were shut and blocked. She couldn't get out. Maybe if she could get up above…

The sound booth!

The sound booth where Sparky had been playing the records.

Up above everything, they used the room to play music for various stage productions, and it also housed the spotlights. Situated just above the entrance to the caf, it would be perfect. Not necessarily a way out, but if she could get there she could maybe barricade herself in. Wait it out until someone came to help.

But how could she get to it? The one and only way in was from the stairs that led up from the cafeteria floor. She would have to cross the floor. Reluctantly, she considered it again.

Those things were out there. The things that had killed Hassy. Killed Steph. All the others. No, that wasn't exactly true. Some were still alive, because she could hear the weeping and moaning. Still, the dog-beasts attacked anything that moved.

She drew her attention back to the carnage. She wanted to see if anything distracted them, but no, it didn't seem so. But they were doing something different now. In a way, it seemed even worse than just attacking.

They seemed to be setting her classmates up. Arranging them.

Marcia shook her head. No, she wasn't seeing what she was seeing. She couldn't be.

But she was.

The beasts would very purposefully throw up a sickly stream of vomit and then arrange the still-living bodies in it like a stone setting in a ring. Like a fly in amber.

As though making a museum display of the mutilated bodies they had created. A sculpture.

An obscene sculpture. Marcia could see there seemed to be a purpose, a design behind it.

Every one of them has a…hole of some sort facing up. Why?

Some of her classmates were arranged with their genitals facing out. Some had their mouths propped open, gaping wide, unnaturally, jaws broken wide. Some had holes torn into them and ripped wide.

Then the worst realization hit her. Tears sprung to her eyes and her gorge rose. None of the arranged were dead yet. That was where the crying and moaning was coming from.

The students who she went to school with every day. What in God's name was happening?

Steph got off easy, she thought. She fought down the rising gorge, shivered again and clasped her hands around her, partially for warmth, partially for comfort.

She had to get to that booth, but there was no way she could cross that floor. She'd be…set up like the others in seconds.

She looked to the sound booth again.

Gonna paint a Michael-fuggin-Angelo onna roof!

More like you'll be swingin' from the damn rafters.

Marcia looked to the ceiling of the cafeteria. At the metal supports that ran from the stage area straight back to the far wall. Straight back to the sound booth. The supports ran in parallel lines about four feet apart.

Thirty feet up.

"Inna gadda da vida, baby," Marcia whispered. Her voice quavered.

No way. There was no way she could do it. She wasn't a lover of heights. Not a suck, but not a fan either. *There's nothing to grab up there*, she thought.

Okay, that was wrong. There was a lot to hold on to. But if she lost her grip…

Thirty feet straight down into hell.

No way. There had to be another solution.

Marcia looked around again. Doors frozen, cafeteria floor a definite no-no. And to make matters worse, the dog-beasts looked like they were finishing up. Some looked like they were scouting for more sculpting projects.

Fuck.

Marcia was a reasonably good Catholic girl. Not one of those virginal Billy Joel Catholic girls, and definitely not one of those Frank Zappa Catholic girls with their strange fascination with TELEFUNKEN U47s. Just a normal girl who really didn't swear too often. When she did, she wanted it to be worth the trip to confession.

Well, this one was going to be worth confessing. *Bless me, Father, for I have sinned. I was stuck on a stage watching my friends get eaten alive and I determined the only way out was to go hand-over-hand thirty feet above them. So I said "fuck" three times.*

Fuck.

And while we're at it, I took off my bra in a plan to tempt an ex-boyfriend but it went all wrong and now he's probably dead.

Shut the fuck up, she thought. *Okay. Four times.*

As much as Marcia didn't like it, there was no other way out of here.

At the back of the stage hung a rope ladder used to get to the stage lights. Marcia briefly considered just climbing up and pulling the ladder up behind her and waiting it out until help arrived. She looked over to the cafeteria floor and listened to the wails and cast that idea aside. Besides, there were all these curtains around her, and those dog-beasts looked like they had some seriously nasty claws. She figured she'd have to watch for them climbing the curtains, but she didn't think they'd be too hot on metal rafters. She guessed they couldn't really grip unless they had something they could sink their nails into.

Of course, she based all this on what she could observe through the dark from several yards away.

It was time to go.

"Inna gadda da vida, baby," she whispered one more time and grabbed at the rope. Then she hauled herself up, one swaying rung at a time.

Marcia took more care this time. She didn't want to find out if she could survive a second fall to the stage. After climbing a few feet, she stopped and pulled up the dangling portion of the rope ladder from below her and looped it over her shoulder. There was no way she was going to let one act of stupidity or carelessness be her downfall.

Her hands already ached, so cold her fingers creaked as she climbed higher and higher, praying to God in Heaven that nothing saw her. She felt completely exposed, ripe for the picking. She tried to keep all the slack rope tightly looped so it wouldn't wave around like a flag.

Though it seemed like hours, Marcia made it to the ceiling in a couple of minutes. Her numb fingers stiff, her arms quivering, her breath fogging out in huffs, but sweating despite the cold.

She pulled the rope up and looped it around the rafter, making sure it wouldn't fall and cause a surprise later. She wanted to take it with her, but it would throw her off-balance and she didn't think she could have unknotted it anyway. Besides, there was no way Marcia would have trusted any knot her frozen hands would have been capable of tying at this point.

She wrapped herself around the rafter and rested as best she could, getting a feel for the beams she would be riding. The metal support was actually a large hollow I-beam with diagonal supports welded in at forty-five-degree angles that reminded Marcia of grinning triangular teeth all in a row. Like a shark.

Like the dog-beasts.

The sweat cooled rapidly, especially where her belly made contact with the cold metal, making her shiver more violently, almost wobble. Theo would have called it a piss-shiver.

That's not good, she thought, but she didn't know if she meant the shivering or the thought of Theo. She took a deep breath and set her mind on her desperate endeavour.

♦♦♦

LAURA TEASED THE lighter higher in her pocket as she angled toward the door. The injured thing on the cabinet followed her moves like the two of them were in some kind of Spaghetti Western stare down.

She made as if to break for the door, but at the last second she faked the thing out, swung her arm in a quick arc, and smacked the paintbrush handle sticking out of it. The beast snapped and wailed and thrashed. Laura seized the stick and pinned the dog-beast to the tabletop like a butterfly specimen, her lips pulled back in a grin that was all malice, no humour. If she could have driven the paintbrush into the countertop, she would have, but she could apply enough pressure to hold it down. Laura grabbed the paint thinner and thumbed the cap off—thank god Ann Marie always forgot to tighten the lids—and upended the canister over the spitting creature. The sudden sharp odour made her eyes water. The room was filled with the noise of her grunting to hold the dog-beast down, its squealing, and the bong of the metal paint thinner can.

When the canister ran dry, Laura tossed it clanging into a corner and she dug into her pocket

(milk and honeycomb cereal)

for the lighter. As her attention went briefly to getting a flame, the thing twisted and clamped down on her forearm. She let out a wail of her own, but didn't loosen the pressure on the stick.

She thumbed the wheel and watched the sparks. Finally, a flame. She torched the creature. *WOOF!* Laura smelled burned hair and knew she was missing eyebrows. The hair singed off her arm before she could even let go of the stick. The dog-beast opened its mouth wide to scream and Laura yanked her arm back.

It didn't so much burn as melt and shrink away—almost like the light of the flame was doing more damage than the heat. The creature's frenzy grew exponentially, and in the confusion, the lighter was knocked from her hand and spun off into the tangle of stools and easels.

The dog-beast gave a final lurch and snap of its jaws, then it was dead. Just the sound of her breathing and the odd pop and spit from the burning meat of the creature. Her ears rang like they did after monitoring duty at a school dance.

She limped over to some artfully draped fabric on a pedestal, took it down, and tore some strips to wrap her leg and arm.

As she made the last knot around her calf, Laura's ears cleared enough to hear the screams echoing down the darkened corridors. Ensuring the thing was dead, she used the rest of the fabric to smother the flames.

She sopped up the fluid and bundled the fabric into a ball, the dog-beast in the middle of it.

Then she dropped it to the floor and stomped on it until it was flat. Only then did she leave the room.

♦♦♦

LAURA LIMPED DOWN the hall into a scene more hellish than the one she just left. Constant wails pounded her ears like the roar of the ocean. They seemed to be coming from the cafeteria.

Robert Bostash—Stash—lay in the middle of the lobby in a circle of his own blood. His foot looked like someone had taken a chainsaw to it. She guessed the chainsaw had been small, black, and carried huge dentures. Dennis Bussik—the Toad—appeared completely incoherent. She heard him saying something under his breath, but it could have been Japanese for all she knew.

Thelonious Clarke—Theo—arguably the most intelligent of the three (at least while Bostash was unconscious) and the one she would have voted Most in Charge of His Senses also looked zoned. He didn't have the same look that Dennis had. His was more a look of someone who had been dealing with way too much, way too fast. The look of someone who needed to get off the ride for a while. At least to get away from the sounds of human pain coming from behind the cafeteria doors.

It was the same look Laura guessed had rode her own face not ten minutes earlier.

Theo and Dennis stared at the cafeteria entrance. She heard a crack and, though her eyes were still adjusting to the lack of lighting in the lobby, she knew where to look. That's when she saw the

(holy christ where did all the ice come from)

ice around the doors. Big bands of it, like the trunk of an old tree.

Theo said, "We gotta *do* something!" Apparently, he meant to get in there.

"We can get a torch from automotive to melt it," she offered, "but those doors may be so cold we might be able to crack them with a battering ram, if we can find one."

Theo and the Toad spun like they'd heard a ghost talking, and it was then that she realized they hadn't noticed her coming up at all. She thought, with all her hopping and limping, they couldn't have missed her. Then again, with all the screaming and ice cracking, why would they?

"Sorry guys. I didn't mean to scare you. You look like you've both had enough of that already."

Theo just nodded. The Toad stared at her with wide eyes, his lips moving soundlessly. *Jesus,* she thought, *they're just scared kids.* For all the wishing and acting and posturing they did every day to prove how adult they all were, these people were still kids, barely a couple of thousand days into their teens. That was sometimes hard to remember.

For all of that, Laura would never forget the looks on the two boys' faces at that moment. It scared the hell out of her.

"They're trapped," Theo said.

"Who's trapped?"

"Students. The guys doing the…uh… "

"The sets? For the musical? Hassy…Mr. Hasselton? Those guys? How many?"

Theo was nodding. "Lots. I don't know. Marcia…Steph. Steph's in there. Her face…" Tears started. Fourteen Stephanies were enrolled at Clarington High that year, but when Theo said the name he could only be referring to one. Laura knew Theo had a crush on her. Hell, everybody knew that. Half the guys in the school had a crush on her. And Marcia…Theo and her had been an item, too, hadn't they?

"Look, let's get down to auto and get a torch and a big toolbox. Maybe we can pound our way in."

Theo wiped his tears with the heel of his hand and sniffed once to clear his nose. Big breath and he was sort of in control again. "What about Stash? We can't leave him."

"Dennis?" Laura looked at the Toad, but he shook his head

furiously, pupils as big as olives behind his glasses. No way was he staying here alone, that was obvious.

Theo turned to him, talking to him as he would a young child. "Then go with Miz Davis."

"Laura. Call me Laura."

"Okay. Go with Laura. Can you do that?" The Toad took a second to ponder. His lips stopped their recitation. One nod, quick, like he had to get it out before he changed his mind.

"Then go. Hurry."

They went, Laura still limping, but striding with more purpose and intent than she really felt, the Toad loping after, trying to look in all directions at once, hands clutched together tight to his chest. His boots made loud squelching noises. His lips were moving again.

♦♦♦

MARCIA DISENGAGED HER right arm from the support and reached ahead, getting a firm grip on the next diagonal. Then she pulled out her left leg and hooked it back over the support a little further up. Then the other arm and the other leg.

She was on her way.

Her breath still fogged out, her hands were frozen into claws, but for all intents and purposes, she was safer up here.

She tried to get into a rhythm so she wouldn't have to think. She couldn't really look down because she was hanging from the rafter, belly up, the ceiling maybe two feet above her, and that was probably a good thing. She didn't want to think about what was happening thirty feet below her. She didn't want to consider anything about *anything* thirty feet below her.

Down there, she had eaten lunch earlier that day. A ham-and-cheese sandwich with tomato and lettuce and Dijon mustard, a fruit cup and a milk to wash it all down.

Thirty feet below her, other things were eating right now.

Thirty feet below her, stage sets had been sculpted out of papier-mâché, but now, her friends were the set.

Thirty feet below her, she had been in an assembly not two weeks ago, not really caring what it was for, only that it had got her out of French class. She had heard about the school winning some computer competition. She had heard about some fundraiser for the school band. She had heard Mr. Austin play the piano while Nicole Davidson had sung that Boomtown Rats song, "I Don't Like Mondays." She had heard the whispers around her. There were rumours about those two. Mr. Austin had made some comment about Nicole helping him with the sheet music. Yeah, they knew what he meant. "Sheet music." No kidding!

Thirty feet below her, the whispers were now shrieks. The song was one of pain and suffering and unimaginable terror.

Marcia tried to picture a tunnel, or some endurance test from gym class. She did everything she could to convince herself that the ground was just a few inches below her spine. That's all, just a few inches, because if she believed that, really believed it, she could manoeuver across this beam easy as you please, a caterpillar on a branch, nothing to worry about, no big deal if she messed up.

Marcia tried to think of other things. Last year she had been in this cafeteria at a school dance. That was the first time she had really noticed Theo. She had seen him around, and everyone knew about his old man, but she had never really *noticed* him.

But then the DJ had put on a slow song and she watched all the hungry looks come onto the boys' faces. She stood there swaying to the music, waiting to be asked, because good Catholic girls *never* asked boys to dance, at least according to her mom. She had watched with barely disguised horror as

Marty Wormser made his way over to her. She did *so* not want to dance with the Worm.

But that's when Theo had saved her. She had turned and he had been there. A slight smile on his lips, like he knew what he was saving her from. She noticed how good he smelled when he leaned in close to ask her to dance. She noticed that he really didn't look too bad in his dress cords—jeans were never allowed at a school dance—and when he put his hands on her hips, it was like they were meant to be there. No light-touch, do-I-or-don't-I? crap. A confident hold.

Even when he sang along to "Night to Remember" by Prism—a thing she normally hated—she was impressed. He knew all the words and he could carry a tune.

Yes, she had noticed him that night, all right.

He gave her a ride home, even though it was the opposite direction to where he lived. That's when they started dating.

Marcia had been a virgin when she and Theo had been dating, and she didn't let him get too far. They would neck for hours on end, until their lips and tongues were sore, but that was it for the longest time. After a month or so, she began to let him touch her breasts from the outside—no under-the-shirt stuff, no flesh on flesh. She didn't trust herself that far. Sometimes—okay, most times—even those extra layers of material weren't enough.

But when she told him to stop, Theo would. Wasn't that what good boys were supposed to do?

Only, when she told him to stop, she wasn't sure she meant it. She waited for him to offer up some argument, some token excuse, no matter how flimsy, just so she could run with it.

Theo never offered one. She would say no, and he would accept it. Breathlessly and obviously regretfully, but always politely and immediately.

Wasn't she worth some resistance? At least a token show of wanting more?

It left her wondering if Theo really wanted her or not. He said he did, but he didn't play the game right. She felt like he didn't want her enough, and she was sure Theo felt her interest wane. Though his never seemed to fade, Marcia felt her own desire sputter and die like a candle in the rain.

Then came Crouch. The complete opposite from Theo, he generally didn't accept no as an answer and he always had an excuse handy. Marcia hadn't really wanted to do it with Crouch—when she lost her virginity all she could think of at the time was Theo—but Crouch had played the game right and he got the prize. At least she had known he was interested.

But one Sunday afternoon, as she lay in his sweaty bed staring at his airplane drawings, she began to realize that Crouch was really only interested in himself. He would thrust and moan for a few minutes, and sometimes it even felt good to her, but then he would be finished. He'd strip off the sodden condom, drop it on the floor, then go smoke a joint and leave her with the cleanup.

On this particular afternoon, she had cleaned herself up and crawled back into the still-warm bed. Crouch was somewhere else in the house, getting stoned. And, alone in her absent boyfriend's bed, Theo's disinterest began to look more and more to Marcia like respect. She began to think maybe it was her, not Theo, who wasn't playing the game right.

She found herself longing for another dance with Theo. Him in his cords, singing softly in her ear.

Just once more in the darkened cafeteria.

Thirty feet below her.

♦♦♦

THEO TURNED HIS back to the cafeteria doors and sat down cross-legged beside the semi-conscious Stash. The screams weren't dying down, but Theo told himself there was nothing he could do right now. He tried to shut out the noises, but with no success. He squatted and, placing a gentle hand to his friend's shoulder, he looked down at Stash.

"Buddy, I'm gonna get you outta this. Honest to god I am."

Stash—no, Bobby. Bobby. The poor bastard was maybe dying, so he should at least

(no-no he's not gonna)

die with someone respecting his name.

Theo checked the tourniquet to make sure it was still snug, not that he had any real idea if it had been applied correctly or not. It seemed okay. No fresh blood. That was okay, wasn't it? Christ, he hoped so. He and Sta—Bobby—had been through a lot together. Of the group of them—Theo, Stash, Crouch, and the Toad—Theo and Stash were the tightest. They liked the same girls, the same music, the same TV shows. They were "buds." They knew all the words to Billy Joel's "Scenes from an Italian Restaurant." When they got to the "Brenda and Eddie" part, they sped it up to an auctioneer's pace to see who could get it out faster. Hell, they could even play off each other to "Bohemian Rhapsody," Stash taking the

(oh, mama mia)

low parts, Theo on high

(mama mia figaro)

until they broke out in hysterics, usually over the face one of the two was pulling at the time. Two guys who wouldn't dare sing in public had no problem singing right into each other's faces.

And Stash stood up for him. Showed him he could stand up to his father without having to be afraid.

Bobby's eyes rolled and opened slightly.

Theo moved a little closer. "How ya doin', man?"

Bobby's voice was high and thin. "Get the number...whaddyacall...truck that hit me?" They both smiled.

"Nah. If I had, I woulda got him to back up an' finish the job."

"Prick."

"Matter a' fact, it's a rather big one. Your mama said so last night." They both smiled wider, and Bobby was out again. Theo's smile dropped away immediately as he checked Stash's pulse, then his own to compare because he really wasn't used to doing anything like that. Bobby's seemed a lot weaker. "Thready" was the term that popped into Theo's head.

Jesus, we gotta get outta here! Theo thought again. Twelve years of school, and he had no real idea how to save his best friend. What good was the ability to calculate acceleration on a frictionless surface now? What the hell good was the ability to sink a basketball, all net? What the hell good was school when there were things that came out of nowhere and chewed half your leg off? Here Theo sat, not having a clue how to ease his friend's suffering, only able to crack the same wiseass jokes that had been said so many times before.

"Fuck," he said. He got up, lifted

(use your legs not your)

Stash in his arms, and walked him to the boys' washroom, having no desire to see what was left of Crouch in the girls'. He checked every inch of the room to make sure there were no more surprises and made Stash as comfortable as he could. Then he ran to the nearest classroom and took a desk. He used it to block the inner door to the washroom. Extra insurance.

Hopefully, nothing would go in there until they found a way out of this mess.

Theo had never felt so helpless in his entire short life.

At least until Mr. Austin and Nicole Davidson burst through the doors from the north stairwell.

Chapter Nine

As soon as we get into that cafeteria, I'm hauling ass to third floor. Please let Tom be all right.

Laura and the Toad were in the automotive area of the tech wing. She'd had a real hard time entering the darkened room, but there was a big, rubber-cased flashlight right by the door that helped to push back the shadows. She had listened a long time before going too far into the room. No claw-on-concrete noises.

The room smelled of grease and metal. An eviscerated 1973 Mercury Meteor dominated the room. Most of it was gold, but there were large patches of purplish primer sprayed Dalmatian-style over its dying body. They looked like bruises. The colour always reminded Laura of the desert.

Her lips were pressed into a thin line as she picked her way over to a portable blowtorch. It looked pretty damn small when compared to the ice on the cafeteria door. *Screw it, take a couple and move on. Tom's waiting.*

Dennis—why the hell they called him the Toad, she had no idea—stood in the doorway, just rocking back and forth. Her late husband would have said he had a "fucked-up pumpkin." All she knew was that he wasn't talking, and he sure as hell wasn't helping.

"You wanna get in here and help me with the tanks and this toolbox?"

The Toad just shook his head, his rocking never altering in speed or intensity.

Laura shook her head and dropped two blowtorches and the tanks on the top of a bright-red toolbox with a big oval STP sticker in the middle. What did "STP" stand for anyway? All she could think of was "stinky toilet paper." On the side of the toolbox were other stickers: FRAM, Quaker State, Hot Wheels.

Boys and their toys.

She walked back to the doorway, kicking a path through the debris, praying there wasn't another dog-beast looking for a snack. If she found one, it was going to be toasted worse than the last one she had met.

After she had cleared a path from the toolbox to the door, she turned to the Toad. She raised her eyebrows, her hands outspread.

He continued to stand, rocking and muttering.

Nope. No help there.

Sighing, she turned and walked back to the toolbox, getting herself around behind it. She planted her hands on each corner and pushed. It was heavy as hell, but it rode on wheels and moved reasonably easy. She had to be careful that the tanks didn't drop off. If one of those cracked open, it would turn into a bullet. She rolled the toolbox right out the door and kept on going right down the hall. The Toad fell in behind, not even attempting to assist her. Why the hell had he even come?

His mumbling chewed at her nerves.

♦♦♦

THEO HEARD THEM pounding down the stairs just as he came out of the bathroom. A deep masculine voice that sounded panicked enough so Theo couldn't immediately place it. Austin and Nicole blew through the north stair doors just as Laura and the Toad pushed through the doors separating the tech wing from the lobby. Theo finished blocking the washroom door and ran to catch Austin just as Laura bumped the door open with her butt, then she and the Toad heaved the toolbox through the doors, her back to the action.

"Jesus, Theo, next time send someone who's gonna help a little, huh," Laura said between exhausted breaths. Then she turned and saw Mr. Austin.

Theo managed to get himself in front of Austin just before he rounded the corner to the lobby and became the latest contestant in Puke-o-rama. It looked like he aimed to run out the front lobby doors and drag Nicole with him. Austin had a wild look about him, his stylish haircut twisted and mussed into flying wings. His eyes constantly shifted this way and that, looking for demons or a way out.

Nicole was locked in his grip, an unwilling passenger on the flight. Her long brown hair hung in her eyes as she kept her gaze intently on the floor. Though he could not look into her eyes, Theo could see the blotchy red marks on her cheeks that let him know she had been crying. Her breath still hitched in her chest.

"Gary?" Laura prompted. There was no response from Austin. She grabbed him by the arm and lightly shook him. "Gary!"

His eyes tracked around to her, stopped briefly, then continued, as though he was trying to bend his sight around that final wall and outside. Laura shook him once again, and suddenly had his full attention.

"Laura!" he yelled. "We've got to get out of here! *I've* got to get out of here. There's…things in the school and they're killing everyone and Nicole and I were talking in one of the classrooms and they came in and they just started attacking us and I managed to get us out and then they chased us and—"

Laura slapped his face to bring him back. The sharp crack acted like one of those clap-on, clap-off switches. His barrage of words stopped as his mouth snapped closed. He took a breath, tried to smooth back his hair, and said, "Laura, get out of my way. Nicole and I are leaving."

"You can't go out there, Mr. Austin," Theo said. "As soon as you get a look out there, you're gonna blow your lunch."

Nicole stood meekly, still locked in his grip. She didn't seem to react to anything.

"I'm going," Austin said. "I've already seen outside, and I know what you're talking about. But it's just some sort of fog. I'll get help."

Theo's bullshit radar shifted into overdrive. Austin didn't look like someone who was running to get help. He just looked like someone who was running.

"Nicole, honey?" Laura said. "Do you want to go with Ga—with Mr. Austin?"

Nicole continued to study the floor. Then Austin said, "Fuck this," and started forward, dragging her with him.

Theo, Laura, and the Toad all tried to stop him, but Austin bullied his way past them, stopping just short of the final corner. He turned to Nicole. "Close your eyes." She immediately closed her eyes. *Jesus Christ*, thought Theo. *Does she even use her own brain anymore?*

"Gary, why are you doing this?" Laura asked. "Stay with us, we'll find a way out. Nicole, you don't have to do this."

"Yes she does!" Austin yelled, veins pulsing at his temples.

"Why?" the Toad asked, bringing shocked looks from Theo and Laura.

"Why?" Austin said. "You wanna know why?" He shook Nicole by the arm, belying the object of his panic. "She's gotta go because we have to go together. That's why!" As though this explained everything.

"Gary," Laura said. "I don't underst—"

"She's knocked up," the Toad said, really finding his voice now. "Right, *Gary*? You knocked her up, didn't you?"

The expression on Austin's face said it all. "Oh, Gary," was all Laura could say.

"We've got to get out of here. Together," Austin said. "Because if we don't go *together*, some little *bitch* says she's going to *kill* herself." He punctuated his sentences with violent yanks to Nicole's arm.

Theo readied himself to stop Austin. He didn't like what he was seeing. He kept flashing to his own parents with each vicious tug he witnessed. The Toad also moved toward Nicole. Austin must have sensed it somehow, and before anyone had moved more than an inch, he bolted, dragging Nicole behind him.

Theo and the Toad ran after him, but both fell to their knees, retching, as they rounded the corner.

Austin, though a complete and perfect bastard, drew a small measure of respect from Theo due to his ability to push through, dragging himself and Nicole along, both puking, their bodies heaving and bucking like cats coughing up furballs. Eyes watering, Theo still saw that they had both pissed themselves, and it looked like Austin even harboured a special delivery package in the rear end of his Underoos.

"You smell…shit?" the Toad asked, confirming Theo's observation.

Though it killed him, Theo stole quick, retch-inducing glances to chart Austin's progress. He heard the two of them bang through the front entrance doors. He glanced up to see them lurching down the angled walkway that normally led to the parking lot. Now it led to…nothing. He angled his eyes downward again, his stomach doing everything it could to escape his spasming abdomen.

"Where'd he…gah…go?" the Toad asked.

Theo looked up again. *We've got to get her.* Nicole was out there on her own. *She looks like bait,* was his next thought.

♦♦♦

GARY AUSTIN WAS having a hell of a time keeping it together. His whole plan had been to get out of the building, get into his car, and get Nicole out of town.

Get out, get gone. That was the full plan, as far as it went. Or it had been.

He had expected to encounter other staff and students. That didn't even bother him much. He knew how word travelled in New Hope. By breakfast tomorrow, he would be the talk of the town—the asshole who knocked up one of his students. Happened all the time, didn't it? Could he help it if they threw themselves at him? He knew no one would understand, but he figured he'd at least make it to his car. Even with that damnable fog that had encompassed the school.

But he had found himself getting more and more panicked as he stood dealing with Laura and those kids. His brain grew a nagging itch that told him to run, just leave the pregnant bitch and run. But if he did that, she'd kill herself. She'd said so, and Austin figured her to be just nuts enough to do it. Over a goddamn cluster of cells the size of his thumb! Christ! Give him a coat hanger and ten minutes and the problem would be gone, flushed into New Hope's septic system.

When he couldn't stand the itch in his head, or all the bleeding hearts around him, he ran, taking his knocked-up ball and chain with him. He intended to fix this one way or another, and he wasn't going to let a little puke get in his way.

He dragged Nicole along—thank god she wasn't resisting—and cracked his hand on the doors, getting some distance between him and bleeding hearts.

He was disgusted with what was happening to him, covered in vomit, piss, and crap, but he couldn't help himself, finding the view so disorienting that he could barely remain upright, doing so by taking only the most necessary and judicious peeks to fix his position.

As he got farther from the school, he realized this was no fog he was running into. It looked smooth and translucent. *Kind of like a colourless pearl.*

That would prove to be his last coherent thought before something horrible tore him from Nicole.

♦♦♦

NICOLE STAYED LIMP. There was nothing left to give.

Gary had always been so kind, so sweet. He'd made her feel special, like there was no other girl in the world. At least, no other girl for him.

And it had all been so romantic and exciting, in a Romeo and Juliet kind of way. They'd been the forbidden, secret lovers she always read about, stealing away for those treasured moments of passion, where he would always swear his undying devotion. He would whisper words of love in her ear, first in French, then English. The translations were always beautiful, but it was the French, the language of love, that had ignited her and opened the doors to the affair.

Her friends told her to be careful, but she always knew Austin would take care of her. He told her so.

Then came the day she missed her period. That had been over two months ago. She hadn't said anything because, well, she'd only really been having them for a couple of years, and they had never seemed to settle into any sort of rhythm like some of her friends. In fact, over the next few days after her monthly visitor didn't come knocking, the first time, she managed to convince herself that this had happened before. She was sure of it.

She just couldn't remember when.

When it didn't show the next month, that was a different story. There was no way she could convince herself that she had ever missed two in a row. She had been thinking of trying to get over to the next county to get a pregnancy test done when she began getting another visitor—morning sickness. After that, there was no need for the test. She knew how bad the mornings had been for her own mother, having been reminded of it every time Nicole failed to live up to her expectations. "I carried you for nine months for you to end up like this?" she'd say, her eyes squinting behind the ever-present cigarette. "I barfed up breakfast every morning so you could hurt me like this? You caused me so much pain back then I should've known it would never stop!"

The morning sickness convinced her. She had talked it over with Danika, one of her closest confidants, telling her all the wonderful things Gary had told her. Danika assured her that she could talk to him about it and he would make it right. Danika had painted her a beautiful picture.

Gary had taken that picture and torn it to shreds.

She had approached him this morning, telling him that she was pregnant and that they needed to talk. They agreed to meet in his class after school hours, and she knew immediately that it was not going to go well.

"You've got to abort this thing," he had started. *This thing!* This thing was his *child*. She couldn't believe the caring, passionate man she knew and loved could talk like this.

The conversation went from bad to worse. She would not get an abortion. He would not hear otherwise. And worse, he seemed to be placing all the blame squarely on her shoulders. After being accustomed to his deep, mesmerizing voice whispering silken phrases, his yelling and stamping now shocked and scared her.

"YOU'RE GETTING AN ABORTION! DEAL WITH IT!" he had yelled.

"No," she said quietly, the tears sliding down reddened cheeks. "I'll kill myself before I'll kill my baby."

"WHAT?" he roared. "WHAT DID YOU SAY?" She looked up to see him bent over her, his hand out, palm flat, in preparation to descend in an arc that would end on her face. He would have done it, she knew.

But the power had cut out. Then all hell broke loose. Nicole had never seen so much blood in her life.

She didn't know how they escaped, and she wondered that he even took her at all. In his rage, she truly expected him to leave her there to die. Her and her *thing*.

But he had pulled her along like a trailer with no wheels. Her legs were battered from where she had tripped on the stairs. Gary hadn't even slowed, just kept dragging her down, her calves and heels pounding the stairs like she'd been hitting speed bumps.

By the time they had met up with Theo and the Toad, she was beyond caring. Her world had crashed down, her hopes of a bright future—her, Gary, and their baby—were gone. She had lost everything in minutes. A dark, evil thing that wasn't Gary, it only looked like him, now held her hand.

She knew, one way or another, she was going to die. Either Gary was going to do it, or she would take care of it herself, but she would not live beyond the night.

With her mind made up, an unusual calm fell over her and Nicole was able to detach from the argument. She knew Gary was roughly yanking at her arm but the feeling was remote, distant, like she was anesthetized. There was nothing left to do but wait for death. She could go no lower.

There was nothing left to lose.

She caught a look outside when they rounded the corner, and, like everyone else, she too vomited, but lately that had been a constant morning companion, so it didn't bother her overmuch. After that, she did her best to close her eyes. The feeling of the contents of her stomach settling warmly into her sweatshirt was uncomfortable, so she did her best to not repeat it.

Nicole blindly followed Gary, then he was gone, roughly pulled away.

Then, he came back.

♦♦♦

THEO TRIED TO watch Nicole as best he could, and had begun his own trip to the doors in hopes of getting her back inside.

That's when Austin came back. He twisted in from an unknown altitude as though he had gone on some magical

(think happy thoughts)

Peter Pan flight. The window wobbled, but held as he first flew into it, then stuck, like a squeezed zit on a mirror. His clothes were gone, but Theo could still see the demarcations where the waistband of his underwear and socks had been, the skin slightly redder and dimpled from the fabric. His face was pressed up

(steph)

against the glass, his mouth a soundless "o" as he hung there, not touching the ground, not touching anything. Pressed almost dead centre in the floor-to-ceiling window, Theo then heard cracking noises. He thought it was the glass and backpedalled. Another gag-inducing glance told him it wasn't the glass.

Austin's fingers made squeaky noises on the window as his fingers spread, then contracted, spread and contracted, as though he was waving bye-bye to them. It wasn't until more and more of his naked body became visible, pressing to the window as though he was Silly Putty, that Theo realized he was hearing Austin's bones cracking. His face pressed flatter and flatter against the glass, his eyes so tight that they could only register pain and shock but not move. They darkened as blood and bodily fluids began to seek exits, Austin's body no longer able to contain the same amount as usual. A slight pop and one of Austin's eyes leaked obscenely down the glass.

He's being squeezed like toothpaste! Theo got an image of the Toad mashing his banana, remembered how soft the inside was as the Toad sluiced it into his mouth, then looked on as Austin's insides began to squelch out of his body in thick clotted rivulets that rolled down the window. His eyes, ears, nose, mouth, and penis all became exits for Austin's interior workings.

The glass never cracked.

Tears pouring down her face much like Austin's guts on the glass, Laura begged them to leave. "Oh god, Theo. Dennis. Please, I can't stay here!"

"Nicole!" Theo said.

"She's gone, Theo," the Toad answered.

He was right. Another gut-wrenching scan showed no sign of Nicole. She was gone.

They never saw her again.

CHAPTER TEN

"LET'S GET THIS going, okay? I want to get up to the third floor and check on Tom—Mr. Popper. He was supposed to be working late tonight."

The tone of Laura's voice and her grim look told Theo that, a half-hour after Austin and Nicole, she was still shaken by what they had witnessed, but no matter how he approached it, she refused to talk about it.

The three of them had pulled themselves back around the corner, out of sight of the lobby windows and the outside. Leaning against the rough brick of the inner lobby, they waited until they heard no more sounds. They waited until the only sounds were the hitching sobs of Laura bringing herself back down.

They waited beyond that silence. When Theo mentioned checking on Nicole, they decided to wait longer still.

An interminable time later, Theo got up and checked, knowing that if he began talking about it, they would never move. Feeling his pulse beating in his head, he gathered himself, took a deep breath and shot a glance around the corner.

"Whaaaa?"

"What?" the Toad said. "What's goin' on?"

Theo came back around, gasping for air. "Gone."

Laura pushed herself up from the floor. "What do you mean, 'gone'?"

"He's gone," Theo repeated. "Nicole too, but...Mr. Austin...there's nothing left. No blood, no marks. Like it's been wiped clean."

"Or licked clean," the Toad said. His eyes held an unnameable dread.

Laura shook her head, as though shaking out that last line before it could stick, then grunted once, softly. And, just like that, the subject was closed off. Laura got herself together, dusted off the seat of her pants, and turned them back to their original goal.

The cafeteria.

♦♦♦

THEY STOOD IN front of the caf doors once again, this time armed with the toolbox and the tanks.

Laura grabbed one torch and Theo the other. He turned the nozzle and heard the gas. "Give me the lighter."

Laura stared at him, head cocked slightly to the left.

He held out his hand. "The lighter. The sparky-thing. To light it." He hefted the hissing torch.

"What, these things don't have a lighter built in?" She reached for her pocket. "Where the hell is my lighter?" she said. Then Theo saw the light of memory. "The art room." Her head dropped. "Shit," she said.

Theo cut the gas. "Well, these are useless, unless there's one in the—"

He tried a drawer on the toolbox. Locked. "You never tried the drawers to see if they were locked?"

"Do I *look* like a mechanic, Theo?" Laura said. "I could've used some help, but didn't get much." She made eyes at the Toad.

The Toad at least had the decency to mumble a quiet apology.

"So we can't get into the toolbox?"

"Nope," Theo said. "I'm guessing most of the stuff that would help us get into the toolbox—" he rapped the metal lid with his knuckles "—is in the toolbox. We got a big paperweight."

"Okay, look at the ice. It's way too thick anyway," Laura said, "so why don't we ram it?"

Theo and Laura rolled the toolbox as far across the lobby as they could. They all positioned themselves: Theo on the left corner, the Toad on the right, Laura in between.

"On three," Theo said.

"One.

"Two."

Deep breath.

"THREE!"

The box picked up speed fast as they accelerated it across the

(frictionless surface)

lobby floor and braced themselves for impact with the ice-laden cafeteria doors. Faster and faster. Almost wanting to back off a bit, but not. Getting ready, here it comes here it comes here it—

CRACK! Metal splintered ice into a million shards, as unseen tools rattled ineffectually inside the toolbox. But that was it. All they had for their effort was a banged-up toolbox, tingling arms, and a lot of ice on the floor. Nothing else.

"Damn it," Theo said. "Now what?"

"Nothing's gonna get us through those doors. Need a howitzer or somethin'," the Toad answered. "Or a bigger battering ram."

Theo and the Toad stood pondering the problem. It took them a minute to realize Laura was standing there smiling at them. *She's smiling,* Theo thought. *Has she forgotten Austin and Nicole already?* Theo could see there was no happiness anywhere in her eyes. Only determination.

"What?" Theo asked.

"You need a big bullet?" She turned and lifted one of the acetylene tanks. "I got your big bullet right here."

♦♦♦

A QUICK RUN back to the auto shop netted them an assortment of large, heavy tools. They chose a particularly large wrench—none of the hammers looking like they had enough heft, and there wasn't a sledgehammer to be found.

Back in front of the cafeteria doors, the Toad handed the wrench to Theo.

"Why me?" he asked.

"Why *not* you?" The Toad's voice held a slight note of indignation.

"Jesus," Theo replied. "I thought slavery was abolished a few years back." Still, he kept the wrench. Laura helped him position the tank about five yards from the frozen doors, the nozzle facing away from the caf.

"So...what? I just give it a whack?" Theo asked.

"I guess."

"Okay." Theo wrapped his hands tightly around the forged steel, spread his feet, lifted the wrench high above his head, and swung with all his might.

The wrench bonged off the valve assembly, leaving a divot but little else.

"Shit!"

"Hold on," Laura said.

"What?" the Toad said.

Laura pointed at the tank. "See how he knocked it around when he hit it?" The Toad nodded. "What if it goes off in the wrong direction?"

"So what do we do?" Theo said.

"Dennis," Laura said, "do like I do." She sat down on the

floor and spread her feet about a foot apart, then scooched her butt up so her feet rested lightly on sides of the tank. The Toad got it and did the same from his side. The tank sat contained between their feet, a makeshift guide. Then the Toad looked up at Theo.

"Hit it again, dude. You'll do it this time."

Again, Theo planted his feet, swung up and then down, again impacting on the canister, again, with no effect.

"Shit!"

He did it again.

"Shit!"

And again.

"Shit! Shit and damn!"

One more time, his face red and shiny with sweat. Nothing.

"You know," the Toad said. "These things are probably designed to kinda *not* break easily."

"Not helpful right now," Laura said.

Theo snapped. Cursing and swearing, he dropped to his knees and began to pound on the canister top, sparks flying, hacking at it as though trying to chop down an enormous tree. The halls rang with the sound of metal striking metal.

Laura and the Toad both leaned away from Theo, though he could still see them from the corner of his eye. Suddenly, Laura turned and put a hand up to catch the Toad's attention, her eyes wide. Theo continued to bash away at the valve.

"What?" the Toad said, raising his voice over the din.

"What about those students inside? If this hits one of them…"

Realization dawned in the Toad. "Theo!" he yelled. "Dude! Wai—"

Theo looked up as his arms swung down. The wrench caught the valve at the correct angle, and the weakened assembly cracked and blew back, pinging off the back wall, taking a chunk of the brick out before imbedding itself.

The canister itself leapt forward between Laura's and the Toad's feet, a mostly unguided missile rocketing toward the cafeteria doors, hitting the floor only twice, each time with a high-pitched *BING* and a spray of ice shards.

All three turned away, eyes shut tight, expecting, anticipating, the sudden stop that didn't come, only the rush of frigid air. The canister impacted the left door about a foot from the bottom and peeled it inward like a pop tab, the obstruction barely slowing its forward momentum.

One by one, they opened their eyes as the canister continued to rattle around in the cafeteria, finally expending the last of the fuel and banging to a stop somewhere deep inside, well past the doors they had broken through. The caf door shuddered on abused hinges, finally coming to rest wide open, beckoning them inside. The cold air rolled out, laying a fine fog on the floor just outside the door.

After the cold, it was the smell that hit them next.

One by one, their eyes widened, first in shock, then wider in horror.

Laura spoke in a whisper, but the other two heard it just fine.

"My god," she said. "I think we just broke into hell."

Part Three
Through the Dark

"I have seen the dark universe yawning
Where the black planets roll without aim—
Where they roll in their horror unheeded,
Without knowledge or lustre or name."

Nemesis
H. P. Lovecraft

CHAPTER ELEVEN

THEO, LAURA, AND the Toad stood frozen in the same position they had when the door smashed open. Their rapt silence was cracked when the Toad turned and vomited the last remaining

(diced carrots why is it always diced motherfucking carrots)

contents of his stomach on the broken ice shards. Wiping his mouth on the sleeve of his jean jacket, he said quietly, "I don't like the dark." He turned and walked back to the wall and sat down facing it, gently placing his hands on his head, rocking back and forth.

Laura looked up at Theo and shrugged. "Looks like it's you and me, kid." She sounded so calm, like they were just going to walk into the cafeteria like any other day. Theo envied her. He envied anyone with the courage to stand up to their fears. The thought that she might be scared shitless never crossed his mind until much later.

Theo swallowed. "Okay," he said, trying to project the same calm It didn't come close, not from his side of the fence, anyway. He considered saying no, but he was so accustomed to taking orders from someone older than himself, even from an asshole like his father, that he discarded the thought immediately. He didn't question it. They were going in. That was that.

Going straight into hell.

♦♦♦

THE RATTLING CRASH scared the poop out of her. Then there was the distant sound of banging. She tried to ignore it, and it actually wasn't that hard.

Marcia's hands ached from the cold. It was getting harder and harder to make her fingers work. She felt like the Tin Man when Dorothy first discovered him, frozen up and needing some oil to get him moving again. Her fingers were frozen up. Her ears hurt from the cold. Her legs were cramping. She had to pee.

And there was nothing she could do about it because she was thirty feet up. And it was nine-point-eight metres per second per second straight down. She didn't really know what "per second per second" meant. Sounded dumb. But she remembered it.

I could never remember that for an exam. Why can I

(doin' it all on a night to)

remember it now?

Marcia never got a chance to answer that. Yes, the rattling crash had scared the poop out of her. But it was the earthshattering explosion of sound and light from the door below her that shocked her so bad she jumped.

She felt her punished and freezing fingers lose their grip on the beam.

♦♦♦

THE SCENE WAITING for them in the cafeteria could have been ripped from the fevered, sweaty dreams of a psychopath. The big room hid its atrocities in a darkness deeper than they would have expected. A quick glance above them confirmed that all the emergency lights had been pulled down. Theo could see one on the floor ahead of them. It had been destroyed. Not just smashed—more like someone

(something)

had a personal grudge against the units.

From the minimal light dribbling into the room from

(the outside nothingness)

beyond the smashed doors, the space became a dark impressionist painting in deep tones of blue, grey, and black. From the darkness came warped, disembodied shrieks, moans, and panicked pleadings for help, for release, for death. Off to one side, near the cafeteria doors, lay a bloody mass. A body. It looked like it had been beaten with a bag of bricks, then run through a paper shredder. Theo hoped he didn't know who

(not steph no it's not steph)

it was, and didn't go over to check.

Their eyes took a few moments to adjust. Then the full weight hit them, burning into their heads, permanently tattooing the pain and horror onto their brains. No matter how long they lived, the memory would never leave them. The scene would occupy a good portion of their thoughts until they died.

The cafeteria was now more like a cave. Smashed papier-mâché sculptures from the musical. Paint and water and blood and shredded pieces of meat on the floor. Stalagmites

(or stalactites which is which?)

grew out of the floor.

But the bodies…oh, the *bodies*. And the *sounds*. Crying, yelling, howling, screeching, so that each voice—except one strident call for help that rung out like a bell before being swallowed by the din—blended into a seething wall of noise.

Now that Theo and Laura had gained their night vision, they saw more than they wanted. Theo didn't want to see any more, but like a car wreck, he couldn't stop looking. For all the terrible sights, he couldn't look away. It drew him in like some sick carnival sideshow, past the gruesome displays. Floating deeper into the room on a wave of revulsion.

"What the hell is going on here?" Laura whispered, her voice quivering. Theo had to lean close to even hear her. If they were going to talk, they were going to be forced to cup their hands and yell into each other's ear.

"Look," said Theo. "Look at the bodies!"

"I know. I feel sick!"

"No! LOOK! Look at them! They've been arranged."

"Arranged? What do you mean? Arranged for what?"

"...I think they've been arranged...*positioned...*" Theo faltered, his hands waving vaguely.

"Tell me!"

Theo took a breath. "It looks to me like they've been set up for...easy entry." The last was said as though someone had shit in his mouth. He didn't know how else to say it without being crude.

Laura looked around, then back at him. The expression on her face told him she wasn't getting it. The gloom didn't help. *Fuck!*

"Jesus, look at them! It looks like they've been set up so they can be easily fucked. No. Raped, actually."

Laura looked around again. Theo saw her mouth open to a silent "oh" as she looked again at the insanity surrounding her, saw her finally get it. Lower torsos set into semi-liquid altars, legs spread wide. This one female, that one male. Over there, a face

(i think that's rachael from history class)

trapped in a similar altar, her eyes pleading, her mouth forced open, her tongue gone. To her left, a body stripped of all but the left arm, a large gash in the abdomen that had been ripped and spread wide. Over to their right...behind them...ahead of them...

Chunks of flesh. Just big chunks of flesh. Each with some sort of orifice, open and spread wide.

And every one of them was somehow still alive. Their bodies still quivered from the pain. They still moved. Their eyes beseeched Laura and Theo.

Most of the them should have been dead.

But they weren't just alive. They were conscious.

Their minds still worked.

Theo heard more screaming and moaning, like someone had turned up the volume. Loud, penetrating screaming in his ears. The screaming came from Laura. And she couldn't stop.

♦♦♦

THE CAFETERIA DOORS boomed and ice shards exploded into the room. A big bullet rocketed under her, skittering and sliding across the floor before banging to a stop just short of the stage.

The unexpected crash was enough to make Marcia jump and release her tenuous grip on the beam. Her stiff fingers scrabbled at empty air as she began her descent.

Reflex caused her legs to tighten up on the ice-cold metal and instead of dropping the thirty feet to the cafeteria floor, she swung like a panicked pendulum in a grandfather clock. Her legs scraped painfully against the flanges and her ankles protested at the weight that had been thrown on them with no warning. Her heart jackhammered in her throat as the blood rushed to her head.

Surely whoever was down there would see her. Surely they would save her!

"HELP!" she cried, her body still swinging.

The wailing of the broken students below blocked any other noise, but she saw two people enter. The room was murky and her eyes watered from the cold but it looked like…

Yes it was.

Theo. He's alive! Theo had come to save her.

Someone else was with him. A woman, but Marcia couldn't make out who.

Marcia yelled at them, but they wouldn't look up.

Why won't they look up?

Then realization sank in. The situation was too horrible down there. Why would they look up in the dark when they had more than enough to deal with right in front of them? It kept all their attention focused on what was happening on the floor.

Marcia yelled again. Really howling, veins and muscles cording on her neck, her arms and chest tight, that gravelly feeling in her throat, her head throbbing with the rushing blood, her body swaying with the effort to make herself heard.

They didn't hear her. They *couldn't* hear her above the din of the suffering souls ten yards below her.

And then they came deeper into the room. Where were the dog-beasts?

They must have retreated when the door was smashed in. Marcia knew Theo and his partner had no idea what they were walking into. She also knew she would be no help to them if she dropped to the floor like a sack of potatoes.

She tried to reach up to the beam. Her outstretched fingers fell well short of their target. The blood continued to rush to her head, giving her a pulsing, skull-full-of-cement feeling.

"Help!" she yelled again, but weaker.

Why can't they hear me?

There would be no help from below. *So get off your butt and get going!* Marcia tried once more to reach up, the muscles in her stomach and abdomen squeezing and bunching painfully, but it was no use.

Slowly, she lowered her arms until they dangled down below her head. She swung them back behind her, then quickly ahead, starting a controlled swing. Her legs howled in protest. She grunted with the pain of exertion, but otherwise ignored their pleas for mercy.

She still wasn't getting high enough. She checked on the pair on her next backswing.

Theo and the girl moved deeper into the room.

Marcia threw all her weight forward. Up, up, but not quite there.

She swung back and forth a couple of times. She was tiring too fast. Too fast! She only had a few more swings in her.

She flexed her legs just a little, modifying the positioning. Not too much. She didn't need to lose her grip, just loosen it slightly.

Back.

Forth.

Back again, arms cranked back for maximum swing.

And forward, arms outstretched, stomach tight, *willing* herself to rise up, just a little more, just a little—

Her fingers closed on the edge of the beam. Her hands immediately complained of the cold, but it felt wonderful right now. She pulled herself back into an intimate wraparound hug of the beam and willed herself to calm down. She was sure she could feel the rafter vibrating with the disco beat of her heart.

Where are Theo and the other one?

Angling her head just right, Marcia could see them leaning into each other, cupping their hands, alternating back and forth.

They seemed struck dumb by what was all around them, and oblivious to the danger. They went still farther into the room.

"No no NO!" Marcia knew very well they weren't hearing her at this point, but she couldn't stop yelling anyway, like her dad yelled at the TV during football games. She just got more and more frustrated as she added to the white noise.

God! If only she had brought the rope! She could have lowered it, signalled them somehow.

She was getting frantic because she knew what waited for them, just out of sight. What could she use to catch their attention? What?

Marcia was in a frenzy, not thinking straight, because she looked down and saw them being surrounded. They didn't know. They couldn't, because they weren't reacting.

Then it looked like the girl discovered something, because she seemed to snap. Laura saw her mouth open, eyes shut tight, hands to the sides of her head.

And all the while, the dog-beasts crept closer.

♦♦♦

"LAURA! *LAURA!* GODDAMMIT, shut *up*! We got fuckin' problems."

Theo stood in front of her, arms on her shoulders, shaking her. He kept it up for a few seconds until the screams began to subside. He looked around nervously.

"Laura, we gotta get out of here. We're in some deep shit." They had, in their shock, unknowingly moved further into the caf. Though they were still in the area of the faint light spilling through the doorway, it really wasn't much. Theo could see their lower legs and feet better than he could see Laura's face. Theo had figured out that they had maybe come in too far just around the same time he noticed the hell-rats starting to move their way.

Neither Theo nor Laura had noticed them when they came in, and they had forgotten about them once they became caught up in the sights of this house of horror.

"Theo?" Laura said. "What are we gonna do?"

"Get out of here." Their voices were hoarse, loud whispers. Slight exhalations of breath in each other's ears, nothing more, but it was like they had tuned into each other's frequency and could suddenly hear each other that much better.

"How?"

"We walk. Slow and easy." The things were getting closer. The screeching, nerve-grating sound of claws on stone just audible over the wailing.

"And if they attack?"

"Then you don't wait. Run like fuckin' hell." Theo remembered the old joke about two people being chased by a bear. *You don't have to run fast. Just faster than the other guy.* It came as a bit of a shock to him that he was willing to be that other, slower, guy for her. "Don't look back. Let's go."

Arm in arm, they slowly turned and started moving slowly, oh so slowly, to the entrance. The little bastards were all around them, circling them, boxing them in.

Theo and Laura were cut off. They couldn't get out.

They were screwed.

♦♦♦

THEO AND LAURA turned so they were back-to-back, facing the demons.

"If one comes close, kick the fucker."

Their hands clasped, and even in their present circumstance Theo felt a slight thrill.

"Try and move toward the door," Laura said.

One step, and Theo caught the darting motion from the corner of his eye. He reacted without thought. His foot shot out and he heard a satisfying crunch and what seemed to him to be a surprised yelp. Scrabbling noises, but going away. That was good.

Then the bones in his hands were ground together painfully as he felt Laura's body tense. She jerked and screamed. "Get off me! Getoffgetoffgetoffget*off*!" Theo tried to disengage his hands. Tried to get around and help. Get the little—

There was a painful splash of light in his eyes and a ring of squeals around him. Theo's eyes teared up, causing the twin lights to halo and blur out of focus. He heard Laura's confused "Wha?" as she spun and wrapped her arms around him. The thing must have dropped off her with the assault of light.

Theo blinked away the tears as the light drew closer. The Toad! It was the Toad! He came in, parting the hell-rats like the Red Sea. He had one of the emergency lights cradled against his chest, like a precious baby. The twin lights were angled out and down, making two large pools of light to either side of him. The hell-rats kept a respectful distance, but not too far.

Theo's eyes finally adjusted to the light as the Toad drew nearer, and he realized something was wrong. The light wasn't really white—more like an orangey colour. *Shit.*

He checked out the demons. *Yeah. Fuck.* They were circling closer.

"Toad! Hurry up, man! The battery's dyin'!"

As he approached, Theo and Laura could hear the familiar mantra: "...weaselpopgoestheweasel*dontlikethedark*pop..."

The Toad reached them, and the light was visibly weakening, growing more orange by the second. The whining and scrabbling increased. The hell-rats scrabbled closer, getting bolder, like they could smell the dying breath of the light.

Then, for apparently no reason, they stopped. Weirder still, they began backing off from the three terrified comrades. Now, for the first time, Theo heard the violent cracking sounds overriding the others.

"What the hell?" said Laura.

"I don't—" started Theo.

"Oh shit. Ah shit! Ah *fuck me*!"

Theo and Laura turned as the Toad's voice scaled higher and higher. That's when they saw what the Toad was freaking over. The door they had knocked open was gone now, the opening made wider and taller, chunks of ice and concrete and twisted metal littering the floor. Yet, that wasn't the worst of it. No, it was the thing that had done all that damage. The thing now blocking the entrance. What was left of it.

The Demon.

CHAPTER TWELVE

IT CAME THROUGH the doorway they had just broken through minutes before, doubling the size of the opening. Metal and ice and concrete fell like rice at a wedding. Theo got an instant visual of the Tasmanian Devil buzzing through a tree, leaving a Tasmanian Devil-shaped hole behind. Only this thing simply walked in, its bulk, its mass, and its momentum clearing away anything that obstructed its path.

The cafeteria—already trashed, iced, blood-soaked—was an abattoir. As the Demon entered, its scent flooded the room—cabbage and cinnamon and cat piss—so cloying and thick that the three companions' eyes watered up and they began to gag, their stomachs heaving uncontrollably made all the worse because there was nothing left to purge.

The Demon cleared the doorway, then advanced into the cafeteria, wading through the waves of screams.

"That's it," whispered Laura. "That's what the room was...prepped for. That thing." Theo realized the room had gone quiet, as though the thing's loyal subjects knew to not anger it. And he knew Laura was right.

Theo lost all concept of words and could only think, *Holy fuck. It's big.* Black on black on black. Some of it seemed almost transparent, wispy as smoke, like those cartoon genies from a lamp that are smoke from the waist down.

Some of it was as solid as granite, black and shiny, like

black metal. It had no eyes. Theo couldn't see this from where he was, but he knew

(the hell-rats are its eyes yes yes)

it to be true.

For all the beast's presence and threat, perhaps the most horrible feature was its genitalia. "Penis" was too polite a word for the monstrous, wicked thing hanging between its legs. The organ was massive, a tree trunk, black and veined and scabrous and fetid and studded with small, back-angled barbs spiking from the head like feelers on a catfish. No, not a penis. This was an instrument of pain.

It's meant to go in, but rip its way out, thought Theo. He looked around again at all the people trapped in the room. *Sweet Jesus!*

As they watched, the organ began to engorge. It got a hard-on just walking into this hell. They had their confirmation. Theo looked around one more time at the people he had shared his classes with. *Steph's in here somewhere. Marcia's in here somewhere.*

And there wasn't a damn thing he could do to stop what was going to happen.

♦♦♦

REMARKABLY, IT WAS Dennis who got them moving. He kicked Theo—his arms still full of dying light—and angled his head in the universal let's-me-thee-and-she-get-the-fuck-outta-Dodge gesture. Theo nodded and tugged at Laura's arm.

"We can't just leave these guys here with that thing."

"Laura, we can't stay. We leave now and get it another time." There was pain in Theo's voice and tears in his eyes, and Laura suspected he was thinking, *Steph is in here somewhere. Marcia is in here somewhere.* Still, he shook it off, ducked his head to look her in the eye, and said, "This isn't the hill we're gonna die on." Then he grabbed Laura and they backed away from the monster, toward the stage and away from the entrance. Theo and Dennis were back-to-back, Dennis leading the way with the quickly fading emerge-light held out in front like failing holy fire.

"Where in the hell are we going?" Laura said, talking more to herself. "There's no way out from here." They were going deeper into the room and would soon be backed up to the stage.

"Oh, okay, there's the exits from behind the stage. As long as they aren't locked. Aren't they usually locked?" she said. She sneaked a peek in that direction. There was a gruesome chorus line of the dog-beasts along the rim of the stage, their heads bobbing, their mouths snapping at the empty air, as though gobbling it would bring the three of them to their jaws faster. Dennis swung a fading beam of light in their faces and they retreated. But not enough. This wasn't going to work.

Laura looked at the smashed sets around her, trying to avoid the panicked eyes of the broken people. Just the sets. *The Sound of Music* sets.

"The hills are alive with the sounds of screaming," she muttered as she turned her attention back to the dogs following them. They jumped forward when Dennis had moved the light, but jumped back again when he brought it back down. But they were getting braver as the light dimmed.

Laura sucked in a quick, surprised breath when Dennis suddenly wasn't a pressure at her back anymore. Theo spun, ready to kick some demon ass, and they both saw Dennis opening a storage door at the front of the stage, his hands shaking visibly even in the murky light. Theo grabbed the emerge-light to ward off the demons and butt-pushed Laura toward the opening, her eyes not wanting to leave the creatures still following close behind.

♦♦♦

MARCIA HUNG THERE, suspended like a sloth. Cold, exhausted, and scared shitless. She was sure she was going to see Theo die right before her eyes, completely powerless to stop it or to intercede in any way.

They were surrounded. Until the Toad came in and, somehow, armed only with an emergency light that he cradled like a baby, managed to get the dog-beasts to back off.

They don't like the light! That's why they smashed the emergency lights back when they first hit us.

But things just went from bad to worse.

As she hung there, she saw the three of them turn. Even in the dark, she could read the Toad's lips, could see the frightened expression on the woman's—Miss Davis, the art teacher, she realized—face. And she saw Theo, first confused, then shocked, then disgusted, then scared. The emotions dropped from his face like masks falling off one by one.

But she couldn't see why. Whatever the thing was, it was right below her. She could only catch a glimpse out of the corner of her eye.

She wasn't getting much, but even her peripheral view began to set off alarms. She couldn't see what it was, but she could sense that it was big. And black. Darker than the surrounding blackness. It stank.

And the room, for the first time, went blessedly quiet.

Her first instinct was to yell for Theo now that he'd be able to hear her. Even got as far as opening her mouth and drawing a breath, but then realized, if Theo could hear her, so could that thing.

Her next instinct was to move. To get going, to get away from the thing before it looked up and snatched her down like an apple from a tree. But no, no she would stick where she was. There really was nowhere to go except farther along the rafter, and that would really do her no good. In her panic, she might make a mistake.

No. No stupid mistakes.

So she stayed quiet and gripped the frost-covered metal of the beam, hugging it tight like a lover. She would not move, would not breathe. She would become part of the structure. It would pass under her and never notice.

She fought her trembling. *I am not cold. I am not scared. I will not shiver.*

She closed her eyes tight and repeated her magic incantation.

I am not cold. I am not scared. I will not shiver.

She kept her eyes closed. She had a flash of childhood memory.

"Got my eyes closed, Daddy. You can't see me!"

Her eyes were squeezed tight as though she was trying to fuse the upper and lower lids together. She did not want to see anything right now. If the big, bad monster was going to get her, she wanted to be surprised. If her boyfriend was going to die, she did not want to watch. If anything was going to happen, she did not want to be aware of it.

I am not cold. I am not scared. I will not shiver. I have my eyes closed so you can't see me.

But she could still hear, and she could not make out whether the sounds coming from the floor were from the previous victims or from three new ones.

Then, somehow, she was aware of the presence moving away from her. There wasn't the same sensation of mass below her. She had to work to crack one eye open, it had been closed so tight.

She saw the…what? The *thing* that had been below her had walked right past her, never noticing, or not caring, that she was there. Her magic spell had worked!

But Theo, the Toad, and Miss Davis were gone.

The dog-beasts must have caught them near the stage. There was a mass of them there. The last time she had seen them mass like that was to rip Stephanie to shreds. They must have swarmed the three of them like flies on a corpse.

Was she going to be the only one to make it?

Oh Lord, please God, please help me get out of here.

While their attention was diverted for the moment, she continued her way along the beam as fast as she could.

♦♦♦

SHE WAS IN, then the Toad. Theo glanced back at the Demon—he was beginning to think of him as the Big Dude—and everything seemed okay in that department. The monster continued to advance, but it wasn't spewing hell-snot out of its nose or anything, thank Christ. Just getting a woody that would humble John Holmes.

But, Theo wondered, *have we just boxed ourselves in?* He thought they just might be a big fucking TV dinner. Just heat 'n eat.

We're fucked, he thought as he slammed the door behind him.

CHAPTER THIRTEEN

MARCIA HAD WORKED her way to the wall and now had to make a decision.

The first choice was to try and get into the sound booth as she had originally planned. She had hoped to hole up there until help arrived, but now had serious doubts of that happening in the near future. If help was coming, why was it just Theo, the Toad, and Miss Davis? Where were all the adults? Where were all the people? Nobody else had come through the door. Had that thing killed everyone?

Even if she stayed in the sound booth, she had only counted on keeping out those little dog-beasts. She didn't think there was anything that could barricade against that big thing. Surely it was a beast from hell itself.

Or maybe I'm dead and this is *hell.*

And suddenly all those Sunday sermons came back to her full force. She began to tremble again.

Nerves, cold, and fear were taking their toll. Heaven or hell, she had to get out of this room. Now.

She studied the sound booth, her easiest route. She could get into the room with relative ease, but once in there was only one way back out and that was through the door and down the stairs to the cafeteria floor. Once she reached the floor, she would have to run halfway across the cafeteria to the doors. Too far. Way too far.

She was cold and exhausted. There was no way she could win any foot race against the dog-beasts and there was now the big…Demon to consider.

The other route, her only other choice, was to get over to the scaffolding that stood just to the right of the cafeteria entrance.

But that meant she had to cross from one rafter to another, then another. Then, another. Rafters that were about four feet apart.

How was she going to do that? She had to make a decision, and quickly.

Maybe she could do the sound booth. It depended on what the dog-beasts and that big thing were doing.

She looked back at it, just to check its position and—

OH MY GOD!

Its back was to her, but it didn't take any stretch of imagination to understand what it was doing. It was pumping its hips in a savage, methodical rhythm. It was…

Oh it was…

And the screaming, the pain it must have been inflicting…

Marcia looked away, silently gagging.

No! I will not throw up. I will not. She clenched her jaw tight, swallowed hard, and concentrated on breathing through her nose. Deep breaths.

In. Out. In. Out.

But that just brought her back around to what she had just seen.

Fuck it. I can't go to the booth. It's gotta be the scaffold. And it's gotta be now!

She brought both hands around to the same side of the rafter, and then, holding tight to the burning cold metal, she heaved first one leg, then the other, and got both legs hooked over the beam. She then gave herself a few moments to get her breathing under control, then closed her eyes again and released her hands.

She fell backward and ended up hanging upside down like a bat. Again. Her bruised legs bore her full weight at the crook of her knees. Quick glance to her left. Violent pumping. She blew air out silently through her mouth. Okay, while the creature was still occupied.

She pulled up hard, her thighs shaking, but caught hold of the beam with her hands. Clutching it in a death grip, she transferred her legs to the other side of the beam, getting her a few precious inches closer to the next one. She gave herself a count of ten, then dropped her arms to hang head down yet again.

Marcia arched her back and flung her hands back and forth to start a swinging motion. It hurt like heck on her knees. She adjusted her legs so that the weight rested more on her calves, and tried again. Yeah, that was better.

She didn't rush, though every bone in her body said to do so. She built up the arc, increasing the rocking motion slowly, building momentum. She wanted to get it right the first time.

Her calves burned with the punishment, the hard edge of the beam cutting into her with each downswing. But her outstretched hands were almost there. Swing again. Almost there, brushing the metal of the next rafter on the last pass. One more swing. *Jeez, haven't I already passed this screen test?*

Back.

Forth.

Not enough!

C'mon! C'mon, Marce! You've done this! You can do *this!*

Back again, arching her back, putting everything into it.

Forward again, shooting her arms down to gain speed and momentum and then she was swinging up, up.

And got it! Her fingers closed on the lip of the beam and braced against the downswing that threatened to tear her grip away. A soft "ungh" was the only noise she allowed to escape. Her fingers held tight and she improved her hold, the pads of her fingers flat against the lip, her thumbs a vice on the bottom side.

Then, before she could think about any consequences of failing, she confirmed her grip was solid under her fingers, then let go of the previous beam and her legs swung free.

Not allowing herself any rest yet, she worked to translate the back-and-forth arc to a side-to-side and got her right leg up to the rafter, hooked it, and got the next one up.

Only then did Marcia take a breath. Her long brown hair was stuck to her head from sweat, and her breath burned in her throat.

But she smiled.

One down, two to go.

♦♦♦

THEY WERE IN the crawlspace under the stage. For all of ten seconds, it was good—nothing but the sound of their own breathing.

Then the scratching started at the door. It sounded just like Theo's last dog Rufus when he'd finished his business and wanted back in the house. Then it became more insistent, more desperate.

They didn't wait around. The Toad moved to take the emerge-light—even though the power was so low it was almost reduced to mere glowing elements within the bulbs. Theo stopped him.

"No, leave it. Point it at the door."

The Toad looked pained. "I don't like the dark," he said matter-of-fact. Theo would have laughed at him had they been in almost any other situation than this. Instead, he tempered his sarcasm. He didn't need the popping weasel thing to start up again.

"I know, buddy, I know." He looked into his friend's eyes,

again using that tone of voice reserved for the very young. "We gotta leave it, okay? It's gonna keep those things back a bit longer. Okay?" The Toad nodded, reluctantly.

The light was left on the floor, and Theo angled both lights at the door just as it began to tilt open. It was good enough to hold back the hell-rats…for now.

They had to move.

♦♦♦

MARCIA HUNG FROM the rafter by her fingertips. Her punished digits were blue from the cold and she couldn't feel anything with them anymore. Her arms shook. Her entire body rocked with erratic, uncontrollable jerks from the exertion. She was finished.

She let go…

…and dropped to the scaffolding platform.

It had been brutal, each crossing taking a larger bite out her reserves. The last rafter had been the worst. She had grabbed the beam and found herself unable to get her legs up. She had made the last ten feet by sliding her frozen fingers along the lip of the beam, inch by inch, her weight supported completely by eight numb digits.

But she had made it.

And now Marcia was lying prone on the platform. She was still twenty-five feet above the floor, but she was suddenly so much closer. Those five feet felt like victory.

She tried to slow her breathing, knowing it was coming in harsh sobs. She didn't want to draw any unwanted attention, but from what she could see she didn't rate high on the importance scale. The big thing seemed to be moving methodically from one sculptured victim to the next, its need apparently insatiable.

She turned back to her own problems. Her crabbed fingers were locked, palsied from the torturous journey. She had to pry them back by setting her fingers to the rough pressboard platform and pushing. They began to bend, each with a painful pop. She did the other hand, then worked them to relieve the stiffness as her breathing slowed.

She took a few extra moments—more than she really should have—to rest herself, giving herself the excuse that she needed to plan her next steps. That was BS, really. All she had to do was climb down the scaffold and run five feet to the door, and if she couldn't run right outside the school, then at least she could find somewhere to hide in case anything followed. She was thinking the girls' washroom. It was close, just across the lobby. But so were the outside doors.

It would be a fast decision. Left to outside, right to the washroom.

Okay, so her plan was in place. No more stalling.

She made the mistake of looking off to her left. To the monster.

She'd pushed it out of her head, doing everything she could to ignore it, pretend it wasn't doing what it was doing as she Spider-Manned her way across the ceiling of the school. Her aching muscles and numb hands and fear of falling did much to occupy the majority of her brain.

But now she had found a respite from all that. Now, to her horror, her mind could focus on the beast and what it did. She desperately wanted to look away, to unsee what she now saw, but she couldn't.

She watched the thing, this beast as it approached a person—she was pretty sure it was a boy, but couldn't identify him—then it reached out a large, scabrous hand and slid a claw-tipped finger into the victim's mouth, stretching the opening to its limit. The beast's finger went in, then it stopped, apparently reaching the limit of how far their lips would stretch. She shuddered at the look on the thing's face. It didn't smile, but she knew it drew pleasure from what it did next.

It pushed deeper. Slowly.

Marcia watched as blood drooled down the boy's—with a shock, she realized it was Marty Wormser—down Marty's mouth and his eyes widened. She couldn't hear his noises over the restarted cacophony in the room, but she saw the strain in his neck, the sheen of his sweat in the too-cold air. The widening, then tight closing of the eyes, reacting to each movement of the forearm-thick finger that pushed down his throat. Then, finally, the beast withdrew the finger, brought it to its queerly-flattened nose. She watched its chest rise as it inhaled the scent deeply.

Then it put its finger in its own mouth, sliding it out slowly, sucking the slick blood off it. Marcia gagged and needed to turn away. Desperately wanted to turn away.

Couldn't turn away.

Then she watched what came next.

♦♦♦

LAURA SAID, "WHAT the hell are we supposed to do now?" They were trapped in a box less than four feet high. The sounds of their feet scraping the raw concrete came back echoey and weird. The dust they were stirring up was remarkable. The Toad sneezed and wiped the snot-rope on his sleeve and, in a notable show of silence, made no comment about it whatsoever.

"Follow. M-me," he said. Theo could tell how much effort was going into stringing a coherent sentence that didn't mention weasels. "We can. Get. Out through. The tech. Wing. Doors." His voice squittered over the words. Theo could see the weakening light reflected in the Toad's aviator-style glasses. And his teeth.

(big nasty teeth)

Damn. His teeth. That meant he was freaking. He always got that stupid smiley face when he was snapping. The last time Theo had seen that was when they watched *The Exorcist*. The Toad was never big on horror movies and Theo guessed he now knew why, though he had never heard the "pop goes the weasel" thing before.

The movie got to the Toad on a level much deeper than Theo would have imagined. The movie had been scary—that sure as hell was true—but the Toad, with his strict Catholic upbringing, had been sure he was seeing a true and literal demonstration of Satan's power. So he had snapped. Popcorn exploding, hands flying, smiley face smiling in a big toothy display, he ran from the movie house and didn't stop until he was all the way home. Luckily, it was only two blocks. Any farther and Theo thought the Toad's heart would have exploded much like the popcorn had. Hell, the Toad probably even stopped jerking off for a couple of weeks.

So, though he had indicated he knew the way, the Toad made no move to get them out of there. The door they had just come through swung wider as the hell-rats found their courage with the darkening of the light. No longer able to see him clearly, Theo swiped his arm in the general area of the Toad's location and made contact.

"Go!"

He went, Theo scrabbling simultaneously for the Toad's belt loop and for Laura's arm. Amazingly, he managed to snag both and they started, a ragged, hunchbacked parade of three.

♦♦♦

MARCIA GRIPPED THE rough wood of the scaffold platform as tears streamed down her face and pooled under her. Even with the blurring of vision the tears afforded her couldn't hide the enormity of what she witnessed.

The beast dropped its hand, the finger still glistening moistly as it reached for its cock, standing out from its body, but not rigid. It clenched it with a fist and began thrusting, the obscene head rising and leaking some fluid in vile sprays. Marcia didn't want to guess what it was, but seeing some gobbets that seemed a little more solid made her think more bodily fluids from its victims than…than…what had Crouch called it? Jizz juice?

The thing extended its other hand to Marty, now spitting blood, a shameful twin to the clenched organ in front of him. Its hand engulfed the entire top of the boy's head, covering his scalp, leaving only the face and some tufts of hair visible. The small dog-beasts seemed to go into a maddened frenzy, jumping at the beast's feet, nipping at its lower legs, tearing at its flesh, but the beast not bleeding, not acknowledging them.

Instead, it guided the barbed head of its cock toward the boy's mouth. It pushed and the boy's mouth was forced open, wider, wider, then Marcia watched as the boy's eyes went wide and his lower jaw dislodged and popped wider, his throat distending obscenely. The thing pushed again, Marcia seeing the musculature in its torso and legs flex and tighten. It got the same look on its craggy, hideous face as it had earlier.

Pleasure.

It thrust deeper still, and Marcia, against her will, imagined those barbs pushing down her throat, sinking deeper. Then the thing pulled back and what was left visible of the boy tensed, tightened, and tried to rise with the obscenity in his mouth, but he remained trapped in the substance from the dogs.

This time, even above the din of the room, she heard him.

The thing thrust again. And again. And again.

As it built to a rhythm, gouts of blood and gore slid out with each pull until the boy was blackened with it from the eyes down. Then the beast looked upward and roared. The dogs went maniacal, running and snapping at each other, at the beast, spinning in circles, the outward embodiment of the thing's orgasm.

Then, finally, it was done and pulled itself free, not without some difficulty. Large broken chunks of Marty's insides followed the barbed cock out and tumbled down the front of the boy.

Who was, somehow, still alive.

Marcia turned away finally, covered her mouth enough to mask the sound, then vomited violently onto the scaffold. Tears rolled freely down her contorted face. She felt the small chunks of food not quite digested roll up her throat into her hands, and she saw the bigger chunks of Marty rolling down from the boy's rent face, and her body bucked as she vomited again and again, each time doing what she could to muffle the sound.

Gasping and finally done, she slid away from the sick and put her cold, sweating head down on the platform. Just long enough to catch her breath.

She wanted to send out a prayer of thanks that she hadn't been that poor boy. That God had saved her from being any one of those people down there.

Instead, she prayed for their souls. Fervently. When she finished, she pushed herself up to all fours, wiped her hand on her pants, and sighed heavily.

Time to escape from this hellhole.

♦♦♦

MAKING THEIR WAY as quickly as the Toad could lead them, each with a hand on the next, they got a reasonable distance before hitting an obstacle. It was cold, hard and metallic. "Chairs," Theo said.

"It's where they store all the chairs for the audience when there's an assembly," Laura said. "Are they blocking us?"

"Yeah," he said. "We've gotta backtrack and skirt the block."

Laura gave a soft "ah fuck" as the last reddish glow faded off the emerge-light, and they were dropped into total darkness.

Dennis went south. Laura felt him stop, then drop to the dusty concrete with a whimper. Then, it started again. "Popgoestheweaselpopgoesthe…" They heard the scrabbling behind them, so Theo didn't waste any time. Placing Laura's hands back on Dennis, he took the lead. Between the two of them, they pushed and pulled Dennis through the structure.

"I can't see a goddamn thing," Theo hissed. "Ya got a match?"

"Yeah, sure—" Laura reached to her pocket for her lighter, but once again, the familiar bulge

(burn you little fucker burn burn BURN!)

was gone.

"Shit. No, Theo, I don't—it's gone." She almost sobbed the last two words.

Somewhere behind them, scrabbling noises. They were coming. High gear time. Trying to make their way in total darkness, they prodded Dennis. Theo had a hold on his arm and Laura brought up the rear, pushing on his back. Dennis had a rhythm going.

"…goestheweaselpopgoestheweaselpopgoesthematchesp-opgoesthe…"

"Jesus Christ! Will you shut the fuck up?"

But he wouldn't stop. He just kept it up, the mantra he was hanging what was left of his sanity on.

"…weaselpopinthepocketpopgoesthematchespopinthepoc-ketpopgoes…"

"What? Laura, what's he saying?"

His voice took on an urgency. Laura stopped him and listened. He was rocking with the cadence of the syllables.

"...the*matches*popinthepocketpopgoesthe*matches*popin*thep-ocket*pop..."

In the pocket. Matches.

Matches!

"Matches! He's got matches in his pocket!" Laura stopped his motion and he immediately dropped to the floor, flat on his back like a submissive dog. *Why the hell didn't he mention it when we were talking about the damn lighter for the torches?* But he had been freaked out then.

There was a strange, awkward moment when, in searching blindly in the dark—*doing my best Stevie Wonder,* Laura thought—her hand patted firmly on Dennis's crotch. It wasn't an immediate recognition. Shapes were different in the dark. Her hand lingered for a moment on the bulging denim before she realized and continued on.

Neither of them ever acknowledged it.

♦♦♦

LOWERING HERSELF BACK onto her stomach, Marcia slid herself backward, her feet dangling out over the floor so far below. She continued back and when she got to her hips, her legs swung down and she placed them on the strong aluminum support. She made a quick check. None of the beasts seemed to notice. It looked like there was smoke coming out from the stage. She didn't know why, and really didn't want to right now. They were ignoring her for now.

Good, let's keep it that way, girl.

Now that her feet had purchase, she could move faster. She got her upper body out and then she was vertical, hands and feet on the scaffolding rungs. She started down.

And immediately stopped.

The scaffolding was shaking. She had never been on it before, and didn't realize how it jiggled with almost any movement. She hadn't noticed when she dropped to the scaffold simply because she was grateful to have something to lay on. The sliding hadn't caused too much movement. But now, it seemed any movement sent a shiver through the framework. It wasn't loud, but it did make noise.

She'd have to go slow.

Marcia carefully placed a hand on the next rung down. Then she lifted her foot off and dropped it slowly, deliberately, to the next rung. Then the other hand. Then the other foot.

Twice she stopped dead because it seemed the big beast was becoming distracted. Each time it turned back to the task at hand, but each time it seemed to take a little longer to do so.

Marcia felt like Jack in *Jack and the Beanstalk,* trying to escape the giant without him noticing. Only that giant didn't have hundreds of little dogs running around. Though there seemed to be less of them. Where had they gone?

And the smoke from the stage was increasing. *What the heck is going on over there?*

Whatever it was, Marcia was grateful for the diversion.

At last, her left foot touched the good, solid tile of the floor and her eyes welled up with tears. She took a second to look back along her route. If anyone had told her this afternoon, when she had been eating her lunch with Patsy and Danika, that she would be playing Spider-Man across the ceiling not five hours later, she would have laughed her brains out.

Then again, if someone had described what the cafeteria would look like at the time, she would have laughed at that too, after saying they were sick.

She wasn't laughing now.

With nothing paying her any attention, she sprinted over to the broken cafeteria doors, tears still in her eyes, and crossed over the threshold.

I made it! I did! I'm free –

There was still a ghost of a smile as the first wave of nausea hit her, dropping her to her knees. Whatever was left of her lunch sprayed out of her mouth like water from a sprinkler.

♦♦♦

THE HELL-RATS were scurrying about, all scratchy clawing and squealy grunts. *Shit, they're getting closer,* Theo thought. He picked up some small object off the cold concrete and threw it in a vicious side arc. He heard it connect with a wooden support, maybe fifteen or twenty feet away to his right. The scrabbling went right in a flurry of heard, but unseen, motion.

So they can't see too shit-hot in the pitch-black, Theo thought. *Then again, neither can we.*

The diversion didn't last. The demons returned almost as fast as they had left.

There was a brief spark, then a tiny but somehow powerful flame.

"Quick! Light something!" Laura looked around for something that would burn. The flame crept toward her fingers.

"Don't let it go out! If it goes

(pleasepleaseplease don't let it go)

out, we're dead." Theo's voice was taking on a hysterical edge. Too much adrenalin burning too hot.

"It's not going out, Theo!" Laura yelled. "Shut the hell up!" She spied a canvas tarp to her left, and movement further behind. Shielding any errant breeze with her palm, she hunch-walked to it and held the flame to a corner. The canvas was dry and lit immediately.

"Theo," Laura said, "tear some off! We're gonna need something to keep 'em off us."

The canvas was old and frayed. Theo was able to grab a corner and start ripping. The Toad made a half-hearted attempt, then gave up. Theo glanced at him out of the corner of his eye. The Toad seemed to be coming back a bit with the light from the flame. Smoke and long-undisturbed dust filled their breathing space, making them sneeze. The flame reflected off the Toad's glasses. He grinned humourlessly. Theo had never seen anyone so pathologically afraid of the dark.

As one, the three started forward.

"Toad! You gotta show us, man! Where is the goddamn door?"

"Keep going…watch floor…tracks in dust lead ya…right to it…follow yellow brick…road."

That threw Theo, causing him to give the Toad a fast double take. Was that humour or reflex?

The hell-rats backed away from the growing flame, keeping to the shadows that jumped and writhed as though alive. The tarp was burning damn fast, and the stage's supporting framework and the boxes stored there had ignited as well, the flames growing. The blackened wood gave off clouds of choking smoke that had nowhere to vent.

"Cover your nose and mouth," Laura said. Theo and the Toad cranked their shirts out of their pants and covered their faces as best they could, being on all fours. In the flickering orange light, Theo watched Laura do the same and caught a flash of abdomen and bra.

Jesus! How can that get me going in a fucking situation like this? Theo thought. *I'm a goddamn sicko!* Then he thought of

(did you at least keep your bra on)

Marcia.

The crawlspace was so bright now, there was no need to follow tracks—the door was obvious. The Toad was the first one through, then Laura, and Theo came last. The hell-rats made a rush for the door, but Theo dropped the burning cloth on a stick just inside the door and slammed it shut. He threw the bolt.

"Woo! We made it!" Laura said.

"That won't hold them long. Help me get this table over."

Laura and Theo flipped a large wooden table—"Christ, how much does this thing weigh?"—on its side and dragged over to the closed door. Then Theo grabbed hammers and a bucket of large nails—"Quick, pound these in!"—and the three of them got to work.

"Go ahead and try and push through that, y' bastards! See what a face fulla nails does for your complexion!" Theo and Laura grinned like idiots, like maniacs. They stood quickly and she hugged him. Theo returned the embrace awkwardly, not used to affection or the feel of another body against his. Marcia never felt like this. The spontaneity of the gesture fell away and they both held on a little longer than either had expected.

"It'd really…open up your pores," the Toad said.

Theo and Laura looked at the Toad like they were just noticing him for the first time. Then they looked at each other. Her hold loosened as Theo turned back to the Toad. He released her reluctantly.

"What? What are you talking about?"

"I said, it would open your pores. A face full of nails. Would open your pores."

It took a second, but then it sunk in.

The laughter came fast. To anyone else, it would have sounded maniacal.

CHAPTER FOURTEEN

MARCIA DISCOVERED WHAT the others already knew. Looking outside completely messed up her head.

Propped up on her hands and knees, she spat the bad taste from her mouth. She knew that her gut had clenched and that she had vomited as soon as she had looked outside, but she couldn't understand why. Yes, it was different out there—no parking lot, no cars, no trees in the distance—but how could looking out a window do that to her?

She looked up again.

Her body bucked and heaved, threatening to offload vital organs if she didn't stop looking outside.

She was convinced. She would not look again. There was no escape that way. She closed her eyes, moved her hand to push herself up and placed it squarely in a warm, lumpy puddle of her own yarkings. That almost set her off again, but she got up and ran toward the washroom. There were no windows in the washroom.

She could rest in the washroom.

Marcia ran, arms outstretched, eyes shut tight once again. Distances became strange with no sight. She hit the cool concrete of the wall and slid herself along to the left. There! A doorframe. She pushed and the door swung open.

She knew there would be an inner door as well. She didn't expect the desk that was propped in front of it. With her eyes still closed, she slammed her already-bruised leg into it. Pain jangled all the way up to her hip and her eyes popped open. She tensed, girding herself against another bout of nausea that never arrived. The outer door closed with a muffled *thunk.*

Why in God's name is there a desk in here? It almost looked like someone was trying to lock her out. *Or keep something in here.*

Marcia decided it couldn't really be too much worse than what she had already been through. Unless it was one of those dog-beasts but, placing her ear to the inner door, she heard no noises. She figured those things would have either chewed their way out by now, or would be freaking out as they tried. And besides, at least this time she was prepared.

Sort of.

She lifted the desk and pulled it back as quietly as she could. The desk wasn't really heavy, just awkward. She got it back far enough that she could lean over it and push open the inner door. If something was going to rush her, she wanted the desk between them. It would also give her a quick peek at the inside of the washroom.

As she opened the door, the sight of the room confused and disoriented her.

This wasn't the girls' washroom!

It was the boys'! She had misjudged and overrun her target. But why the barricade?

Nothing came running out at her. But she thought she could hear breathing.

♦♦♦

THEY WERE IN the tech wing—the lair of the grease-laden. The scratching at the storage door was insistent. They moved away from the barrier they had made.

Theo had never been in the tech wing before—his subjects leaned toward the maths and sciences. It was a wholly different, not-unpleasant smell in here. Wood and oil and metal and the ever-present scent of teenage sweat. It was a bigger room than any of his classrooms, and in the relative quiet, ignoring, for the moment, the hounds of hell behind them, things echoed, but in a way that set him a little more at ease. He couldn't put a finger on why, but he felt comfortable here. Safe.

This was obviously the electrical end of the wing, with all the various electrical things Theo recognized but could not name on sight: resistors, capacitors, transformers, and the like. He saw a couple of big things that he guessed were generators. Off to the left hung rolls and rolls of various gauge wiring hung from the wall on things like big toilet paper rolls.

The wire he had heard about before. Crouch had liberated a substantial amount for his own personal use. He'd run the wire from the stereo in his bedroom, out his window along the house, then down the driveway and through a trench he'd laboriously dug in the lawn to the lake, where he had then attached his speakers. That had satisfied him for a while, but soon he became irritated with having to go in the house every forty-five minutes to flip the cassette. Playing records was out of the question, because then he was flipping the LP every twenty minutes or so. And 8-tracks were just passé to everyone in the group except the Toad, who was still pissed that he couldn't get the first three Cars albums in that particular format.

Because he viewed the record- and tape-flipping thing as such a pain in the ass, Crouch eventually replaced the six-foot power cord on his stereo with two hundred feet of Clarington High's finest heavy gauge to bring the entire stereo system down—minus the turntable, of course. Wouldn't want sand getting in the album sleeves and scratching the records.

As far as Theo knew, it never once occurred to Crouch to simply purchase an extension cord to do the same function. If it took longer, was more technical, and had a good chance of buggering up, or it simply was not feasible at all, that was always the solution Crouch went for. Theo guessed the large quantities of alcohol and marijuana Crouch consumed contributed to this mindset. But Crouch was like that.

Was.

Not anymore. Crouch was dead now. *Fuck.*

Suddenly, Theo was so very tired. He looked to his friends. They both had a blown-out look. He knew if he looked in the mirror, he'd see the same thing reflected there.

"Is that a generator?" he asked, pointing.

"Yeah," said the Toad. He seemed to be almost all the way back now.

"Anyone know how to use it?"

"Yeah," said the Toad. "I had to learn them when I worked for Hydro last summer."

"You think we could rig some lights? Give ourselves some downtime to figure out how to get out of here?"

♦♦♦

"WHO'S THERE?"

Marcia's voice sounded raw and too loud after not talking for so long. Her throat grated with the hoarse noise and it echoed around the tiled enclosure.

No response, but still, she heard the sound of laboured breathing. She slid the desk along in front of her, not willing to give up her security blanket just yet. A few feet further into the room and she saw a pair of denim-clad legs, one bloody, looking like it had been chewed on, sticking out from under one of the stalls.

Someone else is alive!

She pushed around the desk and flung open the stall door, not caring that it banged against the wall, not worried about any noise at this point.

"Bobby!"

Bobby Bostash looked bad—horrible, in fact—but he managed to raise his head and focus on Marcia with bloodshot eyes.

"Hey Marce. You look like shit."

She smiled. She had always liked Stash. He was one of the few guys in the school who talked to her like she was human, and not just another potential conquest.

"Yeah, well, no offense, but you don't exactly look like Travolta right now, either."

Stash twirled his index fingers lethargically. "Ah ah ah ah stayin' alive." He smiled, but there was a river of pain running just under it.

Marcia sat down on the toilet. It wasn't comfortable, but it was a place to rest, and it was a warmer room than the one she had just escaped. "What happened, Bobby?"

"Not sure. Went to take a whaddayacallit piss. Something ripped Crouch apart..."

"Ben is dead?"

"Shit. Sorry, Marce."

She blinked away tears as he continued. First Theo, now Ben. *Damn it!*

"Anyway. Thing attacked me. Ripped me up good," he said, pointing to his leg. "Theo an' Toad saved me."

There was silence for a moment.

"Theo."

He looked up, meeting her eyes.

"He's dead, right?"

"Yeah, Bob. I'm pretty sure he is. Him and Toad and Miss Davis got swarmed in the caf by a bunch of dog-beasts."

"Little nasty-ass rats from hell? Yeah, that's what got my leg. Theo an' Toad saved me." She didn't point out that he'd just said the same thing. Maybe it was emotion, or maybe it was his injuries.

"I'm sorry, Bobby." It was all she could think of to say.

"Yeah," Stash sighed raggedly. "Me too."

The two of them sat quietly for a time, absorbing the death of their friends and lovers. Both blinked away tears. Neither seemed too eager to talk any further. From here, the screams were very faint. Marcia could almost forget they were there at all. She closed her eyes and rested her head in her hands, elbows on her knees.

♦♦♦

"HEY TOAD, REMEMBER that party out at Crouch's last year?" Theo asked as they ran the lights.

"The one where he was in the lawn chair on the roof?"

"Yeah, that one. Remember him discovering the ring around the Earth?"

Both Laura and the Toad looked at him with "whaaaat?" expressions.

"Serious! Crouch got stoned, and I found him and some girl—can't remember who but it was before he hooked up with, uh…with Marce—and he crashed on the grass in his backyard staring up at the stars."

Everybody who came to New Hope always remarked at how incredible the night sky was. With little pollution and no big city lights to ruin it, the stars ran rampant in the sky. Theo used to go out and watch for satellites passing by. He could usually spot them with his naked eye.

"Yeah, the two of them had been playing tonsil-hockey or something, but at one point, I guess Crouch looked up and saw this big ring of stars—"

"The Milky Way?" Laura asked.

"—yeah, the Milky Way, and he was so shit-faced that he was convinced he had discovered a ring around the Earth, just like Saturn's." Theo shook his head at the thought. He hung the last of the lights in place.

"It took me almost an hour to convince him not to call NASA. The girl, whoever she was, was no help at all, by the way." He smiled, then remembered again that Crouch, discoverer of astronomical phenomena, wasn't alive any more.

"Anyway, I just wondered if you had heard that one." They all turned back to their individual tasks. Theo couldn't help but remember the conversation that had occurred just after that. It had eventually turned to parents, and to respect.

Theo could still see Crouch from that night: the peach-fuzz beard, the dopey, lopsided grin, and the ever-present cowboy hat—a fixture ever since that *Urban Cowboy* movie had come out.

Crouch had been on his back, the hat pulled low over his eyes, the girlfriend having long since grown bored of the discussion, and moved inside in search of beer or another tonsil-hockey player.

"People look up to you more than you think, man," Crouch had said, out of the blue.

"Yeah, right." It wasn't the most creative response, but Theo had been trying not to laugh more than anything. *People look up to me? Ha!*

"No, seriously, dude," Crouch continued. "Your dad's an asshole—no offense—but you still keep pounding away. Take a lickin' and keep on tickin'. Yer like a fuggin Timex..."

Theo felt weird knowing all of this came from Crouch's heart. Theo wasn't used to people opening up like this. But he was also keenly aware that the path from Crouch's heart to his brain was currently well lubricated with alcohol, and Theo had a deep mistrust of booze-talk.

"My old man's cool, don't get me wrong," Crouch said. "But sometimes, man, I just wish he'd clue in. Hell, half the damn town knows I'm Damage, Inc., but my old man—the guy who figures out how people died—doesn't."

Theo did find it amazing that the guy didn't have a clue. Shit, all those street signs in Crouch's room? Really. Think about it. Do the math!

"And remember that time I got in the fight with Moose? And we ended up punching a couple of holes in the walls? I told Dad it was a bat that got down the fireplace an' I tried to kill it with a broom. I mean, Jesus! A *BROOM*!" Crouch's head bobbed up and down, his body physically reacting to his disbelief.

Shit, Theo realized. *He's* trying *to get caught!*

"Just once, I wish he'd call me on it," Crouch continued. "Call my bluff. 'Geez son, that's a great story, but I do believe I'm smelling a heapin' helpin' of bullshit, don't you?'"

Theo snorted. "Don't complain. I'd trade your situation for mine, any day."

"Either way, we're both sorta missing out on the whole parenting package, aren't we?" Crouch tilted his hat back and propped himself on one elbow. "And ten years from now, probably, we'll be parents."

"And seventeen years after that," Theo said, "our kids will be sitting in the yard, bitching about how shitty their parents are."

"No doubt," Crouch said. He played with an empty beer bottle that had been carelessly dropped in an earlier moment of passion. "But for now, here I am, Joe Beerhead." He waggled the bottled between the two of them. "And then there's you. You don't have anything to be ashamed of. Nothing. Nada. Zip." He stopped, regarded Theo seriously.

"I got something I need to confess to you, man," he said.

That scared Theo a touch. "What?"

"When I grow up, I wanna be just like you," Crouch said, a ghost of a smile crossing his face, slightly curling the fuzz on his upper lip.

"You ain't gonna hug or kiss me, are you?"

"Fuck no," he said. "Only if you were a whole lot better lookin'."

"You should be so fuckin' lucky," Theo replied. "Your face, my ass, no difference."

"The permanent vertical smile, buddy."

Theo had known right then, booze or no booze, that he really did have support. Crouch, Stash, the Toad—they were all his support system.

But now his support system was dying by degrees. Stash was dying. Crouch was dead. The Toad kept slipping into catatonia. How was he ever going to survive without them?

Goddamn, I'm gonna miss you, Benmont Devenish. You and everyone else. He banished the thoughts and concentrated on the task at hand.

♦♦♦

THOUGH THEY WERE all exhausted, it didn't take long to rig the lights in a rough circle. They finished the work in silence, surrounded, and haunted by, their own thoughts.

Finally, Theo held the connection. "Here comes the sun...and, if I do say so myself..."—he made the connection—"it's all riiight!" Meant as a joke, it came across as hollow, forced.

Looking at their handiwork, ignoring the attempt at humour, Laura said, "That should keep them out for a while." Her voice betrayed their exhaustion.

They collapsed in the bright, relative safety of the ring of lights.

♦♦♦

MARCIA JERKED UP with a start. One of those full-body jerks that instantly doubled her heart rate and left her wondering what had caused it in the first place.

Then she remembered. *The washroom. I'm in the boys' washroom.* She hadn't fallen asleep so much as she had zoned out for a few minutes. She registered the deep, rhythmic breathing beside her and took a few seconds to check out her new haven. It wasn't every day a good Catholic girl got to see the inside of a washroom designed for the opposite sex. Then again, a good girl wouldn't fall asleep alone in a room with a boy. Her mother would have been mortified.

Though she was no longer a virgin, and for that one her mother would *really* be mortified, the male sex organ—in the rare times her mother did call it anything other than "disgusting," she referred to it as a "phallus," thinking it was the nicest of the rude things it could be called—was still mostly a mystery to Marcia.

She checked out the urinal. *How in heck do you pee standing up?* She just didn't get it. There was a pungent smell in the room that she wasn't accustomed to. Urine. Filthy boys peeing on the floor.

She realized that almost anything she knew of the opposite sex was flavoured by a comment or observation of her mother's.

If I ever get out of this, some things are going to change, she thought. That was followed closely by the sudden realization that she really had to pee. Badly.

Marcia got up quietly, every little sound echoing off the tiles, and moved to the next stall down the line. The last thing she needed was for Bobby to wake up and see her making water, her bare bum hanging out for anyone to see. Besides, she didn't think she'd even be able to go with him that close, unconscious or otherwise. She still locked the door when she went for a pee at home, even if she was the only one in the house.

She closed the door to the stall as quietly as she could, but she couldn't prevent the faint squeal of the hinges. She pulled down her pants and sat on the cold seat. As she urinated—her mother would have said "tinkled"—she checked out the bruises on her legs. Yes, they were purpling up nicely. It would be a while before she could wear shorts or a bathing suit.

That was assuming she'd ever get the chance to wear them again...

She finished and wiped herself with the wretched sheets of paper. There was no water in the toilet, so she didn't attempt a flush. She left the stall wishing public washrooms had lids on the toilets, so she could at least be more discreet when she couldn't flush.

Marcia went back to where Bobby lay. She looked down and realized he was sitting very still. With a start, she realized she couldn't hear him breathing anymore. For a short moment, she wondered if he was dead too, but no, she saw his chest rise and fall. Every so often, his face would screw up in a wince of pain. She looked him over and saw that most of the damage seemed to be to his foot. It didn't look good. There was a blood-soaked tourniquet on his leg, just below the calf.

She reached out to touch it. There was something familiar about it. Then she saw a small area of white in the field of red. It had been white. With a wide blue stripe, now turned black with the blood.

A white jacket.

Theo's white jacket.

Damn.

The tears welled up again, and spilled down her cheeks, making dark circles on the denim of Stash's pants.

Oh Theo, I'm so sorry. I'm sorry I disappointed you. I'm sorry I made you mad. I'm so sorry.

She sniffed and wiped away the tears with the heel of her hand. She pulled off two or three toilet tissues and blew her nose. *Why can't we just have rolls of toilet paper like normal people?*

The tears just didn't seem to want to stop. She pulled more tissues and wiped at her eyes.

"I think he still dug you, Marce."

She looked down at him, embarrassed at having been caught crying. "How long have you been sitting there watching me blubber like a baby?"

"Not long," he said, a small smile curling the corner of his mouth, making her blush with the thought he might have heard her…tinkling. "I'm serious. I know you two had some kind of a fight back there in the whaddayacallit caf after the whole hands-on-the-shirt thing, and I know he was always chasing after Steph—"

"You all were." She didn't have to ask, she knew he was talking about Theo.

"Yeah, well. But Theo still had feelings for you. If he didn't, he wouldn't care enough to fight with you. Crouch never did, did he?"

Marcia considered his words.

"You always know what to say, don't you?"

"What can I say?" Stash smirked. "It's a whaddayacallit gift." Stash got his hands under him and pushed to change position, wrinkled his nose to walk his glasses back up and failed as usual.

"Bobby, I don't know how long we've been here. I think we both fell asleep. But I think there's still a lot of trouble on this floor. And we can't go outside right now." After seeing his puzzled expression, she explained why. She left out the part about putting her hand in her own vomit. That was just gross.

"So what do you want to do?"

"Do you think you can make it upstairs? If the coast is clear, we could get you to the second floor. Danika's locker is there, and she's got half a pharmacy going on in there."

Stash gave her a look.

"Migraines. So she says, anyway. We could get you something for the pain and we could get away from those things."

"I don't know, Marce. I don't know if I can get up those stairs. Why don't you just go on your own?"

"Because I've just lost a lot of people who meant a lot to me. I'm not losing another one. I swore to myself that I wouldn't make any stupid mistakes, and I'm not going to start by leaving you behind. Now, let's go."

"I ever tell you I like dominant women?"

"I ever tell you I could kick your butt?"

"Ass, Marce," Stash said. "It's 'kick your ass.' If you're gonna whaddayacallit swear, go all the way."

"Bobby."

"Yeah, Marce?"

"Shut up and let's get going."

"Yes ma'am. You're making me hard."

Marcia rolled her eyes and said nothing further. She knew he would never let her have the last word. No male did.

♦♦♦

THE THREE OF them sat on the cold floor for what seemed like hours. No one spoke. They just stared off to the middle distance, listening to the occasional weak scratch at the storage door. Or their breathing. Theo eventually became aware that they were all situated in a way that they all touched each other somehow. An arm against a leg here, a shoulder to a foot there.

It was Laura who finally broke the silence.

"Toad...Dennis, can I ask you something? You don't have to answer, but..."

"What?" he asked, sitting up, cross-legged.

"I was just wondering...'pop goes the weasel.' What does it...you know. Every time it gets dark, you..."

"Freak out?"

"Yeah. Listen, you don't—"

"No. It's cool, it's cool." Theo could tell it was anything but cool, but didn't stop the Toad. He drew in a long, ragged breath, ran his hand through his blond bowl cut, and blew out the breath again.

"I used to have this babysitter. It was before you came to New Hope, Laura. His name was Tim Ambrose—"

Theo sucked in a breath. "The same Tim Ambrose who had his head—"

"Yeah, him. Anyway, my mom used to play bingo two or three nights a week—"

Shit, thought Theo, *she still does.*

"—and she used to have Tim come over and…you know…babysit me." The Toad shifted position, getting more comfortable.

"So he'd always be real cool while mom was still there, all smilin' and shit, and pattin' me on the head and stuff, makin' out like we were best buds or some shit. And I, I'd uh…" He sniffled a bit, took a deep breath.

"Dennis, you don't…"

"No. I'm okay. I've just never told anyone this before, and I guess I really want to. Don't know if we're gonna make it out of this shit show, so…it's time." He adjusted his glasses.

"So anyway, yeah, I'd have to act like I was diggin' him bein' there too, when I really hated him. I *hated* that fucker." Theo watched his friend's face darken at the thought.

"So mom would leave, and he'd just go and sit in front of the TV and watch *The Dukes of Hazzard* or somethin'. The big smiles were gone. I remember my dad used to say some people had a liquid smile, cuz it would just wash away like it was never there. That's what Tim would do. 'Stay off my case, fuckface,' he'd say." He huffed out a humourless laugh.

"I'd usually go outside and hang out on the swings, praying that Mom would hit it big and come home early. I prayed to God every time. She never did, though."

He looked down at the floor, his limp blond hair shadowing his face.

"She never ever did," he repeated. "Not once." Theo saw a single tear slip down Laura's face, but she held her silence.

"So I'd stay out there 'til about 7:30 P.M. or so. Then he'd call me in with that sweet-ass 'Den-nis. Time to get ready for be-ed' shit. I guess that was for the benefit of the neighbours, not that Mrs. Kroeger would care. She was always drunk by then."

Mrs. Kroeger was the Toad's next-door neighbour. Theo and the guys used to ride the Toad about thinking she was hot—shit, she was pushing sixty and not very well—and he was constantly bugged about getting her juiced and having his way with her. "Giving her the Toadstool," they used to say.

Theo came back around to what the Toad was saying. He looked grim, but he continued to slog through his tale. Theo listened, though he wasn't sure he wanted to.

The Toad continued. "I'd come in, and he'd make me get undressed

(skinny little shit ain't ya)

right in front of him, right down to

(shit you ain't got hardly no dick)

naked and he'd take me into…into the, uh, into the closet and he'd shut the, uh, door, so's it was almost completely dark. Just a little crack of light at, uh, at the bottom." He sniffed, swiped at his nose.

"Then Tim would, uh…touch me."

"Dennis," Theo said, "don't—"

"Just shut up, okay? Just shut up." He took off his glasses and rubbed the two red spots on either side of his nose. His eyes were red-rimmed. He took another breath and continued.

"So, like I said, he'd have me naked in the closet—I'm, like, seven at this point, okay? Seven years old. And he's touchin' me...my dick and stuff. And stickin' his finger in my...

(let me check yer temperature denny)

"...you know.

(now suck it suck it suck my finger you fuck)

"It made me feel real weird, cuz some of it sort of felt good, but it mostly felt real *wrong*, y'know? Real bad, like the shit your mom tells you you're gonna go to hell for. I felt bad because a little tiny part was sort of enjoying it, you know, the stuff that sort of felt good, and because he was paying some sort of attention to me instead of out playing fucking bingo every fucking night."

The Toad was in it now. Theo could see he wasn't telling it. The Toad's eyes were closed, tears slipping down cheeks that still had traces of baby fat. He wasn't telling it anymore, he was living it.

"And I can hear him. He's close enough that I can feel him jerking. But all the time he's doin' this shit, he's singing, 'All around the mulberry bush the monkey chased the, uh, the weasel. The monkey...' you know. That stupid fucking nursery rhyme."

Theo thought, *Oh god no.*

"And I'm sitting there, naked in my own closet while he's singing and touching me and jerkin' off and I can hear his voice getting lower and lower and hoarser and hoarser and he's breathing heavy and singing that stupid song over and over and his breath I can feel it on my face all warm and moist and he's huffin' and I'm waiting cuz I know he's gonna come it's gonna come and no matter where he is in the song he always says '*pop* goes the weasel' and this warm shit comes on my face and it feels oh god it feels so bad so wrong so...so...fucking...goddamn...wrong..."

He stopped, his chest heaving. Theo didn't know what to do or say. He looked to Laura, who was looking at the Toad with more tears standing in her eyes. As he watched, another slipped and tumbled down her cheek. She leaned forward and embraced the Toad, almost as mother to child.

"I'm sorry, Dennis. Oh Jesus, I'm so sorry."

The two of them sat like that, sharing an embrace. Laura made soft, reassuring noises as his sobs slowly fell away. Theo, not knowing what to do, did the only thing that felt right. He put his arm around his friend and said nothing, feeling his friend's and his own breathing slow back to normal.

♦♦♦

"YOU OKAY?" LAURA asked, after a time.

"Yeah, thanks," the Toad replied, slowly drawing away from her embrace. Theo saw the darkened stain of tears on Laura's shoulder.

"You wanna know the worst part?" the Toad said, wiping his nose on his sleeve. "The worst part of the whole thing?" *No,* thought, Theo, *I really don't. I don't want to know any more.*

"What was it?" he heard himself ask.

"The waiting. The waiting for that shithead to shoot his load in my face. When we were under that stage back there and it went all dark, all I could think was, 'When's he gonna touch me? When's he gonna stick his finger in my mouth? When's he gonna cream in my face?'" He paused, blinked. "I know you guys think I'm nuts…"

Theo and Laura both shook their heads.

"…but that's all I ever think of in the dark. The fingers coming out of the dark. Then the…other." He shook his head, almost as though to shake off the thoughts.

"After he was finished, I'd hear him zip up and he'd open the door to the closet real cautious-like, and again I'd pray that once, just once, mom would be there. An' he'd look at me and tell me to get my faggot-ass face cleaned up and get to bed. He told me if I ever said anything, nobody'd believe me. They'd just think I was some fag and they'd take me from Mom and put me in a home with all the other faggot kids who'd all blow their loads in my face. So I never said a thing."

He never had. Never even gave a hint of it in all the time Theo had known him.

"For three years and five months, I never said a thing. Then, it just stopped."

"What happened?" Laura asked. "Why'd it stop?"

Theo knew how it ended.

"Tim's dad was supposedly cleaning his shotgun when it went off by accident," the Toad said. "It took Tim's head off, is what I heard. The thing is, Tim's old man always cleaned his guns in the garage, but this time he was in the woodshed. And from what I heard, the spray pattern went *down*, but he usually sat down with the barrel pointed up."

Theo thought, *Fucker got a taste of someone shooting a load on his face*.

"It was ruled as an 'unfortunate accident.' I think Mr. Ambrose found out somethin' about his little Timmy that didn't sit well. I've seen him in town and he always gives me this nod, like, you're-okay-now sorta thing."

Pop goes the weasel, thought Theo.

No shit.

Chapter Fifteen

IT WAS A pain in the butt, but Marcia got Stash to his feet—or more precisely, his foot—and they struggled out of the washroom. Marcia steered them off to the right, where the doors to the stairs would be. It was damned scary, popping out of the washroom with their eyes closed and no idea what could be waiting just on the other side. She imagined the dog-beasts all out there, waiting for her. As they eased open the last door, Marcia was convinced there would be the entire horde from the caf out there. They would have smelled the blood and her puke, followed her trail, heard the two of them talking. They would know Marcia and Bobby would be coming out defenseless and tentative, and they would be sitting there, silent, staring with their big black bug eyes, saliva runnelling down their oversized black razor-teeth. They would have the patience of an executioner's blade. She could see them, quiet as death, anticipating their appearance.

Her hands shook as she exited the room. Stash gave her a slight squeeze that told her he was in the same mind-place.

All was silent. The two of them stumbled awkwardly to their right and toward the entrance to the stairs. They made it through the doors without incident.

"Okay Bobby, I think we can open our eyes now." Marcia screwed up her face and cautiously cracked one eyelid. Her stomach fluttered in reaction to the memory of that terrible sight just beyond the school windows, but it held tight. *Good.* She blew a sigh of relief.

Stash looked at the stairs and a pained expression crossed his face. "You really want the second floor? Couldn't we just stop at the landing and you could go on from there?"

"The pills are on the second floor," she said. "Let's get going and see how you make out, all right?"

"I've never had any complaints."

"Complaints? Bobby, what are you talking about?"

"You said you wanted to see how I made out. I've never had any whaddayacallit complaints."

"I can leave you here, you know."

"You can, but you won't. You like me too much."

Again realizing she could not win, she smacked Stash lightly on the back of his curly haired head and got him moving.

♦♦♦

THEY WERE BURNED out. Too much fear, too much adrenalin, too much running, too much emotion.

Too much.

Out of desperation, Theo felt he had to change gears, get away from the heavy and into something that required a lot less brainpower. He had been moving around the room, looking for anything useful that might assist them in getting the hell out of…well, hell.

Without stopping his search, he spoke up.

"So, Laura, what kind of music do you listen to?"

She gave Theo a look. "Theo, I'm not *that* much older than you. I can still rock out, you know."

That brought a smile to both Theo and the Toad's lips.

"Oh yeah? 'Rock out,' huh?" Theo said teasingly.

"Uh-oh, there's gonna be a gunfight," said the Toad. "Look out, Laura, he's gonna give you the quiz." His voice was still quavering, but his demeanour was more tranquil now. He was able to move outside of the lights to help Theo in his quest for weapons or tools.

Laura brushed the hair from her face and squared her shoulders. "Bring it on, baby." Nobody seemed to cotton on to the fact they were talking rock trivia while in hell. It just felt good to deal with something familiar for a while, however brief that time might be.

The Toad, getting into it, whistled the theme from *The Good, the Bad, and the Ugly*. Theo began firing questions, machine-gun style.

"Who's your favourite singer?"

"Bryan Ferry, Roxy Music."

"Drummer?"

"Stewart Copeland and Neil Peart, in a tie. John Bonham for sheer power."

"Bass?"

"Ooo. Geddy Lee, Rush. Though McCartney's way up there, too."

"Guitar?"

"Clapton."

"Clapton?"

"Clapton."

"Uh-oh," said the Toad.

Theo stopped and turned to face her. "Clapton. You're serious."

"Yeah, Clapton. What's the matter with Clapton?"

Theo made a face. *Let her keep her delusions.* "Never mind. Band?"

"Beatles, no question."

"Good choice. You had me worried there for a second."

"Clapton played on the *White Album*."

"Ouch," said the Toad, obviously enjoying this. "She knows her shit, dude."

Oh, she's asking for it. "Okay, yeah, he played on the *White Album*, and they thought so much of it, they didn't even credit him." Theo dropped a coiled length of rope in the area where Laura was sitting.

"True, but—"

"And then he ripped off Harrison's wife."

"And wrote one of the best songs ever about it."

"Yeah, yeah, 'Layla.'" Theo stood over her, hands on hips. "Okay, I'll give you that, but he's also got some bad dumbshit songs, too."

"Like?"

"Like that dumbshit one…uh…Toad, what is it again?"

"The 'Rainbow Has a Moustache' one?"

"That's it! 'The Rainbow Has a Moustache.' Dumb dumb dumb."

"Actually guys, it goes, 'the rainbow has a beard,' and yes, Clapton plays on it—it's a Cream song—but he didn't write it. Jack Bruce did."

"Damn, Theo, she *really* knows her shit."

"Picked it up from my husband." Laura paused, her eyes downcast. There was silence again. "He was a freak for guitar heroes. He worshipped Hendrix," she finished, without much conviction.

And with that one statement, the one mention of another dead soul, the mood was broken. And uncomfortable silence wedged itself between them.

Shit, thought Theo.

He tried to salvage the mood. *Just keep them talking.* Keeping a light tone in his voice that he really didn't feel, he said, "Y'know, that song just makes no sense. 'Rainbow has a beard.' What's that mean? Makes no sense."

"Sort of like the situation we're in right now," the Toad mumbled as he gently added some lights to their growing pile of supplies.

Theo tried to ignore him. "Doesn't that song have a stupid name, too?"

"Yeah," Laura said, disinterested. She had her arms around her legs, her chin resting on her knees. "'SWLABR.'"

"Swih-lahber?" asked the Toad.

"Close enough. Just run it together faster."

"Swlabr."

"That's it. Stands for 'She Was Like a Bearded Rainbow.'"

"See? That doesn't make sense," said Theo.

"So let's kind of make it tie together!" The Toad sounded almost excited. "We got a song that makes no sense, and we got a senseless situation with a big-ass monster—"

"The Big Dude," said Theo.

"—yeah, whatever. Let's christen the fucker."

"What do you mean, Dennis?" Laura asked. Her head was off her knees. He had her interest.

"I mean we're running from a big, ugly son of a bitch, and we don't even know what to call it. It don't make sense. Like a rainbow with a beard makes no sense. Let's call him 'Swlabr.'"

Theo considered it. Laura just smiled. It was weak, but it was a smile.

"Why not?" she said. "It's as good a name as any other."

"Stupid song, stupid beast, stupid name. I like it,' said Theo. He stood up, raised his arms. "I hereby christen thee Swlabr, The Shitpile That Walks Like a Man."

"Now all we have to do is figure out how to get away from that particular shitpile," Laura said, her head sinking back to her knees.

Again the silence.

Shit, thought Theo. This time, he let it go, and the silence descended like a fog, clouding their thoughts.

♦♦♦

IT WAS SLOW going. Stash couldn't put any weight on his damaged foot, so he had to hop up the stairs one at a time on his good foot. Marcia could see it was taking a lot out of him.

"Come on, Bobby. A few more steps and then we'll take a breather."

Stash gave her a pained look. She could see his curls beginning to stick to his forehead from the sweat. He didn't say anything, just wrinkled his nose, hunkered down, and hopped to the next step. Then the next. And the next.

They got to the landing—the halfway point between the first and second floors where the stairs turned back in the other direction—and Stash collapsed on the dirty floor, sucking huge, whooping breaths.

"Oh Christ! I'm dyin' here! Marce, you're killin' me."

"Let's just rest, Bobby. You're doing fine."

Stash looked down at his foot, bending his knee to bring it up closer. He wrinkled his nose to move his glasses up his face. It didn't work, so he did the finger-poke.

He examined the wound with his teeth gritted. Sucking in a sharp breath with a quick *sssssst* sound, he turned his ankle this way and that.

"No," he said softly. "No, I don't think I am doing fine. I think I need to take some of the pressure off this tourniquet."

"Let me help." Marcia went back down a couple of stairs, turned, grabbed his pant leg, and gingerly eased it up. Stash caught the stick and slowly released the pressure.

"Ah, that feels better," he said.

"Yeah, but not too much. You'll start—oh gosh, see? You're bleeding again. Tighten it a bit." He did as he was told. "We'll have to tighten it again before we move you."

"I hear you." They sat quietly for a few moments, Stash rubbing the circulation back into his leg. But the blood was too much, so he tightened the loop again. Then he extended his leg back out straight, taking care to lower his foot to the ground lightly.

Marcia didn't know what to say, how to make it better. She didn't have Stash's gift.

"You'll be okay," she said, knowing immediately how lame that sounded.

"Yeah, but I'll never be able to play the whaddayacallit piano again, dammit." His head was resting back using the bottom step as a pillow. His eyes never opened and his face was a mask of buried pain. Marcia wasn't even sure he was aware of what he said.

Could've been a joke, she thought, *or it could be he's hallucinating.*

They rested as long as she dared, then she wrestled Stash back to his feet.

"No," he said. "This isn't going to work."

"Bobby, we need—"

"I'm gonna sit on my ass."

"Pardon?" Then she watched as he sat back down. And she got it. He planted both hands on the stair above, pushed, and heaved his butt up one riser.

"Okay," she said. "That works too." It seemed easier on him, though he still had to be careful dragging his injured heel up until Marcia clued in that she could support it.

"I always wanted a woman to wait on me hand and foot," he said. "At least I got the foot part now."

She didn't dignify the comment with a response. What was the use?

♦♦♦

THE TOAD—IT seemed kind of strange to think of him as 'the Toad' after what they now knew about him—was the one who broke the silence again.

"Okay guys, seriously…what are we gonna do? We gotta get out of here. And what about Stash? And all those guys in the caf? They're not dead. We can't just leave them there."

"What are you saying, that we should wade in there and somehow put them out of their misery?" Theo asked.

"No, but we have to do something. They're suffering, and they looked like they were in there to be…to be…"

"Impregnated." Laura's voice betrayed her distaste.

"Yeah. That."

"I don't think we can save them, Theo." Laura looked pointedly at the other two. "You both saw them."

"So what do we do?" Theo said.

Laura reached into her slacks and brought out the Toad's crumpled book of matches.

"Burn 'em," she said, her voice flat.

♦♦♦

"MARCE! HOLD UP. You're killin' me here! We gotta stop."

Marcia had gone up to the second floor to scout ahead. She wanted to be sure they didn't walk into another nasty surprise. There had been enough of those today, thank you very much.

Now she looked back down the stairs to where Stash stood, leaning against the concrete wall, panting like a dog. His hair clung to his head like a bather's cap. Sweat stains darkened his T-shirt. His foot was propped on the riser.

There was no way he was going to be able to make it to Danika's locker.

Damn.

She did her best to hide her frustration. In his condition, Stash probably wouldn't have noticed anyway.

"Okay, Bobby," she said, trying to keep her voice light. "Let's at least get you up to here. We'll hole up in Mr. Corrigan's class for a bit."

"Think if I make to Corrigan's room, you could see your way clear to getting me a drink of water? Better yet, how 'bout some milk and cookies?"

"How about a nice cold beer, Bobby?"

"Oh, you bitch. You're such a tease." Marcia was glad to see he had a smile on his face. He seemed a bit more himself when she got him moving. She came down the steps and reached out an arm to help support him. He gripped the handrail and readied himself. Then Marcia felt him hesitate.

"What?" she asked, concerned. "What's wrong, Bobby?"

Stash looked as though he was going to get all serious on her. His eyes were looking at her differently. She watched a drop of sweat roll down his cheek to his jawline. He seemed to hesitate. His mouth opened and closed. Then his expression changed again, back to normal Stash.

"It's not nice to tease, Marce. You've been a bad girl. Go to my room."

She smiled, and he immediately turned back to the task and began hauling himself painfully up the stairs.

But he left Marcia wondering what he had been going to say.

♦ ♦ ♦

"YOU CAN'T BE serious!"

"What have you got that's better? I'm not leaving them there. These are people we know. I'll tell you right now, if I was in there, I sure as hell would rather be dead. Wouldn't you? You saw that thing—that Swlabr—come in. What do you think it may be doing right now?"

Theo was silent. He didn't know what to say. Laura was right. He knew she was, couldn't see any other way out of it. But still.... Jesus.

The Toad put his hand on Theo's shoulder. "Let's put them out of their misery."

Theo jerked his shoulder away. "All right! Fuck! All right, I'll do it. Just don't fuckin' ask me to like it. I don't. It doesn't feel right."

Theo looked at the two of them. "But after that, we do a fast fucking search of the school for survivors and we get the hell out. Somehow."

"Survivors?" the Toad asked. "You really think there's more than us?"

"And Stash."

"Oh Jesus! Tom!"

Theo and the Toad looked at the panic-stricken Laura. "Who's Tom?"

"Tom! Mr. Popper! He was going to be in his class! He must still be up there!"

♦♦♦

THE THREE COMRADES raided the woodworking shop and the other tech classes and assembled a small arsenal of flashlights and portable welding torches. And gas. A lot of gasoline from the auto shop. They were

(the right thing are we)

going to make the biggest bonfire they could, so they needed the fuel.

As they gathered the various articles, Laura and the Toad kept up a small banter, nothing serious, but they were talking. The Toad had obviously bonded with the art teacher since he had exposed his soul in front of her. Now, in spite of what was going to happen—or maybe because of it—they chatted about light topics. Students, music again—

"Boston's the best band in the world, man. They're kickin' everyone's ass right now."

"But every song sounds the same."

—the bell curve, why Mr. Trask was still allowed to teach when he was such a pervert—

"No, he never came on to me, but he did try to pick some imaginary lint off my blouse a couple of times."

—cars, shit, and art—

"So what's the deal with abstract art? Another thing that makes no sense."

Through it all, Theo kept silent, his mouth a grim line, his eyebrows furrowed. He followed behind the other two, quietly picking up the items they thought they might need and neatly stacking them under the artificial joy of their lighted safety area.

To the other two, it looked like he was concentrating on the tasks at hand but that wasn't it at all. He just kept going over the same thought again and again.

Are we doing the right thing? Are we?

Each one of them had learned to respect each other's quiet periods and knew enough not to interrupt. Laura and the Toad left Theo alone, speaking to him only when necessary. He would come around in a while.

In the meantime, they loaded the items on a large dolly, taking care to place everything neatly. The last thing they needed was a propane gas canister falling off and breaking the valve assembly. They had already seen one turn into a big, uncontrollable bullet, and while it had served its purpose, none of them wanted to deal with something like that again. They had enough problems.

They wheeled the dolly out into the hall and started back toward the cafeteria. Still, Theo was

(doing the right thing)

quiet. In fact, everything was quiet. Too damn quiet.

Where were the Chihuahuas from hell?

But running like an underground current through Theo's mind, deep and cold, the same thought, over and over again.

Are we doing the right thing? Are we?

Chapter Sixteen

Maybe ninety minutes after their escape, the three of them stood back in front of the ruined doors leading into the cafeteria, careful not to look anywhere near the windows. Even still, all three felt their stomachs churning. Theo spied fresher vomit just outside the caf doors.

Must have been the Toad offloading one last meal before coming in to save us, he reasoned.

The air was coppery and pungent with the sharp smell of fresh blood and old vomit. The sounds were now more reserved. *Tired,* Theo thought. More whimpers and mewling, like kittens.

They're giving up, Theo thought. He thought about the thing's—Swlabr's—huge dick slowly coming up, barbed feelers out, and he felt…what? *Sick?* No, sick didn't do it. *Repelled? Unclean?* Closer.

Yes, they had to be put out of their misery. But still, it didn't feel right.

Are we doing the right thing?

"So who's going back in there?" the Toad asked. He was losing his calm again, out and away from the safety of the lights. His voice quivered slightly.

The other two were a lot more lenient toward the Toad now. Theo wasn't going to force him into a dark room again and, when he looked over to Laura, he could tell by her expression that she wasn't about to either.

So. It came down to Laura or Theo.

Fucking-A, Theo thought. He still had that nagging voice going on in the back of his head:

Are we doing the right thing? Are we?

One more time, for his conscience: "Guys, listen," Theo said. Laura turned to him, her face a grim mask. The Toad had that nervous grin back on his face. "Do we really wanna do this? Seriously? I mean…we're really gonna *kill* all those guys? People we go to school with? Really kill them?"

Theo looked from Laura to the Toad and back again. They searched each other's eyes for…what? Determination? Or for the first one to back down? Theo didn't know. All he did know was that he was really struggling with the decision. It all felt bad, and dammit, Theo couldn't seem to articulate it. Maybe if just one of them said no, that maybe they should wait, then maybe they would stop for a minute and reconsider, or someone would come up with another idea, or…

Something. Anything. Theo opened his mouth. He would be the one. He would be the voice of reason.

Another voice cut through their thoughts like a gunshot. A girl's voice—

(…marcia? steph?…)

—ragged with fear and pain.

"OH GOD CAN'T SOMEONE HELP ME?"

They all jumped and Theo saw the Toad's pupils dilate just like his cat's used to.

The girl's voice bounced through the empty corridors. Corridors used to happier sounds.

Laura's eyes turned to stone. She faced Theo with a look that was as terrifying as the sound that had just been torn from the caf. His mouth closed silently. He had not uttered a single word.

"This is going to happen, Theo. They're going to be put out of their misery." She stalked closer, her finger punctuating her words into his chest. "And if you won't help me, I'll do it myself." She turned to the cart, grabbed a gas can in each hand, and marched through the caf doors.

No hesitation whatsoever.

Fuck, Theo thought. He grabbed some more gas cans and followed her in, leaving the Toad to guard the cart.

Theo half expected the cafeteria to be scorched from their last pass through. He guessed the fire under the stage went out once all the oxygen was used. He also walked in half expecting a fight—demons big and small, but...nothing. *Where are they? Is this another trap?*

The last thing Theo wanted was to be surrounded again. He knew they got lucky last time and he couldn't count on it again. *No more stupid moves. No more stupid mistakes.*

But there was nothing in the cafeteria except victims. Theo and Laura and the others, all tortured in their own way.

Laura was off to his left, running a thin trail of gas from one grisly structure to the next. The floor was dark and slick with fresh blood. She was snuffling and awkwardly wiping her nose on her upper sleeve. Theo assumed it was less from the fumes and more the sights. He walked over to her.

"Laura." She kept walking and pouring. He walked behind her, maintaining her pace.

"Laura," he said again. "Listen, I—"

"Do you need this other gas can?"

"No," he said. "I left a couple more by the door. I—"

"Should probably get going then." She snuffled again. "We don't know when those little fuckers'll be back." She moved away from him.

"Yeah," Theo said. "Yeah, I guess you're right." What else was there to say? Better to get it over with as quick as possible. He blew out an exasperated breath and walked back to retrieve the gas.

Theo grabbed the tanks and walked to the opposite corner from Laura. He did his best to not look at the people he was passing. One of them could be Steph. Steph who was ripped screaming from the window, the skin of her cheek the only reminder that she was ever there. One could be

(night to remember)

Marcia.

Reaching the far side of the room, he bent and unscrewed the cap from the tank. Everything was in slow motion.

He blew another breath.

"Okay," Theo said to himself, "let's do this."

♦♦♦

STASH AND MARCIA stopped at the doors that would gain them entrance to the second floor of Clarington High. Stash focused on getting his breathing and pulse rate to something near normal. "Concentrating on truckin' right," as he put it. Marcia took the time to press her face to the cool glass in an attempt to see down the hallway. It brought back the memory of Steph in the caf, but with effort she pushed it back down.

There was no sense in thinking about that. She couldn't help Steph anymore. She had to worry about herself and Stash now.

Seeing nothing in the gloom down the hall, she cracked the door as quietly as she could. She didn't hear anything out of the ordinary. That was a good sign, wasn't it?

"C'mon, Bobby. Let's get you in the class so you can rest." She wasn't whispering, but she kept her voice low enough that it stayed between the two of them. Stash's response was to limp toward the class.

They crossed the hallway, Marcia feeling like one of those targets at the circus arcade. *Hit a lame duck, win a stuffed bear.* With her hand on Stash's lower back, she gently propelled him toward the door.

"Be careful of the windows. Don't look at them."

"What are you gonna do about them, Marce?"

"The windows all have curtains. I'm going to shut them. Hopefully it'll be good enough."

They entered the room, their eyes squeezed shut. Marcia left Stash near the door and headed over to the far wall where the windows were. Navigating was an exercise in blind faith and memory—an exploration by finger and shin. She remembered the basic layout of the room, having had classes here before, but this was a whole different ballgame.

She remembered a game she used to play as a kid. Her backyard went back quite a ways before ending in a white picket fence that her dad lovingly painted every three years. There were two big trees inside the fence. The game was to stand near the patio doors of the house and close her eyes. She would then try and walk a straight line to the back fence, avoiding the trees.

In the dozens of times she tried it, she had never been able to walk a straight line, or make it to the fence without cracking open one eye for at least a second, just to get her bearings.

Now, in the classroom, she had no choice.

And what if there are those little dog-beasts from the caf in here? Oh God, what then?

Marcia felt her flesh creep at the thought of one of them hiding under a desk, just waiting for her to walk by. She remembered hearing that, sometimes, when a shark bites, it happens so suddenly, so efficiently, that the victim doesn't even feel it at first. Maybe the thing would just take a snap at her and she wouldn't feel it until she went to put her foot back down and found it gone, realizing only when her bloody stump impacted on the dirty floor, the bone grinding into the linoleum…

She let out a sound, like clearing her throat, almost involuntarily, but mostly from nerves.

Oh Lord, stop it! You're gonna drive yourself nuts doing this!

Her outstretched hands touched the cool, painted concrete wall. *Thank you, God!* She slid to her right to find the corner of the room where the pull cord would be hanging. There! She pulled it and listened carefully. She couldn't tell if the curtain was sliding toward her, or away. She gave a longer pull. Definitely toward her—the wrong way. She pulled the loop in the other direction and heard the sound of small plastic rollers on aluminum, the curtains sliding closed.

That was one. Now she had to go to the back of the class for the other one.

"Bobby? How you doing?"

Silence.

"Bobby? BOBBY?"

♦♦♦

TRY AS HE might, Theo could not help but pick out familiar faces, all beseeching him with wounded, terrified eyes.

Ann Marie and her brother Charlie (who insisted on calling himself Chas). He was a guy you knew would simply be a fuck-up all his life. A guy who would end up in a dead-end job that he'd invent some stupid, impressive-sounding name for. Sanitary engineer for garbage man, that sort of thing. Ann Marie would always be embarrassed by her association with Chas. She would always try to overachieve to make up for his failure, as though her successes would balance his boners. But her overachievements would backfire, leaving the impression that she was fussy and too particular. High maintenance.

Sparky, the stereotypical nerd: thick glasses, skinny form, tousled hair with more than a hint of dandruff, but possessing a keen knowledge of...something. Science, electronics, classical music. Who the hell knew? Very few. Maybe the teachers, who would use any latent ability to assist in, say, the sound booth for the musical, something like that. But rarely would that knowledge or assistance gain him any recognition. But he would take any crumb they would throw, craving any approval he could get.

Bob and Anna. Both shared the same nickname—Bobanna. The most tempestuous relationship in the school, prone to fiery outbursts at drinking parties, usually over some perceived—but usually incorrect—alcohol-fuelled indiscretion. They were slated for marriage right after graduation. That meant one of two things: a messy breakup in their final year of high school as one of the Bobannas developed cold feet, or they would manage to hold it together with enough spit and tissue to go through with it, only to divorce within a year or two. A messy breakup either way. Billy Joel's "The Ballad of Brenda and Eddie" all over again.

Ralphie, one of those high-profile students. Not too bright intellectually, but he excelled at extracurriculars—both in and out of school. Always a lead in the musical, always dating one of the more popular girls then moving to the next. He would remain friends with the previous ones, though, in a case of mutual understanding that they may need each other later on if one fell out of favour. A hard drinker, he nevertheless had enough friends around to bail him out. He never really got into serious trouble. High school would be his peak. He would end up some store manager in a mall somewhere, marry someone much further down the social ladder than he ever would have accepted in high school, and fade into obscurity.

Gerry. The lovable loser, just clumsy enough to be viewed as funny but not clumsy enough to be stupid. He was the one who started with the teenage drink/party/sex life later than most of his peers, so fell victim to pranks usually played on teens one or two years younger. He would be the one who could not hold his booze and throw up on a treasured rug or bedspread, leaving the host with a lot of cleanup and explaining to do. But it wouldn't be a normal throw up. It would be one of almost biblical proportions that it would go down in the history books of the local teens. It would become mythical. "There was this guy that used to go to this school who threw up so much/so far/so high..." He would be the one who would decide this was not what he wanted his legacy to be and better himself after escaping the town. He would become a respected and successful citizen. One described as having roots in the community. He would rarely talk of his teen years, except as a lesson in the dangers of excess.

Theo walked by them all, flashing on his times with each, the interactions he had had with each. And as their past and once-future lives passed before his tear-filled eyes, he became more and more lost.

They would have no future, all these people. Their lives were ending. Theo and Laura and the Toad were going to be responsible for the end of their lives. All those possibilities, gone. Futures washed away like the most grandiose sandcastles at high tide.

All this death. All this death on our hands.

His tears ran unchecked down his face and fell into the gasoline, where they would have no effect on the coming flames.

All his tears were useless. They could not save these people.

♦♦♦

LAURA WAITED AT the entrance as Theo emptied the last of his second can. The smell of gasoline was overpowering. The moaning sounds were less now. From exhaustion or anticipation, Theo didn't know.

The Toad came up to them. He looked at the ground, avoiding both the room and their eyes. "Is it...did you...?"

"It's ready, bud. We just have to light it."

Without a word, the Toad's hand came up, palm out. A book of matches sat there, waiting to be used.

Theo took them from the Toad's sweating palm and looked at them, like he'd never seen

(close cover before striking)

matches before.

He heard Laura as if from far away. "I'll do it," she said.

Theo's voice seemed equally distant as he answered.

"No..." Theo said. "No. I got it."

Flipping the cover of the matchbook as he walked back into the caf and to the nearest structure, Theo pulled the little cardboard stick from the bundle. Numb fingers manipulated the match to the scratchpad. He succeeded only in breaking the tip of the match off.

Theo pulled a second match.

Scratch.

Nothing.

Scratch again.

Nothing again. *Fucking dud.*

Off to his right, a moan.

Fuck.

Fuckfuckfuckfuck.

Another moan.

"I'M DOING THE BEST I FUCKING CAN, OKAY?"

His hands shook as he pulled the third match. He went to flip the book and dropped it. Other hands picked it back up.

"Theo. I'll do it."

Theo looked up into the Toad's—Dennis's eyes. There was a look there—a determination—that Theo had never witnessed before. It was dark in here, but the Toad was holding it together. No popping weasels. Hell, he was holding it together a lot better than Theo right now.

"Okay bud." Theo tossed the offending match away with a shaking hand. "It's all yours."

Theo walked out the cafeteria doors, a scratching sound whispering behind him. It sounded damn close to the claws of the little hell-rats on flooring. As Theo approached Laura, there was a loud extended *WOOOOMPH* and a hot wind that blew their hair around.

The Toad came stomping up seconds later, grinning ear to ear. "I did it!" he said. "I feel like the Human Torch! FLAME ON!"

That idiot smile only lasted until the wailing started again.

CHAPTER SEVENTEEN

STASH STOOD JUST outside the door to Corrigan's class, his back to the cool concrete. He was so thirsty. He couldn't stop thinking about the half a can of 7-Up he had tossed at lunch because he didn't have time to finish it. He would have killed for that half a can now.

He listened as Marcia bumped and banged her way to the curtains. He had almost broke down and told her how he'd felt about her. How he had felt about her for so long. How he dreamed about her, how he had wanted to go out with her for so damn long. But Theo and Crouch had always beaten him to the punch. *But they can't do that anymore.*

And that had stopped him. The guilt of using two of his best friend's deaths as an opportunity to get in with Marce. He wasn't going to remind her of two dead boyfriends.

Still, she seemed to be doing okay—not great, but okay. She had a lot of balls to be going into a room with her eyes closed. Stash didn't think he could ever enter a room feeling safe again. Not after what he had seen. Not after Crouch. He had looked like he had been run through a paper shredder. When Stash first saw—

What was that noise?

It came from down the hall, and it didn't sound like the nasties.

He could take a short hop down the hall for a looksee, couldn't he? Besides, there was a water fountain just around the corner. His thoughts seemed to come at him all scrambled. Like opening the box on a jigsaw puzzle, the entire picture was there, but it was jumbled. Somewhere in the back of his head he was aware of this and felt he should be worried, but mostly he was too overstressed to do more than just sit back and enjoy the ride, and too thirsty to think of much beyond getting a drink.

The thought of the water fountain galvanized him, made him feel funny. He was so thirsty! The thought of water washing over his dry, thick tongue and sliding down his constricted throat…oh Christ! It would almost be better than sex. His body did a quick piss-shiver dance and he knew he needed that water. He would go and check out the noise and get a long, cool drink of water. A drink and a look. He could do that. Surely he could do that.

Just a quick look.

A drinky-drink and a looky-loo.

He squeezed his eyes tight and stuck his head just inside the door.

"I'm just going around the corner for a drink, all right?" He kept his voice low, just in case other ears were listening. At least, he thought it was low. Hell, in his current state, he might be yelling, or just mouthing the damn words. But he thought he heard a response—almost a grunt—and took it as approval. He knew Marcia was deep in concentration and didn't want to bug her.

Using the wall to take the weight off his bad foot, he shuffled and slid along until he came to the spot where the wall began to curve. He cautiously pulled his head out and looked down the hall as far as he could. It wasn't very far, considering the curve and the darkness. Like looking down a deep, dark well.

A well full of water.

Water.

The fountain was just past the angle of the wall. It sat there, snug against the wall, its cool white porcelain curves beckoning him with the promise of pleasure. It invited him like a lover.

"Put your hands on me. Touch me, make me gush. I'll give you anything you want. Oh yes." Stash's eyes began to water as he slid along the wall, hardly able to control his shaking until he could reach it.

Oh, this is gonna be so damn good.

"Anything you want."

A nice shot

"Oh yes. Yes!"

of cool wat –

What the fuck?

He turned the knob on the side of the white porcelain but no water came. He caught the sound of gurgling from deep down, made transistor-radio tinny by the distance travelled through the pipes.

"No." Stash's eyes watered up. "No," he repeated.

No fucking water today. *Yes, we have no bananas,* he thought stupidly. He felt like crying. He felt like yelling and stamping his feet. He wanted to have a temper tantrum. But he didn't do it. No, Robert Bostash, the perfect son, the perfect friend, the perfect student, kept it together.

He was about to turn back and see how Marcia was making out. Anything to take his mind off the fucking he had received at the water fountain. He looked at the fountain one last time, the virgin white picking up some unseen highlight.

"Next time, kiss me first before you fuck me like that."

But then he heard the sounds again. Human sounds.

He was sure of it.

They were coming from the next class down the hall. A furtive whispering, like there were several people involved in a frantic discussion at low volume.

He slid along the wall, the damnable fountain almost forgotten, his passage making dull, hollow noises on the lockers, like secrets pounding against the metal to get out.

♦♦♦

THEO COULDN'T STAY there any longer. He couldn't listen to that horrifying sound again.

He watched as the Toad's face ran through a series of emotions almost too fast to follow. He had just sealed the fate of thirty-odd classmates.

"Laura, let's go find Mr. Popper," Theo said, knowing she didn't want to hear the wailing any more than he did. He figured mentioning Popper's name would kick her into gear. The Toad looked like he would take any excuse.

It only took a few steps down the hall for them to clue in that they had way too much equipment to get upstairs.

"So, what are we going to do with it?" Laura asked.

After a quick debate, they decided to load it all into the boys' washroom down the hall where they had stashed Stash. Theo thought it would be safer out of sight, out of reach from the fire in the caf, and away from those big-ass teeth

(wind-up dentures)

with legs. It gave them a chance to check on Stash at the same time.

He thought about checking on Stash after mentally kicking his own ass for forgetting the poor bastard all this time. *How the hell do you forget a friend like that?* he wondered. *Fuck, I'm an asshole.*

They pushed the dolly the short distance through the lobby to the washroom. Theo opened the main door.

"Oh Jesus! Stash! Oh Jesus Christ!"

The desk had been moved.

"Aw shit, Stash, no."

Theo pushed the desk to one side, grabbed the handle to the inside door and pulled. He didn't care what was waiting for him inside.

"I'll kill you fuckers! I'm gonna fuckin' kill every fuckin' one of you!"

But his threats bounced off empty tile and porcelain. There was no one in the room at all.

Laura came up behind Theo.

"Stash's gone, Laura."

She swept a light around the room.

"Theo, there's very little blood. His foot was torn up, right?" Theo nodded, his eyes still searching the room as though he might have missed Stash somehow, that he was still here.

"Okay, so if his foot was torn up, there would be some blood. You set him over there, right? So there's some blood. But not a lot. They didn't come in and shred him like they were trying to do to me."

"So maybe he's in the caf," Theo said.

That seemed to catch her off guard. She hadn't considered it.

"No…no, I didn't see…he wasn't…"

"I didn't really

(liar liar caf's on fire)

look at anyone either. I just poured the gas and left," Theo said.

"No, he couldn't have been in there," Laura said, worry creeping into her voice.

"Yes, he could. Why couldn't he? Jesus Christ, Laura! Those monsters were looking for as many fucking wet holes as they could find! And I left him right here, right out in the open! Why was I so fucking stupid?"

"Theo—"

"NO!" he roared. "I did this! I'm responsible! We were sitting under those goddamn lights getting all warm and fuzzy with each other and Stash was getting…aw jeez…he was…"

Theo dropped to his knees. Laura placed her hands on his shoulders.

"Don't take this all on yourself, Theo. There's two more of us here that should have thought to help him too. *I* should have thought of Tom a lot sooner than I did!"

"But he was my best friend. He wouldn't have forgotten me."

"And you didn't forget him, either. Theo, look what's happened to all of us today! We needed downtime to regroup. None of us are thinking straight."

Theo looked up at her as the Toad came through the outside door.

All these people dead. Steph dead. Crouch dead. Stash dead. Marcia dead. All dead.

"Not thinking straight," Theo said. "No shit."

♦♦♦

WHERE IN GOD'S name has he gone?

Marcia finished up with the last curtain, ensuring it was closed before opening her eyes.

When she was sure she was going to keep down whatever contents were left in her stomach, her next thought was that her chest was killing her. She let out her breath in a whoosh, not realizing she had been holding it so long. Her breathing slowed to normal, but her heart continued to thud.

Where in God's name has Bobby gone?

She looked around, blinking stars away, some seeming to pulse in time with her heartbeat. Had her eyes really been closed that tight? Yes, they probably had.

Bobby. Where was he? Where had he gone. And why?

She sprinted the length of Mr. Corrigan's classroom and stopped at the door, one hand on the frame. She took one more glance around the class, ducking low to see under the level of the desktops. Bobby definitely wasn't there.

Marcia turned back to the hall and looked out, hoping he was just outside the room. No such luck.

Where would he go?

She eyed the stairs briefly, but she was sure he wouldn't have gone that way. He was too weak.

In fact, she was sure that he had gone of his own volition, just because he would have cried out if something had attacked him. But then again, wouldn't he have said something if he was going somewhere?

What if he had? What if she hadn't heard him?

Stop with the what-ifs! What if you just sat here not doing anything?

It was enough to get her moving again. She exited the class and turned left, down the darkened hallway. The washrooms were to her right. Maybe he went in there.

She crossed the hall to enter the boys' washroom. Her palm pressed flat on the door to push it open, but it jerked back when she heard Bobby's voice. Slurring and thick, almost as though he was drunk—and she had seen him drunk many times—but definitely Bobby's voice.

"Marce. Over here. There's people."

Marcia looked down the hall and saw Stash's head stuck out of Miss Helmsley's English class. He had a big dopey grin on his face and beckoned with his free hand.

♦ ♦ ♦

THEY LOADED EVERYTHING into the washroom. Again, Theo said nothing through the operation, only glancing a few times at the blood staining the tiles. Once that chore was done, they armed themselves with a couple of flashlights each, and the small blowtorch.

Theo stuffed the flashlights into the pockets of his jeans, looked at the drying blood on the floor one last time, and said, "All right, let's go get Mr. Popper." His tone said he was not going to let what happened to Stash happen again.

Then, cautious as hell, they started up the stairs to the third floor.

♦♦♦

"BOBBY! YOU SCARED the heck out of me! What are you doing?" She moved down the hall at a quick jog. Stash ducked back into the classroom and Marcia followed him. "What's going on?"

The classroom was so obviously Helmsley's room. The books and author's photographs and illustrations. The quotes on the walls and the windows. It looked to Marcia that these quotes had saved them from the stomach-churning void outside.

Saved by literature. Who could have guessed?

Over in the corner, Miss Helmsley sat with a beefy arm wrapped around the necks of two students. It looked like some dumb move from one of the cheesy wrestling shows the Toad watched. Miss Helmsley didn't seem to notice that her too-tight miniskirt was hiked up far enough to see her lack of underwear. It was thankfully murky in the dark room, but still quite obvious. Marcia looked away in distaste. Her mother always said dirty girls didn't wear underwear.

(did you at least leave your bra on?)

Stash didn't seem to notice.

"What happened here?" Marcia asked.

"I don't know," Stash slurred, his eyes heavy-lidded. "I just came in and saw them, then I heard you in the hall."

Miss Helmsley's face was feral, like a rabid cat. Her voice was low and grumbly, like she hadn't talked in a while. Her teeth showed when she talked. As though she snarled the words.

"Get me out of here. Now."

This image of Helmsley contrasted sharply with the usually smiling, heavy-set woman with the nervous giggle who did more to advertise her insecurity about her weight than all the clothing with vertical lines that she wore. Vertical lines "slimmed" the full-figured woman, according to Miss Helmsley, though she tended to describe herself more as "Rubenesque" in the personal ads she placed in the big city newspapers. She thought no one knew, though several of the students had sent her bogus responses back as a joke.

From the angle of the grip, Stash and Marcia could not figure out who the two unfortunate headlocked students were.

Then Marcia noticed the creamed-corn and mushroom-soup trails that sputtered across the classroom floors and desks. They told the tale of two people desperately trying to block out the sights peeking through the dialogue covering the windows.

Marcia got a mental image of Helmsley as a short, nasty Sumo dragging the students to their tasks. "Do it or I lift the skirt again!" she would say in her best dirty-girl voice. Marcia's stomach rolled and she thrust the image away.

"Miss Helmsley," Marcia said, "why don't you let go of the students?" The kids seemed strangely calm. They might have been sitting in that position for hours now. Marcia moved deeper into the room to see if she could help them.

"DON'T COME ANY CLOSER! NO CLOSER!" Miss Helmsley yelled. *"I DON'T TRUST ANY OF YOU!"*

Marcia and Stash stopped, twin expressions of disbelief on their faces.

"GET AWAY! AWAY, I SAID!"

Stash moved to sit down on one of the desktops, his leg obviously causing him pain.

"NO YOU DON'T!" Miss Helmsley screeched, her voice like a nail on the side of a car. *"DON'T YOU SIT SO CLOSE! OVER THERE! OVER THERE!"*

Miss Helmsley whipped her head viciously to the left in the direction of the far end of the class, her jowls jiggling like Jell-O. Marcia and Stash backed off, scared that her heavings and jerkings were going to break the students' necks.

"WHAT DID YOU KIDS DO TO THE OUTSIDE?" she continued. *"I PUKE WHEN I LOOK OUT THERE!"*

Stash was getting visibly agitated, whether from the volume or the near-madness Marcia didn't know.

"Please Miss Helmsley," Marcia said, "please keep it down."

"I CAN'T KEEP ANYTHING DOWN, GODDAMN IT!" Helmsley hugged the students tighter, drawing them in under her heaving breasts. Their arms flopped about as though trying to fly from her clutches. *"MY STOMACH'S ROLLING LIKE A BINGO-BALL SPINNER!"*

Marcia saw Stash crack a slight grin. She knew Miss Helmsley was a big bingo player at the local church hall. From what Marcia's mom said, Miss Helmsley's pointed lack of undergarments had boosted the participation of the male population at the old folk's home. She remembered the Toad referring to them as "taco watchers." It apparently disgusted the Toad's mom, but it sure didn't seem to curb her visits any.

"Okay, Miss Hel—"

"DON'T YOU TALK DOWN TO ME, LITTLE MISS!" Helmsley's large frame wiggled and shook as she bellowed. Her captive students had seemingly given up on ever escaping her chubby clutch. *"I KNOW WHEN I'M BEING TALKED DOWN TO, AND I WON'T STAND FOR IT! NO! NOT AT ALL! IT'S MOST DEFINITELY NOT APPRECIATED!"*

Marcia's hands made placating gestures as she spoke. "I was just going to ask you to lower your voice a bit."

If anything, that statement had the opposite effect.

"DO NOT TELL ME WHAT TO OH MY GOD WHAT'S THAT?"

That was two of the little demons with all the teeth who had just strolled in as though they were checking out a new café. It was the first time Marcia had seen one up close. The sight of them reminded her of how they'd gone for Hassy's face and made her feel like she was going to pee her pants.

Marcia was scared stiff—literally not able to move. She couldn't even breathe. She knew what these things were capable of. Her eyes darted to Stash. He seemed frozen, too. She knew he had his own reasons to be afraid.

Miss Helmsley was a complete contrast to Stash and Marcia—she went completely over the top, bellowing at the top of her ample lungs as she maneuvered her tree trunk legs under her—giving Marcia another unwanted peek at her murky privates—and hefted herself to her feet.

Her unwilling passengers didn't struggle. They didn't move. They looked like Raggedy Ann dolls.

Oh Lord, they're dead!

Questions whizzed through Marcia's head almost too quick to register. *Did Helmsley kill them? Who are they? Why won't Helmsley let them go?*

Questions. But no answers.

As soon as Miss Helmsley got to her feet, the toothy beasts only had eyes for her. With no hesitation, they accelerated down the space between the desk rows.

Helmsley saw them coming and she pitched first one, then the other, ragdoll student. Cynthia. Then Moose. As the creatures skittered over the bodies, Marcia saw purplish bruises under their eyes. Moose's tongue hung out like he was trying to catch a taste of one of the scampering demons ripping over his face.

The demons paid the bodies no attention as they lunged for the wildly flailing Miss Helmsley. Her arms pinwheeled like a cellulite windmill, any sounds from her mouth reduced to shrieks.

Then they leaped on her, digging into her flesh, clawing their way up, their teeth gnashing at her calves, her thighs, her stomach, her breasts.

Marcia's eyes teared up, then she found herself shoved violently toward the door. She opened her mouth to scream, but she couldn't. She couldn't yell, she couldn't breathe. She looked back and Stash pulled his hand away from her mouth.

"Go," he mouthed.

She went, hauling him behind her. They'd almost reached the door when their exit was noticed. Miss Helmsley still stood, quivering and squealing as they ate her alive. Her movements seemed to go unnoticed by the feeding creatures.

Lunch on the run, Marcia thought.

One demon paused, a large, shiny red slab of flesh dangling from its mouth, and made a low growl at them. The other stopped, pulling its head out, dripping and gore-caked, from a particularly large hole it had created in Miss Helmsley's neck. Blood gouted unnoticed as it turned and prepared to spring at Marcia and Stash.

"Marce! Run!"

They bolted for the door and Stash pulled it closed behind him just in time to hear a muffled thump of a small body impacting on the other side. His hopping threw him off-balance and he dropped to the floor. Marcia did a quick scan of the hallway, but didn't see any other demons. Turning back to Stash, she noticed his leg bleeding again. *How had he run on that?*

"Bobby, let's get back to Corrigan's room. I'm right behind you."

She hefted Stash to his feet and pushed him back the way they had come. Watching to make sure he was going, she then crossed the hall to the janitor's station, grabbed the mop soaking in the grey water, and quickly mopped the thin jagged line of blood that Stash was trailing. She didn't know if these things operated on smell or not, but she wasn't taking any chances. No stupid moves.

Marcia quickly worked her way backward to Corrigan's classroom, made one last, quick check for any missed spots, cleaned the area around the door, and threw the bloody mop back out into the hall. She wouldn't keep it in the room with them.

She shut the door quietly. Only then did she allow herself to breathe again.

Sinking to her knees, Marcia clamped a hand to her mouth to keep the sobs in. Moose and Cynthia! Stash had parked himself on a desk and had his head down, arms wrapped around it as though to shut out the world.

Horrible sounds assaulted them from the next room over. Feeding noises.

Stash's voice was soft and muffled as he spoke.

"Now what?" he asked.

CHAPTER EIGHTEEN

THEIR MOVEMENTS WERE echoey and seemed overloud in the darkened concrete-and-metal stairway. The Toad put his hand on the stair railing and quickly pulled it away, as if burned. He wasn't far off.

"Fuckin' thing's so cold it hurts!" he said, popping his fingers in his mouth. The entire stairway was rimed with a light dusting of frost. *Colder than a walk-in freezer,* Theo thought. Their breath fogged as they huffed up the stairs.

The group heard noises from the second floor, decided they weren't human noises, and kept climbing.

They reached the third and final floor and stopped to listen. All seemed reasonably safe for now. Theo hooked one of the flashlights on the handle of the door and pulled. He figured the door handle would be just as cold as the railing was and he didn't want to leave

(steph's hand and face peeling off on the window leaving)

layers of his skin behind.

They entered the hallway on the third floor at the northernmost end. From here, it curved off to the left. Normally, from this vantage, both the boys' and girls' washrooms and the door to Mr. MacNamee's English class could be seen, as well as the dull orange lockers following the curve of the hall.

Only, today, things had changed.

"Looks like someone redecorated with a wrecking ball," said the Toad.

He was referring to the boys' washroom, or rather, the hole where there used to be a door that displayed a Gumby-like figure indicating the male species could relieve themselves inside.

All that remained was a rampage of twisted metal and chunks of concrete. They had seen this sort of entrance before.

The door to the caf now looked like this. They approached the opening with caution.

"What in the *hell* happened here?" Laura wondered aloud.

"That hole's about the same size as that big black fucker—"

"Swlabr," said the Toad.

"—as Swlabr. He came through here," Theo said.

"What, it had to take a monster piss?" said the Toad.

"No. Actually, it looks like Swlabr came *out* of here," Laura said. "Look…see how the rubble is all sort of blown outward from the door? That makes me think it broke out of the room, not in." Her flashlight beam swept outward, indicating the direction.

"Yeah, right. That thing just showed up in a third-floor shitcan. Sure it did."

"Okay, Dennis," Theo said, "you're so fuckin' smart. Y'know what? It doesn't really matter *where* it showed up, does it? I wanna know *how* it showed up. And *why*."

"So?" Laura asked. "Who goes in this time?"

♦♦♦

MARCIA TURNED TO Stash.

The poor bastard panted like a dog. Tears stood in his eyes as he raised his head. His hands shook. Blood seeped from his shredded foot. He was in bad shape.

"Now what?" he repeated. Marcia had no answer for him. Instead, she changed the subject, partly due to desperation, partly due to how Stash looked.

"Are you okay?" she asked, knowing he wasn't.

"No, Marce," was the reply. "I'm really not okay."

She knew he was worse off than he looked then. For Stash to admit any substandard grade was unheard of.

"You in pain?"

"Yeah. Foot's hurtin' bad. I thought it'd be numb with this thing Theo put on, but it hurts. Walkin' too much."

Marcia bit her lip. If they were ever going to make it out of here, Stash had to be mobile. There was no way she was going to leave him behind.

She chewed so hard at her lip that a large chunk of skin ripped off and she started bleeding. She licked at it, then pressed a cool finger to it to stem the blood. She felt the dull, salty throb under the pad of her finger.

She knew what she had to do. She just didn't want to do it.

C'mon girl, make a decision! Poop or get off the pot!

Stash seemed to forget she was there as he stared off into space. He was zoning out.

Or he was going into shock. She had heard the term but had no idea what someone in shock looked like. And she wanted to be a nurse. Cripes, she couldn't even help the one person in her care right now!

She looked back to Stash's trembling hands.

Yes, she could help him. She could!

And she would.

"Bobby, I'll be right back. Don't go anywhere."

"I ain't movin', swear to god." He made a feeble attempt at crossing his heart, but missed totally, not really getting his hand much higher than his belt.

She noticed the tremble in his voice as he said, "Where you goin'?"

"I'm going to raid Danika's locker. She's got some migraine pills. I'm going to get them for you." She reached down and took off her shoes, leaving on her socks.

"Isn't she…other end of hall?"

Marcia's throat constricted, her voice tight as she answered. "Yeah."

"Bring back…7-Up."

"Yeah, Bobby," she said, carefully closing the door behind her. "No prob."

Out in the hall she stopped all motion, willing her breathing and heartbeat to silence as she listened for the demons. There were still noises coming from Helmsley's class. As bad as that was, it was good. It meant they were occupied. She would creep past the door and hit Danika's locker. If she had to, she would go up to the third floor, cross the hallway, and come back down the south stairs to avoid them. In fact, that sounded like a great idea. God knows she was good at going above the things. She'd already done it once. This one would be a cakewalk.

Moving with exaggerated care, she began her silent trek down the hall.

♦♦♦

THE WASHROOM REMINDED him of a sewer, dark and damp. Theo was sick and tired of dark and damp. It smelled of piss, sweat, and toilet mints. But underneath it all ran a familiar coppery smell.

Theo's feet made splashing noises on the ceramic tile floor. With all the damage, the flashlight cast large shadows behind the concrete remains, like a full moon on a graveyard. Theo couldn't see worth shit and he stumbled over rubble. He angled left, where the urinals should have been. A couple remained on the wall, but the bowl part was missing. The broken porcelain glittered in the beam of Theo's flashlight like big, broken teeth.

To his right, where the bathroom stalls used to be, it looked like a giant hand had flattened them against the wall. All the toilets were gone, pulverized into dust. Nothing left but the holes in the floor.

"What's going on in there?" The Toad's voice sounded tinny as it echoed off the walls.

"Nothing, man. Place is trashed."

"Is this where the thing came from?"

"Who the fuck knows? All I'm sure of right know is I'm about ankle deep in piss."

Laura was saying something else, but Theo cut her off. "Hold up. I see something. Give me a sec."

Theo could see a shape. The only reason it stood out in the moist semidarkness was that it had a less jagged outline. Amid the carnage of broken concrete and twisted metal, this shape was smoother, more organic.

It looked somewhat human.

Theo moved over to the shape. It was against the wall where the sinks had been. One of the four mirrors that used to occupy the wall above those sinks remained surprisingly intact and it reflected the beam of his flashlight at weird angles.

As he approached the shape, Theo became more confused. It *looked* human, but not completely. The other thing messing with his senses was the fact that the shape seemed suspended in mid-air.

There's gotta be some sort of ledge or shelf or something, Theo thought, even though he had been in this washroom many times. There was no shelf. No ledge.

Fuck. It's floating.

"What's happening?" the Toad asked, making the light in Theo's hand jig in surprise. His voice was distant and it echoed in the darkened washroom.

"Jesus! Shut up and give me a minute here!"

"Okay! Shit! Don't get your panties in a knot, fer chrissakes!"

But Theo wasn't hearing him anymore. The shape *was* human. Male. And it *was* in mid-air.

And it was a student. But then again, it wasn't.

Whoever it was, they were smashed up. But it went beyond that. They were *changed.*

The floating body was naked, yet parts of him seemed to be covered in a shiny black substance, almost like

(swlabr skin)

plastic, or an insect coating. There was now a large horn poking out of its forehead, just left of centre, like a drunken rhino. The face though…it was hard to tell in the beam of the flashlight, but damn…he sort of looked familiar. One eye rolled over to take in Theo, an eye that looked more like a cat's—the iris green and full, allowing no white to show, the pupil slashed instead of round—a demon eye.

Is it…?

This…thing's broken body was bent over almost double. He looked *folded.* But he wasn't bent at the waist. He was bent higher, around the bottom of his ribcage. And he wasn't bent forward—*he was folded backward!* His shoulder blades touching his buttocks, like he had a hinge on his spine at mid-back. Theo could see their stomach expanding and contracting as he took breaths, saw the spread of his ribcage, flowered out so there were inches between each rib as they arced around the unnatural backward bend. Some of the ribs had broken through the skin, gleaming yellowish under Theo's flashlight beam.

Sweet Jesus!

But worse than that were the things growing out of his genitals. Tentacles…no. No, that was the wrong word. Tendrils. Tendrils grew out of his groin and ass. They rose up and waved around, touching the walls, the ceiling, caressing his head, his chest, sliding over his ribs, exploring the immediate environment. They waved and swayed like seaweed. It made Theo want to puke. It made his stomach roll over.

Theo swallowed bile, closed his eyes, and took a breath.

Please please please.

Opened his eyes. Nothing had changed. The cat eye still watched him. It watched him. It breathed. Theo had to say something.

"Pete?" he said. "Peter Wilson?"

One or two of the tendrils scooted out as though to touch Theo. He was reminded of a television show he'd seen where a blind person "looked" at someone else by touching their face. He jumped back with a splash. No *fucking* way that was going to happen here.

"Pete?" he said again, this time with more edge in his voice.

"Who's there?" Peter said in a voice that was also changed. Lower, rumbling, like a warning growl from a guard dog. Theo saw Peter's stomach constrict sickeningly with the syllables.

"It's me, Pete. Theo. Theo Clarke." Peter's head rotated with the sound of his voice, like he was trying to locate Theo, tendrils waving. The eye never left him, but Theo realized Peter couldn't see him from that eye. *What's watching me?* he thought.

"Thelonious."

"Yeah, Pete. It's Theo."

"Why are you here?" Peter asked, his voice like concrete sliding on concrete. "How did you find me?" He sounded almost disinterested. *Maybe you'll tell me, maybe you won't. I won't care either way.*

"We're trapped here, Pete. Some fuckin' monster has us trapped in the school. And it's taken the school someplace…someplace else."

"Yes. Carcosa. Can you see the black stars?"

"Black st—are you talking about outside? We can't even look outside without puking. There's nothing there. Nothing."

"Perhaps we are closer to Azathoth's domain…the idiot dreamer's blank canvas."

"I don't know what the fuck you're talking about." He took a breath. "And right now, I don't give a shit. There's a big black thing that's—"

"My Demon."

"Your Demon." Theo stopped and took a breath, the information slowly rolling through his brain. "*Your* Demon!" *Pete's Demon?* Theo felt a thick, burning rage build in him.

"Peter," he said, and he didn't recognize his own voice.

"Yes, Thelonious?" The tendrils waved as though in a rapid underwater current. Theo reached out and grabbed a bunch, viciously yanking them.

"What the *fuck* did you do?"

CHAPTER NINETEEN

SURROUNDED BY THE delicate plinks of dripping water and weird echoes, Peter's tone was one of weariness, like he had lived far longer than he had ever anticipated. Like he had seen far more than he had ever expected. His tone ached of one who just wanted it all gone.

"It caught me when I was vulnerable. I was weak and it took advantage."

"What do you mean, 'vulnerable'?"

"I mean I was consumed with the idea of revenge. I was searching for the best method to murder my father."

That caught Theo. The casualness of how Pete tossed out that fact, yet it was something he knew. He knew because everyone in New Hope had heard of Stinky Pete's weird old man. About how he had gone bugshit after Peter's mother finally gave up and left. Theo's dad called him a "weird sumbitch."

Wasn't that the pot calling the kettle black?

"Yeah, I've heard your old man was kinda messed up."

"There were many incidents that defied reality," Peter said, that weariness scaling up a notch. "I doubt you could imagine..." After a thoughtful pause, that strange cat eye staring at him, unblinkingly, he said, "Then again, maybe you're the one person who *could* imagine."

Yeah, word got around. Theo knew people talked about his dad too. The town drunk who'd fuck his own mother if the hole was wet.

"Yeah, my dad ain't no angel, either." That made Peter laugh. A low, wet smoker's laugh, thick with clots. His stomach stretched and constricted obscenely.

"Is that why you invited me to poker? When was that?"

"Yeah, Pete, you looked like you needed a friend. That's why I invited you. Earlier today. It was for tonight."

"Yes…earlier today…hmph. Your request seems like ages ago, Thelonious."

"I know what you mean. Why did you say no? You looked like you wanted to come."

"Indeed I did. I was quite willing to give up my thoughts of revenge and throw in with your crowd. However something—I presume it must have been the Book, or possibly something behind the Book—stopped me. I never got to thank you for extending the hand of friendship, Thelonious. Please accept my gratitude now. I only wish I had been able to take you up on it. Now it looks like it shall never come to pass."

"So, you wanted to…what? Get a demon to kick your dad's ass?"

"Yes, the theory was to raise a demon who would then be indebted to me. My own genie in a bottle. Only this beast didn't look anything like that woman on the television show—"

"Barbara Eden," Theo said automatically.

"—yes, her. It was bigger than expected. And quite duplicitous, much like the Book that helped me summon it."

"We've met. The Toad named him Swlabr."

"Swlabr? Why?"

Theo made a face. Was this something he really wanted to explain right now? "It's a Toad thing. Long story. Don't ask. Do you know its real name?"

"Indeed. But it shouldn't be spoken. It's better that you don't know. Once you know it, it knows you. It can find you, wher*ever* you are." Theo didn't miss the emphasis, but didn't ask about it.

It sank in slowly—probably due to the unreality of talking to a thing...a person who he used to see slinking the hallways that now was so...not real—but Theo was only now starting to hear Peter's choice of words. His phrasing. This wasn't the normal New Hope patois. Peter didn't talk like Pete. Theo ignored it for now. He needed information.

"So what happened to you then?" he asked.

"I called and it came. I found the Book had not given me enough information." The tendrils jerked and snapped in the air. "It will do that, you know. Not *lie* to you, but hold back essential truths. I needed to know that I required a word of protection. I now know that something ensured the Book held that back, and...Swlabr...took advantage."

"You mean there's a word that will protect us?" Theo was excited. *One word? One magical word may protect us?*

"No. Not a word. A word. Of protection." Theo again heard the emphasis, that little *oomph* that Peter put on it. *Like the difference between* god *and* God, he thought. *Same word, same letters, but a whole different meaning.*

"So this word of protection...it's like a spell or something?"

"Yes, exactly so. A binding spell the summoner casts to bend the Demon to his will and protect him from harm. It didn't show me that."

"It it it! What the fuck is 'it'?"

♦♦♦

MARCIA PADDED DOWN the hall, her socks making only the barest of whispers on the fake granite tiles. She was more concerned with her breathing. Would she ever get it under control?

She approached Helmsley's door. The noises were more muted now, but still there. Wet noises. She heard a pop and jumped, clamping both hands to her mouth before a sound could emerge.

She imagined a bone being pulled from a socket, and had to stop. In the half a second the thought roiled in her head, she got a flash of an ivory bone, stained in places with red, as it pulled out of a grey cartilage-lined socket. That was enough, just that half-second glance. She would never be a nurse she decided, then and there.

I'll be happy flipping burgers at a McDonalds if I can just live through this. I swear to God, I will.

She kept going past the door, expecting it to fly open at any second and the two beasts to be on her, shredding and tearing…

Stop it!

She guessed she got lucky that Helmsley was the victim. With her size, it would take them longer to eat her. Then she felt guilty for being so selfish and cruel. *But with things so small, how could they possibly eat someone so large? Where does it all go?* Then she felt guilty for wondering about something so stupid when a teacher was being consumed not two car-lengths away from her. She banished all thoughts of Helmsley and tried to pick up the pace. She was getting sloppy, she could feel it. And she was going to make a mistake. She could feel that too.

Marcia stopped, pulled her blouse up, and wiped the sweat from her forehead. She closed her eyes, took a deep breath, and mentally reset herself.

Okay, let's do this, she thought.

♦♦♦

THEO TURNED AT the interruption. Peter's tendrils jerked in surprise at the sound, then reached out.

Theo had been so engaged in the conversation, he had not heard Laura and the Toad come into the room.

"Jesus Christ!" Theo said. "Don't sneak up on me like that! How long have you two been here?"

"Just before *I Dream of Jeannie,*" the Toad said. "What is this 'it' you keep talking about? 'It' caught you when you were weak. 'It' didn't tell all the truth. What the hell is 'it'? Some kind of book?"

"Thelonious? Who's there?"

"Who's—" the Toad started as he entered the lighted area. "Whoa! What the hell?" Catching sight of Peter, the Toad jumped backward, splashing through water and tripping over debris. Laura caught him before he landed on his ass.

"Toad!" she said. "Theo, what's going on?"

"Thelonious?" Peter repeated.

Laura saw him then. "Oh my god," she said.

"It's Peter Wilson," Theo said. The Toad stared at the waving tendrils. Theo leaned close to Laura and the Toad. "Stinky Pete," he whispered.

Laura took on an unreadable expression. The Toad likely would have puked if he'd anything left to give. *This isn't going to help his fear of the dark much,* Theo thought.

When they both appeared to have some semblance of control, Theo turned back and said, "Sorry, Peter. It's the Toad and Laura Davis, the art teacher."

Peter shifted a bit, his head lolling to one side. The cat's eye continued to scan the three of them. "Dennis. Miss Davis. I apologize for the situation that you're in. I'm afraid it's my doing." Again, Theo was struck with the realization that Peter had never talked like this. Hell, no one in the school talked like this except for Theo's whacked-out English teacher, Mr. MacNamee. And even he referred to his speech pattern as an "affectation."

"So you did this, Peter?" Laura asked. "I know why, but how?"

"Yeah, and what the hell is the 'it' you keep talkin' about?" the Toad added.

Peter's tendrils waved as leaves in the summer breeze. His voice, low and grumbly, took on a remorseful air. For some reason, Theo was reminded of Winnie the Pooh. *Oh bother.*

Winnie the Pooh with a cancerous smoker's rasp.

"The 'It' I refer to is the Book. And the Book allowed me…actually educated me and showed me how to call forth a Demon. The one you call Swlabr."

"So what are all those little shits with the teeth?"

"They are lower demons whose purpose is to act as Swlabr's eyes. He's blind. So they go out ahead of him, studying the area, looking for appropriate subjects, and of course, any threats, not that there is much in our world that can threaten a being of its power."

"Appropriate subjects?" Theo asked, flashing on the cafeteria.

"*Subjects* may be the wrong word. Vessels. Living bodies that can accept his seed. Once he enters a new environment, his essential purpose is to procreate, to multiply, to conquer the area, then procreate even more and conquer a larger area. More progeny for his father."

So they had been right. The bodies in the caf had been arranged for…what had Peter said? Procreation. Theo closed his eyes and took a breath. Procreation. Didn't matter how you wrapped it up, it still meant they were fucked.

Theo didn't have time to think it over any more than that. The Toad had splashed over to Peter and took two big fistfuls of those waving feelers drifting around his body. Peter shuddered, but made no sound.

The Toad was shaking. "You fuck. You stupid *fuck*! You wanted to grease your dad, so you brought this thing into our fucking school? Our school, Pete! Do you know how many people are fucking *dead* now? And the school is…fuck! I don't even know where the school is now, because every time we look out a window we puke our fucking guts out! Crouch is dead! Stash probably too! And all those guys in the caf…" His voice caught. Even in the darkness, Theo could see the tears standing in his eyes. The Toad released the tendrils with a violent motion.

"We had to burn all those guys in the caf…just to put them out of their misery."

The tendrils stopped waving abruptly. Had they hit a nerve? *What? What did he say?*

"You set fire to the Demon's vessels? Had the Demon got to them yet?"

"Yes, he must have. We had to take off under the stage to get away from him."

"Yeah," the Toad added. "Him and his rampaging hard-on."

Theo could almost see the thoughts as they skittered through Peter's mind. The tendrils would jerk, then stop, then jerk again. Even floating in mid-air, Peter seemed agitated. The cat's eye rolled, not fixing on anything. Peter's jaw muscles worked, bunched, worked some more. Then he took a breath.

"You are certain? He definitely got to those people before you burned them?"

"Yes yes yes!" the Toad snapped. "Asked and answered! What the hell's the problem?"

Theo was getting an edgy feeling and that same question came back at him.

Did we do the right thing? Did we?

"Peter," Theo said, "if you've got something to tell us, please, just tell us."

"If…Swlabr…got to them as you say, then their souls were already his. The burning did nothing to save them."

"What are you saying?" The Toad shook with a rage Theo had never seen in him before, his hands clenched into fists. Theo wasn't too far behind him.

The Toad's voice quavered, barely constrained. *"What the fuck are you saying, you fucking freak?"*

"I am saying that all those people are still conscious. His seed has been destroyed, however those people? They are still alive and they are trapped in the Demon's domain, feeling everything he has done to them…and all that you have done as well."

That horse pill took a few moments to digest. It was just too big to swallow all at once.

They're still alive? Steph? Randy? Marcia? All of them?

And still feeling all the pain they had been in before. Theo, Laura, and the Toad had just added to it, made it worse.

"They will experience the pain and horror for all eternity. The pain will always be fresh. It will never go aw—"

"Shut up." Laura begged.

"Oh Jesus," Theo said, his head dropping.

"You stupid goddamn motherfucking murdering asshole!" The Toad wailed. Theo had to hold him back, hooking his arms under the Toad's armpits and hauling the bigger boy backward.

Peter's voice was calm, like he was discussing the lunch menu. "You are right. As I said, the Book caught me when I was weak, confused, and It took advantage. It filled me with promises and delivered half-truths. I accept full responsibility. I am ashamed."

"So give us the goddamn book and let us send this fucker back where it belongs. Give us the book so we can release those souls."

"It would not work for you. I am the summoner—it was my duty to put the controls—the limits, if you will—on the beast. I failed and it now has free rein. It would take someone with a much higher magnitude of knowledge, skill, and ability to bring this beast down now. I do not have any knowledge of how to release the souls. I have extreme doubt that the Book would help you." Peter's tendrils twitched.

"As I said, the Book is not to be trusted. You can see my current state. Swlabr left me for dead. I used the Book to try and heal myself, to try and find a way to banish the Demon. I succeeded in getting myself to this state: blind, mutated."

"And floating," Theo said, still in shock.

"Yes. Each time, I believed the Book provided me with the answers I needed. Each time, I only succeeded in exacerbating the problem. The Book did allow me to heal myself sufficiently that I would not die, but ultimately, death would have been kinder."

"*The Monkey's Paw*," Theo said.

"What?" The Toad looked confused, jumpy. Maybe the dark was getting to him.

"*The Monkey's Paw*, Dennis," Laura explained absently, her mind far off. "It's a story where anyone can get a wish, but when their wish comes true it's not what they expected. It was a lot worse."

"Be careful what you wish for. You just may get it," Theo said.

"Exactly so," said Peter.

"Where is the Book?" Theo asked.

"You are better off without It," Peter replied. "It will not assist you. Do not trust It."

"Maybe we can't use It to kill Swlabr, or free those people, but maybe It can show us how to get home."

"The Demon will bring you home. When it finds a way to procreate, it will transport the school back from...this space, this time, and back to your own universe."

Your universe, thought Theo. *Not ours, yours. He doesn't even consider himself human anymore.*

"The Book, Peter. Where's the—"

Theo didn't need to complete the sentence. The Book rose from the ground behind Peter and purposely moved around his shattered body to stop in front of Theo. It hung there at chest level. It must have been sitting in the debris and water, yet It showed no sign of water or any other damage.

Peter seemed to sense the Book as It revealed itself. His voice rose, and his tendrils whipped around like a cat in stalk mode. *Snap snap snap.*

"You've found It, haven't you?" he said.

"Yeah, sort of," Theo replied.

"The Book has chosen you, Thelonious." His voice sounded resigned to the fact that Theo was the Book's new owner. "As It chose Talia. As It chose me."

"Talia?" Laura said. "Talia Davis? My niece?"

"Spooky Talia's your niece?" the Toad said.

Peter ignored them. "You may as well take It, as It will follow you until you do. But don't believe It. Don't listen to It. Destroy It if you can."

Theo reached out for the Book. Before his fingers could close on It, Peter began talking again, faster, like he had no time left.

"Please know that I never meant for any of this to happen. It was my dad—" and here was when Peter's voice changed, sounding slightly guttural, but more like Stinky Pete Wilson "—my fuckin' dad. He did this! Him and the Book. I never wanted to hurt anyone. Just him. I just wanted him to pay. I'm so sorry. I'm so—"

Theo's hands closed on the Book and ownership was transferred. Theo felt it as a tangible thing. Peter screamed as his self-imposed spells were twisted out of true and he was suddenly far more human again, still broken, the tendrils turning shit-brown and dropping off him like leaves in the fall. Peter was left to revisit all the pain of his original wounds from the Demon.

As the sounds throttled out from his tortured throat, Peter's neck corded like a stalk of celery, his body rigid and every muscle banded and rippled and threatened to break free of their straining host. His eyes bulged in their sockets, his nostrils flared to suck in more air to fuel his song of pain. The broken bones of his back ground and slid against each other, adding a crunching, cracking counterpoint to the high-pitched Siren scream.

Then, as suddenly as it came, it stopped, like a switch had been thrown. Peter's battered form ceased its trembling and thrashing. The upper half of his body rose to face the three survivors, the bones of his severed spine grinding like tectonic plates. Peter's eyes seemed to have a faint glow. He began to speak, but the sounds were coming too fast and too foreign to decipher. His tongue shredded as his teeth bit into them to produce the sounds required for this language of the dead. Blood flowed freely down Peter's neck and chest, shining blackly in the flashlight glare.

His head whipped around to face Theo, his teeth red and dripping and matted with chunks of his own mouth. "More friends will die at your hands." His head snapped to Laura, splashing her with blood and saliva. "You lack the courage to save the one who needs you most." Spinning to the frightened Toad, he spit, "You will profit from the Demon, does that please you?" He turned one more time to Theo. Grinning a horrible, blood-blackened smile, he said, "The wolves will steal something essential from you." Finally Peter leaned back, his vertebrae grinding horribly. He raised his arms like some biblical prophet addressing his flock of true believers. "And when you believe you have beaten all'Gueroth, he will rise again. Nyarlathotep will see to it." And then, with no warning, his broken body crashed to the floor of the washroom with a heavy splash, a small grunting noise escaping his lips as the air was punched out of his lungs.

As his body contacted with the water, the filthy liquid seemed to shiver and shy away from him before erupting in iridescent flames, as cold as they were beautiful. They consumed him in less than a second, then seemed to seek out new victims even as they burned down to nothing.

"Ah! Jesus!" The Toad yelped as the flames made tentative contact. "The fuck? I can feel it burning me on the inside." He punched Theo on the arm. "Dude! We gotta run!"

Theo didn't notice. His hands trapped the Book in a death grip. His head was thrown back and his teeth ground together in a rictus.

He began shaking, big body tremors that made the flaming water splash around his ankles, and through his clenched teeth a noise tore free, a sound somewhere between a moan and a whine, quickly building to a full-out Siren wail that made Laura and the Toad squint their eyes and hunch their heads into their shoulders in reflex. As bad as what had come from Peter's dying throat, this was worse.

He felt his body rise out of the water, his feet lift free from the filth. He knew he hung suspended in the air something like Peter had, but he didn't care.

Theo screamed like he was never going to stop.

CHAPTER TWENTY

PETER WAS SAYING something about being sorry, about not meaning to hurt anyone. Theo tried to listen, but the words, while familiar, came at him like agitated insects, leaving him hearing more of a low buzzing from Peter. Louder was the insistent whispering, a sibilant dull roar of sound. It had to be coming from the Book.

The Book fascinated and revolted him at the same time. It told him lovely, nonsensical things, as a mother coos to her baby to calm him.

~...iiiit'ssss aaaallll riiiight eeeevvvveryyyythiiiing iiiis aaaallll riiiight...~

Peter had said something about...

~...nooothiiiing'ssss gooooing toooo huuuurrrrt yooooou...~

Peter had said something about...what?

~...theeeere theeeere iiiit'ssss ooookaaaay...~

Theo's eyebrows bunched with the effort of concentrating on a single coherent thought.

~...doooon't...~

It was there, right there on the tip of his tongue. Don't...something. There and gone.

~...aaaallll riiiight iiii'llll prooootect yooooou...~

He really wanted to look inside the Book. It could help. It would save them. Theo could get them out of here.

~...nnnnooothiiiing wiiiillll haaaappen toooo yooooou evvvverythiiiing'ssss ooookaaaay...~

Theo really wanted to look in the Book.

But he didn't want to touch It.

♦♦♦

WHEN THEO WAS ten, he had a cat. His name was Dammit, the perfect name for a pet, as far as Theo had been concerned. *Come here, Dammit. Here's your food, Dammit.*

Dammit was probably the best friend he'd had up to that point in his short decade of life. Theo and Dammit would hang out together. Theo's father used to say the goddamn cat didn't need legs because Theo carried him everywhere.

Then there was the day Theo came home from school to find Dammit on the front lawn. He had been hit by a car and had died trying to crawl back home.

Theo didn't know what to do. He just stood over the cat, looking at his butterscotch fur, now matted with blood and dirt. Dammit's teeth were bared in death and his tongue lolled out.

Theo couldn't remember how long he'd stood there, staring down at his dead friend, but eventually he was aware of his dad coming up behind him.

"Stupid fucker went and got his ass killed, did he? Well, don't just stand there, he ain't gonna get himself off my yard. Get a goddamn garbage bag and get rid of him."

Theo stared at his father. He couldn't move. At ten, Theo didn't have the words to explain that he couldn't pick up his cat anymore. He couldn't tell him that this wasn't his cat anymore. It was a container that life had spilled from, and that, somehow, death had poured into.

At ten, Theo couldn't explain that it wasn't the absence of life, but instead it was the presence of death that overwhelmed him.

Now, as Theo stood staring at the Book, he had the same feeling again. There was a presence of death in this Book. It was filled to the brim with hurt and death and pain and suffering. Theo didn't have the words to adequately describe it at ten, and he still didn't, years later.

Theo just knew the Book was *wrong*, like when he saw pictures of Charles Manson. When Theo looked at the cult leader's eyes it was plain to see there was something *wrong*. It was the same, here and now.

Peter droned on about courage and or some damn thing, but the Book washed the words away before they could take hold in Theo's head. The Book whispered to him, enticing him to reach out. Theo fought this with everything he had. *I'm not going to touch It.*

He wanted to turn to the Toad, turn to Laura, get them to help him, but he couldn't. Couldn't turn his head.

Could only look at the damn Book.

With his gut, his heart, his head—hell, everything—telling him he was an idiot to do it, Theo reached out and took the Book.

Bad move. Seriously bad fucking move.

Theo had thought the screaming from the caf was bad. It was a lover's cry of pleasure compared to the wailing that tore its way from his fingers up to his head, ripping through flesh, slamming its way into his skull.

Every soul ever condemned to hell used this Book as a direct-dial to scream into Theo's brain. Every soul.

Every.

Soul.

There were thousands. Vampires. Werewolves. Demons. And humans. Thousands of humans.

Faces, people, lives rocketed across his mind.

Theo got fast glimpses of the events leading up to all these damned creatures' eventual demise. Death. Death in so many variations that he couldn't have even conceived. A how-to manual on getting into Hell.

And somewhere behind all of this, a dark thing, a Demon of a thousand names, a thousand forms, pulling the strings, manipulating the Book. Creating more death. More lives consumed.

Then, without warning, something changed in the parade of lives and deaths. Suddenly, Theo was seeing people he knew. Faces from school, people he had seen every day but didn't necessarily know. One, two, ten, faces he could identify, people he could name. More and more and more.

A young girl that he somehow knew was Talia's sister. Then her mother. Her father. Others.

Then he saw Crouch.

Then Hassy. Then Ann Marie. Then Chas. Sparky. Bob. Anna. Ralphie…others.

Then Steph.

He saw her burning. He heard her screaming. And then…

(are we doing the right thing?)

oh, and then…

(are we?)

then he realized the true and terrible horror…

Theo began to scream in chorus with all those maddened voices in his head.

♦♦♦

"THEO! THEO! WAKE the fuck up!"

He woke up coughing, soaked through to the skin. Looking around in panic, his eyes unable to fix on anything in the darkness, it was the splashing water behind him that gave him a clue as to where he was. Just outside of the washroom. Laura and the Toad were bent over him, concern in their eyes.

"What hap—" No, wrong question. Theo knew what had happened. And that was a place he didn't want to go back to yet.

"How long was I out?" Theo asked between coughs.

"Not long. Peter was talking, apologizing. Then you grabbed the Book and freaked out. You were shaking and screaming and Peter...I don't know...died maybe?...and dropped to the floor, then disappeared. And you kind of freaked and passed out." The Toad furrowed his brows. "Theo," he said. "Dude, there was friggin' fire – " and he raised his arm, seemed surprised there was no marks there " – and you actually rose *up.* Like, your feet left the water before you zonked out."

"By the time we got to you, you were on the floor, out cold."

The Toad reached down to Theo's left. "Was it the Book?"

"DON'T TOUCH THAT!"

He jolted back.

"Sorry, man. But I'm serious. You don't want to touch It. It ain't a normal book – It gets in here," Theo said, pointing to his head. "That's what made me freak." He wiped at something from his nose. Blood. It was fresh.

"What do you mean, 'gets in your head'?"

"Toad, bud, I know you've got some weird shit going down in your melon right now. 'Pop goes the weasel,' and all that stuff... "

The Toad blushed and turned away. Theo continued.

"...but seriously, the stuff that's in that Book is serious hardcore shit. I'm not demeaning anything you've gone through, honest, but...this is...dude, I think my mind was raped."

He looked like Theo had just burned him. Laura had a curious look on her face, trying to figure what Theo meant.

He didn't mean to bring up that stuff with the Toad. He didn't want to open that door. That was like picking a scab.

Damn! Theo had, in the past few hours, experienced a shitload of stuff. Stuff that he really didn't want to know. Stuff that he would never want to revisit again. Stash. The caf. The Toad. The hell-rats. Swlabr. But he knew somehow that he would. Theo would need to relive all of this again. All of this and more. If he was ever going to exorcise this stuff from his head, he would have to drag it out and sort through it.

"Look," Theo said. "Just take my word for it, guys. There's some bad kinda mojo goin' on with that Book. More than Peter let on. And I learned stuff from It that…well I'm not really ready to talk about it yet. I will, I swear to god. But please, not right now, okay? Not now. I can't."

"Nothing, Theo?" Laura said. "You can tell us nothing?"

He looked down at the Book, then looked back at them, doing his damnedest to make his face unreadable. "Let's just get out of here, okay?"

Nobody objected when Theo grabbed the Book. Maybe It knew how reluctant he was about taking It, because he just got a twinge, but no flash flood of images.

Thank Christ.

♦♦♦

THEY PICKED THEO up and stumbled over the wreckage in the hall outside the washroom, the beams of their flashlights swinging in crazy arcs over the walls of the hallway. Now that he was back among the living, Laura and the Toad shut the lights off to preserve the batteries. No one mentioned Peter. There was nothing to be done anyway, he was gone.

Theo didn't want to have any more to do with Peter. The legacy of the Book was enough, hell more than enough. It had gotten into his mind. And Theo was very scared of what his mind was going to cough up next.

I've been hit enough, let me up.

Theo did his best to ignore both the splash of the water that had seeped from the washroom and the tickle of the Book in his mind, like a nasty itch under a cast that can't be scratched. He said nothing to Laura or the Toad, and prayed that it would just go away. The Book was bad enough news. He didn't need the added worry of dealing with Stinky Pete Wilson and whatever hell he was in now. Carcosa. The chaotic realm of dreaming Azathoth. Wherever.

The hallway was still in that funky semidarkness that had been their nemesis since all the bullshit started, but after the washroom, it felt like they had stepped out into golden sunshine. It was weird, but a good weird. Just to be able to navigate without the flashlights lifted Theo's spirit.

The three battle-weary comrades continued down the hall in silence. The silence was, in part, because they were being cautious as hell, but part of it was trying to get hold of the thoughts swirling and roiling in their heads like a storm-tossed ocean. No one seemed too interested in talking.

Following the long, slow arc of the hallway, they eventually came to the final curve and the last of the classroom doors down the hall were visible. Mr. Popper's was the one on the left. The south stairs lay just beyond, the doors pulled away and left bent and twisted in the hallway. *Obviously the Demon got downstairs this way,* Theo thought.

Theo and the Toad both slid sidelong glances at Laura, but the only betrayal of emotion visible was the way she chewed at the tender skin on the inside of her lip.

What the hell are we gonna find in there? Theo thought. The Book remained silent, as a parent is silent while waiting for their child to unwrap that one big Christmas present. Its silence was anticipation.

This is not gonna be good.

Theo touched her arm. "Let me," he said.

"No," she replied. "I'm good. Let's all go."

Theo raised his eyebrows—the monobrow, as Stash used to say—in a you're sure? look. She gave him a curt nod that left him with an answer, but not the one he was looking for.

"All right," he said. "Let's go get Mr. Popper." Theo's voice held a lot more enthusiasm than he really felt. To be honest, he was damn sick of entering rooms in this fucking building, not knowing what the hell would jump out and eat his face.

♦♦♦

"OKAY," THEO SAID, "we don't wanna get into another pukefest in there." It would be a long time before he could face any window again without feeling his stomach lurch. It had to be assumed that the nothingness was still out there.

"Here's what we should do," Theo said. "Toad, you hold this end while I go in." He began wrapping one end of some rough nylon rope around his waist. Rope that the Toad had thought was a waste of time bringing. He had even called Theo the "rope dope" a couple of times.

Yeah, well, I'm not going to get my ass chewed off without a fight, Theo thought.

The Toad grabbed the offered end, looking a little chagrined. "You hear anything go wrong, you start yankin'," Theo said. "Don't forget, I'm gonna have my eyes closed through this whole thing so I don't do the Technicolor yawn, okay?" The Toad nodded his assent.

"We ready?" Nods all around. They seemed a little more energized with a job to do.

"Cool. Let's see if he's in there."

Theo stuck his head around the door jamb, his eyes closed as tight as he could make them. He didn't want to put a bandanna around his eyes, in case he needed to get out fast. At least then, puke or no puke, Theo could see to get out. He was pretty sure Popper was long gone, one way or the other, but didn't want to say anything for Laura's sake.

Still, they had to try. He moved deeper into the room.

"Mr. Popper? Tom?"

A low moan to the left.

"Tom? Is th— "

"GET ME OUTTA HEEEEEEEEERE!" Definitely Mr. Popper. Theo felt a sight tug on the rope. Good, that meant the Toad was sharp. Ready to go, but not panicked.

Then, behind Theo, Laura said, "Tom? Tom! We're here! We're gonna get you out. Hang on!"

Easy for her to say, Theo thought.

"Where are you? Tom?"

Another moan. Theo began to move in that direction, carefully feeling for chairs and desks. He tried to keep himself angled to the wall away from the windows, just in case he had to sneak a peek. A bang and a scrape, and Theo had a new bruise on his leg. He bent down to feel for where the desk had gone, his hand batted empty air, and eventually hit a surface. He began to work his way around it, when he heard

(swlabr's eyes)

a small scratching.

"Tom? TOM!"

A moan. "Over here… "

"Tom, this is real important. Did you just move in any way? That little scratching noise, did you make it?"

"…n-no…why…?"

Fuck, Theo thought.

"It's a little thing with a lot of teeth."

Theo spun in the direction of the voice. A different voice.

"What? Who?" he said stupidly, caught off guard by the unexpected presence. He took a quick breath and composed himself. "Who's there?"

"It's me. Joe. Joe Barrett. There's something in here with us."

Joe Barrett. Crouch's cousin. He was a minor niner. Theo caught a memory of a tall skinny boy with red hair and freckles.

Fuck me hard. *Two to get out. And one to get around.*

"Laura, listen, can you get a couple of those flashlights powered up and shine 'em in here?" Theo tried to keep his voice as even as he could.

A small skittering.

Laura asked, "Why? Aren't your eyes closed? Can you see something?"

Another skittering. *Goddamnit! Okay, screw the warm and fuzzy…*

"Don't fuck around here! Get some lights on! Now!" *Jeezuz! Why can't anyone just listen to me?* "I've got two people in here, okay?"

Now to find out the damage. "Tom, are you okay?"

"Yes. Passed out, but think I'm okay now."

"Good." He swung his head the other way, attempting to locate by sound. "Joe? You okay?"

"Yeah. Got myself barricaded behind some desks. But every time I open my eyes—"

"You puke. I know. We're gonna get both of you out." He turned back to address Popper.

"Tom, you *gotta* listen to me, okay? Do. Not. Move. Got it?"

"…yeah…ain't goin' anywhere…"

"Joe, you too."

"All right." Joe's voice was small and trembly. How old was he? Fourteen?

The scratching skittered closer. Theo didn't move a muscle so he could try and place where the little bastard was. What worried him was whether there were any obstacles between him and the lower demon, or if it had a wide open path to him. He also wasn't sure if there was only one. What if there were a few?

Theo could hear Laura and the Toad fumbling with the flashlights in the doorway. He fought the urge to scream at them to hurry up. He could almost see her, biting her lip, her eyes closed against the horrible emptiness outside the windows of the class, shining lights around the room.

"Tom," he said. "Say something so Laura can find you."

"...hey Laura, what took you..."

"Laura, shine the lights in his direction. Keep them there."

"'Kay." Tight. Firm. Nervous as hell. Damn! Theo wished he could see!

More skittering. The little fucker had patience. More than Theo.

"C'mon, you little shit," he whispered. "Come out come out wherever you are. Ollie ollie oxen free."

Theo tried to edge over to where he figured Popper was. Popper seemed to be more in the open. Joe seemed to be off in one corner. It was damn hard keeping his eyes closed, knowing that thing was in here with them.

Another desk. He edged around it. More scratching noises. What was it doing? Why hadn't it attacked by now? It was obviously in the room before them. Why hadn't it got Popper? *Where is it?*

Why the hell didn't I get more information out of Stinky Pete?

Theo could tell he was getting closer to Popper because of the stench of fresh vomit. Shit, hadn't this crap started with someone vomiting earlier today? *Crouch.*

Joe's cousin. *Yeah, now he's dead.*

"Tom, where you at?"

(maaaaaarrrrr-co...)

"Here."

(poooooo-lo...)

Theo moved closer. His foot hit something.

"Ow."

"Tom? Tom!" Theo bent down and felt his leg. "Laura, I've got him! Can you stand?"

"Yeah, I think so."

"Then get the fuck up and let's get outta here! Joe, I'll be right back, I promise. And keep your eyes closed."

"No problem with that."

"Laura," Theo said. "Try and track us with those li—"

A huge scrabbling behind them, coming fast. Theo didn't think, just reacted. He gave Popper a massive push toward what he hoped was the direction of the door. Flailing his arms, still conscious of the teeth behind him, he hooked a desk and overturned it in the direction of the sounds. He heard it skitter to avoid the projectile, then continue to come at him. Another desk.

"Laura! Lights! Lights!"

Skittering. *Pick my target. Be the ball.*

Skittering, closer, faster.

Coming up. Maybe three feet…

Now!

He flipped the desk over, hoping to nail the thing. Not letting go, Theo drove it into the tiles and felt it rock on something that gave slightly.

Bingo! We have a winner, folks!

Theo pushed the desktop down hard, throwing all of his one hundred and fifty pounds behind it. He was going to squash it like the big nasty bug it was. He was rewarded with a satisfying screech worse than nails on a blackboard. He smiled.

"Got you, you bastard!"

He jumped and landed hard on the underside of the overturned desktop. Something crunched. Jump. Again. Again. "DIE, MOTHERFUCKER, DIE!"

The screeching got weaker, and the crunching got louder. It was like stepping on a June bug, but better. Theo was sure the thing was long dead, but he kept it up a little longer. Just in case.

Finally, he stopped. Breathing heavy, he waited, still standing on the overturned desk, his heart thumping in his ears. All else was silent.

Then Laura said, "Theo, you okay?"

"Yeah…yeah I am."

Theo stepped off the desk. No other noises in the room. He called to Joe, letting him know the monster was dead. He heard the desks scraping across the floor as he freed himself of the makeshift fortress. Theo guided him over to where he stood, then guided them both out of the class.

Theo didn't open his eyes until the door closed behind him.

♦♦♦

MOVING AS SILENT as a prowling cat, Marcia glided down the hallway. She passed other classrooms that she refused to look into. Any flash of red was enough to avert her eyes. The demons seemed to be on a mission.

Marcia followed the curve of the hallway, cautiously looking ahead until she could see straight down to the south stairs. In the stillness, she caught sounds emanating elsewhere in the school. There was a commotion going on somewhere nearby. She was glad she wasn't there.

Danika's locker was on the left, seventh from the end. Marcia had no idea what the number was, but could have identified it from the smell of perfume and makeup emanating from the small space. It was also the only locker in the vicinity that had a small pad of paper taped to the door, and a pen on a string.

The school had requested the removal of the pen and paper on numerous occasions, however Danika's social butterfly wings had refused to be clipped. She would take it down, and two or three days later the pad would be back again.

When the school had threatened more severe punishment, the message board was removed again. Then the school janitors began to bitch about having to clean messages written directly on the locker door in pen, marker, lipstick, or anything else at hand. Then came the one that said, "Wher the fuk is yur pad?" This concerned the school officials for two reasons – the defacement of school property, and the literacy level of the vandal.

Eventually, the school officials relented and reversed their decision, allowing the pen and paper back. The only condition was no profanity. That hadn't been a problem, as far as Danika had been concerned, because the only time it had happened they couldn't even spell it right.

Marcia padded up to the locker and automatically read the message there.

Marcia – See ya 2nite!
Everyone else – have a great weekend!

It had been written in Danika's big, unselfconscious loops, all forty-nine characters written to engulf the entire page. There were two quickly drawn flowers around the periphery and a little smiley face in the "d" in "weekend."

"Have a great weekend!" *Yeah, right,* Marcia thought. *It's starting so well…*

She looked at the little smiley face again and felt a sob starting deep in her chest. Was she going to make it out of here? Was she ever going to see Danika again?

Breathe, Marce. Cool it. Her breath fogged out in front of her. It was getting cold.

Carefully, she cradled the combination lock in her hand to avoid making any noise. She turned the little dial, knowing the combination as well as her own. The hallway was quiet enough – despite the far-off noises of something going on that she really didn't want to know about – that she could hear the faint noise of the lock's inner workings clicking into place.

The quiet unnerved her.

Marcia twisted the dial to the last number, held the arch of the lock firmly in her left hand, and gently pulled down on the round base, careful to keep the entire operation as quiet as possible. The lock opened with a muffled *snik* and she allowed herself to breathe again.

She never realized how often she held her breath during crisis moments. Then again, she had never had so many of them piled up in one day before.

Danika's door could sometimes stick, and there were times when Danika just threw her stuff in the locker and slammed it shut, putting temporary stop to an avalanche of binders and texts.

Marcia slowly and deliberately opened the locker door. It did not stick and there was no avalanche. Marcia raised her red-rimmed eyes to the ceiling and mouthed a silent thank you.

As she swung the door open, she deliberately placed a hand over a photograph she knew was taped to the inside. Taken on one of the last good days for skiing a few months back, it showed Danika and Marcia leaning into each other, eyes squinting from the sun. Their cheeks were pink from the crisp air, and were bunched up in big smiles. In the background was a perfect deep-blue sky that Marcia was losing hope of ever seeing again. The ski hill was so white it had a slight blue tinge and was dotted with the colourful garb of the other skiers.

Danika had a gloved hand behind Marcia's head with two fingers extended in the peace sign. Marcia had a finger pointed below Danika's nose, as though poised to mine for booger-nuggets.

Mining for booger-nuggets. That was one of Theo's expressions.

The photograph had been taken not too long after her split from Crouch. In fact, it had been one of the first happy days she had experienced after their breakup.

She kept her hand over the photo as she checked the top shelf for Danika's migraine pills—her mind-blowers. Danika's menstrual cycle played havoc with her and migraines were just one of the side effects.

She remembered laying in bed with Crouch once, telling him about it, confiding to him some secret information. That's what lovers did, right?

"Jesus!" he had responded. "Does she grow hair and bark at the moon, too?" At that comment, Marcia clued in that she shouldn't have said anything. When he asked Marcia if she could score him some of the pills, she knew for sure.

Marcia had to push away those thoughts because it could only spiral off to, "Crouch is dead." Or, going a different route, "Why did I put up with Crouch after Theo?" Which would inevitably lead to, "Theo is dead." There was a lot of road no matter what path she took, but it all led downward.

She found the pills toward the middle of the top shelf, back behind a plastic yogurt tub that held a small can of hairspray, a brush choked with Danika's hair, and a riot of brightly coloured hair bands and elastics.

She must have been in between periods, Marcia thought as she carefully moved the bucket and retrieved the pills. *Otherwise they would have been front and centre.*

Turning the bottle slowly, she took inventory: five pills. That wasn't going to carry Bobby too far, but it was a start. She started to push the bottle into the pocket of her jeans, then reconsidered. Five pills would rattle in the bottle.

Marcia pushed down on the childproof cap and removed it. She tipped out the pills onto her palm and deposited them to her pocket. *Won't rattle now.*

She allowed herself a tight little smirk—not quite a smile—at her ingenuity. She had to admit that she had done pretty well, considering the circumstances.

I'm doing better than a lot of my friends, she thought. Then the little smirk faded.

♦♦♦

THERE WAS A moment, just a brief, heaving moment, when it all went still. Mr. Popper sprawled on the hall floor, slimed in his own juices. Laura crouched over him, head down. The Toad bent over, hands on knees, butt against the wall, his gaze to the floor, his face unreadable. Joe off to one side, his expression dazed but still alert.

And there was Theo, sitting on the floor, back to the lockers, legs splayed, chest heaving. A brief moment when all five were all lost in their own minds, far away from the fuck-up.

Theo's hand moved to the Book on the floor next to him. As his fingers made contact, he heard a voice, soft and whispering.

~...iiiitttt coooommmmessss...~

He knew he was the only one who had heard it. Lifting his head like it weighed a hundred pounds, Theo heard the words come out of his mouth, flat and hard.

"We gotta get outta here," was all he said.

CHAPTER TWENTY-ONE

MARCIA HAD JUST begun to work her way back down the hall to Bobby when she heard an explosion of noise above her.

She had been careful about making sure the locker door was closed and relocked, and even considered leaving Danika a note on the pad. Then she realized she had no idea where the school even existed anymore. She didn't know if the rest of the world even existed beyond the school walls anymore. There was a scary moment when she considered that maybe the school was the only thing still left. That the world, maybe the entire universe, was gone, leaving her and Bobby as the only survivors in a perverse cat-and-mouse game.

Jeez! What was she thinking? *Stop it! Stop it right this instant!* Marcia took a deep breath and laid her hand on the locker door. She had no idea whether she was ever going to see her friend again.

It wasn't until she had gone to all the trouble of closing the door and locking it that she realized she really probably didn't need to do that at all. She shook her head. So much for keeping her head on straight and thinking right.

Okay, okay, in the grand scheme of things, it was a minor slip-up.

One last glance at the locker door, with its pad and pen and happy note, and she was on her way. She had been away from Bobby too long already. He was probably freaking from the pain.

Two steps away from the locker, she heard screaming. She stopped and cocked her head to try and make it out. It sounded…

It sounded like it was more people in trouble. More people dying.

Marcia dropped her gaze to the floor and bit her lip. *Time to go!* She had to make the two of them a priority. She started her quiet sock-glide again. The noises from the floor above ricocheted down the hallway.

Then came a massive bang, like the world's biggest gunshot. Then it got quiet.

Marcia didn't know what to do. Should she sneak up the stairs just behind her? She could look through the windows, not even enter the hallway itself, just to see what was what. Maybe she'd find someone else who could be saved.

Her brain told her she should go and see if she could help them, but her gut told her she'd only be putting herself in another situation like the caf. Or Helmsley's room. If she was going to get Bobby and herself out of this, she had to be selfish.

Both rooms had been scenes of carnage. She flashed back to the cafeteria. She couldn't imagine any survivors from what she had seen back in that hellhole.

But what if there were survivors? Helmsley had somehow survived, why couldn't others? Obviously some had, from the noises above her. What if it was her up there? What if someone else heard her noises and didn't try to help her? Besides, the sounds above seemed human, not nasty, squealing, and demonic.

Marcia stood frozen, paralyzed by indecision, torn between getting back to Bobby, who she knew was suffering, or seeing if there were others more in need.

What if it was Theo up there, Marce? What would you do then? I wouldn't even hesitate, she thought to herself. *Not for a second.*

Despite their earlier words, Marcia had come to realize how big a part of her life Theo still occupied. Even when she was with Crouch, she had never stopped thinking of him. Even now, with both Theo and Crouch dead, she still compared them, and Crouch came up lacking in almost every area.

No, if it was Theo up there, she wouldn't hesitate.

It was enough for her to make a decision. Marcia decided to take a fast, quiet trip up to the third floor to see what the fuss was all about. She turned, began to walk back and, seconds later, dropped to the floor in shock.

♦♦♦

THE LOUD CRACK

(the caf! shit oh shit the caf)

sounded oh so familiar. Theo, Laura, and the Toad tensed, knowing immediately what was happening. Picking up the vibe of the other three, Popper and Joe got more nervous, their eyes searching for the source of the danger.

"God*damn*it!" Theo said. "Are we never going to get a fuckin' break here?"

From down the hall came heavy moving sounds, like a bulldozer trying to negotiate the too-narrow corridor. Above that, high scrabbling noises played a rough counterpoint.

"The stairway door's frozen," Mr. Popper said. "How did that happen?"

The south stairs! Theo turned to stare in awe at the ruined doorway. The gaping hole that had faced them before was gone, replaced with a wall of bunched and knotted ice. It looked like one of those horribly fake *Star Trek* alien-planet sets Kirk, Spock, and McCoy would overact in. But it was real.

Shit, that takes care of our option to run away, Theo thought. *How the hell does it freeze something from a distance?*

Ignoring Popper, he glanced at Laura. "You get the lights."

He looked at Joe. "You help her." Turning again. "Dennis."

The Toad's head snapped around.

"Start rippin' the lockers open. We need something to fight these things. Get anything you can find. Shit, maybe even lunches will slow them down."

The Toad, to his credit, didn't say a word. His eyes were a little wide. Could have been fear, could have been panic. Either way, Theo didn't care, as long as it got him moving. The Toad spun, grabbed a crowbar from their supplies, and attacked the first locker. The cheap steel caved under his panicked onslaught, bending open to reveal its contents like an eviscerated abdomen. He tore three open quickly, then dropped the crowbar.

As the Toad pulled the guts of the first locker out onto the floor, Theo grabbed the crowbar and went at the next three with just as much gusto.

The noises were getting closer. Fast. Too damn fast!

"Hey! Major Tom! Up off your ass and help Laura and Joe!"

"I..."

"NOW, YOU SON OF A BITCH!"

Popper got up off the floor. Laura threw him a light, not giving him a chance to protest.

The Toad wasn't finding anything and moved to the next locker. Mere seconds had passed, but with all the noise they were making, and all the noise that was advancing down the hall to them, it seemed like hours.

Theo ripped at another locker. The Toad looked at him, his face red and sweating. "Anything?" he asked. Theo handed him the crowbar for the next locker.

"Nothing." *Jesus! All these kids that go hunting half the year! Doesn't anyone keep a gun at school?*

Then the first of the hell-rats came around the curve.

Swlabr's eyes.

That meant they had been seen.

The Toad didn't hesitate. Just as he had with Stash's attacker, he ran at it, crowbar in his hand completely forgotten, jumped, and came down hard.

Missing it by inches.

It snapped at his leg. He stomped at it, his teeth gritted in effort, his blond hair flying. The Demon kept dodging him.

Theo ran to the lights and popped one on. "Crowbar!"

The hell-rat froze in the light. The Toad took its toothy head off with one clean swipe of the crowbar. He looked up and immediately spun and ran back to the rest of the group.

"Joe," Laura said. "Keep going at the lockers!" Joe moved to obey. Popper was frozen in place, almost as though the ice the Demon threw at the doors had claimed him as well.

The Toad skidded to a stop. "There's a fuckin' *ton* of them! We're dead!"

Laura's voice was tight. "Joe! Anything?"

Joe glanced around at the rough-strewn inventory. "Nothing! Pencil cases, books, a lunch, a camera, some records and tapes, and—"

Laura and the Toad got it before Theo.

Camera?

Camera!

"Joe! Any flash cubes?"

"Yeah, one…YEAH!" It hit him about the same time as Theo. Laura had told Tom and Joe of their hatred for light as they recounted their experiences while recovering.

Laura dived for the floor beside Joe just as the horde came into sight, a big, black cancerous mass crawling, spilling, roiling over itself like some sort of mutant avalanche.

"JESUSLORDGODALMIGHTY!" Popper was just about out of his mind. "What in god's name is that?"

Swlabr lumbered toward them. The lower demons surrounded it like a police escort, forming a circle. Its mass filled the hall, but the corridor walls almost seemed to shrink from any contact with the Demon. Swlabr was so massive and profoundly dark that it seemed to be a black hole, sucking any residual light from that end of the hallway, shrouding the advancing demons in layers of malicious intent.

"Holy Christ!" Joe said, almost dropping the camera. Laura grabbed it from his hands.

"Toad! Lights!" Theo and the Toad rushed to get all the lights on. They seemed to hold the demons at bay.

For now.

The demons knew the light wouldn't last forever.

The survivors knew the light wouldn't last forever.

Who would blink first?

"Okay guys," Laura said. "I've got it."

She surreptitiously hefted the little Kodak Instamatic, shielding it from the other team. Like demons were going to know what a Kodak Instamatic was. There was a little blue flashcube perched on the top like a cherry on a police car.

"There's only three flashes left. One's used. I think I've got it on right. When I say go, run."

"Run? Where?" Popper asked.

She bared her teeth. "Through them."

"It's the only way out," Theo agreed.

Popper was panicking. "No way—"

"One..."

"Laura! There's too ma—"

"Two..."

"LAURA! FOR GOD'S S—"

"THREE!"

♦♦♦

THERE WAS A bang like a cannon, like thunder, like the fist of God slamming and banging its way through the school. Maybe it was. Maybe it was God's own punishment for the events that had transpired here. For all the needless deaths. Yes, God did that, didn't He? Punish the sinners? Jericho? The Tower of Babel?

Clarington High?

But then she realized that she had heard this sound before, not long ago—a couple of hours maybe. Back when the world had made some sort of sense.

Back in the caf.

Yes, the huge cracking noise was something she had heard before. The doors of the caf, freezing rapidly, ice building and layering and rippling like her father's arms as he chopped firewood.

Ice.

That meant dog-beasts.

That meant the big one.

She only thought she had been paralyzed before. Now she was.

She lay sprawled in the middle of the hallway, her face to the now-frigid floor telling herself that she had to get up, to get away.

Get up, Marce! Damn it, get back up!

♦ ♦ ♦

THE LITTLE FLASH popped, exploding light down the hallway. They ran, Theo and the Toad each taking one of Popper's arms. In their rush to go, Theo was aware of a few things happening all at once:

Joe taking off like a sprinter, his foot catching a binder and sending it spinning back toward the ice-covered stairway entrance.

Popper trailing behind Theo and the Toad, not quite resisting, but not quite complying either, his leg catching one of the flashlights, pounding it into the floor with another flash and a loud electric *pop.*

Laura holding the camera at arm's length in front of her as she also took off into the squealing mob.

The demons, screeching, recoiling from the powerful, compressed blast of light, brighter than anything that had been thrown to them up to now. They turned their heads in an almost human gesture, squinting against the light.

But it was Swlabr's reaction that almost made Theo halt in his tracks. The Demon seemed to break apart, to spew out and away from the light like tissue paper shredding in a hurricane. The shredded chunks seemed to be as weightless and ethereal as smoke.

The shredded wisps seemed to spray to specific

(shadows it's hiding in the shadows)

locations.

That gave them all a half-second pause. One second, they had to dodge around a monstrous beast, the next second it was gone. They had a relatively clear path, except for the teeth.

They ran.

Once the light dissipated, Swlabr came back, reformed and solidified, big as life and twice as ugly, as Theo's Uncle Floyd would say.

But now the little band of five was so much closer, in range of those teeth and claws.

"Again! Flash 'em again!"

Theo heard a muffled click, but no flash. *What the hell?*

"Laura, pop the goddamn—"

"It's jammed. It won't—"

"Advance the film! Spin the thumbwheel and it'll flash!" yelled Joe.

Amid all the confusion and squealing and scrabbling and pounding feet, Theo heard a faint grind of plastic gears.

POP!

This time Swlabr wailed. The light was closer to it, stronger. Laura had hurt the thing.

Again it shredded away. Again, it came back.

It came back swinging.

"Theo! Mallard!" the Toad yelled.

Theo ducked lower, pulling Popper down with him, and missed the massive arm that swiped just above them.

Woulda taken my head off! Fuck!

"Run! Runrunrun!"

There was a sickening thud, and squeals from the lower demons, and then they were past the horde, Laura now angling the camera behind her. "Last one!" she yelled.

Click. No flash.

"FUCK!"

"Do it again. I think that was the used bulb. You only had three." Again the grinding of cheap plastic gears, Laura's thumb flying over the small, inset dial. Her finger stabbed at the shutter button.

POP!

With the last flash, some of the lower demons tried to run down the hallway away from them, but there were still flashlights on down there. Theo thought he saw a couple fall over, whether stunned or dead, he wasn't sure. There was a large heap to one side, lower demons everywhere on it. A pile of their own dead? Were they feeding on each other?

But nothing came for them anymore.

Even as Swlabr solidified again, it stood facing them, but not making any attempt to advance. Those last couple of flashes must have hurt.

Theo couldn't help letting a small smile slip past his lips as he turned to the stairs.

♦♦♦

MARCIA HAD ABSOLUTELY no idea what to do. She knew that, ten feet overhead, hordes of demons were ripping and shredding any survivors they could find. She knew that all of the measures they had taken to stay alive up to this point had been in vain. Was that how she and Bobby were going to end up? Push and push and fight against the evil just to find out it had got them nowhere at all?

No, damn it! That was *not* going to happen to her!

She pushed herself up, hearing the commotion working its way down the hall, back the way she had come. Toward the north stairs.

Toward Bobby.

She had to move.

♦♦♦

KEEPING AN EYE on the demons behind them, they ran for the north stairs and flew down the steps. Theo wasn't aware of his feet touching anything, navigating more by the cold handrails than anything. They didn't stop running until they got back to the compound, chests heaving, screaming for each burning suck of air.

It wasn't until they reached the compound that they noticed one of their own hadn't made it.

CHAPTER TWENTY-TWO

SHE GAVE UP any pretense of being cautious or quiet. A whole lot of noise had blown by the second storey on its way to the first. It sounded like the 3:15 P.M. Friday stampede all over again, all feet and voices, rampaging sneakers and raging hormones. Next stop: parties and pot, sex and drugs and rock and roll.

Had that really only happened two or three hours ago? Somehow, it had.

This time though, unlike the stampede sound she was used to, she thought she heard wild, uncontrolled panic as well. It sounded like the cafeteria all over again. So there *were* other survivors. But would they survive for long with those things chasing them?

Better to look out for yourself for now, girl, she thought. *You and Bobby.*

Marcia slipped and slid down the hall, half running and ready to hit the emergency brake, not knowing what she would see around that next curve. The trip that had taken her so long to go one way took a few seconds the other.

She blew by Helmsley's class, her nanosecond glance into the room registering that Helmsley had either dragged herself, or had been dragged to, the desk with stuff hanging out of her. Then Marcia realized that Helmsley's door was open.

It was *open*.

So if it was open…

...that meant...

"Shit!"

(forgive me father for I have)

"Shitshit*SHIT*!"

That meant those things were out. And if they were out and she hadn't seen them, there were only two places they could have gone: to the stairs...

...or to Bobby.

Taking her chances with whatever may be lurking around the corner she barreled on, her sock feet making soft noises somewhere between a thump and a slap on the hard tiles of the floor, her hair flying wildly, strands sticking to the corner of her mouth.

She was prepared for almost anything. She had already angled herself to grab at the mop she had tossed aside earlier. She ran the various scenarios through her head, clicking through her different options with the efficiency of the computer that occupied a room on the floor below her.

She was prepared for anything, except what she ran into rounding the last curve.

♦♦♦

MARCIA TORE AROUND the last corner, then immediately pinwheeled her arms and backpedalled, her socks slipping uselessly on the slick floor as she tried to throw herself into reverse. It occurred to her in her moment of panic that, to any outside observer, it would have looked quite comical, like a scene from *The Three Stooges* or something, maybe how Moose would have looked as he ran drunk and naked down the street.

As dark as the hallway was, the end was darker. The large shape at the end of the hall seemed to suck any light out of the area. The hairs on Marcia's arms rose in hackles, partly from the sub-zero temperature, mostly from the living, breathing piece of hell that stood ready to greet her.

The Demon. The big one.

The last time, she had been above the creature and it had been imposing. Now, slipping and sliding in her socks toward it, it was so much worse.

The floors were slick and she simply couldn't stop her forward motion. She fell to her butt, banging the side of her knee painfully on the floor as she landed. Her feet kicked in a total rejection of her direction.

All that effort proved futile.

♦♦♦

"WHERE THE HELL is Joe?" Laura yelled.

"Oh Lord," Popper said.

In the confusion, no one had noticed that Joe was not with them.

"We gotta go back for him!" Theo said.

"But we don't know where he is," Popper said.

"Could be anywhere," said the Toad. "Maybe he wiped out on the stairs or something."

Theo grabbed up more lights. As he did he ran through the past five minutes again. The flash. The running. Swlabr blinking out and coming back. Another flash. Still running. Ducking. Running. Another flash, looking back, seeing some of them fall. The pile to the one side.

Sounds: squealing, screeching, claws *taktaktaking* on the floor, the yelling, the lights popping, the thud as he ducked under the swinging arm—

The thud.

The pile to one side.

"...oh shit..." Theo said quietly.

The other three looked at him.

"Swlabr. Swlabr got him. Toad told me to

(mallard)

duck, and I pulled Popper down with me, but I guess…I guess…"

"Ah, damn." Laura hung her head, her chest heaving. Theo placed the lights back down on the workbench.

"If he hadn't found that camera…" the Toad said.

"He saved our asses back there," Theo said. He was still bent over the workbench, lights and tools strewn over it from their earlier searches.

"GODDAMMIT!" He slammed both fists down, making the power tools jump. Then came the tears.

Laura came over, putting her arms around him from behind.

"Theo…"

"He was only fourteen fucking years old, Laura. Fourteen!" He shrugged out of her embrace, finding no comfort there.

"I know. I know."

"Dude," the Toad said. "There was nothing we could have done."

"We could have watched out for him better! *I* could have—"

"Theo," Laura said, turning him to face her. "You couldn't have. You had your hands full."

No one looked at Popper. No one needed to.

Theo straightened and shook off Laura, more gently this time. He wiped his eyes dry. At this point, no one would have disputed his word. He was their leader.

"No one else dies."

He looked at the other three in turn, as though placing the responsibility on each of them individually.

"No one else dies," he repeated. "No one."

He turned his back on them and, picking up the Book, walked away, getting some distance from the group. They let him go, looking at each other.

No one else dies.

♦♦♦

MARCIA SLID INTO the beast like she was sliding home at the bottom of the ninth. Her feet hit one of the beast's legs and she responded as though the touch was electric, jolting her legs and careening off the beast, back the way she came, arms scrabbling for purchase on the smooth floor, hands making squeaking

(you're making the floor laugh)

noises on the tiles.

The Demon stood, watching, something clutched in one black claw. An ebony statue, it seemed in no hurry to do anything other than watch Marcia's mad scrambling.

Watching her. As though it possessed eyes.

As Marcia got first to her knees, then to her feet, she looked behind her to see what the massive creature was doing. What she noticed instead was the blood. All the blood that trailed from the creature in a jagged, panicked line to her. Straight to her.

Marcia looked down at herself and it was only then that she saw that she was covered in blood. Her blue jeans were dark purple. Her maroon blouse was almost black.

Her scream ripped the air and threatened to tear her head in two.

♦♦♦

IN THE RELATIVE safety of the compound, they rested again and let Popper get back some strength. Running down the stairs to the compound, he'd been nothing more than a boneless chicken. Laura and the Toad raided more lockers. They fed on peanut butter and jam sandwiches, cold soup, cookies, and chocolate bars.

Theo, still smouldering with rage, refused the food and went off to one corner to study the Book.

Laura approached him like she would an unknown dog, smiling, but ready to run at the first sign of danger. "Theo?" No response. "I brought you this," she said, placing a knapsack-style book bag at his feet. "If we have to move, you'll need your hands free. I thought this would help."

He had not yet opened the Book. He leaned up against the wall, the Book on his knees, his palms flat on the dark cover. He looked up at her, his eyes red and punctuated with dark circles. He said nothing. She changed gears.

"Theo," Laura said, "we've been at this for hours. You've got to eat." She held out a sandwich and a chocolate bar.

"Why?" He wiped his nose. "So we're nice and fat when the witch comes to eat us?" His voice was flat, monotone.

"No," she said, continuing to hold out the food. "We've all got to keep our strength up. If we're really going to kick this thing's ass, we need to get some food in us...so no one else dies."

Theo sat there, looking up at Laura, her long blonde hair spilling down one shoulder. He considered what she said. Had it been anyone else asking him to eat, his stubbornness would have kicked in. Part of him fought to do just that—sit in the corner and sulk like a little child.

"Theo, you're going to get us out of this." She smiled. "I know you are."

He sighed and rubbed his eyes. Up to today, only his mom had ever been successful in pulling him out of a funk. Now there were two.

"What's on the menu?" he asked, his voice subdued.

Laura's smile widened. "Locker surprise."

He reached out and took the items from her hand.

"We've got some Cokes and 7-Ups over there, too," she said gently. "Come and get one when you're ready." She turned back to Popper and the Toad, leaving him alone.

Biting into the sandwich, he turned back to examining the Book. No one else was going to die from his lack of knowledge or his lack of attention. He was going to get information out of this Book if it was the last thing he did. He *would* get them all out of here.

He hefted the Book onto his lap. It was the biggest book he had ever seen, and Its warmth disturbed him. There was death and pain and suffering in there, but It felt alive. His fingers touched the cold metal corner of the cover. He took a deep breath and opened It.

The first thing he felt was relief. The Book behaved Itself—no skull-bursting visions. Next came amazement. Theo found the same thing that Peter had discovered two months earlier: he would turn a page and the calligraphy would swim before his eyes, rearranging into recognizable words and sentences. It made his eyes water just to watch it, but he persisted. There were questions he wanted—needed—answered.

Through his investigation, he found the Demon Peter had raised and, though he already knew it, he confirmed Peter's warning—as far as he trusted the Book, at least—that it was better not to speak the Demon's name aloud. The actual warning stated to avoid this act "lest It seeke thee and impregnate body and soul with Its damnable, unholy seed." Good enough for Theo.

He found out that Swlabr was the progeny of Nyarlathotep, also known as the Haunter of the Dark, as well as hundreds of other names. The Haunter, a being possessing a burning, three-lobed eye—whatever that was—had come to Earth several times, but most notably through the Church of the Starry Wisdom. But they'd used some damn thing called the Shining Trapezohedron. Whatever that was.

Strange and fascinating stuff, but ultimately useless. He moved on.

He found that the little fuckers with the big teeth—the *dæmons lower*—were indeed Swlabr's eyes. They ventured out, getting the lay of the land, finding suitable vessels, and generally chewing through anything else they could find.

But what was it that had saved Joe and Popper?

It took Theo a while, but eventually the Book reluctantly offered Its secrets. Theo didn't want to think what the cost was going to be, so he pushed it to the back of his mind. Instead, he concentrated on the swimming lines of handwritten text and drawings.

He found that the lower demons had an unusual blindness. If there was movement, they saw it. If there was not, they effectively could not see. They could still rely on other senses, but primarily it was sight, both for themselves and for Swlabr.

Theo closed the Book and stood. He put the Book in the bag Laura had given him, then rejoined the others. Laura looked at him as though welcoming him back. He nodded imperceptibly. *Thank you.*

Turning to the other two, he said, "Popper, what happened in your classroom? I mean from the time everything went to hell in a handbasket until we showed up." He couldn't keep a note of contempt from creeping into his voice when addressing the teacher.

"Well, let me recall…" Popper began fidgeting nervously. "I was grading papers at my desk. Then the power cut out. At that point, I wasn't overly concerned. As you know, it happens quite often. I knew—" his face reddened slightly "sorry I assumed—Laura was coming to my class, so I continued to work by the light from outside. Then I felt something…very strange, hard to describe…"

"Was that when the school moved? Lurched?" Laura asked.

"Yeah. It, like, flexed," the Toad added.

"Yes, either term is adequate. I felt a lurch and the light in the class was different, terrible. I turned to look outside. That's when I…soiled myself." His face went very red and his voice quavered. "I guess I also passed out from all the excitement—my blood pressure is slightly higher than normal—and I regained consciousness just as you were entering the room."

"What about Joe?"

"I have no idea. I have to assume—"

"He must have come in to escape whatever was out in the hall while you were out cold," Theo said, cutting him off. *That gets them both in the room.*

"So you probably didn't move once you fainted," Theo said.

"Presumably not."

"That's what saved your ass." When Popper looked at him questioningly, Theo continued. "You weren't moving. The little hell-rat came into the room, but nothing was moving. I was calling to you in there for a while before Joe even spoke up."

"He must have been scared stiff," Laura said.

"The lower demon could probably smell you, or the puke, but couldn't place you. Joe had set up a barricade of desks, so he was safe too. It probably couldn't see any of the little movements he might have made."

"Why wouldn't Joe have set up a barricade around the two of us?" Popper asked.

"Probably thought you were dead," the Toad said.

"So he ignored you, too," Theo said, dismissing the thought. "My guess is the demon sat around waiting for something to happen."

"And then you came," Laura said. "Theo, I'm so sorry."

"Why? I killed it. I got Joe out." He looked over to where Popper was standing in the ring of lights, half a stale peanut butter sandwich in his hand. "And Popper."

She smiled at Theo, but her eyes were pained. Theo thought she looked genuinely sorry for sending him into danger. He knew she must be feeling just as shitty as he was for losing Joe.

The realization that he would do almost anything for her once again dawned on him. It didn't surprise him this time. It had been coming for a while.

"You got all that from the Book? I thought you said It was all terrible and stuff," the Toad said. "'Do not touch' and all that."

"I did and It is. I'm sorry bud, but there's shit in here I didn't want or need to know."

"Like what?"

Theo paused, chewing on a SNICKERS bar, weighing what should and shouldn't be told.

"I picked up a lot of

(more no more no more no more no more more)

what was going through the

(leggo my fuckin' eggos, you fuck)

heads of the others who used this Book. I experienced a lot of what they experienced. Like watching a movie on high speed."

Theo flashed on Stinky Pete, cock in hand, masturbating in the washroom. He felt what Peter had felt, that it wasn't a hand jacking him off…

"Peter had a lot of issues with his old man. He was an asshole to Peter, and…well you know the rest. But there's so much more in there. Hundreds of lives like that. Thousands. All the people who used this Book, and all the ones who

(steph thumping on the cafeteria door screaming the room dark and behind her theo and dennis standing just a few feet from the door why aren't they helping why aren't they moving why is this happening and the pain as the skin of her face and hand rips from her body she sees it as she is dragged away from the door and something is digging at her stomach and there's a warm gush and pain and pain and pain and they didn't help oh god why didn't they help they left us here to die and her vision narrows and as it goes

black the last thing she sees is black teeth ripping at her face and a tug as something is pulled away they just left us here to)

died from its use." He closed his eyes, hoping to clear the images there. They didn't go away. They burned afterimages into his head. They would never go away.

Theo got quiet. *All this death. All these people dying, who I should have been there to help. Crouch, Steph, Stash, Joe. All those people in the cafeteria.*

The others seemed to grasp that there was more going on than Theo was letting on. They left him alone.

♦♦♦

AFTER AN UNCOMFORTABLE silence that stretched far too long, the subject of escape came up. Theo made it clear that they could not and should not count on the Book for an answer. They all agreed. They had seen Peter and knew what It had done to him.

After they ate, they worked out a strategy. Popper asked a lot of questions about the behaviour of the beasts, and he provided most of the plan that ultimately emerged. It wasn't the best plan Theo had ever heard, and he really didn't want to trust anything coming from the man, but the Book wasn't giving him the answers he needed and no other plan seemed to be forthcoming. Theo had serious doubts as to whether it would work at all. Still, it seemed like the only workable solution. They couldn't trust the Book.

It had to work because if it didn't, they would be stuck in this damned circle of hell forever.

Part Four
To the Night

"Searchers after horror haunt strange, far places."

The Picture in the House
H. P. Lovecraft

CHAPTER TWENTY-THREE

"SO THIS IS the crux of the situation," a somewhat rejuvenated Mr. Popper said. "We're going to need someone to flush the big creature...Swalliber?"

"Swlabr," the other three said.

"Whatever. Flush it out and into the trap."

"A lure," Theo said, dryly.

"Um, yes, I guess you could put it that way."

"Okay, fine. Who's that?" Theo said. *As if I have to ask,* he thought.

The Toad hung his head. He would not go. Theo looked at Popper. He was a couple of inches shorter than Theo, with a neatly trimmed beard and a handsome face. *He sort of looks like GI Joe,* Theo thought. Popper returned Theo's gaze evenly.

"It will not be me," he said simply.

What?

Theo blinked at him. Before he could begin to frame a question, in jumped Laura.

"Not going to be you? Not you? Why? Jesus Christ! We just risked a lot—Theo more than any of us—to get you and Joe out of a room you would have died in. Alone!"

A room you could have crawled out of by yourself, too. If you hadn't thrown up and passed out. Theo was losing respect for the man by degrees.

"I know, and I thank—"

"No. No, absolutely not." Laura's hand shot out, one finger

stabbing at his face, warning him to shut up. Her face reddened. She was pissed.

"Are you *trying* to piss me off, Tom? Don't even say 'thank you' because it's bullshit. You are really honest-to-god saying that you will not help get this thing out in the open? Christ, it's mostly *your* plan!"

Popper stepped back from her finger and paced around the little compound, away from Laura's assault. Theo noticed he never strayed one inch out of the ring of lights. Even the Toad would venture out for short periods of time. But not Major Tom.

"Yes, I guess that is what I'm saying. I'm not proud of it, but I'm not going. Knowing I was in a room with one of those demons took a lot out of me. Seeing Joe die took a lot out of me. No, I'll stay back and take care of the rest of the details with Dennis."

Took a lot out of him? He didn't see Joe die! He'd been too damn busy saving his own ass. For a guy nicknamed Major Tom and who looked like GI Joe, he sure wasn't living up to either image. Theo couldn't feel sorry for him. They had all experienced so much worse than one little demon in a room. Hell, it hadn't even drawn blood from any of them before Theo killed it. Theo's band of three had experienced so much more death and horror.

Theo couldn't feel sorry for him, but he was getting restless. And another thought had dawned on him just recently. A thought that was probably incorrect, but it had given him some hope, nonetheless.

"Laura," Theo said. "Don't sweat it. I'll go. It makes sense. I've got the most experience with the lower demons and the Book and all—"

"Fine," Laura said, her voice hard as stone. She looked at Tom, at Theo, then at Tom again, dismissing him. "Fine. It's me and the boy."

Theo saw from her face that she meant no slight against him calling him "the boy." He and Popper both knew damn well who it had been directed at and why.

So, instead, Theo allowed himself a small, private smile.

♦♦♦

THIS WAS IT.

Marcia's mind had locked down to a white expanse of nothing. A polar bear in a snowstorm.

Back when she used to be a living, breathing human being, Marcia never understood the rabbit-in-the-headlights thing. It had just seemed so *stupid* that an animal could watch something coming at it and not do a thing to prevent it. She had watched horror movies and thought, *Oh for gosh sakes, just run, will you? Why do you just stand there?*

And yet, here she lay, covered in blood in the middle of the hallway on the second floor of Clarington High School, five painkillers in her pocket, her body locked up with mind-wiping fear.

It had all led up to this. All the death. All the terror. All the running and puking and bleeding and pain. All the caution. All to come down to this.

All for nothing.

One stupid mistake.

All to come down to her watching as the Demon dropped the body of a boy—*Is that Joe Barrett?*—and slowly, gracefully, glided down the darkened hallway, its massive arm out to her as though asking if might have the courtesy of this one last

(doin' it all on a night to)

dance. Marcia's only response was a slight quiver of her lower lip. She found she couldn't even blink.

The Demon drew closer still, blood running off it in rivulets. Was it the Demon's blood? Was it hers? Was it

Bobby's? Was it Joe's? She couldn't even formulate the questions. She could only watch as the Demon came closer and closer.

One stupid mistake. All for nothing.

Then it stood right in front of Marcia, towering over her. The air darkened. Gooseflesh tightened the skin on her arms, the back of her neck, her scalp, her breasts. She breathed in the beast and her lungs recoiled, but could not breathe it back out, like thick viscous oil coating her tongue, her throat, and finally settling in her lungs. It affected her every sense. She shivered violently though still paralyzed.

The Demon bent to her, face to face. It had no eyes. But it could see her.

No eyes. She was going mad.

Its breath washed over her face, cold and stinking of despair and desecration, wisping her hair and numbing her lips and ears. Its nostrils flared as it breathed in her smell. Her eyes watered, yet she could not blink.

It reached out a hand and gently, gracefully cupped the back of her head and brought it forward to touch its own. As Marcia's head connected with the Demon's, her unblinking eyes rolled back and her shivering stopped. She went limp, staying upright only due to the support of the Demon at the back of her neck.

The white expanse that had been the landscape of her mind turned black, charred by the fires of the blackest hell her chosen religion could only ever hint at.

♦♦♦

...AND WE MOVED to Beh-ver-lee.

Theo had made a conscious effort to push Joe to the back of his mind. Like the others, he would deal with all of it when he got out. In the meantime, as they packed the necessary supplies for Popper's plan, *The Beverley Hillbillies* theme song wormed through Theo's head and he couldn't get that line out. It kept repeating like a broken record.

"Why do they say a broken record? Why isn't it a scratched record?"

The three others looked at Theo like he'd lost it — a very real possibility, under the circumstances, but not the case right now. It was a lot more homegrown than that.

Theo's mom used to go through various chains of thought, one thing leading to the next, like dominoes. Then she would come out with something that made no sense whatsoever to Theo — like *The Beverley Hillbillies* to scratched records to Theo's mom. Chains of thought, strung together with gossamer strands, nearly invisible to any outside observer.

The three of them continued to stare at him. He cleared his throat self-consciously.

"I've got *The Beverley Hillbillies* theme song going through my head, over and over, and I was thinkin' 'Why do they say something repeats like a broken record?' A broken record won't even sit on a turntable properly. And you can't play it; it'll screw up the stylus! But a scratched record can be played, and it does skip. Like my *Bat Out of Hell* record, right Toad?" The Toad nodded. He knew where Theo was coming from. "So why isn't the expression, 'repeats like a scratched record'?"

There was silence for a second or two. Popper and Laura continued to stare. Then the Toad chimed in.

"Just doesn't have that same zing, y'know? *Scratched* record. *Broken* record. See the difference? *Scratched* record. *Broken* rec — "

"Will you two shut the fuck up?" Laura stood, hands on hips. "Get this shit loaded so we can get the hell out of here!"

"Jeez! I was just sayin'," Theo said, slightly stung.

"Laura, when did you start using so much profanity in your everyday speech?"

"Tom?"

"Yes, Laura?"

"No offense, but will you shut the fuck up too, please?"

Theo and the Toad turned back to their duties, shit-eating grins threatening to split their faces.

The Toad bent to Theo and brought his hand up as though to block Popper from hearing what he said. The stage whisper he used, however, allowed for anyone in the room to hear

"I'm sure she meant that in the nicest possible way." Both attempted to hide their smiles. Both failed miserably.

Swimmin' pools. Moo-vee stars.

♦♦♦

A HALF-HOUR LATER, Laura and Theo were looking for the nasties. *Be vewwy vewwy quiet.*

Goddamn! Why was his mind floating to all these stupid things? First the Hillbillies, now Elmer Fudd. Theo thought maybe it was a survival instinct: Don't think about what's going to come out from around the next corner and chew my leg off.

The two of them had already done a quick loop to the northernmost end of the school, the far end of the tech wing. Nothing. The lower demons had been there all right, but nothing now. They continued their search.

Theo opened his mouth several times, as though to say something, each time closing it again, saying nothing.

"What's on your mind, slim?"

Theo chuckled. "Slim?"

"Yeah." She smiled. "It was something I used to say to my husband. He was built a lot like you. Long and lean."

They carried on out of the tech wing to the main lobby. The caf's broken, torn doors were on their right and the gym to their left. They had to cross that big expanse, and the lobby windows looked out on the stomach-lurching emptiness.

Great choice, Theo thought. *Look out the windows and puke or look toward the caf and puke.* The smell coming out of the cafeteria was sickening, gasoline and burned meat and unrelenting suffering.

He had to get his mind on something else. Laura grabbed his hand.

He looked down at her. That tingle was back.

"Let's close our eyes and just feel along the wall," she said. "We'll get through this together. Just keep talking to me, okay?"

"'Kay." He really didn't want to go across the expanse again. He could still remember exactly where Stash had been hit. And now, thanks to the Book, he had memories of being on both sides of the caf door.

Stop it! Get your mind off it!

"So, what happened to your husband?" *Oh yeah, great topic. Bring up her dead husband why don't you? Fuck I'm stupid.* "I'm sorry. That was dumb. Forget I said that."

They were still holding hands, and with her free hand, Laura picked out their way along the rough brick of the wall. They should have been coming to a glass case that was full of trophies soon.

"No, Theo, don't apologize. It's okay. I've dealt with it. Jude had a heart attack. Simple as that. One second I'm married, the next I'm a widow."

"Wow. Yeah, I never thought of that. Widow. That sounds so…"

"Old?"

"Yeah, I guess."

"I think so too. I still feel like I'm too young to be a widow. Not that there's a good age to be a widow." Theo heard her smile.

"So were you gonna have kids?" *Oh* Jesus! *Again with the stupid questions! Geez, why not just ask which position she liked best when her dead husband was throwin' her a hump?*

"We talked about it." Her voice held no annoyance, and that eased Theo's mind a bit. "Jude wanted a lot. Five or six. Plus we were supposed to take in Talia as well. I was leaning more toward two. We were still in negotiations when he died."

"I'm sorry." *Sorry for all the dumb questions.*

"Don't be. Like I said, I've dealt with it."

Theo knew she was sincere. He really wasn't screwing up with her. He was just overthinking everything…as usual. *Let it go, dude. Just talk to her.*

"So, Jude, huh? As in 'Hey Jude'?"

"Jodiah, actually. With one brother named Charlie and one named Glen, he could never figure out how he got saddled with Jodiah."

Theo chuckled. "His parents never told him?"

"Just that they were looking for a unique name and they liked that one."

"Yeah, that's like my cousins, but kind of the opposite. They're Signa, Twyla, Una, Joobal, and Jennifer."

"Oh gosh," she said. "That's bizarre. Yeah, Jude hated Jodiah. He was okay with Jude, though. Loved the Beatles. I already told you he was a music nut. Oh! Here's the trophy case. We're almost there."

"Good."

"What about you? Thelonious?"

"Yeah, the obvious. Thelonious Monk. The jazz piano player. My dad's a jazz freak. Sounds to me like they're constantly practising or tuning their instruments or something."

Laura's laughter washed over him like sunshine. He smiled in return.

"I'm told that an appreciation for jazz comes with middle age."

"Yeah well, Steely Dan's about the closest I'm ever gonna get to jazz."

"No piano-playing in your future?"

"No. The only musical thing I can play real well is the stereo." She laughed again. He was on a roll.

Theo wondered why it took a disaster of this proportion, all this death and pain, for him to finally be able to talk normally to a woman without concentrating on her tits. Hell, even his last conversation with Marcia had been about her tits.

Maybe it's because my eyes are closed. Or maybe it's that middle age creeping up on me. Next, I'll be digging jazz.

"Here's the door's to the stairs," Laura said. "We're in the hallway now."

"We made it?"

"We did. Thank you, Theo." She gave his hand a squeeze and let go. Theo deflated as she released his hand.

♦♦♦

THEY CONTINUED SOUTH, past the stairs, past the principal's office and main admin on their left, and entered the science wing. Chemistry, physics, biology.

Nothing. All the plants and fish and hamsters were gone from the biology lab. It looked like this floor was clear. They started to breathe again.

Until Theo realized something.

"Shit," he said.

"What?"

"The gym. We didn't check the damn gym." That meant going back through the lobby.

"Okay, so we do it now."

"Yeah, great. We do it now. We check out the biggest room in the school and probably the darkest. Where do I sign up for that one?"

After one last check to make sure all the various flashlights worked, the two made their way back through the lobby and to the steps leading down to the gym.

♦♦♦

THE GYM WAS the big area that the rest of the school seemed to bend around. The tech wing arched away behind it to the north and east, the main hall and classrooms curving to the south before moving off in a different direction.

Like every high school gym in the world, the Clarington High gym was simply a big, reverberating box, smelling of sweat. In the dark and quiet, the room seemed to hold the sound of every shoe that had ever squeaked on the hardwood floors, ready to send them echoing back with the slightest provocation. For Theo, it also held the despair and embarrassment of every time he had screwed up in some sort of athletic competition. Spiking the volleyball into his side of the net, flubbing a crucial layup during a basketball game, never quite able to get the puck during floor hockey. Memories of the looks he got every time that happened, barely held at bay. Memories of some stupid jock, blessed with all the athletic prowess Theo could only hope for, levelling a withering glance at him with a cocksure yet pitying smile, shaking his head.

It was the same smile Theo got from his dad on a regular basis. A smile he'd learned to despise.

But now, entering the gym with Laura, it felt all different. The echoey room was in total darkness. Laura closed the door behind them as quietly as she could. As she made her way to Theo, he felt her hand grab hold of his again, soft and cool. The empty feeling left Theo again.

Is she feeling the same thing at all? he wondered.

"Okay, Theo, I'm gonna turn my light on."

If she is, she's sure hiding it well.

The powerful beam stabbed at the darkness. It revealed so little. Theo turned his on at a right angle to hers. The dark receded grudgingly.

They picked out details in the half-light. The stripes across the parquet floor, marking the relevant areas of the various sports. The volleyball nets strung across one wall. The mats used for wrestling—always so cold against bare skin—hung against another wall like padded art. Over to the right, large netted bags held basketballs and volleyballs.

The little bastards could be anywhere. Hell, in this dark, that big bastard could be in here. Standing in the corner, waiting. All they had to do was miss one section. Just one. Walk by it and the fuckers would be on them like flies on shit.

They stood where they were, swinging their beams around the room. Laura was squeezing tighter on his hand. They scanned as much of the room as they could from that one point.

"Let's go," Theo said.

"'Kay."

He tried to lighten the mood again.

"This is, of course, where the expendable crewmember would be killed on *Star Trek*. Those red tunics are fatal."

"Very funny," she said. They started forward, eyes watching for any movement. Ears tuned to any foreign sound.

Was that skittering?

"Was th—"

"WHAT?" Theo said, way too loud, his voice thundering around the room. "Jee-zuz! You scared the shit right outta me! Was that what?"

"Would you keep it down?" Laura hissed. "Did you hear that noise? Was it those little things crawling around?"

"I don't know," Theo said. "I can't tell cuz one of us keeps talking. Stop and listen."

They stood still, letting the residual sounds die. No movement. No breathing. Twin beams of light swept the room in great arcs. Nothing. But Theo felt her hand, slightly sweaty now, but not unpleasant, tighten its grip on his yet again.

A minute passed. Two.

Bupkes. Diddly. Nada.

Theo let out a breath. "I don't think there's anything. I didn't hear anything."

"I think you're right. Let's go."

Laura took a step. There was a soft, light scrape.

"There! It's—" She took another step. Another scrape. Step. Scrape. She let his hand go and was spinning in a tight circle, looking for anything that was coming at her from any angle. "Something's *following* me."

Theo pointed the beam of his flashlight to her feet. "What?" she said, panicked. "What? Is there one…"

Theo couldn't help his reaction. He laughed. One of those laughs that bubble up out of nowhere. Deep, gut-shaking, belly laughs. He tried to explain. It came out gibberish.

"It'ssss…itsyer…ssssssss…sh…shhhhh…oooooozzzz…"

It only heightened her panic. She began to dance a jig.

"Where? Where…is…it?"

Theo, unable to speak at all, could only point at her shoe.

She lifted her foot, and her untied shoelace slid across the hardwood floor. The little plastic tabs scraped lightly across the tiles. Laura stared at it unbelievingly, still trying to equate it with one of the demon dogs.

Theo lost it. Hands on his knees, eyes squirting tears, completely silent, lung-sucking laughter.

"Not that fucking funny," she finally said.

That did it. Theo fell down. She was killing him.

♦♦♦

ALL WAS BLACK. All was gone. All was pain. That thing was killing her.

The nothingness outside the windows was the nothingness in her mind. It poured in like mercury and filled each crack and crevice in her brain.

She could not feel. She could not cry. She could not think.

Marcia was in hell.

CHAPTER TWENTY-FOUR

LAURA AND THEO re-entered the compound. Laura was obviously trying her best to look pissed at Theo, but every once in a while he caught a little smirk squeaking out. It was too damn funny.

Popper and the Toad were busy loading items on another rolling platform. Popper still seemed to ensure he remained surrounded by the ring of lights. No doubt he had never left it.

The Toad pulled his glasses off and wiped the sweat from his brow with the sleeve of his shirt. He had two bright-red spots on the bridge of his nose from where the glasses rested. His eyes looked too far back into his blond head without the magnifying effect of the lenses.

"What's the scoop?" he asked.

"There's nothing on this floor," Laura told Popper and the Toad.

"Except a killer shoelace," Theo added.

She spun, her finger in his face. "You, shut up."

The smirk was back. Theo smiled back for a second, but the smile ran away when he remembered Steph doing the same finger-in-the-face thing to Stash and the Toad just a few hours before.

Toad flashed a look of confusion, not understanding what either of the other two were talking about, and chose to ignore it. Popper just looked annoyed.

"Swlabr and his buddies must still be on the second or third floors," Theo said. "Why they didn't chase us down the stairs I don't know, but they sure as hell ain't here."

No one wanted to think it might be because there was another cluster of people trapped somewhere on those floors. Another caf situation. More death.

"Must have been the flashcubes," the Toad said.

"Must have been," Laura said, nodding.

"No help from the Book?" Popper asked.

"No." Theo hefted the small book bag Laura had given him. The Book now rode in there, never leaving his side. Theo thought he felt It shift every once in a while, almost like It was trying to get comfortable in Its new resting place. He wasn't going to tell Popper he didn't even try using the Book. He avoided the vile thing as much as he could, now that he had dredged up whatever information he felt he could safely glean from Its monstrous pages.

"So, I guess we set the trap on the first floor and see if we can bring it down?" the Toad asked.

See if we can bring it down. We. Like that's gonna happen. Theo held his tongue.

"Yep, sounds like a plan, Stan," Theo said. He hated that expression, but still used it all the time. *Damn you, Paul Simon!*

Laura looked right at Popper. "So I guess Theo and I are going to be the bait? Again?"

Popper looked down. Not really embarrassed, more like he was just avoiding the obvious answer. The silence stretched and bunched like an elastic band twisted too much.

"We'll get things set up down here," the Toad said. "Give us ten minutes and we should be good to go."

"Fine." Theo was getting to know that tight-lipped expression on Laura's face very well by now.

♦♦♦

"HERE KITTYKITTYKITTYYYYYYY..."

"Theo?" Laura said.

"Yeah?" Theo answered.

"Shut. The fuck. Up."

"You're sayin' that a lot lately."

"Shut the—"

"Sorry."

"Don't mention it."

Theo and Laura had walked the length of the school one more time on the ground floor just to make sure there was nothing there, and to also make sure they knew exactly which room Popper and the Toad had set up in. They left Popper and the Toad behind to finish the trap and took the south stairs to the second floor, opening the door as quietly as possible. There were monsters around here somewhere.

♦♦♦

POPPER AND THE Toad finished dragging all the equipment into the computer class and were ready to set it up.

"Okay," said Popper, "we've got to leave a space big enough for this thing to get in between the lights, so make sure you space them far enough apart. We'll set up the generator behind the lights so it can't get to it."

"I think we have enough cable that we can even run the generator out the door and across to the other side," said the Toad. "We'll just have to duct tape the cords to the floor."

"Even better. Good thinking, Dennis."

"Thanks, Mr. Popper."

"Call me Tom. 'Mr. Popper' sounds too close to a soft drink. And I really don't like 'Major Tom.'"

"You know about that, huh?"

"How could I not? I've even had some parents call me that, albeit inadvertently." He stopped, seeming to ponder. "At least

I believe it was inadvertent." The Toad had never seen anyone ponder before, had never thought of anyone actually pondering. Most of the people he hung with didn't even think, let alone ponder. But Popper was different. If anyone were to ponder something, it would be Popper.

"I'm just not sure of the reference. Does it have to do with the GI Joe resemblance?"

The Toad's shocked laugh tumbled out of him. Never in a million years would he ever have expected to be talking to the calculus teacher about this.

"GI Joe? You know about that, too?"

"I'm not hearing impaired, Dennis."

"Yeah." The Toad cleared his throat. He knew he had contributed his share to the GI Joe and Major Tom monikers. He wound the electrical power cords around and around his arm nervously.

"Actually," he said, "the 'Major Tom' thing is from David Bowie." He stopped, expecting Popper to pick it up immediately. He didn't.

For a smart guy, he could be stupid sometimes. Popper was still looking at him. Time for an explanation, obviously.

"Bowie? You know…'Ground Control to Major Tom'?"

Nothing. Blank stare. Popper was just standing there, hands full of lights.

"'Space Oddity'?"

"Ah, the Kubrick film?"

"Who's Kubrick?" The Toad shook his head. How could someone not know Bowie, but know some Kubrick joker? "Really famous song? 'Bout a guy in space? Ever heard of it?"

"Regrettably, no. My taste runs more to classical recordings. This…Major Tom…it's one of his songs?"

"It's *two* of his songs. 'Space Oddity' and 'Ashes to Ashes.'" Popper had obviously never heard of it. No use trying to explain. "Anyway, that's where the Major Tom thing comes from. David Bowie."

"Thank you for clearing that up, Dennis. I'll have to investigate that once we extricate ourselves from this predicament."

"Yeah, what you said," the Toad replied. *Why couldn't he just use normal words?*

They set to work, the Toad running the power cords, Popper setting up and positioning the lights.

"So, why this room, Mr. Popper?"

"Call me Tom. Please."

"Okay…Tom."

Popper smiled. "I decided on this room because it's one of the smallest in the school. No windows. Before we put the computer in here, we used to joke that this would be the perfect prison for any unruly students. Of course, with *that* monstrosity in here," he said, pointing to the computer, "there isn't a whole lot of room for anything else."

"Except maybe a demon from hell."

"Yes. Hopefully."

The Toad looked over at 'the monstrosity' Popper referred to. It was a marvel of technology, able to run both FORTRAN and COBOL computer languages. At about ten feet long, it was one of the smaller computers on the market. The school had hand-picked some of the brightest students to participate in a test class for computer programming. Only the best and the brightest.

Steph had been in that class, the Toad remembered. The Toad had not even been considered. But the only thing that would have interested him would have been Steph anyway, so it was no big loss.

"You know much about these things, Mr.…Tom?"

"Some. Most of the math and science instructors had to take an introductory course for some basic knowledge. I can tell you, these things are the future."

"Why? What are they good for?"

"Lots of things. You can program it for various tasks, like figuring out averages, totalling large quantities of numbers, that sort of thing."

"So it's a big calculator?"

"Yes. But think about all the things you do in my class, or in Mr. Corrigan's functions class. Students used to use a slide rule. That's going to be a dead art in a year or two."

The Toad remembered seeing a slide rule that his dad had. He could never figure it out. Thank god for calculators. Popper continued.

"The same will happen with computers. One day, functions and operations that would take hours to do will be done in minutes. Hook this computer up to a machine and it will perform the same task over and over again, never getting bored, never needing a break—except for periodic maintenance."

"Sounds more like it's gonna put a lot of people out of work." The Toad eyed the computer suspiciously, like it would be the next demon he would need to conquer. Popper continued on, oblivious, in lecture mode and not stopping for anything. *Hell, there are demons in the school and Popper's* still *lecturing!* He still concentrated on the task at hand, placing the lights, but his mouth kept going.

The Toad was sure he was one of those people who could walk and chew gum at the same time. *What does Laura see in this guy?*

"There's even some exciting work being done by connecting computers together much like we do right now with phones. It's called the ARPANET, and it's a network, though ours will utilize the USENET."

"So, what, they form one big superbrain or something?" The Toad remembered hearing, or reading, a story like that. Everyone in the story died and the computer took over the world. Something like that, anyway.

Popper smiled again. "No, but linking them up allows them to communicate with each other, or allows the users to communicate with each other. You can type messages and send them to another connected computer. That user can read your message and send one back."

"Like a computerized letter."

"Exactly! I believe it's called electronic correspondence. Queen Elizabeth was apparently one of the first to receive one of these letters and that was almost five years ago. 1976, if I remember right."

"So this is some pretty hot stuff, huh?"

"Absolutely. It will revolutionize the world someday."

"Yeah, well, I'll stick with the phone. It's easier." The Toad didn't want to hurt Popper's feelings because he seemed so hot on the idea, but it seemed this wasn't anything he couldn't do himself with a calculator and a phone. Whatever cranks your corn, as his mother always said.

They finally got the generator situated in the room across the hall, the wires carefully taped to the floor and connected to the carefully placed lights. It looked like everything was set.

"Okay," Popper said. "Let's do a quick run through and make sure everything works."

♦♦♦

THEY COULDN'T SEE more than thirty feet down the hallway because of the fucking curve that some fucking architect thought would be so fucking modern.

Thanks, asshole, Theo thought. *Never thought about a goddamn demon when you were planning your sightlines, did you?*

Blood trailed from one end of the hall to the other. He shared a cautious look with Laura, then turned back to the slick floor.

Someone rolled out the red carpet for us, Theo thought. *Oh Jesus, what's the matter with me? This was in someone's fucking veins not too long ago. Shit, it could just as easily be my blood on the floor.*

They walked past the empty classrooms, where Theo had spent so much of his life.

Mr. Nelson Ledden's algebra class. Nels had an unconscious habit of screwing his face up into a ridiculously wide grimace whenever he concentrated on something. Theo and his buddies were guilty of taking things up for him to explain just to get him to grimace. It was Theo who grimaced now, though. Blood was splashed throughout his classroom like someone had hooked it up to a lawn sprinkler.

Mr. MacNamee's English class. MacNamee was truly bizarre weirdo who was never seen without his walking stick and purple-tinted glasses. His wife, also a Clarington High teacher, wanted to be reincarnated as a cat. MacNamee taught Theo's class about utopian societies through *Brave New World, Animal Farm,* and *1984*. Theo had enjoyed that class for the most part. The room was clean, except for one overturned desk and some papers on the floor.

"Ohmigod! What's that smell?"

Miss Helmsley's English class. Better known as Miss Piggy. She washed her hair once a month so as not to destroy the pH balance. From the condition of her class, she would never have to worry about it again. She was on the floor, her miniskirt hiked up to her chest. Her vaginal area was slimed with the contents of her eviscerated abdomen. Sausage-like shapes formed a foul-smelling loincloth that made them both gag from the hallway. Laura shut the door, her free hand covering her mouth and nose.

French class. Economics. Law class. Theo had been in them all, often not giving two shits what the instructors had tried to teach him. He'd been in the classes reading the latest Stephen King or Graham Masterton novel instead of learning about stratocumulus cloud formations or the Magna Carta. He'd played poker. He'd slept. He'd done everything except pay attention to what was being taught. They had tried to teach him, to engage him. Every one of the teachers had tried their best to instill knowledge in him but he'd known none of it was ever going to be applicable once he hit the real world.

Well, here it was. This was the real world, in a fucked-up sort of way. What good was the Pythagorean theorem now? Theo could recite pi to fifteen decimal places, but who gave a shit? Would that put the blood back in veins? Would it put Helmsley's guts back in her body?

He realized he had been completely right all along. None of the lessons they'd been given were ever going to help him. There he was, justified in his beliefs at the ripe old age of seventeen. A hollow victory.

All Theo wanted right now was to sit in one of those classes again. Wanted one of those teachers doing what they could to get through to him. Hell, he wanted to sit in a class with his friends and let that teacher bore him. Bored would work well for him right now. He wanted to be away from these dark, echoing halls. Away from the heavy smell of his own fear-sweat. Away from the infernal weight of the thing in his backpack. Theo wanted back that shiny, happy world of what could be. A world rich with endless possibilities.

Correction: he wanted that world, but without his old man.

"Peter did all this just to kill his dad," Theo said, looking around at the carnage and darkness.

"Yeah. It's too bad some people don't have respect for their family."

"Or themselves."

"Or themselves," Laura agreed. "Good point." She looked over at him.

"Your father's no saint, is he, Theo?"

Theo huffed. "No, he sure isn't. My dad's a whore. A drunken whore."

Laura didn't seem to know what to say, so she said nothing. Sometimes listening was just keeping your mouth shut.

"I mean, I don't get it," Theo said. "My dad's one of the smartest people I've ever seen. Way smarter than me. I wish I had half his brains."

"Now, Theo—"

"No. I mean it! I've watched him working on the car, and sometimes there's an area he can't reach, or some part in an awkward position. Instead of tearing half the engine apart, he'll go into the garage and build the tool he needs to get the job done. And it's not any half-assed thing either. He knows exactly where the stress points are, how the leverage will work, everything. He just knows." Theo tapped at his temple.

They continued down the hall, briefly checking rooms as they went. Still, she stayed quiet, giving Theo the stage.

"When I was young, he used to build things for me. Little things out of wooden thread spools and elastics. When I got older, it was airplanes. Then it was a hovercraft."

"A hovercraft?" Laura asked, incredulous.

"Yeah! He got the frame welded for a one-man hovercraft. That was when I was about eleven. Mom pretty much had a shit-hemorrhage, but we were bound and determined to do it."

Theo paused, reliving the memory, chewing on it like a bit of food discovered wedged in his teeth. He didn't seem to like the flavour.

"He'd been an ass before then, but we managed to get along. Then he started drinking. Then he started fucking around. At least, that's when I noticed it. Maybe it was getting worse. Maybe I was just getting older and more aware. Mom says he had been doing it for years. I guess it was getting harder to hide." He paused. "You know what smell immediately triggers a thought about my dad?" Theo asked.

"No. What do you remember?"

"The smell of booze. A smell that oozes out his pores. A sort of sick-sweet smell. It's always there, to the point where I guess I just sort of accept it as one of those normal family smells. Like Marcia. She smelled of some soap…Jergens, I think. Every time I smell it, I think of her, y'know? And, as fucked-up as this is gonna sound, whenever I smell that sick-sweet booze smell, part of me feels comfort. It's the smell of my father, you know? The smell of family."

"Yeah," she said, "Jude had a smell too. I loved it." She abruptly cut off and Theo assumed that was a deep cut she didn't want to probe.

"Anyway," Theo said, "his whoring got out of hand a few years back and now we get threats all the time. Guys calling saying they're gonna kill him. I'm a joke at the school cuz of him."

"Theo, that's not true."

"You know what they call him? Dick Clarke, on account of him thinking with his dick. They say it behind my back, but I hear it." His eyes watered up.

"Theo… "

"You know what someone told me once? 'You can pick your nose, and you can pick your friends, but you can't pick your family.'"

Laura smiled. "That's so true," she said.

Theo shook his head, as though shaking the thoughts away.

"Whoa!" he said. "This is getting too heavy." He straightened up, wiped his eyes with the back of his hand, and said, in a terrible Monty Python accent, "Roight! A change of topic is in orhdah! Roight!" As fast as it came, the accent was gone.

He looked at Laura with more seriousness. After a pause, he asked, "Why did you start teaching?"

Heavy sigh. "Good one." She looked at him. "I was strapped for cash when my husband died. He was going to take care of me."

"Then the real world hit you right between the eyes."

"Something like that, yeah." Her smile was forced, weary.

"Do you like it? The teaching?"

"Most of the time, yeah, I do. Every once in a while I see real talent, and I get excited. Maybe one day, I think, that one student will make something of themselves, and in some little way I'd be part of the creation."

"Yeah, but that's every once in a while. What about all those other times? I've been in your class. I've seen the other shit. What about then?"

"Well, I actually thought that when I had you in the class. You were my every-once-in-a-while kid."

That screwed him up. He feigned surprise at the statement.

But it was a lie. Theo knew he had talent. He could draw. It was just about the only thing he could do and feel a sense of peace, a sense of worth. A glimmer of what could be. Laura was one of the few who had actually encouraged him. But Theo was too busy being the angry young man to pay any notice, even though the positive attention felt so good.

"Thanks," he said.

"Don't thank me," she said, stopping to face him. She put her hands on Theo's shoulders, lightly shaking him. "Do something with it! If we ever get out of here, do something with it! Dammit Theo, you're a smart kid, and you can do so damn much. Don't let life pass you by. One day you'll wake up and find out ten or twenty years have gone by. You can never get them back. Don't waste them."

"So what are you doing, then? Are you wasting yours?"

"No." She smiled. A genuine smile. "I'm getting you and Dennis out of here."

He smiled back. But at the edge of his peripheral vision, Theo noticed something.

"Oh, Jesus Christ," Theo whispered.

"What? What is it?" she whispered back. She probably thought there were creepies about. She was wrong.

♦♦♦

THE NOTHINGNESS PERVADED Marcia's entire being. Around her and through her, a universe full of emptiness.

Fading…

Fading…

And then, with no warning, a sensation.

After nothingness, any sensation was a powerful and painful experience, but this was pain in its own right, delivered with surgical skill and loving detail.

The nothingness blew away and blinding, white-hot brutal agony flooded in.

It was pain, but it was *something*. Marcia embraced it as a desert accepts the rain.

♦♦♦

THEO LOOKED PAST Laura to Mr. Corrigan's classroom. There was a large pool of blood just outside the class. And the broken body of Joe Barrett. From the slashes and swipes running through it, it looked like a fight had happened there. But it was inside the class that drew Theo's attention. From where he stood, he could see two legs ending in familiar running shoes. One of the shoes was blood-soaked and missing a heel. Beneath the shoes, a large pond of blood.

"It's Stash."

CHAPTER TWENTY-FIVE

THEO AND LAURA eased cautiously into Mr. Corrigan's class. The curtains mercifully blocked the nothing outside the windows. Corrigan wasn't there. None of the people who had taken Corrigan's Functions & Relations course were in the classroom.

Except Stash, who'd been messed up. Badly.

Theo looked at him and trembled in shock. Stash was his best friend. He couldn't be dead. Not now that Theo had found him.

Laura knelt beside him and felt for a pulse. She glanced quickly at Theo, catching his eyes, obviously stunned to find one. She smiled.

"Holy Christ, Laura, he's still alive!" It didn't seem possible. There was so much blood everywhere. Christ, there were *chunks* of Stash scattered around the room.

Theo remembered watching a special on TV about sharks. How when they got a sniff of blood, they went nuts. The term the narrator used was 'feeding frenzy.' Theo remembered laughing because here they had been showing these sharks going batshit and ripping and tearing away at something that had been alive a few seconds earlier, and this guy on the TV was going, 'The sharks go into a feeding frenzy' in this weird, calm, dispassionate voice. Hell, Theo got more emotion from his old man telling Theo to go to the store and pick him up a pack of smokes.

And yet, here he was, trying to remain calm and dispassionate while looking at his best friend. His best friend who had been the entrée at the last feeding frenzy.

Laura knelt down beside Stash and ripped his shirt open over his thin, hairless chest. Had he been conscious, he would have been mortified. *Figures, a good-looking older woman is ripping his clothes off and he can't even enjoy it.*

Christ Almighty! What am I thinking? Theo didn't know whether to laugh or cry.

"Laura, what're you doing?"

"Trying to assess how bad his injuries are." She pulled away his shirt.

Theo had seen millions of horror movies and slasher flicks, read lots of gory books and comics. At this point in his life, Theo should have been one of those disenfranchised youths desensitized to violence and human tragedy. But one look at the wounds inflicted on his best friend's body—wounds looking like they'd been committed with a dull ice cream scoop—slashes to his body ripped as though from a slow-moving chainsaw—wounds seemingly delivered for ultimate pain.

Theo looked and saw that Stash was like a bag full of broken glass, all points and sharp edges, and that was it. Theo turned and heaved, his recent lunch jettisoning violently from his body.

Swlabr had done this to Stash, and it looked like it had taken its time because it was just so much fucking fun. Theo didn't think he could ever imagine such trauma visited on a living body. And with such obvious glee.

"Theo, you okay?" Laura said. "Look, why don't you step outs—"

"Thee?" They both looked down. "Thee? Tha yoo?" Stash couldn't make all the right sounds with the jagged fragments of teeth left in his head.

Tears sprung to Theo's eyes as he answered. "Ya, bud. It's me. I'm here. You take it easy, 'kay?"

"Nahhhh...hurssss...hurssss baaaad..."

"I know, buddy, I know. But we're gonna get you fixed up. It won't hurt anymore, okay? You'll be good again." Laura looked at Theo, as though to check to see if he really believed what he was saying. He was not.

"Fugyoo," Stash mumbled through his broken mouth. "Doan fuggin lie. 'Sssbaaad. Guh doo sump, 'kay?" Theo could barely understand him, concentrating hard on each syllable.

"Do something?" A slow nod. Theo looked at Laura, then back to Stash. "What do you want me to do?"

Stash took a long time. It was like he was gathering himself together. He swallowed once. Twice. Then he angled his head toward him, shattered bones grinding in his neck. Purposely looked Theo in the eyes.

"I wanyoo t'kill meeee."

♦♦♦

"SO LAURA AND Theo come screaming down the hall..."

"From either direction, north or south," Popper added.

"No," said the Toad. "The south stairs were frozen back when Joe...back when Swlabr trapped us."

"Right. Absolutely. So we should anticipate them coming from the north."

"Yep. With all the hounds of hell hot on their trail." That thought sent a shiver through

(pop goes the weasel)

the Toad. If Popper saw it, he ignored it.

"We scoot across the hall," the Toad continued, "and hide behind the door of Mrs. Parsten's office." He walked over and touched the purple door.

Mrs. Parsten was the school guidance teacher. She was a jovial bleach blonde with small, poochy lips. Those lips fascinated the Toad every time he talked to her. Couldn't keep his eyes off them. All the time he had been setting up the generator in front of her scratched, paper-strewn desk, he could smell the lingering scent of her perfume. He thought of those lips.

He just wanted one more chance to see them. He'd walk up and plant a big kiss on those lips, twenty-odd years his senior. Oh, yes he would. If only he could get out of here.

There was a grey line of duct tape running from the computer room across the hall and under the purple door. The Toad hoped it wouldn't act as a pointer to an all-you-can-eat buffet starring the two of them.

Would you like a little freshly ground Popper with your Toad?

"Yes," said Popper, confusing the Toad, but bringing him back around to the present. "Laura and Theo will enter the computer room and immediately duck to the right and behind the lights." The two of them walked across the hall again, entered the computer room and, with deliberate slowness, angled to the right and behind two large floodlights, pacing out the planned steps like a wedding rehearsal.

"Okay, cool," said the Toad. "We wait for Swlabr to enter, you grab Theo and Laura, and I hit the genny. You sure it's gonna start? If it doesn't..."

Popper's expression was neutral. "If it doesn't, we're all dead."

♦♦♦

THEO LOOKED UP at Laura. "I..." He couldn't make the words. Trying again. "I...I can't."

"Theo, he's in pain." Then, mouthing the words, no sound, so Stash wouldn't hear. "He's going to die. Nothing we can do." Her head going from side to side in an exaggerated *no* motion.

No, *she was saying.* No hope.

(no one else dies)

"But he's my best fucking friend! Don't you fucking get it? I CAN'T DO THIS!"

More friends will die at your hands.

"Yessss. Cannnn." Stash. Stash begging.

~...yessss yoooou cannnn yoooourrrr frieeeennnnd willll diiiie kiiiillll hiiiimmmm...~

"Theo," Laura said, not worrying about being quiet, "look at him. He's dying and he's in pain. We've got to do something."

(no one else dies)

Stash, Laura, the Book in his head, he couldn't take it.

"No. Nonono." Theo sank to the floor. "No more. Nomorenomorenomore." It came out almost as a plea. *Can no one help me here?* it asked. "Can't do it. Can't

(no one else dies)

do this anymore." He tumbled in a spinning black hole. The pit of

(no one else dies)

despair. The valley of the shadow of death. Everything went dark...

♦♦♦

IT WAS A bright, sunny, beautiful August day. Theo's feet made little puffs of dust as he walked down the gravel road, leaving the toes of his running shoes grey. The day was hot enough that he had taken his shirt off and tucked a wad of it in the back of his jeans, leaving a flap hanging over his ass. Printed on the shirt, the Vargas girl from the Cars' *Candy-O* album sprawled seductively across a car, albeit upside down. *Looks better than my ass*, he thought, and it was a lot cooler. Even if his scrawny, hairless chest was out for all the world to see.

At that point, Theo couldn't give a shit either way.

It was about eight miles from his house to Stash's. Theo had stopped crying about three miles into the walk, and now he was just getting more and more pissed at himself.

His mom and dad had been at it again. His mother ragging on his father because he had been caught yet again fucking someone else's wife. Theo's dad, blasted out of his head before noon, yelling incoherent obscenities back at her.

The normal weekend ritual.

Theo couldn't understand why they stayed together. If it was for Theo's sake, it was misguided as hell. He sure wasn't getting any benefit from it, other than learning how not to conduct a marriage.

Secretly, he thought they sort of enjoyed it, in some sick way. Gave them something to do. What else could it be? Why else would a woman stay with a man who consistently cheated on her? Why would a man stay with a woman when he obviously wanted anyone else but her?

Whatever the reason, Theo couldn't handle it anymore. He had walked past them, unseen as usual, got his shoes on, and opened the door. Then he stopped, listening to the two of them verbally tearing pieces off each other, voices ragged and sharp as each tried to out-volume the other one. He didn't know why he did what he did next. He just did it.

Theo went back into the living room and told them both to shut the fuck up.

There was stunned silence for about ten seconds. It was ten seconds of empowerment for Theo. *He* had done this? *He* had managed to shut them up? *He* had created the calm in the storm? *He* had this power?

No. Wrong on all counts.

His mom started in on Theo, screaming that he was just as bad as his dad with his gutter mouth and sewer mind, and that he was going to turn out worse if he didn't smarten up.

Smarten up. Jesus, how many times had he heard that expression? Did they really view him as that stupid? He wasn't the one who fucked and drank and bitched his way through life. And he was at the age where he *was* supposed to be fucking and drinking and bitching his way through life!

Theo's father just let her rant while he got himself upright. That proved to be a chore in itself, and if this was any other time, Theo might have laughed at the sight. Finally vertical, he staggered over to Theo, his expression neutral. For a dim second or two, Theo honestly thought his father might stand up for him.

"Y'know, hon…the boy's right. We're being stupid and hurtful. Let's work out this problem with love, compassion, and understanding."

Maybe a little overboard, but that had been the basic hope running through Theo's mind.

Right up until his father had sucker punched him. A sloppy yet powerful fist that had been so unexpected that Theo found it hard to believe even as the pain swept in after the blow that mashed his lips against his teeth.

Hit him back! Theo's mind had screamed. *Take this son of a bitch down!*

But all Theo had been able to do was stand there, shaking. His father could have done it again and Theo would not have lifted a hand to defend himself. *I'm a pussy,* he had thought.

And this was his *dad*! The thought of hitting his own father was so alien to him, Theo couldn't even form a fist with his own right hand. But still his mind screamed to take him down, to teach the fucker a lesson, to give him back some of his own medicine.

Just *do* something!

But Theo was frozen.

Something that had come so easily to his father, Theo couldn't muster the will to do himself.

His father looked at Theo with all the contempt he could muster, turned, and plopped his ass back down in the easy chair. "Wipe the blood off your face and get me a beer."

Theo's sum total act of defiance had been to ignore his father's request and walk out of the house. That was it. There had been nothing else in him.

So Theo walked. He spat bright-red blood onto the dry, thirsty dirt. And he cried.

And, eventually, Theo ended up at Stash's place.

He walked the length of the driveway, a thin trail through tall trees, to the sound of a buzzing mower. Stash was just finishing cutting the grass. He waved, then ran the mower over the last strip of long grass and cut the motor. He gave Theo a "Hey!" and a wave and met him as Theo walked up the drive.

True friends—someone who will do anything for you with no conditions attached—are rare in this world. A friend will always be able to read your mood from a mile off. They'll take in the obvious fact that you've taken a beating. And a true friend will always know how to react.

"Fuckin' parents, huh?" Stash said. "You look whaddayacallit shitty. Wanna go for a swim?"

And that was that. The situation was recognized and that big balloon of misery and self-pity that Theo had blown up for the last eight miles was popped.

Stash was the best.

Theo borrowed a pair of gawky red Adidas shorts from Stash—the kind with the double white stripe down the sides—and they hit the lake behind the house. The cool water felt good on the rising, bruised lump on Theo's lip. Things got better, and the events of the morning extended farther and farther back in the rear-view mirror.

After a while, the two friends got out of the water and sat on the dock, just soaking up the rays. Stash said, "I'm thirsty. Wanna whaddayacallit Coke?"

"Yeah, sounds good."

Stash's dad had put their old fridge in the garage, and there was always pop in there. Sometimes they got lucky. Sometimes there was beer. Yeah, Theo could use a beer right about now. He could put the cool brown bottle to the bruise on the side of his jaw. *Oh yeah, a wobbly pop would be real nice...*

Theo had been stretched out on the warm wood of the dock when he heard footsteps coming back. "So," Theo said, "what's the scoop? We get lucky today?"

"Oh yeah, you little sumbitch, you're gonna get real lucky."

Dad.

"Get up! Get up, you scrawny little shit, so I can knock you down again."

Theo had turned and got to his feet. He was cornered at the end of the dock. Yes, he could have jumped off the dock, but that would have been too excessive a display of cowardice, even for Theo.

Did he go around to all of my friends like this? Looking for me?

His father blocked the way back down the dock. He was so drunk now he had that rolling pitch going, just to stay balanced.

"Dad, I—"

"Don'tchoo fuckin' 'Dad, I' me! Where do you get off tellin' me andjer mother ta shut up, and then ignore me when I'm talkin' ta ya? Huh?"

Theo could feel that same prick in his eyes. No! He would not cry in front of this asshole. His father would not get that satisfaction from him. Not today. "Dad, look, you're drunk, and—"

"YER GODDAMN RIGHT I AM! AN' I HAD TO GET MY OWN FUCKIN' BEER—"

"Mr. Clarke?"

The voice behind surprised him so much, Theo's father almost went off the side of the dock when he spun around.

Right into the business end of a double-barreled shotgun. Stash had called it an 'over 'n' under' or some such shit.

"Bobby!" The complete change in tone in his father's voice was stunning. Surprise. Fear.

Respect.

"Bobby, lissen. I was just havin' a little family discussion with ol' Thelonious here and uh..."

"No," said Stash. His voice was cool and quiet. It was everything Theo had wanted to be in these situations. "You weren't having a *little* anything, and it sure as hell didn't sound anything like a discussion to me."

"Bobby, put the gun down."

"I don't think so, Mr. Clarke. I saw the thumping you gave Theo there," he nudged the gun slightly over Clarke's shoulder to indicate where Theo was standing, "and I think I might have just cause to shoot you where you stand."

Stash's voice took on a softer, innocent tone as he tilted his head to the side. "Aw, jeez, officer, I don't know what happened. Mr. Clarke just showed up drunk and raving about how he was gonna kill us 'n' all. And what with Theo already being beat up this morning, we were in legitimate fear for our lives here."

Then his voice came back to normal. His head straightened as his cheek hugged the stock again. Theo watched his eyes squint down, Clint Eastwood style.

"Boom," he said, his voice low and menacing.

Theo's dad jumped just a little at the word, though it wasn't said loud.

"Justifiable homicide. Right, Theo? Learned that in law class," he said.

Theo's father turned his head toward Theo. "Yup," Theo said, keeping his voice even. "Self-defense. Get off scot-free."

Theo had to admit the panicked look in his father's eyes made his heart swell a little.

His father kind of ping-ponged between the two teenagers, too drunk and panicked to realize Theo was in the blast corridor if Stash did choose to take him out. Theo and Stash both stood there, not saying a word. *Let him think it through,* Stash's eyes seemed to be saying, though they never left Clarke's. *Don't say anything, let him think it through and he'll clue in in a minute.*

It took Clarke a few seconds, but he finally realized he was beat.

"Okay, boys," he said, running a shaking hand over his whiskered face, "listen, I'm just gonna head on home. Theo and me can finish this up later."

"No, Dad. It's finished now." Theo's voice held, didn't quaver as he had feared it would.

"That's right, Mr. Clarke. It's finished now. And just to make sure, I'm gonna give Theo a present to keep things on the up and up." He patted his back pocket and they both heard the metallic tap.

Stash backed off the end of the dock to let Clarke pass, the barrel of the gun never wavering. As Theo's father edged past him, Stash said, "And you give that pretty wife of yours a big kiss for me, okay?"

By now, Clarke couldn't even talk. He staggered to the truck and blew a plume of dust into the shimmering summer sky as he sped off up the road Theo had walked just two hours earlier.

As they watched him go, Theo's eyes drifted to Stash's rear end. There was no gun as he had promised Theo's father. Theo reached down and pulled the can from the waistband of Stash's shorts.

"I'm supposed to keep him in line with a fucking can of Coke?"

"Yeah, well, we needed something to put the whaddayacallit fear of god into him. Besides, with your fuckin' breath, I figure you could belch him to death."

Theo just stared at him. A little smirk cracked the side of his mouth.

That was all it took. They laughed until they damn near puked.

After it was all over, Theo and Stash sat on the edge of the dock, trailing their feet in the water, sipping their Cokes.

"Hey," Theo said, "I just wanted to thank you. For, you know…earlier."

"No sweat, bud."

"Would you have shot him?"

"Naw. No shells. Thing wasn't even loaded."

Theo looked at him again, and with a whole new perspective. "Remind me never to play poker with you again, all right?"

Stash just laughed.

Theo levelled a sidelong glance at his friend. "I gotta ask. How come you never said 'whaddayacallit' once through that whole exchange with my father?"

Stash smirked. "I only break that out for my whaddayacallit friends."

Theo shook his head and stared into the water for a time. Without raising his head or looking at Stash, he said, "Seriously though. Thank you."

"No problem. You don't need the gun, man. He's just like a dog. If he smells the fear, you're fucked. I just didn't let him smell it. And neither did you. Just keep it up, because he thinks you're one crazy, bugshit motherfucker now."

"Yeah. Guess I fit in with the rest of the family."

"Hey," said Stash, "you know what they say: you can pick your nose and you can pick your friends, but you can't pick your family."

"And you can't wipe them on the back of the couch," Theo answered.

"Yeah, but you can shoot them in self-defense." And that's when Theo realized how much he loved Stash. He had picked good friends.

Theo put his arm around Stash's shoulders without thinking. They were best buds. They were brothers.

♦♦♦

AND NOW, THEO had to somehow kill him.

Chapter Twenty-Six

THEO CAME BACK around to the present situation at the sound of something heavy scraping across the floor. *Oh shit, not them again…*

He spun and jumped to his feet like he had been hit with an electric shock. Laura jumped back. She had a look of surprise on her face, but there was something else there too. A look like she had been caught doing something wrong. What was she doing? Theo looked at Stash. He looked bad, really bad, but he was still breathing.

"What's going on Laura? What are you doing with Mr. Corrigan's desk?"

"Theo," she said, her voice was almost a whisper. "Look, maybe you should just leave for a few minutes." Her eyes pleaded. Her voice had a buttery smoothness that only came out to convince somebody to do something they had no intention of doing.

"Why?" Theo asked. "Why should I leave? What're you doing with the desk, Laura?" He heard his voice getting higher, tighter, but he didn't care.

"Theo—"

"*What* the *fuck* are you doing with the *desk*, Laura?"

She dropped the buttery smoothness. It hadn't been working anyway.

Big sigh. "I've been sitting here looking at the two of you for ten minutes trying to figure out the easiest way to kill Bobby."

"The easiest…what is he? A fuckin' dog that needs to be put down?" His eyes flicked to Bobby. He was out, but his brow was bunched in pain. Then he faced Laura again.

"No, he's a living human being in a lot of pain and he's asking to be released from it. Just like all those people in the cafeteria."

"Yeah, all those people in the cafeteria are going to be in that same pain for all eternity, according to that goddamn Book."

"You're right," she said. She patted at the air, arms spread, palms out, placating. "You're right. But he's different." She pointed to the prone form on the floor between them. "He's been through hell, but that big thing hasn't gotten to him. Yet. Not in any way that's going to damn his soul."

Theo gave her a look. "You willing to bet on that?"

"Yes," she said. No hesitation. "He's begging because he's in pain, Theo. Not because of…of the other."

Theo knew she was right, but still…

"Theo, he's not going to make it out of here, and if we screw up, if we don't make it out, who's gonna help him then?"

Theo stood across from her, looking down at the best friend he had ever had. "Stash taught me everything I know about standing up for myself."

How can I let him go?

"He taught you to do what's right."

"Yeah."

"Then do what's right. Release him from his misery. Like he's asking you to."

"How?" His voice dropped to a whisper. Stash shouldn't be hearing this. The tears came then. *Goddamnit!* He didn't want to cry.

"The fastest and most painless way I could think of was…to break his neck." Her voice took on the same conspiratorial tone.

Theo stared at her.

"Look, I know it sounds barbaric, and it probably is, but what else can we do? I was going to lay him on a couple of desks, leave his head hanging over, and drop that..." she indicated Corrigan's desk "...down to make a quick break. It should kill him instantly."

"You've thought this all through, haven't you, you fucking ghoul?"

"Aw, listen..." Her eyes hurt and watering. Then she tried again. "Theo, listen..."

"No! Jesus! I'm not—"

"You're not gonna what?" Laura snapped, swiping at her tears. "You're not gonna what? Every fucking second we spend arguing, Swlabr is probably doing this to someone else, and *your* friend—your *best* friend—lays there in pain. If you can come up with something else, by all fucking means, because believe me, I sure as hell do not want to have anyone else's blood on my hands." Now her tears came. "I'm just sick and tired of this whole fucking thing," she said.

And with that, they both stood, leaning against desks, suddenly finding the floor interesting enough to stare at. The only sound was the rushing blood in Theo's ears and their breathing.

A loud shriek of protesting metal came from somewhere in the building.

She's right.

Theo scrubbed his hands over his face, pulling them down as though trying to erase the pained expression.

"Pull the desks together," he said with a ragged sigh. "I'll lift him."

♦♦♦

POPPER AND THE Toad sat in the hallway, waiting.

"What in the hell is taking them so long?" the Toad asked. "Christ, I could have covered the whole school by now."

"Dennis, these are extraordinary circumstances. It's going to take as long as it needs. I know Laura. She'll come through."

The Toad looked over at Popper. His normally perfect hair was mussed, his shirttail was out. Sure as hell didn't look like a teacher anymore.

"You and her got a thing?" asked the Toad.

"A 'thing'?"

"Yeah, a thing. Are you guys an item? Are you dating? Swappin' spit?"

"Okay!" Popper said, hand out. "Okay, I understand." He paused for a minute, considering his answer. "I guess we were heading that way. There was definite interest there, from both parties. I don't know anymore. I think it's blown since I refused to go back upstairs."

"Yeah! What's the story there? I mean, hell, you were in a room with one of those things and survived."

"Yes, until I was rescued by a teenager."

"You still survived. There's a lot of people in the caf down there who didn't. Why'd you not wanna go back up?"

Again, the pause. Popper did this when he lectured too.

"I guess, when it comes right down to it, very simply, I was scared. I was just scared."

"Listen," said the Toad. "There ain't nothing wrong with that. I did the same thing. I'm scared of the dark. Get all froze up and stupid."

"Really? Scared of the dark?" Popper's voice held no condemnation. It was more a point of interest.

"Yeah, well, I guess if you want to get technical, it's more a fear of what's gonna come at you in the dark."

Somewhere above them, muffled through the structure, came the sound of shrieking metal.

"Laura will make it. I know she'll make it through."

♦♦♦

STASH WAS LAID across two of the student's desks that had been pulled together. Laura and Theo now had to muscle Mr. Corrigan's desk over to where Stash's head lolled over the edge. The plan was to tip Corrigan's desk up and let it drop. Gravity would hopefully do the rest.

At least, that was the plan according to Laura. Theo couldn't form a coherent thought beyond the realization that he was going to

(more friends will die at your hands)

kill his best friend.

"Theo."

(no one else dies no one)

My best friend. I'm going to ki –

"THEO!"

Theo slid his gaze reluctantly to Laura, his eyes grating, rough balls in his skull. "What." The word came out flat and hard, like he'd spit out a marble.

"Please help me. We've got to move this desk. I know this is hard – god knows I do – but we really don't want to draw this out." She bent, placing her hands under the rim of the desk, elbows tight to her waist. She tilted her head and jutted her chin to the opposite corner of the desk. "Take the other end."

Theo bent and grabbed the other side of the desk, too tired, too numb to argue.

Stash's ragged breathing added a mournful soundtrack to their labours as they scraped the heavy desk across the floor, then, straining, tilted it on its end. Theo heard a great rattling as the contents of the drawers slid to one side.

Examining the angle at which the desk would drop as it tipped over, Laura made some final adjustments by walking it forward a few inches. Finally, there was nothing else to be done. They could delay it no longer.

"Do you want to leave the room, Theo? I'll do this." She made a slight shift as if to take the entire weight of the desk, but Theo shook his head, not meeting her eyes.

"No." Theo moaned. "No, I want to stay."

"You sure? You don't have—"

"I said, I'll stay." Then he moved and Laura did take the weight and balanced the desk as Theo went to his friend. Stash was still, mercifully, unconscious. His glasses were on the floor. Theo picked them up, remembering Stash's constant finger-poke between his eyes to keep them pushed up his nose, even when he wasn't wearing them. Holding them by the gold frames, careful not to smudge the lenses, he folded them and placed them in Stash's left hand, on his chest. Theo's hand rested above Stash's for a few seconds, his head bowed.

"Goodbye, buddy," he whispered. "Love you, man."

He turned back to Laura and nodded, tears slipping down his cheeks. She nodded back. It was time.

"You're sure this will be quick?" Theo asked. "He won't feel it?"

"He shouldn't."

Theo positioned himself behind the desk. From where they stood, they couldn't see Stash. That was a blessing.

"On three."

Theo took a breath.

"One."

God, let this work.

"Two."

Please.

"Three."

They let go of the heavy desk and watched as it arced down toward Stash's head and exposed neck. To Theo, it didn't appear to be going anywhere near fast enough. He didn't think it was going to work. It was the same gut feeling he got going against Crouch in poker. His gut told him when Crouch was bullshitting, and when he wasn't. This was the same. The desk was bullshitting. He knew it wasn't going to work.

It came down with a surprisingly soft thud and Theo watched it shudder, shift, and continue to the floor where it landed with a muffled *whump* as the air escaped from under the flat surface. Theo and Laura were so concerned with its path that it took them both a second to glance back up to Stash.

He was making scary wet sucking noises, the skin of his neck ripped open like a Christmas present to reveal the musculature and inner workings of his throat. Without really knowing, Theo knew they had crushed his windpipe. Stash brought his hand up to his throat—the hand without the glasses—but it was just a useless, mangled thing at the end of the arm.

Stash tried to grab his windpipe and there was nothing there to grab with. Blood pissed down his neck and into his ear and he gurgled and fought and flopped.

"His neck! You said it'd break his neck, Laura!"

Laura looked frantically between Theo and Stash, her hands clasping each other, not knowing what to do. Stash's movements became more violent as he ran out of air.

"Theo…I…"

Theo knew he had no choice. Stash could not suffer any longer. "Jesus *fuck*!" The two sounds ripped from his throat as a wet sob.

He hopped the desk, placed one hand on Stash's heaving, bucking chest. Stash seemed to stop momentarily, then redoubled his efforts to breathe. Theo put his other hand to Stash's blood-slickened jaw, flipped a look to Laura, and pushed as quickly and violently as he could, bending Stash's neck past the breaking point as he bent it down and under the desk surface. Really cranking it, he jerked it until he heard a pop and all the tension fell away.

Stash jerked once more, legs flopping and banging a horrible staccato against the desk, then he was still. No more wet sucking sounds. No more struggling to breathe. No more pain.

No more Stash.

Theo brought Stash's head back up. The muscles in his neck were now loose and pliant as rubber, his head surprisingly heavy. Theo slid him down the desk until his head rested on the surface. He removed his hands from Stash's body and held them out from his own, palms up. One held speckles of blood from Stash's shirt, the other almost black with the mess from Stash's neck. He held them out to Laura as though she could take them away.

He dropped to the floor, hands on his lap, and wept.

♦♦♦

THE PAIN FED her. The pain sustained her.

It was the pain that brought her back. But where had it brought her back to, exactly?

Marcia was sure her eyes were open, but she could see nothing. Not like the nothingness outside the school. This was different. Nothing but black, confining.

A coffin?

No, there's...something, she thought. Some light bleeding through.

She moved to see it better and a hot rod of agony twisted through her. Oh, things were not right in Marcia-land. But the noise she had made! Dull...hollow...metallic.

A locker? Was she in a locker?

Slowly, she brought her hands up and felt cool metal. Yes! She was in a locker!

The hows and whys would come later. She wanted out and she wanted out now.

Pain or no pain.

She heaved against the door with her knees, pushing with everything she had.

No pain, no gain, girl! Push! PUSH!

The door began to give, a few grudging fractions of an inch at a time. She turned her back to the door, putting her weight against it. Her arms trembled and her legs howled in distress.

The door responded with a shrieking anguish all its own, fighting her but losing the battle.

♦♦♦

THEO DID ONE final check of Stash's pulse, placing two fingers to his horribly twisted neck.

Stash was the only guy Theo knew who knew who the Rutles were. He knew who the Bonzo Dog Doo-Dah Band was, and could even sing some of their songs. Stash was the only guy who could see the humour in applauding the key grip when the movie credits were scrolling. Don't applaud the actors, director, or screenwriter. Just the key grip. Maybe the best boy. Stash knew that stuff. Had known that stuff.

There was no pulse.

He slipped a hand under Stash's shoulders and the other under his knees and lifted him off the desks. Stash's head lolled at a terrible angle that made the bile rise in Theo's throat and a wracking sob pass his lips. He saw Laura bring a hand to her mouth and tears stand in her eyes. Gently, Theo lowered Stash to the floor at the front of the class, trying not to bump his head. He walked over to the coat rack in the corner by the chalkboard and lifted the jacket gingerly off its hook. It had hung there so long there was a permanent point where the hook had stretched the fabric.

John Corrigan's wife had bought him the brownish-green corduroy fall jacket last year. Corrigan never had the heart to tell her how much he despised it—though all the students knew and had been sworn to secrecy—so he had worn it for a few days, then just left it at school one day. He let her believe it had been lost or stolen. She had been pissed at him and had decided to punish him by not buying a replacement.

He confided in his students that life had been hell for a couple of weeks, and every now and again she still brought it up, but, considering the alternative was wearing the coat every day, Corrigan figured he got off light.

Theo used the unwanted thing to cover Stash's—Robert Jonathan Bostash's—body. It only covered his head and upper torso, making it look like he was playing some sick game of peekaboo.

"Hey, bud," Theo said. "I gotta go. You take care, okay? Don't you worry about me. I ain't gonna let them smell the fear…cuz I…uh…"

He wiped his nose and eyes, took a long, snuffling breath.

"I'm one bugshit crazy…motherfucker…"

Another big breath.

"And I've got you to thank for it. I love you, man." He put a gentle palm to his friend's chest. "I'm so sorry."

Theo looked up at Laura, hand on mouth, tears in two rivulets down her cheeks. She put out her hands to Theo and said, "He's better now."

He rose, hesitated, then walked into her embrace. They held each other as though in a slow dance, her head on his chest, both of them sniffing and wiping tears. Eventually, she gave Theo an extra squeeze and broke away, never looking at Stash.

She raised her liquid brown eyes to his.

"Let's go get that fucker," she said.

♦♦♦

THE BOTTOM PART of the locker door finally gave way enough that she figured she could get out.

She bumped and thudded her way around to face the door again and was able to get both feet out to the hallway floor. She began to slide down, letting her legs bend any way they could to get out. Then she was on her butt, only the top half of her body still encased.

Marcia rested her face against the cool metal and rested for a moment. When she went to continue, she found herself jammed and twisted at an awkward angle.

"No.

"NO!

"NONONONONONONONO*NONONONONONO*!"

A surge of adrenalin kicked in, fuelling the power to her arms and the locker curled away groaning, her hands an onslaught of white-knuckled fury.

She oozed the rest of herself out, scraping her face and neck on a vicious flap of metal.

"You had to take your final penance, didn't you?" she asked no one.

As she got to her feet something flew by her, bounced ringingly off a locker. A chunk of debris? She didn't know, but it scared the crap out of her.

Then, seconds later, she was pushed up against the lockers as a seething wave of monsters flailed and skittered and thundered down the hall toward the north stairs where the chunk of debris had come from. Marcia thought she heard a loud shout of surprise.

Then she was alone, the wave of sound and fury having passed her by.

A huge rattling sound shimmered from the north stairs. She didn't wait around.

She headed for the south stairs.

CHAPTER TWENTY-SEVEN

LAURA AND THEO left Corrigan's second-floor classroom—pointedly not looking at Joe's remains—and worked their way up the north stairs to the third floor. The cold metal rail bit into their hands just as it had when the three of them came up here to discover Stinky Pete in the bathroom with the Book. Theo wondered how Popper and the Toad were doing.

They entered the hallway again, knowing what to expect to their right. And there it was again: the destroyed remains of the boys' washroom, spilling out into the hall. Peter was still in there.

Theo carefully and quietly picked his way over the rubble to make his way past that irritating, sight-blocking curve again. Seeing all that destruction, knowing what waited ahead, just made him flash back to Stash, one floor below them, and Peter in the bathroom.

"Fucker," was all Theo could say. He couldn't honestly say whether he meant Peter or Swlabr.

"Stop!" Laura hissed. "Hear it?"

"...no, nothing."

Laura bent, picked up a fist-sized chunk of concrete, and lobbed it underhand down the hall. It hit one of those sick-orange lockers about halfway up with a loud metallic *bang*, and rattled down the hall beyond the curve and out of sight.

"That left a mark," Theo said.

"Shh!" she hissed again.

They waited.

Slight, delicate scraping noise. Concrete on granite.

Or claws on granite.

Nothing made a sound for thirty seconds. A minute. Time stretched like a tendon. No sound. Nothing. Theo didn't breathe. Neither did Laura.

Theo turned his head to look at Laura, the air so quiet Theo could hear the bones shifting and sliding in his neck, making him first think of, then push away the thought of, the desk slamming down on Stash's neck. Laura turned to look at him, just her head, no other movement. Total silence. Theo watched a vein pulsing wildly on her neck, sweat on her lip.

Then the bowels of hell emptied, a spewing, screaming onrush of terror coming right at them in a wailing, frenzied wall of black fury. A razor-sharp assault on the senses.

They were caught so off guard that they just stood there, rooted to the spot. A silent "Holy shit" the best they could muster.

To Theo, it seemed to happen in slow motion: coming down the hall, a black storm of evil, just the tip of the iceberg, so much yet unseen. At the first sight of Swlabr, his arm came up defensively. His elbow hit Laura on the way up, jolting her into flight mode. She grabbed his arm, spun, and they were dodging rubble and rattling down the stairs in a barely controlled confusion of shaking limbs, the Demon right behind them.

As they barreled on in their downward flight the stairway began to rain debris, the Demon demolishing the stairs and structure in its descent. Dust, metal, chunks of wood and concrete.

They passed by the second-floor doors and didn't stop. Each had one arm up to ward off the worst of the debris, the other tracing the railing to keep them from falling in their mad dash for the bottom.

"Go! It's coming down, all of it! GogogoGO!"

Then the doors to the first floor were in front of them, and they opened them and squirted through just as a large chunk of third-floor stairway thundered its way to the first floor.

They looked at each other. That thing wouldn't be too far behind.

They turned right and ran.

"Toad! Tom!" Theo yelled. "Get ready! The sumbitch's comin'!"

Laura looked back. Just one second, just one last update.

"Hole. Lee. Shit!"

♦♦♦

MARCIA WANTED TO get back to Bobby, was desperate to do so, but it sounded like that entire end of the school was collapsing. She heard thundering steps that could only be one thing.

So, ashamed of herself, she turned and ran down the south stairs, away from Bobby. She promised she would come back for him, no matter what.

Tears blurred her vision as she took the stairs so she forced herself to be more cautious this time. The last time she went rushing headlong down a hall she'd ran into…

She'd ran into…what?

Something. Something horrible.

But what?

It was enough to slow her down briefly as she tried to remember. It had been terrible, horrendous.

Big and dark, that she remembered. Like that wave that had passed her by. But then again, not.

Screw it. Later.

Right now she had to move.

She reached the entrance to the stairs. There was a cold rime of frost on the doors, but it wasn't like the gym. It took some tugging, but she was able to break the slight seal of the ice, like pulling open a car door on a forty-below morning.

Then she was through and lunging for the stairs.

She picked up speed and ran down the slippery stairs as fast as her socks would allow. Four steps from the bottom, she jumped, landed, and skid to a halt in front of the double doors that would let her into the first-floor hallway.

She stopped dead in her tracks. Somebody ran like all the demons of hell were on his tail.

"Toad! Tom! Get ready! The sumbitch's comin'!"

Theo! Sweet Jesus, it's Theo!

And right behind him, a girl…no, Ms. Davis. *They survived the caf?*

They survived the caf!

They were running right toward Marcia, but at the last moment they deked into one of the rooms.

Because right behind them was…

She dropped to her knees as her memory flooded back.

Oh my God!

♦♦♦

"TOAD! TOM! GET ready! The sumbitch's comin'!"

The Toad and Popper heard the yelling, the panicked running and something that sounded like a pissed-off 747 coming down the hall for them.

"Jesus Christ! You hear that? Are a few hundred-watt bulbs gonna hold this thing?"

Popper had a line of sweat rolling down the bridge of his nose. His eyes were wild, but his voice was strangely calm. "I hope so," was all he said.

♦♦♦

LAURA AND THEO hit the room and threw themselves to the right as planned, scooching in behind the lights, flattening their bodies to the wall, chests heaving. Theo caught a glimpse of Popper and the Toad as they whipped by. They both looked scared, but all there, thank god.

They had all of a half-second before the classroom exploded.

♦♦♦

THE TOAD WATCHED as Laura and Theo dived into the room, ducking off to the right. *Good. So far, so good.* His heart thumped in his chest, head, and throat. He felt like he needed to puke, but he got a handle on it. He would keep it together.

There was a half-second pause and then Swlabr was there in all its rampaging fury, blowing through the doorway.

♦♦♦

THEY HEARD IT before they saw or felt it. The Demon detonated through the door, bringing in most of the doorframe, some of the concrete. Bricks and concrete and metal flew in all directions. The assaulted air screamed. The Demon entered, trailing the stairway railings like seaweed from its ankles. It was so large that when it fully entered the room, it filled it. The creature was

(gotta step outside to change its)

massive.

Theo felt things grabbing at him and a high-pitched squealing. He spun, swinging and punching until he realized it was Popper grabbing at him to get him out. Laura had already gone. *How did I miss that?*

Then they were back in the hall and, though the Toad was right beside him, Theo barely heard Popper wailing at him to hit the generator hit it hit the blasted lights! Popper moved toward the Toad, but Theo knew that would just distract him. They only had a second. Theo lunged at Popper and sent him reeling backwards. It gave the Toad the second he needed.

The Toad was bent over the generator and kicked in the

(please god please let there be)

lights.

The lights seared the very air after the darkness, and for a brief moment, Swlabr was brought out in harsh relief.

The monster reared up and back, obviously in pain, and Theo thought *YES!* then the light seemed to wash *away* from it, bending around the Demon like water flowing around rocks in its path.

"It's doing this!" Theo said, though no one heard. "Swlabr's bending the light to save its ugly ass! Well *fuck* you! That's not gonna do it!"

Theo bent and scooped two of the safety lights, toggled them on, and wielding them almost like swords, not thinking, he ran right at the beast. "Eat this, motherfucker!"

Theo slammed the caged work lamps onto Swlabr's cold, sweaty hide, digging in the hooks. His hands burned at the touch of the beast's skin, immediately bubbling and reddening. He hung on, firmly setting the hooks before the Demon spun, howling an ungodly wail that shook the walls. The light in the room took on a strange quality, somehow thick and curiously heavy, like the light just before a thunderstorm. Then Theo was thrown back, sliding to the wall, the wind knocked out of him. He made a whooping noise as his lungs tried to reinflate.

Still struggling to breathe, Theo watched Laura get a weird look on her face. *It's hurt,* that look seemed to say, *let's finish it off.*

She looked at Popper. He gave an almost imperceptible, almost reluctant nod. The Toad looked from one to the other, grim faces all around. "No," Theo saw him mouth. "No I—"

(pop)

"I just."

(goes the)

"I can't."

(weasel)

But Laura and Popper were gone, grabbing for more lights, dodging desks and ribbons of steel. They hit it from different ends, delivering the lights to the beast and running, leaving it wailing, the sound scaling up higher and higher.

They backed off, hoping the lights, the cords, the generator would hold long enough.

"Die, you fucker!"

"C'monc'monc'monc'monc'mon..."

"May the Force be with us."

♦♦♦

SWLABR THRASHED AND wailed. It couldn't bend the light impacting directly on its skin. It staggered to the other end of the room where the computer sat, darkness trailing away from it like smoke.

It made a lunge at the computer, ripping the lights and lines away with a shower of sparks and sprays of smoky blackness.

The four of them shielded their eyes from the flash and then—

And then—

And then...nothing. No wind, no light, no screaming, no sound save for a high-pitched ring in their ears.

The Toad. "All right! Luke Skywalker and the Rebel Forces! We kicked its ass!"

Theo got up and walked past the Toad to where the thing had been fighting for its life moments before.

"Theo? We kicked it ass, right?" His voice took on a desperate whine. "...please tell me we killed it. Please..."

Popper came up beside him. "What's wrong?" he asked.

"Hear that whine? Just below the ringing in your ears?" Popper cocked his head to one side, listening.

"Yes," he said.

"It's the computer. It's running."

Theo and Popper looked down at the massive piece of modern machinery. Lights flickered and blinked on. And deep inside, a low hum, the sound of big magnetic disks spinning up to the required revolutions per minute.

"It's running with no power in the building."

Theo stared at Popper, eyes blurring with tears. "I think the fucker's in the computer."

Chapter Twenty-Eight

THE ROOM WAS a roiling turmoil of yelling and pounding. Marcia saw two men dash across the hall from Mrs. Parsten's office. One looked like the Toad. Then they were pulling out Theo and Ms. Davis.

Then Theo ran back into the room, the room they'd just been pulled *out* of. Then, all of them came boiling into the room. Lights flashing and weird shadows and then…

And then all was quiet.

She knew they were all dead.

Marcia couldn't make the walk down the hall to see it. She would just sit here and close her eyes and wait for the end. She couldn't run anymore.

What was the use? It was time to throw in the towel.

It was time to die.

♦♦♦

THERE WAS A stunned silence as they listened to the computer whining and humming and clicking. There was no way that thing should have been active, *could* have been active, but there it was.

The Toad lost it.

"What the *hell* are you guys *talking* about? What do you *mean,* it's in the computer? That thing was *huge*! How the hell does it go into a com*pu*ter? Huh? How?"

Popper cleared his throat. "I'm not sure, but we saw the way the light bent around the monster. I know it doesn't like light all that much, but it almost seems to be able to manipulate it to a degree. Possibly as a survival tactic."

"Yeah? So?"

"So…I'm wondering if it was so desperate to escape that it was somehow able to manipulate the device in the card reader to get in." He pointed to a tray device to one side of the machine. "Converted to machine language somehow."

"And how the hell did it do that?" the Toad asked, unbelieving. "Nothing can do that! My fuckin' cat can't see a good Purina commercial and decide to jump into the TV, for chrissakes!"

"No," Theo said. "But your cat also can't appear out of thin air in a third-floor washroom either. Your cat can't bend light."

"Exactly!" said Popper. "We're obviously not dealing with a normal creature here. This is something other."

"'Something other?'" the Toad repeated. "Jesus! You sound like a bad goddamn science-fiction movie!"

"Hey, bud, you were the one quoting *Star Wars* two minutes ago."

"Fuck you, Theo."

"No! Fuck you, man! You weren't the one going upstairs to lure that thing! You weren't the one that had to…to…deal with Stash."

"Theo…" Laura said.

"No, Laura. No." He turned to the Toad. Theo pointed a shaking finger in the Toad's face. "No. Uh-uh. Fuck you, Toad. Fuck you and the weasel you rode in on."

Theo turned away from the Toad and shuffled to a corner of the room, his shoulders hitching.

The Toad stared after him for a moment, then walked to the computer, thumbs hooked in his jeans. He got close to it, but not close enough to touch. As Laura and Popper watched him, he studied the machine. Finally he turned back to them. "Look, didn't we just win? It's in the computer. Fine. Let's just smash the piss out of the computer!"

"How do we know it just won't come back out?" Laura asked.

"We're pretty much out of lights," Theo said, turning from the wall, swiping at his eyes.

"Fine! Why do we have to do anything at all? Leave it in there! Who cares?"

"No, look," Popper broke back in. "Look at the screen."

They all turned toward the monitor.

Laura put her hand on Popper's shoulder. "Tom, what are we looking at?"

"I'm guessing here, but I think it's converting itself to code. It got in somehow, and now it's adjusting itself to the new environment so it can navigate the computer."

"Like I said, Who cares?" Theo fought the urge to say anything else to the Toad. Instead, he picked up a chunk of concrete and bashed it against the wall. *Boom, baby. That's your annoying head!*

Popper looked at him. "We do. Dennis, remember when we were talking earlier, and I told you about an experimental network of computers? Remember the computer correspondence?"

"...Yeah."

"Okay." Popper took a deep breath and faced Laura and Theo. "Long story short: the military created a way of linking computers through phone lines. Eventually, it spread out to a few universities. Remember the assembly? There was a competition and five high schools were allowed to gain access to the USENET network? Some people are beginning to refer to it as a web, due to its shape on a map."

Laura got it first. "We're in that web? This computer is in the network?"

"Yes. This computer is in the network. And that...thing is in the computer."

"So what does this mean?" Theo asked.

"It means we were one of the five schools. It means we're hooked up to the network. So this computer can talk to the other computers in the network—exchange information—just like we do on telephones. And the other computers are in universities and military bases. I'm thinking this Demon will be able to gain access to any of those locations. And if it can get in, what's to stop it from getting back out? You get me? It can get into a military computer."

"But we aren't hooked to any network right now. Remember? We're in never-never land."

"Right," Popper said. "So, the good news is—at least in theory, anyway—it will have to flip us back home to get connected."

"So, that's easy!" the Toad said. "Don't we just wait for it to flip us back, then just disconnect it?"

And that's when they decided to look. There was a series of cables running from the back of the computer into wall connections. And like the cafeteria doors earlier, they were encased in several inches of ice. That explained the cold in the room.

There was enough ice that it would take hours to punch through. Even with the blowtorches, which were running low by now. And as they watched, the rest of the computer was icing up. It was going at a slower pace, almost as though Swlabr knew this was more delicate. It was a slower progression, so as not to stress or flex the casings.

"If it's icing up the connections, it obviously knows what it needs to do. We have to figure this out, fast, before it figures out *how* to do what it needs to do. I figure we've got a little time because it's in a foreign environment. It needs to learn the system. That could take a few minutes."

"A few minutes?" Theo asked. He had been thinking hours. "What the hell can we do in a few minutes?" Christ, the computer already had over an inch of ice on it.

"Tom," said Laura, "how do you kill a computer?"

Theo said, "Yeah, isn't there something about the heads, or the disk drives or something?"

"There's a few ways to do it. The easiest is to jar the equipment with enough force that the heads impact on the disk surface."

"What's that gonna do?"

"You know how a needle sits in a groove on a record player?" The others nodded. "This is the same sort of idea, but the head floats above the disk, never touching it. And instead of the disk spinning thirty-three times a minute, this spins several thousand times a minute.

"Look at it this way," he continued, "you're in a jet going Mach One, but you're only a couple of feet off the ground. What happens if one wing dips and touches ground?"

They all smiled the same *yeah* smile.

"So you can achieve that sort of a crash by applying enough force to the disk drive while it's running. Jolt it, drop it, that sort of thing. Only," he looked at the computer, "that's not going to happen here."

The others followed his gaze. Jesus! In the time they were talking, there was a protective layer of ice over most of the machine now. Inches thick. They'd have to unstick the thing from the floor before they could even jiggle it.

"So how else can we do this?" Theo wanted an answer. They needed one now.

"If we had enough access to the drive, we could drill a hole through it."

"If we had that much access, couldn't we just rip it out?"

"Good point."

"Strike two," said the Toad.

"Shut up," Theo said. He couldn't handle the Toad's shit anymore.

"Fuck you," the Toad responded. "Who died and made you god?"

Almost everyone, you idiot. "Yeah, well, at least I'm contributing a little here. I'm not the one running around saying, 'Ooo! Use the fuckin' Force, Luke!'"

"Hey, y'know wha—"

Popper had a slight smirk on his face.

The Toad looked at him, changing gears mid-sentence. "What are you smilin' about?"

"What you just said. Something about the force."

"Yeah, *Star Wars*. Best movie ever made. So what?"

"So, I'm thinking about force. Magnetic force."

His smile widened. "What do any of you know about magnets?"

♦♦♦

FIVE MINUTES LATER, they had reassembled in the computer room after running in two groups to different areas of the school for supplies and information. They had worried about the demon dogs, but they were nowhere to be found. Maybe, with their master gone to ground, they just winked out of existence.

They hoped.

The group worked fast, the conversation down to efficient two- and three-word commands. "More over here." "Back there." "Couple more spins." "Tighter."

And in a surprisingly short time, it was done. They were ready. All there was left to do was wait.

They all went to take their positions. Laura by the coils of wire, Popper by the monitor, and Theo on generator duty.

The Toad got the first watch, which meant he was out of the class and down the hall by the south stairs, about ten feet from an outside window. He walked down the hall, shielding his eyes from looking outside, so he didn't see the shape at the door until he was opening it.

"Holy fuck!" The Toad spun and yelled down the hall. "Theo! Laura! Marcia's here! I found Marcia!"

♦♦♦

THEO, POPPER, AND the Toad carried her back to Parsten's office and laid her on the couch. She was covered in blood from head to toe, but the only obvious trauma was a nasty scratch running down her face and neck.

"Theo," said Popper. "I don't mean to sound cold or unsympathetic. I know she's your girlfriend—"

"Was."

"Fine, whatever." Popper's face showed a flash of irritation at the interruption. "Regardless, there is nothing we can do for her at this moment, and time is of the essence. We must stick to the plan or none of us will be around to help her at all."

Theo kept looking at her face. Where had she been? They had been all over this school! Why hadn't they found her before now?

Laura touched Theo's shoulder lightly.

"C'mon, Theo," she said softly. "Let her rest."

Theo took a deep breath and let it back out.

"You take it easy, Marce. We're gonna get you out. You sleep now." He stroked her hair, brushing a strand away from her eyes.

Then he stood.

"Okay. I'm all right." One more glance at Marcia. *Where has she been? Whose blood is that?*

"Let's do this."

♦♦♦

THEY WENT BACK to their posts.

The Toad finally positioned himself by the outside window, but didn't look out. He couldn't. He faced one hundred and eighty degrees away from the window, watching the quality of the reflected light on the wall. The Toad was waiting for some change. Any change.

They waited.

Everything was quiet, the only sounds coming from the ice-encased hard drive and their breathing.

There was too much at stake here. It was hard to concentrate. All that adrenalin continued to roil through Theo, screaming at him to not just sit there, to *do* something!

But there was nothing they could do.

It occurred to Theo that Marcia had been sitting right by an open window but there was no sign of vomit around her.

Don't get stupid. She probably figured it out like you did. You're no fucking genius.

But still, where did all the blood come from? Theo had seen too much of it that day. He didn't want to see another drop.

He shifted his weight on his haunches, his hand ready to power the generator. There was nothing else to do.

Nothing but wait.

His palms were sweaty even though it was as cold as a meat locker in the room. Theo blew out and watched his breath fog, then dissipate. Popper's eyes never stopped moving, his movements quick and nervous, his breath blowing in quick puffs.

"Mr. Popper." He was intent on watching the monitor. "Tom!"

"What?" Popper answered, irritated.

"Slow down. You're gonna hyperventilate or something, and pass out."

"Yes, okay, good."

He didn't even hear me. That would be their luck. The only guy that sort of knew what to look for would pass out seconds before they needed him, leaving them up shit creek and bereft of paddle.

Theo looked at Laura, raised his eyebrows, and cocked his head toward Popper. *Can you do something with him?*

"Tom. Tom!"

"What?" Again, the same irritation. The same don't-bug-me-I'm-busy tone.

She persisted. "Tom, can you run me through this one more time?"

Long exhalation. That was better than the hyperventilation. Good, she was getting to him.

"Once we get a sign that the Demon has brought us home, we begin." Then he took a breath and went into lecture mode. "The information on the disks is stored magnetically. By coiling the wire tightly around the drive area, we have created, in effect, a large electromagnet. Once Theo starts the generator, the current will pass through the coils in a current that creates a magnetic force. This, hopefully, will disrupt the magnetically stored information on the disks enough that the Demon will simply be wiped away."

All this was delivered as though he was explaining how to put on a pair of pants.

Theo gave her another look. *Go on!*

"Yes, but, is it going to work?" she asked.

That got him. He turned to her, blinked twice. "I really don't know. I don't know if the current will be strong enough. I don't know if the drives are shielded." He stroked his neatly trimmed beard with two fingers. "I just don't know."

He turned back to the monitor. Laura glanced from Popper to Theo, worried.

Shit! Why did Theo get her to say anything at all? He had seemed so sure when he was explaining it as they ran down the hall to get the wiring. It had all seemed so logical—

There was a noise. A slight change in the whine of the drive. Popper made a little "oyp" kind of noise, and Theo heard a weird hiss coming from the hall. It was the Toad running back to the class, hissing, "We're here! We're back!"

That was his cue. Theo kicked in the generator. It started without a hitch, bless its oily heart. Marcia moaned slightly at the sound. Tom was already yelling at Laura to get back, get back!

At first, there was nothing. A long, frustrating pause of at least one or two seconds of nothing, then the sound of something almost like a zipper being pulled rapidly up and down, up and down. *Zitzit. Zitzit. Zitzitzitzit.*

"That's it!" Popper.

The electric current must have been working, fucking up the works. There was a vague shudder. The ice showed a vein of separation, then a huge crack.

Then Swlabr tried to jump back out. That's the first time Theo noticed the bright sunlight streaming through the west-facing window the Toad had been near. It was a good twenty feet down the hall but it was still bright, reflecting off the dull painted lockers and the shinier floors. It was glorious. Theo breathed deep, trying to suck the brightness into his lungs. The Demon reacted differently.

It exploded out, screaming and spitting, an oily black smoke growing solid out of the crack in the ice, directly off the drive. Then Theo knew it felt the light before it was fully formed. It tried to get back in, but the coils were doing their job and the drive was scrambled like mama's eggs. It couldn't go back, and it couldn't get out. It was half-formed, partially coalescing, but too much of it was left as code on the drive and it twisted into a magnetic spin.

The whining sound spun up faster and faster until the sound dug into Theo's ears and made his eyes water. Theo saw Popper throw himself at Laura and tackle her to the floor as the disk drive began to eat itself, the plastic and metal shredding like wet toilet paper. The wobbling drive began acting as a drill, pounding its way out, before the main shaft holding the disks together disintegrated rather than face all the opposing forces. The individual disks blew off in various deadly trajectories. Two ripped pieces out of the half-formed demon like a chainsaw.

The monitor told its own story as the hard plastic and glass bulged outward, balloon-like, the terminal madly streaming *0*s and *1*s in a frantic plea for logic to be restored. The stream of darkness continued out of the bowels of the computer as Swlabr tried to join itself back together but instead dropped to the floor like tar, or black guts. It made Theo sick to look at.

But it was working! It was fucking working!

Right up until the generator died.

Chapter Twenty-Nine

THROUGH THE BANSHEE wail of the overworked generator and the overextended disk drive and the overwrought group of people fighting for their lives, Marcia slept.

When the generator shut down, she woke up.

She awoke like a gunshot in the night, one moment quiet, peaceful and still, the next a flurry of motion and panic.

What in God's name is going on? Then, right behind that: *Theo! Where's Theo?*

She exploded off the couch, stumbling as she fought for balance. Where was she?

She just got a fix on her surroundings when it all went south again.

♦♦♦

"NO! THIS IS NOT HAPPENING!"

Theo's voice cut through the shrieking din in a bass rumble that was far too powerful for the throat it emanated from.

With the generator now dead, Swlabr redoubled its efforts to reform in the sudden darkness.

(and when you believe you have beaten all'gueroth)

It couldn't happen, Theo knew. This was their last chance. If this thing made it through this time, it was all over.

(he will rise again)

Popper, the Toad, Laura. In the breathtaking lack of options left to them, the three braced themselves. Death was surely coming.

(nyarlathotep will see to it)

If they were going to make it out, it was up to Theo. They were out of solutions that abided by the laws of nature.

It was time to break the laws.

Theo quickly yanked the knapsack from his back and tore at the zipper. It was the Book or nothing.

All the time he rooted for the Book, his mutterings went unheard.

"Damndamndamndamndamndamn…"

Then he had the Book in his hands. It seemed to quiver in anticipation, a virgin preparing to take a first lover. His hands embraced Its warmth as he pulled the infernal Book out to the wintry air.

He prepared to use the Book. But Theo was not going to open It.

"What are you doing?" Laura screamed.

Theo stopped and looked over at the Toad. He felt strangely calm amid the maelstrom. Still looking at the Toad, in a quiet voice that he somehow knew they all could hear, he said, "I'm gonna piss off another poker player."

The Toad nodded. He knew.

"Go get him, Theo," the Toad yelled, smiling. "Leave him naked and running in the street." Then he threw him a double thumbs up.

Theo turned back to the task at hand. Squeezing down hard, as though the Book might squirt out from his hands, Theo's eyes closed. *May the Force be with me.*

He brought up the image of all those people betrayed and trapped by the Book. All those thousands of people back through time who he had never met. All those people in the caf who had been undamned a few short hours ago. He pulled them up, every one, faces and names cascading through his opened mind. The Book trembled, Swlabr continued to take form.

Easy, easy.

Theo sent out thoughts of protection to the Toad, Popper, and Laura. Marcia was safe in the other room.

The Book burned hot in his hands.

When Theo was sure they were all

(how do I know this?)

protected, he focused on the Book, now emanating a freakish light in his hands. It was bright enough that Theo knew Swlabr—*the Dæmon all'Gueroth, progeny of Nyarlathotep*—was aware of it.

Aware of it, yes, but seemingly not concerned. He could almost sense it. *This flesh-meat cannot harm me.*

Oh, but I'm just getting warmed up, you bastard.

Theo took all the pain, all the rage that he could summon, added it to each of the victims' own, feeling it grow exponentially, the rage a gravity well, consuming the pain, feeding and growing on the rage, like a black hole.

But he kept it tamped down, buried under, his best poker face on.

Naked and running in the street.

He's like a dog. Show your fear and you're fucked.

You're a crazy bugshit motherfucker now.

And that was the trigger. The words from the one person the Book didn't own. The replay of Stash's head snapping back as his neck broke, his last breath sliding out through already-dead lips, his chest falling one last time then falling still.

That was it. The point that it all rotated on. Theo rolled all the outrage, all of his absolute

(no one else dies)

total fury, squeezed it down to critical mass, and let it explode.

♦♦♦

ALL OF REALITY went stone-cold silent.

Everything went white. A white so clean and pure that it hurt Theo's senses and took his breath away. But it scaled up, whiter, whiter, his eyeballs seeming to vibrate, until it could not be any more white.

Then it all fell away. The sheer power that Theo released wiped all colour from the world, and he looked around and they—he and all'Gueroth—were standing on nothing, but he could feel the ground, he could touch the concrete walls, smooth with thick layers of paint, yet completely clear. They existed, they were real, but not quite real enough in this new world Theo had willed into being.

There was a faint buzz...no, more than one...a series of vibrations. When he looked hard enough he could see the vibrations—they were a visible thing to him—were his friends. Theo could sense they knew no fear. They were protected and safe and embraced in, yet shielded from, the full fury of his power. They remained safe in the eye of the twister.

His was the power of the Book's victims that carried forth their bright and terrible vengeance.

Ahead of him was the single dark stain in the whiteness, Swlabr, the monster, the Demon that Peter had summoned forth to his world. All'Gueroth. The only other thing visible in this new place of power. It was a black cancer, a tumour struggling, fighting, violating the inescapable vicious purity that ate away at its very form. The luminous purity that Theo held forth against the aphotic corruption of the beast.

Theo sensed its panic, felt its pain and heard its silent scream. And it was good.

There was no sound. All was quiet.

Theo watched it dying, thrashing as if it was a bad dream. His face was expressionless as it melted away.

All was silent.

The creature's thrashing stilled and yet Theo could sense its life. Its evil, blackened soul was not yet gone.

And then it spun, navigating the clarity that Theo had brought down, a specific target in mind.

Marcia!

Theo threw his senses back and realized she was awake and unprotected. It wanted her.

NO.

One thought brought forth the final consequence.

The Book in Theo's hands bulged and split and screamed and shattered out into a million, a trillion, pieces as an unknowable, unharnessed energy – a *rage* – took the fabric of reality and shook it like a dog with a blanket, twisting it and tearing it and shredding it and wrenching it and wringing it until there was nothing to do but ride the storm.

♦♦♦

SWLABR'S MOUTH OPENED and the deepest, lowest tone they had ever heard vibrated in their skulls, beautiful and terrible. The creature lost all cohesion and sprayed apart.

It screamed with all the ungodly power it could muster, shaking the walls, making the floor tremble, and Theo looked and he saw blood squirting from the Toad's nose and Theo touched his ear and his finger came away red and Swlabr's scream went on and on and Theo could feel himself losing equilibrium and Popper and Laura were rolling on the floor eyes bulging and hands clasped to ears and spit sliding out of Popper's mouth and the screaming went on and it was joined by Theo's voice and those around him in an unholy chorus and still it went on and on and Theo fell to one side and hit his head on something and still his mouth was stretched wide as his head was torn apart and finally finally thank god the lights went out in the world as a god closed their eyes and all was dark again…

♦♦♦

POP GOES THE weasel, Theo thought.

CHAPTER THIRTY

THE SILENCE COMFORTED them. The feel of reflected sunlight, the sudden warmth in the room, and a deep, thick pillow of quiet enveloped them like a warm blanket and they snuggled down into it as the adrenalin drained away. They were okay. All of them, beyond a few cuts and scrapes, some bloody noses, they were okay.

They had stared down the beast, looked through the gates of hell, ran through its corridors, and met the physical incarnation of fear. Yet, here they were. They had come out the other side, unscathed.

They sat down amid the ruin and were just still for a few minutes, no one looking at anyone else, lost in their own heads. Theo thought their minds were trying to organize and catalogue the past few hours and put some sort of spin of normalcy on the day's events. Even though he wanted to run from the building into the light—they all did—still, they needed to take a moment. Theo thought, *This is it. If I don't chill out right now and accept the facts as presented, I'm going to snap. I'll fall into my own head and never make it back out.*

This is how people go nuts, Theo thought. *This is how they crack up.* Well, it sure as hell wasn't going to happen to him.

♦♦♦

AS USUAL, IT was the Toad who spoke first.

"So..." he said, "what now?"

Laura looked up, her eyes older and more tired. "There's all those bodies…Stash's body. Joe's body. Benmont's body."

"And all those little hell-rat things, too. What do you suppose happened to them?" the Toad asked.

Theo shrugged. He felt too goddamn tired to even string a sentence together.

"So, like I said, what now?"

Theo was tired but he reacted.

"Let's take it out," he finally said. "Take out the whole school—burn it to the ground."

"Why?"

"Gets rid of the bodies. And the hell-rats."

Theo looked at the five of them, assembled in a rough circle. "You all know no one is going to believe what happened here tonight. No matter how we tell it. Hell, how *would* we even tell it?"

He got varying degrees of acceptance, but he could see they all agreed.

Popper said, "Why don't we go out and check the lay of the land before we make any lasting decisions."

So they did. They found the bodies, and the hell-rats. The rats seemed confused, lost, looking to keep to the shadows, but ridiculously easy to kill, like all their teeth and attitude had been pulled. They exterminated them, and the demons offered no resistance.

"Hey!" said the Toad in a too-giddy voice. "This is better 'n the Whac-A-Mole at the county fair!" His boots were slimed with demon-dog juice that squelched when he walked.

Theo joined in for about five minutes, then stopped. The other four noticed and stopped as well.

Laura asked, "Theo, what's up?"

"I say 'fuck it.' These things aren't a threat to anyone. This is a waste of time. Let someone else clean up, we've done our part. Let's get out."

"Theo," she said, "c'mon, we should—"

"No! No! We shouldn't! We shouldn't have to do this! We shouldn't have had to burn everyone in that goddamned caf! We shouldn't have had to kill Stash! We shouldn't have been here at all! I'm tired, Laura, real tired, and I just need to get outta here." He stared at the ground, hating the tears that slipped from his eyes and ran down his cheeks.

"I need to get out right now."

♦♦♦

THEY FIGURED IT to be around six in the morning when they finally walked through the front doors of the school like nothing out of the ordinary had ever happened. The sky had a luminous quality, like a pearl. The air tasted sweet and somehow lighter. Birds chirped, leaves rustled, and in the distance, cars rumbled along the roads.

They came out of the school as though nothing had happened. But it was obvious something had.

The pavement in the staff parking lot was rubble. The once-smooth blacktop was segmented and fragmented like an old forgotten road. There was a distinct line around the school as well, running in an apparent circle roughly ten to twenty feet out from the walls of the structure. And inside this circle—where the school was—it appeared everything had sunk about six inches. It was like something had lifted the entire school and scooped out some of the ground and then set the school back in like a plant from the pot.

And Theo guessed, in a way, that's pretty much what had happened.

Nobody was there, and that was strange. A whole school apparently disappears for an entire night, with scores of students and teachers, and no one notices? What the hell was that? Stash had always said that the end of the world could come and No Hope would probably miss it, but shit! This was ridiculous.

Theo made some sort of comment to this effect, and Popper cleared it up. "I thought it was morning too, Theo, but look: the sun's setting. This is evening."

"We were in there a long time, but it wasn't twenty-four fuckin' hours."

"No, I think we were in there for however long we were in there, but out here it was a blink of an eye. Maybe a few seconds. That's why no one missed us. Maybe it was some sort of stasis environment."

"Thanks, Mr. Spock," Theo said, more callous than was called for. "Sorry, but I cannot and do not give a flying shit right now. Maybe tomorrow, but not now."

They again stood in that rough circle. *What do you say to the four people who just went through hell and back with you?* Theo wondered. *Catch ya later? Thanks?*

"I don't think we should really talk about this," Theo said. "To anyone."

Marcia nodded her agreement. So did Laura.

"Are you crazy?" Popper asked.

"Maybe. Maybe I am. Maybe we all are. But you tell anyone this and I guarantee—leftover hell-rats or not—they'll think you're nuts."

Popper chewed on that one. Theo didn't know if Popper would really stay silent and, personally, he couldn't care less. Theo just knew he wouldn't say anything. He wasn't even sure what he had done back there, or how he had harnessed that energy.

"Maybe you're right, Theo."

"So..." the Toad began.

"'What now?'" they all finished for him. It was the first time Theo remembered smiling in a while.

"I'm going home," Laura said. She walked up to Theo and

held his face gently in her hands as she looked deep into his eyes. Theo felt a tingle and the Book stirred. Theo could sense Marcia reacting.

Laura kissed him. A little longer and a little deeper and a lot more passionately than Theo expected. *More than either of us expected,* Theo thought. His arms found her waist and, suddenly, Theo didn't want to let her go. As their lips broke contact, Theo began to tear up again. She was crying too.

"You take care of yourself," she said, like she knew what Theo was going to do. Like she knew Theo would never see her again. Like she knew that he would choose Marcia over her. Theo realized she was right—he would choose Marcia over her, and he didn't know why. He felt like he was still on some train that kept on rolling and there was no way to get off. He didn't *want* to choose Marcia. Laura! It should be Laura!

And just like that, the town felt too damn claustrophobic to Theo.

"I found this during our cleanup," she said and pressed something into his palm. Her lighter. Smeared black with soot, Theo wiped the face of the lighter with his thumb and read the words engraved there.

Forever standing next to your fire.

Theo looked back to her face. "Thank you," she said, her voice breaking. "Thank you for letting me stand next to your fire." She smiled through the tears and Theo's heart broke.

"Thank you for everything."

♦♦♦

LAURA AND TOM left the parking lot in Laura's fifteen-year-old rusted-out pickup. She had asked if they wanted a ride, but it didn't feel right. Theo stood and wondered why she'd chosen Tom over him. Theo wondered why he'd chosen Marcia over her.

Theo, Marcia, and the Toad just thanked her and said no. Marcia looked away, but the Toad and Theo watched as the truck left the lot and headed back into town.

Back into the heart of New Hope.

♦♦♦

THE TOAD AND Theo and Marcia walked away from the school, cutting across the grass, stepping over the ripped-up parts with the bare earth showing. More signs of trauma.

They got out to the highway that led back into town, following the same route Laura had just taken. Facing the town, the lake was out to their left and the high school was on their right.

The Toad said, "No Hope, dead ahead."

Theo stopped. Marcia followed his lead.

"What's wrong?" asked the Toad.

"Everything," Theo said. "Everything's wrong. That town. The school. The fact that Stash and Crouch and Peter and Steph and Joe and all those others are

(screaming still screaming screaming in his)

dead. This fucking Book."

Theo threw the bag containing the Book to the gravel at the shoulder of the road. Marcia looked a little scared, and put some distance between herself and the Book. His voice rose.

"What *the fuck* happened here? Christ, this morning I was just hoping to pass the year and get laid."

The Toad got a slight smirk, but it dropped away as he glanced at Marcia. As stupid as it seemed, Mr. Pop-goes-the-weasel's world apparently seemed to be shifting back to normal. Theo's wasn't. He continued.

"But now. Fuck man, There's this...this shit out there." Theo waved his arm to encompass the lake and the town.

"How can I just go on to college, get married, all that shit, when I know there's things like that big black fucker out there? How can I go to bed tonight, knowing what I know? Knowing what I…what we did today?" His eyes found the Toad's, hot tears standing in them.

"Because we faced the dark, my man," the Toad said. "We faced it, and we…you…pushed it back. That's the way forward. For me, at least."

"I can't, man. I *can't.*" Theo shook his head as the tears traced paths down his face. "Once you've seen this stuff…once you're aware that this shit is in the world, you can never go back. You're on the other side."

♦♦♦

THEY STOOD THERE awhile, lost in worlds of thought so alien for their little part of the world. Off in the distance there was a throaty roar, and it was enough for the Toad to look at Theo and Marcia as their minds sorted through the past few hours on high speed. Was it…?

Then the eighteen-wheeler came around the last curve out of town, a couple of miles down the road. Probably hauling lumber out of Madawaska.

Theo looked at the Toad—Dennis—and Dennis looked at Theo. Marcia seemed to understand this was a moment she was not part of.

Aside from family gatherings, which were rare with his family, Theo had never shaken anyone's hand before. None with any sincerity. There had never been a need. And besides, at his age, it had seemed really stupid.

But at that moment, Theo wasn't the young boy he had been when he had got out of bed this morning. Theo was a hundred years old, and Dennis and Theo were going their separate ways. This was a final show of respect.

They clasped hands. "I'm sorry for that shit I said in there," Theo said.

"Yeah, me too. Fuck it, man." He waved a hand, brushing it away. "It's gone. Done."

"Love you, Dennis."

"Love you too, Theo." Then he smiled. He smiled that same stupid ear-splitting grin he got when discussing anything to do with his bowels. Then he turned toward to town. Theo grabbed Marcia's hand and, with the other, he stuck out his thumb out and heard the big truck gear down. It didn't seem to even be a point of discussion that she was going with him.

The truck slowed to a stop, and Marcia, covered in blood and looking like a murder victim, climbed in. The driver looked at her questioningly.

"School play. I'm the expendable crewmember." The driver just shook his head.

As Theo was about to climb into the transport, he looked back and saw the bookbag

~...yoooou sssstiiiillll nnnneeeed mmmmeeee...~

still sitting in the dirt where he had thrown it. "Just a minute," he said to the driver. He hopped back down and grabbed it and a strange thrill and tingle rushed up his arms. Theo turned to look back up the highway to see Dennis still walking. He never looked back as he walked toward New Hope.

Theo climbed back into the cab. He never looked back as he and Marcia ran away from No Hope.

CHAPTER THIRTY-ONE

BEFORE THEY HAD even left the school, Theo had made up his mind. He wasn't going to stick around No Hope anymore. While the others were busy stomping hell-rats, he had raided the school's admin office and committed his first act of thievery: he stole the money out of the petty cash box Mrs. Coppens kept in her desk drawer.

It hadn't been a lot, but it would get him started.

At the time, he hadn't planned on having to support anyone else. Except, maybe, in a tiny little corner of his mind, he had entertained the thought of bringing Laura with him.

Why did she pick Tom? Why not me?

He wondered if his wanton display of power had scared her. It sure as hell had scared him.

(you lack the courage to save the one who needs you most)

The events of the day swirled in his mind as the truck rolled down the highway. He could only stare out the side window as the miles took him away from everything he'd known.

Marcia turned toward him, gave him a little everything's-gonna-be-all-right smile and held his hand. He gave it a small half-hearted squeeze and looked back out the window. He couldn't bring himself to offer the same smile back. It would have felt like a lie.

♦ ♦ ♦

HE AND MARCIA got off at the next town. He made Marcia stand out of sight behind the store while he went in and bought some clothes for them both. They found a faucet at the back of the store. He turned his back to her as she stripped, washed with the cold water, changed, and deposited the old blood-soaked

(goodbye stash)

clothes in a dumpster.

Theo took a walk, leaving Marcia in a restaurant, and found the cheapest motel in town.

He told the clerk he would be staying only one night and yes, he would be alone.

"Thank you, Mr.…Guroth, is it?" Theo didn't correct him. "You have room eight, right at the end."

Theo thanked the clerk, who was not much older than himself, and went back to find Marcia.

♦♦♦

THE ROOM WAS small and dirty and stank of cigarettes, beer, and sweaty sex. The towels hung in the bathroom felt like they would break in half if unfolded too quickly. The bed had a visible dip in the middle. And some idiot had chosen the same sick-orange colour for the walls that Clarington High had chosen for the lockers.

At this point, Theo was beyond caring.

"Theo," Marcia said. He turned his dull eyes to her.

"I just wanted to say…I just…that whole shirt thing…I just…"

"Yeah, Marce, I'm sorry too." It was a long way from mending the bridge between them, and Theo wasn't sure he was even interested in doing so. "Look, why don't we just let it all go tonight and tomorrow we'll try and make sense of the whole thing. Okay?"

"But I...there's so much I need to..." Marcia had never seemed this unsure around him before. Why couldn't she just talk to him like a normal human being?

Like Laura.

"Marce," he said, putting a finger to his lips. "Shh. Not tonight, okay? Tomorrow. I promise."

"Okay," she said. "I'm gonna go have a shower, okay?" Her voice was getting weird. A little higher. Her eyes were red-rimmed. Theo knew he should do something. Reach out. Hug her.

He couldn't.

"Yeah," he said. "Okay. Fine."

He was sure he heard her crying in the shower. He stayed on the bed.

♦♦♦

THEO LAID AWAKE in bed, his thoughts a whirling maelstrom. It seemed he couldn't hold a thought longer than a few seconds before it arced off to another subject altogether.

He thought of Crouch and Stash, friends he would never see again. He thought of Peter and Steph and Joe, people he wished he had known better. Tom and Laura, who he got to know too well.

He wondered about the things people—people he knew and cared for—were driven to do simply to escape. The things Peter did to escape his father. The things the Toad did to escape his memories. The things Theo had done to escape the school and Swlabr. And he wondered what Marcia was trying to escape from, and the things she would need to do so.

Theo wondered about what he had done—what price he was going to pay for the power he had unleashed. He wondered how he had even known he'd had that power to unleash.

He wondered why he was lying beside Marcia right now, her breathing deep and steady, her arm thrown across his chest as though they had been lovers for years. They had never been lovers, though Theo had badly wanted that at one time. They had been high school sweethearts, but had never had their night to remember. Boyfriend and girlfriend, once upon a time, in a galaxy far, far away.

Whatever he had felt for her was now gone, burned out of him like the terrible fire he had unleashed on the Demon. Did he still care for her? He searched his soul and decided, yes, he cared about her. But that was as far as it went.

He wondered about Laura. What was she doing now? Was she

(lack the courage)

lying awake thinking about

(the one who needs you)

him? Did she regret—as Theo did—the choice she

(needs you)

had made?

Or had he scared her with the power he had wielded?

Finally, late into the night, Theo closed his eyes and tried to sleep. He had to find some way to get Marcia to go back home in the morning. He could not stay with her.

His last conscious thought was of Laura. Tomorrow, he would find her and tell her all the things he should have said today.

Yes. Tomorrow.

Tomorrow he would make it right.

Then the darkness took him in its embrace and smothered him until he slept.

♦♦♦

THEO WOKE UP to bright, wonderful sunshine streaming through the tattered curtains of the room. The sun was enough to even make this room look better. He lay there, enjoying the warmth and simple beauty of it. No sense in waking Marcia—he wanted this moment for himself.

Then it got bad. The longer he lay there, the more his thoughts darkened as he considered what he would have to do shortly. He didn't want to hurt Marcia, but he didn't want to be with her. He was going to go away somewhere. Maybe

(load up the truck and move to)

California. Who knew? He didn't. But he didn't need anything reminding him of what he was coming from. Marcia made him feel claustrophobic. It was time to move on, alone.

He finally shifted, stretching the night's stiffness away, but something felt strange.

Like something had dried and caked on him.

It was only then that he looked down, then over.

♦♦♦

"OH JESUS!" HE cried, half jumping, half falling out of the bed.

Marcia was on her back, the covers pulled down to her knees. She was covered in deep, dark red. The bed, the sheets, the floor, and Theo. All red.

It seemed impossible that there had been that much blood in her body. She had been torn open from the inside, looking like a busted watermelon. Whatever had done this to her had taken its time, eating its way out from the looks of it. Not a chest-burster like that *Alien* movie.

Whatever had escaped Marcia's lifeless body had left a ragged trail of torn and shredded pieces of flesh around the room. It must have been looking for a way out.

Why hadn't the thing taken Theo? Why her and not him?

Was it because he hadn't moved?

Or was it because of the Book? His thoughts darkened, his face clouded in anger.

The trail led to the bathroom and, from there, the…thing…had made its escape out through the ripped screen in the window.

Leaving Theo to deal with the cleanup.

He turned back to the bed. Marcia's eyes were closed. Had she even felt it coming? Had she known? Was that why she had been trying to escape?

Had she been looking for Theo to save her?

"'Not tonight,'" he had said. "'Tomorrow, I promise.'"

And here they were. Tomorrow had not come for her.

"Oh, Marce," Theo said, tears brimming. "I'm so

(you lack the courage to save the one who needs you most)

sorry. I'm so…

(shh. not tonight. tomorrow)

sorry."

♦♦♦

THEO QUICKLY SHOWERED the blood off, got dressed, and stood by the bed. He had taken the sheets and covered her up as best he could. He stroked her hair one last time, wishing he knew everything that had happened to her. Wishing he had talked to her.

He bent and kissed her cool forehead.

"Tomorrow never came, baby. I'm so sorry."

Theo walked to the door and opened it.

Just outside the room, he could hear a song playing from a tinny transistor radio carrying through the opened window of the room down from his. He paused for a moment, just long enough to listen to the words. Elton John was singing of shadows in a dark and lonely room, about his eyes mirroring the world outside.

Theo knew the world outside was darker and lonelier than the room he was leaving. Yes, he was sure his eyes mirrored that darkness.

He stood for a moment longer, considering what was next. Then Theo continued on, never looking back as both the song and his old life faded through a blur of tears.

♦♦♦

THEO PICKED A direction and walked away.

Tragedy at District High School

New Hope – June 13, 1981 – The small town of New Hope was rocked this morning by the grim discovery of at least thirty dead at the local district high school.

The local police department received several calls about missing teens—all students at Clarington District High School—last evening. Almost all the students were reportedly staying late to work on decorations for the upcoming musical to be presented later this month.

"Who would do this?" a shaken Nathaniel Bostash, parent of one of the students, and brother to one of the high school staff, asked. "I just don't..."

(Story continues on Page 3. See "Death Toll")

Death Toll Remains Unconfirmed In High School Tragedy

(Continued from Page 1.)

"I just don't understand how this could happen. It's high school. They should be safe there." The prominent local real estate agent was one of the few parents who have received confirmation of his son's death.

"Robert was a good boy. He never got into trouble, and always stood up for his friends," Mr. Bostash said of his son, Robert Jonathan Bostash, 17.

The actual death toll is unknown but estimates have run as high as forty, including some teachers, also reported missing since last evening.

Allan Aubrey, chief of police for Clarington District, will provide no details until the investigation is finished, however comments from the rescue teams indicate that identification is proving difficult.

One paramedic, wishing to remain anonymous, stated: "It's sad to say, but it is probably going to be easier to call the parents and spouses of everyone who was in school yesterday to get an accurate take on who is missing."

But what happened?

"At this point, we have several clues, but no real idea of the events that transpired. There appears to be evidence of arson, vandalism, burglary, as well as significant structural damage…it's a real mess in there," said one of the emergency workers, who also wished to remain anonymous.

Many of the specialists called in to assist in the investigation and cleanup state this is the worst disaster they have ever viewed.

Grief counsellors have been brought in from all over the district to deal with the stunned residents, parents, spouses, and investigators.

"It appears some died due to violent trauma, and others due to a fire in the high school's cafeteria," said Dr. William Devenish, Clarington County Coroner and father to another of the confirmed dead, Benmont William Devenish, 17.

Danika Hilliers, a student at the school, told reporters she left the school shortly before 4:00 P.M. Jillian Nolan, mother of student Stephanie Nolan, 17, arrived at the school to pick her daughter up. Upon arrival, she discovered the school parking lot badly damaged. "I could smell smoke and gasoline," she said. Her 911 call from a neighbouring home came in at 4:28 P.M.

Somehow, forty people died or disappeared in that one horrific half-hour.

Police are requesting anyone with any information surrounding the events to contact Chief Aubrey at 613-555-5116.

The investigation continues.

NEW HOPE TEEN REPORTED MISSING, FOUND MURDERED

Oval Lake – June 13, 1981 – A teen reported missing after the Clarington High School tragedy yesterday was found late this morning by the housekeeping staff of the Century Motel in Oval Lake.

Marcia Denise Mayer, 16, was found in the end unit shortly before noon when Kasy Manton, one of the housekeeping staff of the motel, entered the room.

"I knocked on the door and no one answered, so I thought they had checked out. When I entered the room, I didn't even see her for a minute because of all the blood," a visibly shaken Ms. Manton said.

The room was rented for one evening to a single male.

"He seemed kind of jumpy when I was talking to him," Billy Norton, the night clerk, said. "Kind of like he'd been beat up."

The male is described as approximately 6' 3", approximately 140 to 160 pounds, with medium-length brown hair. The name he used to check in, "Al Gueroth," is believed to be a pseudonym.

In a scene seemingly torn from the popular "slasher" films such as *Halloween* and *Friday the 13th*, Ms. Mayer allegedly suffered "severe trauma" according to Sgt. Flewwelling.

"Preliminary findings point toward sexual assault," Sgt. Flewwelling said. It is not known if Ms. Mayer knew her assailant, nor were the police willing to speculate on whether the murder was related to the grisly events that rocked the town of New Hope, twelve miles northeast of Oval Lake, just a few hours previously.

EPILOGUE

"AND STAY THE hell out! You can tell the rest of your goddamn pack that none of you are allowed in this bar."

Theo slammed the door and stalked back behind the bar. Picking up a cloth that was more holes than material, he went back to wiping down the bar. His motions became more violent, as though he was trying to rub through the bar top. "'The wolves will steal something essential from you,'" he said. "Goddamn werewolves'll be the goddamn death of me."

Out of the corner of his eye, he noticed a couple of the regulars quietly moving away from the bar to the tables and that suited him fine.

Outside the bar, Theo knew, the men who were also wolves took a run at the door and found themselves banished. They couldn't come within six feet of the bar. They just stopped. They'd howl and whine, like some child's story. Little pig, little pig, let me come in. *Not in this lifetime, asshole.* Eventually they'd leave, tails between their legs.

"Fuck 'em," Theo said to no one in particular.

Theo watched as Blind Willie chatted up the new guy. Taco Ernie or Greasy Eddie or something like that. Theo wasn't much for names these days.

Willie was talking low enough that Theo wasn't supposed to hear, perhaps catching the occasional "Ain't that right, Red?" But Theo caught it all. Caught Willie's hushed, almost reverential tones as he talked about Theo. Caught the other guy's—Eddie, yeah it was definitely Eddie—disbelief and his underlying nervousness. He could smell it on him. Theo caught it all. He could taste the words in their mouths, lubricated with his beer. He could feel the sounds of their voices as they trickled down inside his ears and skirted the edges of his memories, picking the locks.

Then Greasy Eddie had asked about a poker game. Suddenly the dam broke free and memories, dusty and untouched for almost two decades, came spilling out as though his mind had been disembowelled. He dropped a full bottle of Jack Daniels at his feet, the amber liquid seeping into the already-saturated floor and taking its part among the ambience of smells already permeating the structure.

Part of him wanted to take the old lighter from his pocket and set fire to the alcohol and stand in the flames.

♦♦♦

POKER. *GOD! HOW long has it been?*

Poker always precluded Theo's perception of the whole Demon event. It was poker that had prompted Theo to even talk to Stinky Pete, and Theo still blamed himself for not pushing Peter a little harder.

If only…

Theo pushed the broken shards under the bar. He'd get them later. As his sneakered feet bulldozed the fragrant glass, he looked over to Blind Willie and Greasy Eddie. They both turned back to their beers and talked in more hushed tones.

Willie had been Theo's first customer, back when they were both a lot younger. Blind Willie had aged a lot since then. Theo had not.

Almost every day since Theo first opened, Red and Blind Willie had come into Theo's bar. Each day, Theo watched the two men gradually age and get closer to death. Saw the lines draw a little deeper on their faces with each passing day. Theo thought of his friends. The last friends he had ever had.

What did they look like now? Theo was, what? Thirty-five? Forty? He'd stopped counting a few years back and now only had a general idea. But if Theo was forty, that would make Laura damn near fifty. He tried to imagine her face.

She had been just as pretty—Laura would never be described as beautiful, but she had an air of attractiveness about her—the last time Theo had seen her. That had been in Los Angeles...what? Ten years? Twelve years ago?

Laura—from what Theo had pieced together—had taken an extended leave from teaching, ditched Popper, and begun painting. Theo was sure it was to exorcise some demons—one, at least—from her memories. She had quickly risen in prominence for her "dark portraits of life in all its sinister beauty and ugly truths," as some bloated critic once described it. Theo still had the *People* magazine with the quote somewhere upstairs in his apartment above the bar.

Then there was the Toad—still going by 'the Toad'—who had also done very well for himself.

The Toad never set foot in the school again, and dropped under the radar for quite a few years. Occasionally, he resurfaced in some dry-out or rehab centre. He contacted Theo once to apologize for not going with him to lure Swlabr and help with Stash. Apparently it had been part of the twelve-step program he'd participated in at the time. Christ only knows what the Toad's therapists had heard over the years.

The Toad knew where Theo was. When Theo had finally decided he wasn't going any farther, he sent the Toad a postcard—no name—just a PO Box and a single sentence: "I've traded my demons for spirits."

The Toad sent Theo a couple of newspaper clippings that he had saved concerning the whole "event." Theo had to laugh, imagining the investigators trying to put together the pieces of this particular puzzle. Theo would have loved to know how they wrote up those nasty little teeth-on-legs hell-rat demons.

The last Theo heard, the Toad had designed a couple of wildly successful computer games. One was called *In the Bowels of Hell* and that had made Theo smile. The Toad still had a shit fetish. The other one was called *The Beast in the Machine*. The Toad had sent him both games. Theo didn't have the heart to let the Toad know he mistrusted electric lights, for chrissakes, so there was no way he was ever going to get near a computer again. A lot of publicity was generated when some big-name music acts—acts Theo had never heard of—did their particular spins on a bunch of kid's nursery rhymes, such as *Mary Had a Little Lamb* and *Ring Around the Rosie* and, of course, *Pop Goes the Weasel*. Theo had read the names of the bands—Type O Negative, Tool, Godsmack, Linkin Park, and Filter—and just shook his head. They just didn't name bands like they used to.

There had been a big publicity event for the unveiling of the *Beast* game that had coincided with a show put on by the designer of the game's artwork, Laura Davis. The Toad had sent Theo a letter almost every day until he agreed to try and make it.

Theo had closed the bar, borrowed Red's old Chev pickup, and drove day and night cross-country to get to LA for the event. Arriving at the gala—events like this were never just parties, they were always galas—he had flashed his VIP pass to security, who glanced at his generic jeans and plain white T-shirt and scruffy hair, assumed he was someone important, and was waved in.

Walking into the glittery room with the glittery people had given him the shakes. The photographer's flashes and the noises from the crowd made him sweat. Then, off to the side of the room, he saw the Toad and Laura. The Toad, now beginning to bald, but with a fashionable spiked haircut and expensive designer glasses, stood laughing with Laura, her long hair now shorter, her face a little wiser. Theo stood there for god knew how long, watching the two of them, still friends after all this time. He heard Stinky Pete's shattered voice then, heard it address the Toad and say, "You will profit from the Demon, does that please you?" Then, as he had done so many years before from a hotel room, he turned and walked away, found the truck, and headed home without looking back.

Why would he intrude on their happiness with his crushed dreams and paranoia? He'd seen too much death. He'd lost too many people. It was easier to leave and never see them again, knowing they were happy, than to walk back into their lives and risk losing them again. It had been bad enough just being there. Theo figured making contact would end up prying loose memories that had been packed away too long ago. He knew the memories would never go back the way they came. It was better to leave them under the dust.

He had driven home again, straight through, never sleeping, never eating, stopping only for gas. He returned the truck to Red, thanked him, and reopened the bar. Theo had never left the town since. The town so far north that night lasted six months of the year.

♦♦♦

AND NOW, AS Blind Willie had told Greasy Eddie, the No Hope bar seemed to be the Mecca for those who lived outside the normal. They came from everywhere and spoke many languages, some known, some not.

But Theo knew them all. Theo found he could speak with them all, and understand them all quite clearly. He tried not to think about that too much.

Then there was Marcia—the other thing he tried not to think about too much, but always did. Marcia, who he had not wanted to take. Marcia, who had loved him with all his faults. Marcia, who he might have been able to save if only he had paid more attention to her.

If only…

But then again, maybe he wouldn't have. He would never know.

Theo would never know because he wasn't sure how he had brought the power—like tremendous pain, he could remember all about it, but not the specific feeling itself. So, while he could guilt himself into believing he could have unleashed some sort of holy cleansing ray to save Marcia, deep down inside, Theo knew he was a one-hit wonder. He knew he would never be capable of any power of that magnitude again. And while it didn't help when it came to Marcia, dead now almost two decades, it did ease his mind a bit to know he was almost normal.

Yes, he could speak any language. Yes, he could banish werewolves from his bar without fear of reprisal. And yes, he could perform simple parlour tricks like lighting the lanterns every night, or pulling ice-cold beer from the case sitting at room temperature. And yes, he had barely aged a day since that horrific Friday. But overall, he was more human than not, by his own estimation. *Bet Stinky Pete would've said the same damn thing about himself, too,* he thought.

Being an owner of the Book, he knew his viewpoint was hardly subjective. Ah, the Book.

The first couple of years he had tried to burn It, shred It, throw It in large bodies of water, including the Pacific Ocean. He had even buried It in the tundra in the middle of nowhere.

Twice.

But through it all, the Book refused to burn, to shred, to

drown, to die.

Somehow, It always ended up back in Theo's little room above the bar.

And then, one day, It was simply gone, leaving him with vestigial power and the ability to not age. Exactly like what It had done with Talia Davis when It jumped from her to Peter.

♦ ♦ ♦

NOT LONG AFTER he'd settled here, the Toad had sent him a clipping from New Hope about the destruction of *The Last Word* bookstore, and the death of both Stan Holt and his son Dan. He had to wonder, did the Book have anything to do with that?

Nothing had been left but a crater.

And Theo could only think, *You lack the courage to save the one who needs you most.*

Had someone else experienced that particular hell as well?

NOW, EVERY NIGHT, when Theo threw out the last drunken customer, he mentally extinguished the lanterns, made his way up the stairs, and always, always, he looked to see if the Book had returned. And each night, it had not.

Every night, as Theo entered into troubled sleep, he cursed himself.

The Book was out there somewhere. Doing what It did.

And damned if he didn't miss It.

AUTHOR'S NOTE

CARRYING ON THE tradition I started in *Bad Blood,* I thought I'd give you some insight into how I came to write this particular beast.

Of all the stories in the Aphotic World series, this one is the oldest. Why? Well, because it's literally the first novel I ever wrote.

Many, many years ago—okay, something close to three decades—I made a New Year's resolution to myself. Kind of a stupid thing for me to do, considering my success rate with resolutions. I mean, I likely make resolutions almost every year, but in all the time I've been doing that, I'd kept one: to not swear for an entire year. That one was made back in high school because I was—and truth to tell, I very much still am—a horrible potty-mouth.

In case you hadn't noticed by the novel you presumably just recently completed.

Anyway, on that fateful New Year's Eve from almost three decades ago, I made my only other New Year's resolution, when I swore I would start writing again.

I'd written a lot through public and high school, but once I left high school my writing fell by the wayside. College, work, hanging out, then later, marriage and children, it all took its toll on my writing. But I found I'd really been missing that creative outlet, so I promised to start up again.

Even signed up for a writing course to get my ass in some sort of gear other than neutral.

Funny thing was, I actually sat down on January 1st, pen in hand, ready to go. I wrote nothing that day. Nothing came.

Same with January 2nd.

By January 3rd, I'd done a bit of prework and actually started a story. Took a couple of days to complete it, but damned if I wasn't actually pretty happy with it. Dug up another one I'd started back in high school. I'd written half of it, then just stopped. I had no idea where I was heading with it originally, but damned if I didn't end up finishing that one too. And I liked it too.

And that writing course I took? I didn't get a lot from it, but what I did get was an instructor who was very encouraging. And that helped me more than anything.

Then, an interesting thing happened. I was watching the animated series *Stickin' Around* with my kids—and yes, after I finish telling you this bit you'll understand exactly why I'm rather embarrassed to say I let my very young children watch this show—and this particular episode involved something about one of the kids' nasty lunches turning into a rampaging monster in the school, wreaking havoc wherever it went. If I remember correctly, one of the kids defeated it either by burping or farting it to death. Quality entertainment, let me tell you.

But it tweaked something in my brain.

I moved to the small town of Barry's Bay, Ontario, right after I completed Grade 10, and did my last three years (remember Grade 13? No? I do!) at the high school in town. In my first couple of weeks at the school, I'd heard the story of one student who, for whatever reason, didn't like the bagged lunches his mom was making for him but decided not to tell her. He also decided to not throw them in the garbage, choosing instead to just mash them into a nasty stack in his locker. Eventually, maggots decided they liked the buffet.

According to the story I heard, they had to seal off the

entire wing of the school to fumigate the maggots and flies out of all the lockers. Sounds a lot like the start of that *Stickin' Around* episode, no?

It was enough for me to start linking the two rough stories. And I also thought, how cool would it be to release some massive monster into my old high school? And then, there's some teachers I could erase like chalk from a chalkboard.

These are the thoughts of writers. We think them, then write them. Saves on the whole trial/jail time.

♦♦♦

THE WORKING TITLE for this short story—yes, you read that correctly, *short story*—was, for the longest time, *School is Hell*. My main character was going to be a monster fighter who had defeated a dragon and stolen its heart and couldn't die, but wanted to. He would come to the school hoping this would be the monster that would best him.

I wrote the first three chapters. Then rewrote them. Wrote them again. It just wasn't working. I was pretty damn close to abandoning the entire thing.

Then I wondered if having a main character who wanted to die might be the issue. So I reimagined the storyline with him out, and one of my minor characters, this Theo kid, as the main guy.

Another side trip here, and this one's kinda dark. This Theo kid? And this Stinky Pete kid? Well, there's a bit of a story there.

During my last year of school, my mother's second marriage—this time to my step-father—fell apart in the span of a few hours. Long story, not worth telling, but believe me when I say it got *ugly* really fast. Unfortunately, my mother and I couldn't afford to move out, so the three of us, mother, stepfather, and me, were trapped in a house full of anger and hate. I witnessed a lot of terrible, horrifying things. And, while I never ever came closer than a basic thought experiment, I will confess to wishing my stepfather dead. If you'd seen the kind of things I saw him doing to my mother, mentally and physically, you'd likely agree it's hard to not have those thoughts.

So, much of that anger and confusion and frustration and...yes...hate...got injected into Theo and Pete. And, just like that, the whole story pretty much fell together.

Except for one part. Thankfully, it's a part I got a good education about writing from.

♦♦♦

I WAS GOING great guns, writing this crazy, sprawling thing that quickly grew from a long short story into something approaching a novel. Then there came the scene toward the end of Chapter Eleven where Theo, Laura, and the Toad are trapped in the caf, and in comes Swlabr, and the whole place is burning.

Yeah, I wrote that, then I didn't write anything for three weeks because I'd literally painted myself into a corner. I had no idea how they escaped.

For three weeks, I did a Winnie the Pooh, and tapped at my forehead, saying, "Think. Think. Think." And for three weeks, absolutely nothing thunk. Now, you have to understand, this was my first long work, and I'd been writing daily for weeks now, building up those words and pages. To suddenly stop, to walk by the computer and feel its disappointed staring? That's an awful feeling.

Finally—and this was the lesson I learned—I decided, to hell with it. I know they have to get out because if they don't, there's literally no story left. So I looked at my notes, at the thing I knew happened next. And I started writing it. What I wrote is now sitting in Chapter Fifteen. And, a funny thing happened as I started to write about them, exhausted, but safely out of the caf…I knew, by the time I'd written no more than three sentences, exactly how they got out. I remembered my school, I remembered the space under the stage, I had their escape hatch.

It's amazing what the mind can do to solve problems unconsciously, jealously hiding the answers away until it has everything pretty much worked out, then it just throws it out and says, "Ta-da! I fixed it!"

♦♦♦

ONE LAST NOTE about the story. I wrote the whole thing and thought, *Yay, I wrote a novel!* Then, just as quickly, I figured out I'd only written about two-thirds of one. It was really short. I needed to add more.

What to add?

As I read through the manuscript, I came to the part where Theo's walking through that damned caf and he's seeing people he recognizes. And one of the ones he recognized was his ex-girlfriend, Marcia.

And I thought, *What if she survived?*

And just like that, I had my final third of the novel.

♦♦♦

THREE QUICK NOTES about many of the supporting characters.

First, this novel is thick with heavily—and I truly do mean *heavily*—fictionalized versions of my schoolmates and teachers. And yes, I truly did have a terrible, unrequited crush on my art teacher. Oh, yes I did.

Second, the Moose running naked in the streets and getting

locked out thing in Chapter One? Yeah, about 95% true. We really did that. Dude, if you're out there, um…sorry, not sorry.

Third, the Jimmy Baldwin baseball bat-to-the-mouth scene from Chapter Seven? Yeah, my best friend did that to me when we were ten. 100% true. Total accident. Buddy, if you're out there, I hope you know I was never, ever mad at you for that.

A couple of interesting last points. Well, interesting to me, maybe not so much to you.

The first is the title of this monstrosity. As I mentioned, initially, it had the working title—that I always hated—of *School is Hell*. Then, once I came up with the name of the town, for most of the next ensuing, multiple decades, it was *No Hope.* But, when it turned into part of a series, that kinda didn't work anymore. So then it was, for a short while, *Demon*. And then I got the brainstorm of linking all the titles with various idioms containing the word *blood*. So, there you have it. How not to name your novel in four easy steps.

The second is, I'd written about two-thirds of the novel, and up to that point, it had all been in first person, from behind Theo's eyes, or Laura's, or Marcia's, or whomever was narrating the scene. And it just wasn't working for me. So I lost a lot of time going back and changing every damn "I" to "Theo" or "he" or "Laura" or "she" and so on. That was a serious pain in the ass.

The last thing is, I knew what the ending to Swlabr had been very early. That whole magnetizing of the computer drives was gonna do it. Trust me when I say I was likely more surprised than any future reader that the wily demon bastard escaped his fate. I'm serious. I was literally writing his escape and whispering, "No, no no…what the hell am I gonna do now?"

It's stuff like that that keeps me writing. I love when my fingers tell the story my brain doesn't know yet, but that scene where Swlabr escapes? Yeah, that was the first time I'd ever experienced it. I think I count that as when I officially became a writer.

Anyway, there's a whole lot of young, insecure Tobin Elliott in Theo Clarke.

I've said this before, and I'll say it again…I've been asked many, many times why I choose to write horror. Over the years, my answer has been whittled down to this soundbite: It's my way of controlling the demons.

And this novel? *Out for Blood*? This is where I learned to control them.

I hope you liked it.

Thanks for reading.

ABOUT THE AUTHOR

TOBIN ELLIOTT HAS written for most of his life. After some unfortunate incidents with walls and permanent markers, he switched to safer things like pens and paper, and later, typewriters and then computers. Though science fiction was his first love, horror has always had a powerful hold on him, even back before he wore big-boy pants. He likes to have the shit scared out of him, and he likes scaring the shit out of others. Somehow, it always comes down to shit with Tobin.

Tobin spent his formative teenage years in a small town about four hours northeast of Toronto. Those experiences, and the magic and wonder of that place, never left him, though he left the town, through no fault of his own. He currently lives within a three-hour drive of the place, and occasionally gets back to top up on his sense of wonder and nostalgia.

Based on that town and surrounding areas, Tobin has written several novels in his Aphotic World series.

Along with those writings, Tobin has been fortunate enough to have had three horror novellas published, as well as seven stories in various anthologies. He has been a board member of both the Writers' Community of Simcoe County (WCSC) and the Writers' Community of Durham Region (WCDR), and, for five years, was an annual participant in the Muskoka Novel Marathon, a 72-hour writing marathon to raise money for adult literacy programs.

Finally, he also taught creative writing for two different continuous learning programs. Tobin writes ugly stories about bad people doing horrible things, and it was his pleasure to show other people how to do the same thing for almost twenty years.

If you're interested in more ramblings by Tobin, well, he's not much into social media. He sees it as a blight on humanity of almost Bookian proportions. And yet, still, he's on there.

Facebook: The Horror Guy (/tobinelliott.horrorguy)

Twitter: @TheHorrorGuy91

Instagram: @tobinelliott.horrorguy

♦♦♦

I HOPE THAT this book captured your imagination, and I hope that this series will turn you into a loyal reader.

Because loyal readers are an author's secret weapon. They can influence other readers…how?

Through reviews.

If you loved this book, and yes, even if you hated it, please also consider leaving a review on the site where you purchased it, and/or Goodreads, or anywhere else. You can also drop me a line at TheHorrorGuy91@gmail.com.

As a reader, you have an immense power to influence others.

Please, use that power.